SONG OF VIRGO

KAT TURNER

CITY OWL
PRESS

SONG OF VIRGO
Coven Daughters, Book 3

CITY OWL PRESS
www.cityowlpress.com

Cover Design by MiblArt. All stock photos licensed appropriately.

Edited by Tee Tate.

For information on subsidiary rights, please contact the publisher at info@cityowlpress.com.

Print Edition ISBN: 978-1-64898-242-2

Digital Edition ISBN: 978-1-64898-243-9

Printed in the United States of America

PRAISE FOR KAT TURNER

"*Song of Virgo* is an intense and perfect combination of magic, mystery, and love!" – *Jaqueline Snowe, author of the Shut Up and Kiss Me series*

"A fledgling witch finds love with a mature rock star in the midst of occult danger in Turner's magic-heavy debut and series launch. Turner sets up a promising world that readers will be pleased to return to in subsequent installments. Paranormal fans should check this out." – *Publisher's Weekly*

"In *Blood Sugar*, readers can expect Turner's trademark snark mixed with magical and metaphysical mysteries, a well-paced plot full of unexpected twists, and two layered and complex characters winning their happily ever after." – *Janet Walden-West, author of Salt + Stilettos*

"Fantastic, vivid writing and great characters make for a fun, sexy, emotional paranormal riff! Get *Hex, Love, and Rock and Roll* as soon as you can!" – *Celia Juliano, sexy, heartfelt romance author*

"Full of witchy goodness and rock n' roll magic, Turner's *Hex, Love, and Rock & Roll* is a steamy, captivating debut. Brian Shepherd sparkles as the sensitive, swoon-worthy (and feminist!) rock legend hero, and Helen Schrader is a go-get-'em heroine I found myself cheering on every step of the way! With her unique world building, smart prose, and sizzling romance, Turner is a welcome new addition to the paranormal romance genre. I can't wait to read what she writes next!" – *Angie Hockman, author of Shipped*

"*Blood Sugar* is as sexy and thrilling as it is dark and chilling. It's perfect for people ready to dive into the Halloween season and be romanced at the same time. Also- zombie squirrel." – *E. E. Hornburg, author of The Night's Chosen*

"Absolute magic. *Hex, Love, and Rock & Roll* delivers thrilling suspense, steamy chemistry, and a sexy British front man. Anyone who's ever had a crush on a rock musician or wished on a star will fall in love with this debut." – *Mary Ann Marlowe, author of Some Kind of Magic*

ALSO BY KAT TURNER

COVEN DAUGHTERS

Hex, Love, and Rock and Roll

Blood Sugar

Song of Virgo

Fallen Angel

＊

COVEN DAUGHTERS ORIGINS

Embers

For Heidi.

ONE

FOR THE FIRST TIME IN SO LONG, TAYLOR LOST HERSELF TO A MOMENT of tranquility. The predawn darkness was still and silent, and the babies had stopped crying. Scents of cedar and detergent filled the bedroom of her cabin and calmed her nerves. These days, she had to take comforts as they came.

Swaddled in bedding and curled in the fetal position, she let in nurturance instead of nurturing. Being the mother of three-month-old twins meant near-constant noise and motion, on top of insufficient sleep. Silence was a rare blessing.

The babies had quieted, soothed yet again by her husband's undivided attention. She stole another peek at the video monitor. On the fuzzy, black-and-white screen, two bundles slept in their adjacent cribs as Julian walked out of the nursery.

Even her chronic pain had finally left her alone.

Useless to speculate why the hurt had lessened, or what injury or malady had wrecked her body beyond repair. She'd never solve the mystery. For now, she was okay, and the cabin deep in the South American jungle was a happy home. Having escaped the weird world of curses and occult experimentation, she was now living sustainably with the clan of shifters who had accepted her and Julian after they'd fled the nightmare of dark magic that had brought them together.

Bed springs squeaked, the weight on the mattress shifting as Julian joined her under the covers. He spooned her, wrapping strong arms around her front, and pressing the warmth of his smooth chest against her back. She breathed in his scent, sighing when his lips grazed her neck, and sent a spray of pleasurable tickles skittering across her skin. White noise from the machine played a soothing, monotonous song.

"Thank you for getting up with them. Again." When a twin woke up crying, one set off the other, turning Malcom and Luna into a perpetual motion machine with an entire night's worth of staying power. Julian had a talent for calming both simultaneously.

"No need to thank me," he spoke into the back of her neck, his deep voice thick with sleep. "Just doing my job."

"How do you do it?" she sighed, arching her back in invitation to continue the contact.

When she got up with the twins, the process took longer. More fussing, and Luna needed lots of patient encouragement to latch and breastfeed, if she even cooperated. The little girl preferred Julian and the bottle, which some "breast is best" advocates might side-eye, but at least Julian was able to take over, allowing Taylor to steal a bit of sleep at night.

He ran his hand down her side, the gentle stroke of his dry, callused fingertips kindling a familiar ache in her core.

"It's luck is all, babe. You're doing everything perfectly. Don't beat yourself up."

A lump lodged in Taylor's throat. Her eyes stung with the threat of tears. "No matter what I do with them, I feel like I'm failing." First the birth that left her torn and bruised, her insides shattered, and now the feeding struggles. Her daughter was rejecting her outright; a bad omen for the relationship.

"You aren't. I promise. Is there anything more I can be doing? Or am I a dick for even having to ask?"

Taylor let out her first good-natured laugh in awhile. In addition to doing most of the newborn feedings, Julian stayed busy with plenty of other things. He made and sold his paintings and craftwork at the market, as well as working as one of the main hunters for the Peruvian shifter community. The horses needed care, and the buildings required maintenance and upkeep. An endless cycle of chores.

The inner circle had been asking more of him leadership-wise, too; increased time commitments at planning meetings. All while Taylor languished, useless, an unproductive eater and a resource user. She'd barely finished her final online class before squeaking away with her bachelor's degree, a steep decline for someone who once aspired to billionaire-under-thirty status.

Lucky for her, at least, she hadn't sensed Julian withdrawing emotionally or growing frustrated with her newfound loser-dom. "You aren't a dick. You're perfect."

"How's your pain today?" He rubbed a circle on her lower belly, the site of endless, baffling frustration.

Her twenty-three-year-old body was betraying her. Neither her midwife or her doula had identified any permanent damage from childbirth, yet the cramps came daily, low-grade versions of the dark, fierce contractions she'd felt while pushing out her babies. Shifter pregnancies were supposed to be easier, the elder women had promised, but that hadn't been the case.

Perhaps the differences had to do with Taylor being an unusual type of shifter, a genetically modified one whose abilities were created through scientific and medical tampering instead of natural occurrence. The fiends who'd kidnapped her had tried to steal her embryos with magic. Maybe they'd cursed her reproductive system. But in the absence of any spiritual disturbances, she lacked evidence for her crank theory.

"I'm okay." She meant it, mostly.

There was an hour or two earlier when she'd been able to walk around without discomfort. Taylor even spent the early afternoon helping in the library, digitizing old letters from the clan's ancestors and binding books while the twins slept in their carrier. It had been one of her best days in a long time.

He splayed his palm beneath her navel, speaking a few soft words to channel the healing magic he'd acquired when they'd travelled through a portal last year. The warmth of her husband's touch comforted her, but the inherent futility of his effort saddened her. His magic was one of the first things they'd tried. He'd saved her life with his power, but he couldn't heal her pain. Maybe nothing could.

"I love you," she whispered into darkness, a plea and a prayer. For the endless night to break, for a new era of lightness and hope to come.

"Love you so much." His breath came hot against her neck, changing into a series of quick and deep sighs while he caressed the plane of skin spanning from ribs to hip points, stopping short of grazing her pubic hair.

Her core softened under his strokes. Tension between her legs heightened.

Julian must've sensed a change in her pulse or breath, smelled a trace of her excitement, because he got hard against her back.

Without a moment's hesitation, she reached behind and cupped him, rubbing up and down on his stiff, silken length. She flipped around, bringing them face-to-face. The unusual stranger from the library, once a reserved man with long black hair and mesmeric brown eyes, was as handsome as ever. Except now, he was hers, and she was his. The father of her children, her one-and-only love.

Taylor kissed his lips while she rubbed and teased his full erection with her palm and fingers. His mouth parted for her, and he tasted as clean as spring water when he slid his hot tongue into her mouth. She slipped him her own tongue, falling in love with their sensual play all over again as they explored each other as if for the first time.

"Let's make love," she murmured into his hot mouth and slung her leg over his hip before he could answer.

"I don't want to hurt you." His voice was pained with memories of failed intimate efforts, words chased by a clipped moan.

His cock throbbed in her hand, his heartbeat an audible drum in the still of night. Julian's mind and body warred, a struggle she related to.

"I want to keep trying. It has to go away eventually. It's been so long." Taylor and Julian hadn't had sex since right before the twins were born—before the pain started. She ought to have healed over a month ago.

She looped her arms around his broad shoulders, then kissed the wolf tattoo on his pectoral muscle. Rain began to fall, tapping against the roof in an increasingly urgent rhythm as if nature mirrored her desire. Streaks of wetness slashed the window glass by the bed, but she sure didn't feel like crying. "Please. I want to."

"You'll tell me if you need to stop?" His excitement showed in the motions of his stiff organ as he pushed in and out of her hand, a rhythm to his hips.

"Promise." They were close. Sex would work out this time, she could feel it.

With a grunt of male lust, Julian urged Taylor onto her back, then moved to kneel between her legs.

She admired the view of his muscled arms and thick thighs, loose dark strands of hair kissing the ink on his chest. His dark eyes glinted in the predawn shadow, the carved bone structure of his facial features cutting an arresting profile.

She lifted her hips an inch off the bed.

Julian responded to the nonverbal signal with a quick dive down, his hair swishing across her inner thigh in silky touches. He grabbed her bottom with both hands, and his face disappeared between her legs. With an absence of buildup or fanfare so stark as to be obscene in the hottest way possible, he worked on her with oral gusto.

His tongue was wet and firm, probing and licking all the right spots in urgent motions. In under a minute, she was tight and tense with expectation, base need and the promise of bliss coiled in congress. The sharp insistence of her noises would've embarrassed her if she hadn't been hungry, desperate. They'd done this act since the difficult birth, but this time was different. Crazed, feral, a brutal surrender to chance. All in. No holding back.

There was something in the air, a wind, rising from deep within her as it wailed beyond the walls.

Soon she was bucking into his face, the slick goodness of his work too much to bear. He dug his fingertips into the tops of her legs as she pressed her inner thighs into the sides of his head. A few more of those steady, medium-pressure laps, and she broke, given over to the sheer ecstasy of a return to what she feared they'd lost.

A burst of electric-blue lightning flashed in the sky, or maybe the blast came from inside her.

He finished and rose, hard as ever, and looked between her legs. "I want you so bad."

"Have me," she ordered in a hoarse, loud whisper, pawing in the nightstand until her fingers connected with an open box, the foil packets inside. She tore off a single, wrapped condom and handed him the small square. "Now."

He ripped the covering and sheathed himself, chest heaving and lips parted, while his eyes roved the expanse of her naked body. "You are so goddamn beautiful. I missed you."

She forced down tears. Tears of gratitude and joy would have to wait. Nothing was allowed to complicate this moment. No crying, no drama.

"Now." Words became inadequate. Only their bodies mattered, and the powerful current surging between them, rich with history, heartbreak, triumph.

Julian lowered and entered her, slow and careful, cupping her head with one hand while gazing into her eyes. "Does this feel good?"

Good? Try divine. Filling her up, claiming her, making her tingle with physical pleasure as well as something more primal: the delight of surrender. "Perfect."

And with her assurance he was moving, thrusting, and it was fucking amazing. She gave in, gave over, blended into oneness with sensation. "Missed you. Missed us."

"Oh, Taylor, you're incredible." His breath came choppy as he picked up the pace, his pushes speeding to a quicker, shallower rate.

She clutched his arms, urging, encouraging, coaxed by a promise deep inside. The base of his shaft slid against her clit as his probes targeted an internal pleasure center, and just as he was reaching the end, her body splintered a second time, a harder time, and she had to wail and groan to get through it.

"Can I finish in your mouth?" he rasped, moving in and out of her like the world would end if he didn't.

She got the point of his request. He craved a skin-on-skin climax, but without the added risk of more babies. Taylor gazed into her man's eyes, communicating her consensus with that one single look. "That sounds awesome."

His groan was broken and high, hungry for what he wanted. Julian disengaged and stripped the condom, tossing the tan scrap of latex onto the floor as he dismounted Taylor and flipped onto his back.

With a hand pressed into his tailbone, she urged him forward, taking him deep into her mouth and throat. He pushed, tasting of latex and musk. She augmented the suction of her mouth with eager lips and tongue.

Julian swelled to impossible stiffness. He grabbed the sides of her head, gaining what little purchase he could find in her short hair, and let go.

She swallowed eagerly until she'd taken all the salty-sweet evidence of his release.

His body went slack. He pulled her close, a light sweat having broken across his brown skin. She smelled herself on him and found a tender closeness in the trace, underscored by the rhythm of his pulse.

"How are you feeling?" Julian asked, skating fingers over her abdomen.

She gave a gentle shove to his shoulder while working to regulate her breathing. "I'm not a delicate flower."

He kissed her forehead. "I know you aren't. You're the strongest person I know."

"Do you ever miss Texas?" The question popped out before Taylor allowed herself to give it much thought. They never talked about their former home. Now and then, she wondered why. Was the unspoken moratorium on discussing the past part of some toxic denial?

He hummed a thoughtful sound. "No, not really. Everything meaningful that I had there, I have here. And then some." He tipped his chin at the babies' room. "Do you?"

Did she? Her sister, Chloe, was almost done with rehab and said she'd come visit once she saved money and got a passport. Her parents were in the midst of a divorce, and after the lies and betrayal they'd put her through, she didn't need to see them again.

Taylor yearned for a piece of fulfilment that her home state symbolized. "I think that I need to find work using my degree."

The shifter community ran eco tours, wooing well-heeled European and American tourists to the jungle with promises of adventure, and maybe even a jaguar sighting. The operation hummed along, sustained by an adequate profit plateau.

Surely they could make use of someone with a strong background in finance and business to increase their wealth margin and comfort level. Taylor had let go of her misguided ambitions to work on Wall Street, but that didn't mean she'd be content to be only a mom and wife. Not forever.

Julian played with her cropped blond hair. "Go for it. What were you thinking?"

She sighed. "I need to kick this pain, get up and around more often, focus on something other than my body and where it hurts. I feel like I'm creating a self-fulfilling prophecy fixating on my insides, you know?"

He nodded. "Any specific ideas? Or would you like to brainstorm?"

Brainstorming sounded good. Taylor could always count on her husband for support. "I'd like to help expand the travel agency. Build the operation's reach. Increase our income so that we're growing our wealth beyond our subsistence baseline level. I'm sure there's potential for market growth in the ayahuasca. There must be vampires outside of this place who would be interested in our plant-based blood alternative."

He nuzzled a sensitive spot behind her ear and palmed the side of her breast, a once-humble B-cup now swollen with milk. "There's my finance tycoon."

She laughed at his playfulness. It felt damn good to laugh again. "I'm serious. I need to use my brain more." Maybe she obsessed over her physical frustrations as a way of sublimating her mental ones. The mind-body connection was a complex and tricky thing.

"I know you're serious." Julian made eye contact. "Let me know what I can do to help." The conviction in his stare matched his confident words of assurance.

A keening wail—Malcom's faster, sharper one—pierced their contemplative bubble like a needle.

It was Julian's turn to release a good-natured laugh. He started to get up. "That's my cue."

She touched his arm. "No, let me do it. I want to breastfeed." A surge of confidence made Taylor optimistic that her latest effort would go well. She'd keep trying.

"You sure?" He brushed his lips across her forehead in a slow, savoring motion.

"Positive." She rolled out of bed, drawing in a cool and grounding breath as her bare soles connected with the warm hardwood floor. So far, so good. She grabbed her bathrobe from the closet and put it on. "I've got this."

"Yeah, you do." He gave her a wide, loving smile, and she returned his affectionate expression.

Things were starting to get better, increment by increment. Taylor just had to keep hoping and not lose her faith. She padded to the babies' bedroom, where their cribs sat side by side against a wall decorated with stickers of giraffes and trees.

Someday, the babies would figure out how to shift into their wolves, and the family could run through the woods together for recreation and rite of passage. How blessed they were, to be born into an accepting community of their own kind.

Malcom squirmed in his crib, his tiny face scrunched up as he fussed.

"Mama's here." Taylor scooped up her son, intoxicated by his powdery baby smell as she walked him to her nursing recliner and sat.

Weird how his cries hadn't woken Luna, but Taylor wasn't about to jinx the small miracle by bothering her daughter. Luna was such a light sleeper that even standing over her crib to peer in could make her little brown eyes pop open.

Malcom latched and cooed while he nursed. Taylor gazed down at her boy and watched him eat. She knew in her heart that she'd be able to feed Luna next. Her fortune was finally reversing.

Tonight was the turning point she'd been waiting for. She couldn't wait to tell Julian about the breakthrough.

Taylor yawned, fading in and out of a twilight pseudo-sleep where dreams merged with reality. Her subconscious fell low, into bleak and frightful dreams of sinful acts and writhing wormy things bathed in blood, forms that never were or never could be haunting the dim lit halls of other places. Silent screams pulsed in time with her brain waves.

A light flashed in the nursery, followed by a thunderous pop that startled her awake.

Watery, shadow remnants of ugly faces appeared and dissolved in her mind's eye as she routed herself back to consciousness, an unwholesome, disturbing energy vibrating all around her. The stares of hateful, inhuman eyes, yellow or red and set in the bodies of those from beyond, danced behind a thin veil keeping them at bay.

She shook her head, ears ringing as she purged the remnants of the strange dream-incident from her tired brain. Adrenaline coursed downward from her center, frying her toes.

Yikes, why was she dreaming of such scary stuff? Especially since the last half hour had been perfect?

The ticks of the wall clock fired in intervals, punctuating the stillness in a humdrum staccato that ought to have eased her distress.

Yet creepy recognition gelled in her as she registered the time. Three thirty-three a.m. An auspicious time. Strange. Witching hour. A chill travelled the length of her spine. Rather than focusing any more on the bad mojo, Taylor glanced down to her son.

Malcom had let go of his mother's breast. He slept, his chest rising and falling, mouth open. Classic milk drunk, a reassuring sight of satiety. She carried him, her steps light with adoration and pride, back to his crib, where she laid him down as gently as possible. He twitched but kept on sleeping.

Taylor pumped a fist in the air to commemorate her mom win. She snuck a peek at Luna's crib. Might as well steal a glimpse, just to check on her baby girl. As long as she didn't get too close, she wouldn't wake the slumbering infant.

Through the wooden bars of the crib, however, she saw only mattress, the plastic slab wrapped in a sheet patterned with cartoon elephants. Taylor's pulse spiked in a jolt of anxiety. Luna had to be tucked in a corner. She did that sometimes. Didn't she?

Holding her breath, Taylor walked closer, her eyes darting as she scanned crib, the floor beneath it.

Her brain short-circuited. Time hardened to stone. Her perception shrunk to the impossible void of her witnessing, the nothingness of those elephant sheets.

Luna wasn't in the crib. Taylor's daughter was gone.

TWO

"Did you bring Luna in here earlier?" Taylor's voice, pitched high and strung tight, trembled. "Lay her down in the bed next to us?" She spoke as if aware her questions made no sense, the strangeness of this sudden intrusion of absurdity threatening to throw Julian into disarray.

As he turned to his wife, a sense of awfulness crept up from the distance, a live wire carrying a current of panic. She stood in the doorway, shaking as she held Malcom. The whites of her eyes gleamed, big orbs igniting the darkness with blazing terror.

"No, of course not." Something was profoundly wrong. He jumped to his feet and ran to her, but stopped short of pulling a sleeping Malcom from her arms. She hadn't lost control of her faculties and wasn't in danger of dropping their son. He refused to catch this contagion infecting the air. They weren't in emergency mode yet. "What are you saying?"

"She's gone," Taylor hissed, her pretty, fine-boned face contorting into a mask of agony. "Someone or something took her from the crib."

Disbelief overloaded his mind with questions even as despair eclipsed his systems and stress chemicals pushed him into fight or flight. His mouth dried, his muscles tensing as surroundings sharpened into stark relief. An eerie, numb calm kicked in and kept him pragmatic.

Running from the cabin screaming wouldn't help find Luna. He needed more facts, more information, before proceeding. A quick check of the nursery confirmed that the window was closed and locked. Same with the rest of the windows and the front door.

The odds of an intruder breaching the boundaries of the jungle community were slim to none. One of their own did this for some foolish motive. "Did you see or hear anything strange while you were in the room? A bump? A crash? Movement outside the window?"

She shook her head even as her brow grooved. "No. I, uh…" Speech monotone, a sign of shock, she trailed off.

Abject panic bit at his heels while he walked to Taylor, but he managed to remain composed. Freaking out might cast a plague of useless negativity and scatter their energies and efforts. He laid his hands on her upper arms, finding her muscles locked, and pinned her with his stare. "It'll be okay, babe. Tell me what you remember."

"A pop and a flash of light," she whispered. "I can't explain it. It felt evil." She squeezed her eyes shut. "Like it's starting up again."

He knew exactly what she meant. Evil, like the kind they had endured, fought, and thought they'd defeated before the birth of their children. If his wife said that evil was back, Julian believed her. But why would mischief reemerge now, after a full year of peace?

No more assessing. Time to move. If supernatural malfeasance was here to shred their lives into gory ribbons again, they lacked the commodity of time. "Put Mal in his carrier. We'll start knocking on doors."

The community would mobilize. Having voted not to institute an official police force, the jungle shifters and the other supernatural creatures they took in protected and served one another.

Clinging to optimism, Julian hopped into jeans, then pulled a shirt over his head. As he tugged socks and hiking boots over his feet, Taylor whimpered.

"Hey." He caressed her cheek with the backs of his fingers, a well-intentioned but futile attempt at reassurance. He had to stay strong for his family and be their rock. "We'll find her. I'm sure there's a simple explanation. Maybe Kathleen wandered over and thought she was doing us a favor by taking her."

Rumors swirled around the camp that the old snake-shifter witch was going senile. Maybe she'd grabbed Luna in a state of disorientation. By virtue of being anything better than the worst-case scenario, the farfetched possibility tempered total despair.

"Or someone came through a portal and snatched her." Tone flatly grim, Taylor buckled Malcom in his portable seat. "Kathleen couldn't have come in. We would have heard her. She would have announced herself."

Julian's stomach dropped. The explanation ruled out his sole theory. He grabbed his keys and pocketed them. "We aren't facing a supernatural situation yet." The bang and light suggested otherwise, but they ought to look in to mundane hypotheses first. "Let's go."

He palmed a flashlight from a drawer in the credenza by the bathroom, then blazed a trail to the front door. Weight of the object assuring in his palm, a potential weapon in addition to a light source, he switched on the beam and opened the door, stepping out into the dirt.

The rain had stopped, leaving outdoor air heady with a tepid humidity peculiar to South America in September. Warm night as sensual as velvet draped the sky. Off in the belly of the jungle, monkeys and bugs sang their layered, nocturnal harmonies. Not one footprint indented the soft ground around the perimeter of the cabin. Bad sign that supported Taylor's hunch. He smelled the air for gasoline or someone's personal scent. No trace of an interloper mingled with the usual wood smoke and fishy smells of the nearby river.

"We'll start with Tim." Julian set off for the clan leader's cabin, twigs crunching underfoot. Tim would kick right into alpha mode, working with Julian to explore the best solutions. Starting with mobilizing the entire community to search the jungle.

"It's the equinox." At his side, Taylor might as well have shouted eureka, though from the sounds of her glum revelation, she was far from elated. "Scarab's finishing what it started, and they want to use Luna. Her blood, her skin. Like they wanted to use mine and yours. Like they wanted to use her while she was still inside of me."

Julian felt ill as he set foot on the stoop of Tim's home, a tiny house made from two upcycled shipping crates, one red and one green in an unintended homage to Christmas. "Let's not go there yet." He wasn't ready to bear the misery of putting the grimmest option on the table.

He knocked as he shoved unspeakable images into the deepest crevices of his mind along with mild resentment toward Taylor for junking up his brain with awfulness.

A faint squeaking noise, like wood scraping on wood, issued from inside Tim's place.

Blood drained from his face as memories flooded back. Of thwarted rituals on that hellish island bunker. They'd put a stop to the shadowy conglomerate's occult misfeasance and kept both of their heads above the rising, poisonous tidewater of doom. "There is no more Scarab. We sunk that place into the bottom of the ocean." Someone had to clench hope. He knocked again, harder.

Surely, Tim could dispel Taylor's monstrous theory. Luna would turn up in short order, they'd lovingly scold Kathleen and forget about the innocent, albeit scary, misunderstanding. A thud from inside. Julian pulled a hangnail. What was taking Tim so long?

Julian bashed his fist into the front door, his blood electric with anxiety. With each passing second, the lack of his daughter hurt worse, the pain intensifying as if a scorching blade slowly penetrated his heart.

Taylor circled back to debunk the theory that Scarab was finished, "We sunk that particular place, yes, but we have no idea if they have more secret locations. I haven't talked to my father since he flew off in that helicopter with Jay Stearns and that woman. Who knows where they went and what they did? It's naïve of us to assume that they just gave up."

Julian slashed a hand through his long hair, the edges of his nerves fraying. Was his baby daughter in mortal danger at the hands of the sinister sorcerers who'd kidnapped Taylor and tried to capture him? Was his precious girl at the mercy of maniacs who, fueled by sadistic magical thinking about the supernatural properties of shifter blood, would have tortured him and his wife to death, then harvested various parts of their anatomy for their twisted practices? The thought made him want to kill. Or die. A scream tore up his throat, but he fought to keep it down and stay strong.

Maybe they'd been lying in wait for an opportunity, plotting. He shook. No. No, no, no.

The wolf tapestry shielding Tim's living room window fluttered. Julian's sigh of relief weighed a hundred pounds. The resulting adrenaline crash kindled a dull headache behind his forehead.

The door stretched open. Tim stood the threshold, his dark eyes bleary and his gray sweatpants wrinkled. "What's this about?" he asked in a groggy voice. Tiredness made his youthful, twenty-something brown face look years older.

"Luna's gone," Julian said.

"She disappeared from her crib while I was in the room." Taylor rocked Mal's carrier, the repetitive motion keeping their boy asleep.

Tim pinched the corners of his eyes. A certain defeat in the gesture, so subtle a stranger would have missed it, stole the largest pieces of Julian's meager hope.

"Has Kathleen been wandering around at night again?" Julian detected the desperation in his own voice, a rawness that might have provoked shame under normal circumstances.

The sag of Tim's broad shoulders and choppiness in his breathing didn't help.

Julian tried again, more for his own benefit, "Maybe Kathleen's delusions are deepening."

"No." Tim's lone, soft word connected as harshly as a body blow.

A red-hot surge seared away every emotion besides indignant outrage, threatening to tip over into fury. He clenched his fists. "You know something vital. I can tell. Why didn't you tell me that something weird was going on? Why didn't you warn us?"

"What do you mean, 'No'?" Taylor raised her voice to the precipice of a shout, every syllable more strangled than the last, then pushed past Tim to enter his house. "I need to get Mal inside before a bug bites him. You're acting like you know something."

Julian trailed his wife until he stood beside her on a circular area rug patterned with black-and-white checkered squares giving the illusion of sinking into a vortex. Fitting, because he'd love to fall through a hole in the ground and pop out in a dimension where this wasn't happening.

Taylor set Mal's carrier by her feet, then rubbed her bicep and tapped her foot.

Tim paced, stopped, then took a breath.

Taylor slapped a hand over her mouth, but the gesture failed to quash her bone-deep yelp of agony. "Is she dead? Oh, my God, I'm going to be sick."

Julian's heart broke for Luna, for his wife, and for himself, but before he opened the compartment where he stored his grief, he pressed for real answers. "The truth, Tim."

"The truth is, I don't know." Tim's speech was laden with weariness and uncertainty yet minimally assuring. The calm conviction inherent, an essence of leadership, made others pause and listen. "I've been active in a closed message board lately where communities like ours have been reporting increased instances of unidentified, inexplicable phenomena. Missing time. Lights in the sky, sleep paralysis complete with entity visitation and even abduction. Your account fits with some of the others. I haven't brought anything up yet in the community because I didn't want to risk drawing additional energetic attention to us. There's some evidence that's how their spells work. I was trying to protect us. But clearly, I failed. I'm sorry."

Taylor stepped into Tim's personal space bubble. "You knew about this but didn't tell us? Who the fuck took my baby? Where is she, and what are they doing with her? And what do you mean, 'communities like ours?' I thought we brought everyone here after the raid on the Scarab prison."

"There were pockets that escaped capture, and they seem to have gone off the grid. Except when they get online to report stuff like this, but even then, their IP addresses are scrambled and blocked behind every firewall you can imagine. As for Luna, assuming that this account mirrors the others, we're looking at an abduction phenomenon."

"Abduction by whom? And to where?" Nausea twisted Julian's guts. "This is a repeat of before, isn't it?"

Tim's tawny complexion paled to a sallow gray. "Maybe, from what I can tell, but more sophisticated. Seamless. Less room for error." He swallowed so hard his Adam's apple bobbed. "Maybe more robust supernatural involvement."

Malcom fussed, a soft but telling grunt of discomfort, and Taylor stooped to soothe him back to sleep with shaky hands. Her voice clogged with emotions, she said, "They haven't given up. They wanted Luna since she was growing inside of me, and now they have her."

When her chin wobbled and her eyes pooled with liquid, Julian crouched by his wife and embraced her. "Do they ever return the abductees?"

Julian knew the answer to his question and wondered why he'd even asked. Perhaps because a dumb bout of wishful thinking made him feel stable, in control, an agent of his fate in an ordered universe.

Tim's somber stare said it all.

A long beat of silence trapped everyone in tense stasis.

"I don't accept this," Taylor said, measured and practical. "We're going to get her back and finish the job we started with those motherfuckers."

Julian raised an eyebrow at his wife and breathed in the oxygen provided by her problem-solving mindset.

She added, "We have until the equinox, right? Like before?"

Tim nodded. "Yeah. Fair assessment."

Taylor rose and chewed a nail. "That's ten days from now. They have events in the days leading up to it where they kill our kind, too, which gives us around five days, seven tops. We can't blindly portal jump. We have to figure out where they are. Like last time, though now we don't have the benefit of that hidden room in my dad's basement."

"The message boards," Julian put in. "We have to start there. Ideally, we'd establish enough trust with one of the participants so we could ask questions privately, but until then we can analyze the posts and look for any trends or clues in those comments."

"A hacker or even someone with computer expertise would be an asset. We have a shortcut to trust building. A method to assess locations quickly," Taylor said.

"I'm not aware of anyone here having those skill sets." Tim furrowed his brow. "But I can start asking tomorrow."

"We don't have until tomorrow. Show me the boards." Taylor turned to Julian, eyes sharp and nostrils flared even as tremors shook her body.

"I can't believe that we weren't on top of this, anticipating this happening."

"We were trying to live our lives and take care of two babies, trying to build a livable life down here. Can you blame us for not being on our toes twenty-four seven?"

Her black, distant glare communicated she did, in fact, have blame to assign. She was saying, wordlessly, that this was his fault. Was it?

She picked up Mal's carrier, then strode to Tim's desk, a neatnik's ensemble armed with the desktop computer and a single pen and legal pad. Beside the supplies, a nub of a potted cactus thrived on neglect. "What's your password?" After setting Mal down, she swirled the mouse and poked a couple of keys.

Julian caught up to his wife and laid a hand on her shoulder. "Please don't shut down on me here. We need to stick together more than ever."

With a shrug, Taylor shirked his touch.

His heart sunk. Though never one to shy away from direct conflict, she'd made her point. And he'd have to give her space to process, because fighting with her was at the bottom of his priority list.

Tim rattled off a random string of letters and numbers, shooting Julian a brief look of sympathy before giving Taylor the address of the message board.

"How did I not know about this?" Walls of text flashed on the screen as she clicked. "There's so much. Where should I start?"

Tim groaned, a noise of unspoken recollection. "Mad Dog Margarita is considered one of the most reliable and reputable posters."

The username promptly appeared in the search bar. Moments later, the account's post history populated.

As Taylor mumbled a string of indecipherable words peppered with the occasional curse, Julian snagged a chair from Tim's kitchen and assumed a station beside her. He wanted badly to plead with her not to reject him in this difficult time, or at least urge her to voice her concerns instead of holding them inside.

She scooted a few inches away from him, the legs of her chair scraping against tile.

"Babe, don't push me away." He reached for his wife's hand, but she conveniently jerked it away before he could catch her fingers.

"Are you reading this?" she asked with crisp formality, like he was one of her damn classmates from business school.

"I'd start with the flurry of posts that they put up around three weeks ago," Tim said from behind. "Work through those, then jump to the newest and read from newest to oldest."

"You could have kept us up to speed on this," Julian let his frustration with Tim slip out.

Tim rubbed his face. "I know. And I accept full responsibility. Like I said, I was hesitant to draw additional energy to us by speaking openly about their plot. But they found her anyway, in spite of my precautions."

Julian sighed. The guy had laid out his reasons for choosing to remain discreet. Steeped in a mix of curiosity and dread, Julian turned to the screen.

Every sentence he read sent him reeling, spinning faster and faster down the weird rabbit hole world of Mad_Dog_Margarita until the outpouring of insanity decimated his composure.

He reread the first post until the words gelled with the horror oozed through his system.

Mad_Dog_Margarita

August 7th, 15:32

Scarab, Inc. is a demon-worshipping death cult. Hence the logo, co-opted from the ancient Egyptians. It's testimony to the transformative power of death. They practice blood sacrifice, blood magic, in their efforts to mutate themselves into other creatures and unlock the secrets to immortality. They want to be able to shift their shapes, change into animals and other people, and change the appearances of others. With or without the knowledge and/or consent of the person mutated. Let that sink in for a second. The ramifications. They're into summoning entities, opening doors, every type of witchcraft and demonology you can imagine. Aliens too, and spells. Think vampires and animal shifters are real only in the movies? LOL.

Mad_Dog_Margarita had plenty of up votes and many cheerleaders, but the occasional zealous detractor intervened to throw cold water on him:

kylesoexxxtra

August 7th, 15:32.

Dude. That's fucking bullshit. Scarab's a pharmaceutical and biotechnology company. You're a paranoid conspiracy freak, Mad Dog.

Mad_Dog_Margarita

August 7th, 15:33

Do your research, bro. I'll wait. Those holdings are the surface, meant for laundering black budget money. The biotech front is a cover for manufacturing live agents of biological warfare, by the way. Mutant monsters. They use mutants in their theme parks too. Money money. Look it up. There are layers, and those layers go straight down to hell.

Julian's throat dried. They sure did go down. Deep below the earth, into a dungeon where impossible beings floated in storage tanks. Where a bloodthirsty monster from another realm chased him and Taylor through dingy hallways. Where sinister strangers performed heinous rites.

kylesoexxxtra

August 7th, 16:07

Okay, maybe you're right about the holdings being fronts, but I'm thinking it's just for drugs or prostitution or whatever. I do concede that it's weird that they own a record label. Not buying the evil arts bit. Sorry, man, but I don't see any evidence for that outside of the ramblings of the tinfoil hat brigade. No offense, lol.

Mad_Dog_Margarita

August 7th, 16:08

To your question about the record label, it's because they're into putting demons into musicians and actors for manipulation purposes and turning them into vampires to keep them young. But yeah, keep on telling yourself that that Chariotz of Fyre guy who hasn't aged in twenty years just has a good plastic surgeon. Sleep tight.

Tim sucked in a loud breath. Taylor and Julian locked stares, except now she looked more determined than upset. No words needed to be spoken. The ageless man in question was Jonnie Tollens, who, along with a woman plagued by a haunting, had come to the jungle several months ago seeking help. In need of an exorcism and an ethical, vegetarian alternative to human blood, they'd gotten what they'd come for and moved along.

"Eve. The woman's name was Eve. I'm Facebook friends with her." Taylor spoke like the notion had promise, which in turn buoyed Julian.

kylesoexxxtra

August 7th, 16:09

Hahah, cool story bro. Why should I believe you?

Mad_Dog_Margarita

August 7th, 16:10

You know what a corporate whistleblower is?

kylesoexxxtra

August 7th, 16:10

yeah man i'm not dumb. so what?

Mad_Dog_Margarita

August 7th, 16:10

That's me.

"Mad Dog Margarita is on. He's online now." Taylor typed in a speedy frenzy, filling in fields, and threw Tim a glance. "Is your IP address hidden?"

"Absolutely," Tim said.

Julian leaned in to get a better look at what Taylor was up to. She'd created an account, her username Shifty_Zoomer_Girl. He got the gist and centered his chair to the screen once Taylor finished, and with a few keystrokes, the online persona truthseeker2784672 was born.

This time, the look that Julian and Taylor shared contained a measure of triumph complete with a nod of solidarity.

Julian clicked the so-called whistleblower's name, followed by the private message icon. If this Mad_Dog_Margarita character knew as much as he or she claimed, he or she would be able to assist in the recovery of Luna. Starting now.

THREE

THE NEW INFORMATION HADN'T LIFTED THE DULL, SICKENING WEIGHT in Taylor's chest, but promising leads curbed the worst of her agony. In her arsenal of options, she had Eve, Mad_Dog_Margarita, and not a single second to waste.

She had Julian, too, even though she still nursed a pang of likely irrational resentment that he'd failed to stop this. She was angry at herself, as well, easily more so.

Blood roared in her ears while she drafted a message to the supposed whistleblower. Hysteria clawed inside of her, but she marshalled every iota of her reserves to stay calm. Calm might solve problems; outbursts would only worsen the trouble.

"You sure you're ready to pull the trigger?" Tim asked with a touch of nerves.

A stretch of silence conveyed what everyone except innocent Mal knew. Once lines of communication with the anonymous poster flew open and thrust Taylor on to the shady stranger's radar, a door would open that might not close.

"We have to start somewhere. This is what we have." She stared at the screen, her finger hovering over the return key, until her eyes burned, forcing her to blink.

Was she about to make a big mistake? Maybe, but dithering could cost Luna her life. She lacked the luxury of evaluating options or strategy.

Taylor drafted a sentence, scowled at it, and tapped the delete key until black characters vanished into white space.

She tried again, pecking keys until she came up with: *My daughter has been kidnapped via portal. Tell me what you know.* "Too adversarial or demanding? I don't want to spook him."

Julian touched her leg and drew a spiked breath as if he started to speak but censored himself. "We have no idea who this person is, no face behind the account. Meaning we can't take everything they say at face value. Not even a little bit."

His words were strong yet gentle, and he was right. An ache expanded deep in her bones, psychic pain threatening, as always, to erupt into the physical realm.

She checked her thoughts before she snapped at Julian. Not fair to blame her husband, but he was the last person to lay eyes on Luna before she vanished. He must've missed something, overlooked a crucial sign. As had she. Frustration without a reference point flew through her. They'd slipped up, dropped their guard, and lost their baby. But assigning blame didn't serve the recovery effort.

She adjusted her weight in the office chair, dull pain cramping her back muscles. "If you have a better idea, please share."

"I'd rather we weren't stuck behind a computer, but until we have a lead on a location, we don't have anywhere to go." Julian drummed fingers on the desk. "Do it."

"Yeah. I agree with Jules," Tim added. "Once everyone is awake, we can assemble as a community and figure out the best ways to move forward."

After pruning her statement down to the barest essentials, she squeezed the proverbial trigger, sending a message into the digital ether: *I need your help.*

A surge of excitement spiked in her when her text disappeared and the word "sent" popped up. She stared at the private message area, her heart thumping. Sweat slicked her palms as her focus and the sum of all emotions inside of her zeroed in on the rectangular gap of white space beneath the blue box containing her sent message.

Her world shrunk. She waited. Those little boxes on the screen held potential.

Horizons contracted into tinier compartments than she'd deemed possible hours ago.

White space, blue space, input from their mysterious maybe-savior. Luna in her arms.

And then, the words with the power to rewire her brain appeared: *Was waiting for you.*

Her own sharp gasp startled her, and she bolted upright. She tried to type a reply, of what she wasn't even yet sure, and deleted a nonsense word.

Julian hovered over the keyboard, his breathing ragged and fast, and hammered out a statement: *If you know who we are, tell us who you are and everything you know about what matters most to us right now.*

Gray dots bobbed in the white space, rising and falling in a wave pattern. Her life, every reason and motivation for existing, swayed with the rise and fall of those dots. Sharp notes of her own perspiration hit her nose while she gazed at bouncing bubbles, her muscles locking, the entirety of her mind fixed in a trancelike state.

Tim's flurry of footfalls marked his advance, and the faint smell of a campfire indicated that he stood behind her.

You're the mutant. They never stopped tracking you. Switched methods was all. The contact's eerie words, along with the hidden subterfuge of it all, made her twitch with dread.

She splayed a hand over her belly, a hunch churning in the unseen realm of her guts. "My pain wasn't natural," she whispered, as if whispering offered any sort of protective cloak. She typed her spoken revelation verbatim, then sent the words to Mad Dog.

No. Not natural in the slightest. No more home surgery this time either. Or you will die.

Scarab had adapted when she'd cut a pair of tracking chips out of her arms. Time gelled into a stew of toxic waste. Revulsion shredded her mind with fiendish abandon. *Why did they want Luna? Why did they take her?*

The prophecy comes. Or so they believe.

A shiver raced over her skin. The supports scaffolding her sanity crumbled. She typed with unsteady hands, beating back an outburst with a brittle twig. *Why are you on here saying all of this? What's your angle*

My motivations are stark and simple. Blow the whistle. Blow them up. Clean out the rot of evil.

Best-case scenario was that they dealt with a righteous keyboard warrior on a vendetta against a former employer. This she could work with, and the theory made just enough sense for her to invest a measure of faith without feeling like a fool driven by emotion.

Taylor scanned the memory logs of her fatigued brain until she pulled up significant things said to her on the day of her capture and detainment in the bunker, when Scarab associates tried to put spells on her and abort Mal and Luna for harvest before she'd stopped the attempt.

She'd stopped them with her gift. Halted their atrocities with her new water magic. They hadn't forgotten. They'd been plotting.

She typed, *They talked about using the fruit of the water witch's womb in their spell. They think that my baby can bring about some prophecy?*

Bingo.

What's the prophecy?

Supposedly involves a powerful demon or demons that they want to free. I haven't seen the Chaos book, the one that supposedly holds The Prayer to Folly, but I've heard that a lot of the details are there. Blood magic, etc.

Her throat closed upon reading the last sentence. Blood. Her baby's blood. Though a piece of her heart withered, she refused to succumb to the paralysis setting in, refused to be terrorized. She had a war to fight and had to hang on to her faculties.

Rational thought. Control.

Where are they keeping Luna?

Underground bunker, location unknown. My sources say Scarab's lair might be hidden beneath one of the major national theme parks that they own. Think after-hours activities.

Can you tell me anything else about this bunker?

The green circle next to Mad_Dog_Margarita's username turned red.

Taylor waited for a response, clinging on for another beat. She knew what the color change meant—her contact had dropped offline.

"Shit." She stabbed the track pad, refreshing the page until the useless action no longer sufficed as a release for her impotent anger, then clenched her jaw, and dove into her racing mind. "A *major* national theme park. There's only two, maybe three places that fit that description. Wonder World and Wonder Planet. Tinsel Studios."

The Wonder parks were slick facilities designed around gender stereotypes and popular among children. World was all pink princesses and enchanted carousels, while Planet offered fighter jets and explosions. Tinsel relied on Hollywood themes.

"If that's true, then at least the scope of our search is limited to California and Florida." Julian rubbed a temple. "My gut says Wonder World because of the feminine theme."

Morning light seeped in through gaps in the drapes to cast a harsh glare on the dark circles under his eyes, evidence of her husband's distress kindling a pang of sympathy. He was hurting. She squeezed his forearm, offering support through touch.

"We can't take Mal with us. It's too dangerous." Taylor glanced at her son's carrier, taking solace in the sight of his light-brown face at peace, the spray of moles dotting his chubby cheek. Her fleeting bit of joy dissolved into anxiety as an impossible choice rolled in like thunder. "But as we know, it's dangerous to leave him here as well."

"If something got in through a portal, there's possibilities for using magic to seal it," Tim added. "I thought it was already sealed. I'm sorry."

"My water magic?" Taylor didn't quite see how such a thing was intuitive or obvious, though not many aspects of magic were.

Not that she'd been practicing her magic since learning of the pregnancy and moving to Peru. Would being out of practice pose major problems? Likely. She bobbed a restless leg, chastising herself for getting lazy about her craft.

"Correct." Tim resumed pacing. "Remember that time we talked about a former community member using magic to stop enemies from transporting here? A literal firewall to keep negative energy from breaching our borders?"

"The protection spell doesn't seem to be working anymore," Julian deadpanned. "Any thoughts on why it failed?"

"I can't say without studying up on Cynthia's air magic, and as far as I can tell, she fell off the grid after she moved away from here." He muttered under his breath. "It could have worn off on its own, or maybe she needed to keep working to hold the spell in place and forgot about it after awhile. Fuck if I know. She took her book with her and vanished. Can't believe it's been two years now since she left without giving her new address." A dry snort from the leader. "Into thin air, if you will. Apropos. Poof."

"Well, regardless, I'd better try my best to seal that portal before they kidnap anyone else." Meaning the time was now to grab her book and start boning up on spells. Down the line, she'd try to establish contact with this possible fellow witch.

"Am I right in guessing that if the portal is sealed, we can't use it to travel?" After refreshing the browser window, Julian turned to Tim.

"Presumably, but I'm not a magic user. You'll have to test it out and see. Fly by the seat of your pants."

"And speaking of flying, we'd have to get up to the states the old-fashioned way. Then go to the park and investigate." She chewed her lip. No point in running around the parks blindly either, unmoored by guidance or a plan. They didn't have either time or energy to spare. Wonder World it was. Julian's theory about Luna being held in the girly park was reasonable.

Julian swirled the mouse on the track pad and clicked on Mad_Dog_Margarita's name. "I'm hoping they come back, and we can get a few more clues. Until then, at least we can try to seal the portal. Which we need to do anyway, like Taylor said."

"I'll call an emergency meeting at breakfast." Tim's stare roved to a window, where sunlight came brighter and with increased abundance. "See if anyone has insight or information they can share. Any tidbit that would help you focus your efforts."

Taylor jumped to her feet, wincing when a cramp clenched her lower belly. The last thing she needed was to get sidelined by her pain and the vagaries of her body. "I'll see if I can figure out a spell."

Malcom stirred and fussed. Julian, his face knotted in concern, picked up the baby's carrier and rocked it. "I hate to see you in pain. I wish I could do more."

"Just keep Mal while I see what I can figure out. Can you represent us at breakfast, and report back anything relevant you hear?"

"Absolutely," Julian said on a heavy breath. He took a step toward Taylor, his brown eyes soft. "I'm here for you. I love you. I love *us*."

She rested the side of her face against her husband's broad chest, soaking in his woodsy, soap-and-nature scent as he enveloped her in a hug. "I love you, too. I love us."

Love didn't have the power to save Luna, but Taylor and Julian had to fight as a united front; support each other, even if their efforts got difficult. There was simply no other way. She broke out of the tangle and looked up at him, seeking centering and assurance.

He nodded once. "We've got this."

Dear God, she hoped. Taylor didn't have much in the way of a spiritual practice, but the present moment might be an opportune time to acquire one while she undertook her crash course in magic. "We've got this."

"I'm gonna go open up the dining hall." Tim's jangled his keys. "You want to come with me, Jules, and bring Mal? There's formula in the pantry and a few bottles."

"Sure. I'll try to stay out of your way. Let me know if I can do anything. Anything at all."

She gave her man one last hug before bolting from Tim's cabin and into the bright break of day. She had her work cut out for her, but she'd conquered difficult challenges before. Time to rise to the latest one.

✴

ADRENALINE COMPOUNDED WITH SLEEP DEPRIVATION BURNED A scuzzy path through Taylor's system.

She dropped to her knees and peered under the bed, halfway expecting to come face-to-face with some salivating monster. Such an encounter would really round out the last twenty-four hours.

Fortunately, all she saw was hardwood flooring, a couple of orphaned socks, and the book. She unclenched her jaw as her fingers brushed the cover. Thick and inscribed with esoteric symbols grooved deeply into beaten leather, the key was in her hands now.

Her initial glimpse of the neglected volume stoked the flame of guilt. If she'd studied harder, would her efforts have saved Luna? Armed her with psychic powers?

With a deliberate yank, she cutoff the obsessive loop playing through her mind and slid the tome across polished pine, a fine spray of dust moles dissipating into the air.

Head in the game, she climbed into bed, the massive heft of printed knowledge pressed into her chest.

Frustration wound her already taxed system tight when she flipped open the cover and looked at the table of contents. She'd barely afforded a passing look to this text, and her negligence didn't bode well.

For all Taylor knew, non-use had caused her water magic to atrophy, like a muscle gone slack in the absence of exercise. Sure, she'd experienced big bursts of initial power that she'd managed to use to escape and tamp down Scarab, but what if that was beginner's luck, a rush of newbie power coming in only to fade away?

She hadn't felt called by the Amazon or received messages, signs, or omens. She certainly hadn't felt empowered to pull any tides or summon massive waves like she had back then.

Hell, on bad fishing expedition days she didn't even reel a single catch out of the murky depths. Maybe she wasn't even a water witch anymore, perhaps she'd blown her shot at taking control of an awesome power, allowed the best gift she'd ever received to slip through her limp, worthless fingers.

Enough.

Self-recrimination didn't help, and at least she had the pages. Some pages they were, warped by moisture damage and stained with inks various colors, inscriptions bleeding down paper in arrested rivulets.

The material was intimidating, foreign. She'd been a quick study in college, though, and her versatile mind promised at least a slim chance at beating this vault of esoteric content.

Taylor located the section devoted to her water element and studied sub-headings marked by handwritten numbers in numerous hues and styles of penmanship. 1. Counter-Balancing...materials needed. 2. Opposition Elements—Pair or Circle Work—Collaboration.

Collaboration. Taylor made a mental note to reach out to Eve down the line, to compare books. She dog-eared the page.

Additional thoughts formed while she read. Speaking of other witches and their books, it was weird that the water text contained sections devoted to other elements.

The creeps crawled over her skin when she chanced a glimpse at the sixth section: Chaos. Mad_Dog had mentioned that in their chat. Taylor brushed her thumb over a chunk of pages near the end but didn't part the stack enough to see more than coy peeps of scrawled words in lush cursive and drawings rendered in indigo ink. For now, she ought to stick with water. The devil she sort-of knew.

The next two sub-headings: 3. Seals—Keys—Moon Phasing—Tide. 4. Oceans or Creature Work [FAMILIAR recommended though spirit-based possible].

Too bad her familiar, Salazar, had flown off a few weeks ago, never to be seen again. Nostalgia for her reptilian friend stuck between her ribs like a pin, but for all she knew, his behavior was consistent with normal migration or roaming patterns.

She had no reason to believe that a giant, winged snake would be loyal, despite Salazar claiming such a thing when they talked with their minds. Ah, well. She read on.

The final sub-section came with a lot of notes, that, like the others, appeared to have been added by numerous contributors. She stole a quick moment to wonder who these people were who'd written in the book, what they looked like, where they lived, *if* they still lived.

Maybe one day she'd meet her predecessors and have a chance to ask them questions, but for now she only had their writing.

Wild writing, ranging from intriguing to confusing to indecipherable. These mystery people had a lot to say. Who knew that water had such sinister ramifications?

5. Boil, Bleed, Poison, Drying, Pestilence, Virus, Contagion [SKULL sympathy...level 7 FOLLY possession...WILL occur, unless (and in rare cases even then) evoked in accordance with collaborative efforts of chaos witchery and under the eye of a high-ranking spirit protection spell of at

least level 8.5. This intervention will borrow alchemy pieces from <u>spirit</u> <u>witch</u> and as such, she must be protected and guarded against ensuing gaps and lacks. Folly WILL fill those gaps and lacks as well. Spirit + Water possessed at level 10 at least.[1]

A footnote and everything. She'd be staying away from the highly opaque, yet obviously super hardcore, insanity involved with number five. Yet, inspired by a rush of curiosity, she continued to re-read the words in that part.

Sure looked like a lot of power to be found there. Power to possess. Kill, even. She twitched, a bit freaked out, yet undeniably enthralled.

Taylor circled back to the part about seals, keys, moon phasing, and tides and split her book to the corresponding section. Decent place to begin, considering that they wanted to *seal* a portal. A musty scent flowed to her nose as she stared into the tattooed belly of her cleaved tome.

Not all the text was in English, but enough was. Grids and etchings accompanied the writing, but the drawings didn't make sense to her. She began with reading the decipherable stuff.

The element water can be utilized to block, disrupt, or scramble energy signals issued from your realm or the other places[2].[3]

Okay. Finally, some good news. The whole "other places" thing was creepy, but not yet an immediate problem. She avoided falling down the rabbit hole beyond the doorway of the second footnote.

Though never a permanent solution owing to the movement patterns of this highly fungible resource, flexibility and an urge to seep and spread, to <u>*storm*</u>[4] *bodies large and small, the very nature of the element water's volatility offers a water practitioner key advantages.*

Water is speech, movement, messaging. Playful and prone to caprice, this element is the most sensitive and receptive of the six. Pull the tides, call down the rain, manipulate bodily fluid or roughen the seas...do as thou will, but accept that your element is the hardest to master.

Interesting and no doubt informative, but still lots of primer and overview-type content. Taylor craved applications and forged ahead until a block of scribbled text prompted her to stop and notice.

Visit nearest body of water and submerge a piece of your anatomy. Establish communion, trust, whatever bond is possible. Listen to the water, for it will express a desire, too. Your relationship must include symbiosis. Do not simply take, or water will punish. Cajole water. Incentivize water. Accept deeply that, despite your best efforts and practice, water spells may produce unintended effects and unpredictable manifestations. Thus is the nature of water, to spread and spill, never contained by vessel or place. If you deem you must, move the molecules.

A spark of insight ignited in Taylor's mind. She'd confirm the exact location of the jungle portal and scramble the signal with river water, protecting the community from future abductions before she and Julian left in search of Luna.

Taylor re-read the section in case she'd missed anything.

Move the molecules.

Marching orders taken, she shut the book with a dull snap and headed for the Amazon River's nearest bank.

---

1. Spirit and Water will move in a synchronous formation using the illustrations in Section 6. Once Folly is channeled, and unless possession complete and inevitable, S and W will enlist C to move F into SKULL, serving as the prophetic key to prevent unlocking of the prism/prison, which shall return The Other One to its captive prison w/Folly attached, sticky and viscous from C+W interdisciplinary collaboration.

2. Other Places house Other Ones, beings attracted to the black goo produced by Chaos magic. Water, A Light Triad element with a similar constitution to her Dark Trinity OPPOSED sibling, Chaos, confuses Other Ones and thus acts as an ideal, robust scrambling medium. Though witches working with Chaos, Fire, or Spirit may, upon identifying the utilization of water in an effort to confuse or misdirect, steal the water magic in question and be able to leverage it to augment their own dark efforts. Beware, for dark trinity practitioners are thought by some to enjoy enhanced psychic abilities such as telepathy, mind-reading, remote viewing, and enhanced mediumship that may empower them to readily identify and subvert water magic efforts that disrupt their projects.

3. Light Triad: Water, Earth, Air. Dark Trinity: Spirit, Chaos, Fire. Lines of Connectivity: Healing, Creative Channeling, ???.

4. Interference and subversion by Dark Trinity practitioners may call for high-level Water spells mixed with a Chaos component (Hemorrhaging, Lighting Strike, Mummify, Flooded Lungs or Fields, Liquid Guts) to halt said efforts. See #5 and explore various means to involve Chaos in your practice.

FOUR

Wʜɪʟᴇ ᴛʜᴇ ʜᴜɴᴅʀᴇᴅ-ᴘʟᴜs ᴍᴇᴍʙᴇʀs ᴏꜰ ᴛʜᴇ ᴄʟᴀɴ ꜰɪʟʟɪɴɢ ᴛʜᴇ dining hall were busy eating, Julian seized an opportunity. He slipped out of his chair, Malcom nestled in the cloth baby wearer strapped to Julian's torso, and walked to the sink where Tim cleaned up.

Mal had finished his bottle and slept soundly. With any luck, he'd be out for a while.

Tim scrubbed pots and pans in the farm sink, blasting each with a spray of water from the removable nozzle. He attacked stainless steel with a scrubber, going at a fry pan like the cookware had called his mother a nasty name. Yeah. Something was amiss.

Normally wielding the calm collectedness of a natural leader, Tim was allowing signs of frustration to slip through his veneer of composure.

Tim knew more than he was saying, and Julian wasn't about to let him get away with secrecy no matter how much he trusted him. Not with his baby girl on the line. He sidled up to the washing station, set Mal's now-empty bottle on the counter, and worked it with a scrub brush.

His tolerance for tact nearing zero, Julian opened with stark honesty. "What are you keeping to yourself here? Judging by how you're abusing those dishes, I can tell that you're holding back." Running water, background chatter, and metal utensils scraping against plates buffered against eavesdropping.

Tim dropped his sponge in the basin. He clenched the edge so hard his knuckles whitened, blue veins and strained tendons embodying tension. "I'm going to level with you because I respect you too much to lie or sugarcoat."

Blurriness wobbled in the edges of Julian's perception, his world contracting into brittle, sharp awareness of the present. Bad news loomed, but he refused to crumble. He had to stay strong for Mal, Luna, and Taylor. "Give it to me straight."

When Tim turned to face Julian, the look in his eyes was hard yet sorrowful. A deeply unsettling portrait. "I think that the effort to recover Luna is too dangerous for you guys and will prove futile anyway." He spoke in the grim tone of a doctor delivering bad news to a patient's family.

While a half-awake and snugly swaddled Mal squirmed against his chest, Julian fought off an outburst in response to the naysaying tumbling from Tim's mouth. Was the guy seriously telling him to give up on saving his daughter? No strong leader touted the message "give up," an indication that Tim might not be much of a leader after all.

"What the hell's wrong with you, man? Why would you say that?" Anguish shook his speech. Fantasies of seeking release in reactionary aggression ushered in hazy daydreams of ruin. His shoulders and arms seized, and if he hadn't been wearing his baby, he might have punched a wall or thrown an object into one.

Tim's dark, drained sigh competed for the dubious honor of the most miserable sound Julian had ever heard, forcing pity to trump violent urges. "It's entirely possible that I've spent one too many nights crawling through the bowels of that fucking conspiracy theory message board and subjecting myself to the ramblings of schizophrenics trapped in the webs of their own delusions."

One unspoken word hung in the air, a talisman of menace swinging like an ominous pendulum. Julian voiced the utterance in question when he ventured, "But?"

"This Mad Dog person is a popular one. Trusted. If he or she is right, telling the truth, then this thing is enormous, complex, and highly coordinated."

"What *thing?*" He spat the second word like poison.

Tim's lips bent into a rictus of disgust, as if confessions gleaned from taboo nightmare fodder loomed beyond the boundaries of decent, allowable speech. "The agenda, plan, operation. Whatever you want to call it. Not only are these monsters sick, they're organized."

"We took down Scarab." Julian swayed side to side, keeping Mal calm with the gentle motion even as Tim's comments made him edgy. He had to firmly grasp his rational mind. "That was huge. We portal traveled and sunk an entire island, Tim. What's special about what they're doing now that's beyond our capabilities?"

"Provided we accept the prevailing theory, the underground tunnel network is extensive, and it runs in a subterraneous system connecting all three parks, along with additional nodes, like basements of front homes. Florida to California, Jules. I don't have to be the one to tell you how much territory that spans. This is vast. Scarab Island, strictly speaking, was centralized and discrete. What if you pick one of those parks to search, and they have Luna at another one on the opposite coast? You and Taylor could easily be intercepted. Killed."

Julian's intuition had a way of piping up when something was off, and right now his inner voice was humming a skeptical tune. "Your reservations boil down to sheer geography?"

Tim fixed a hollow gaze at some distant endpoint before reigning in the thousand-yard stare and looking right into Julian's soul.

The bomb was about to drop. No good. That much he knew. "Tim," he whispered.

Tears moistened the young alpha's eyes, a stark show of vulnerability on someone impeccably put together, cracking the community's pillar of strength.

"I'm sorry." His deep voice, wrenched to pieces by regret, rattled Julian to his foundation. If Tim was this much of a mess, the situation was bad. Good thing he didn't believe in lost causes and refused to give up and fold like a coward fleeing a cavalry.

"Sorry for what?" Julian's mouth ran dry. His words tasted bitter on his tongue. The relentless din of mixed voices made for a disorienting cacophony, transporting Julian somewhere weird, a place dictated by premonitions haunting his racing thoughts. He stood rooted in place while every second dragged. "Sorry for what?"

A low wail from Tim. "I went overboard. Clicking, following links, reading articles, and watching videos. Some of these videos...I wasn't even sure what I was watching. I felt like I was being mind controlled, or that the content was made by an artificial intelligence or spirit. I can't explain it, but after awhile I started hearing voices and seeing things. It was late at night. I logged off for the night and of course had nightmares. When I got back on the next day, there was a message on one of my social media accounts. I assumed it was a prank, a coincidence, but when we stood there behind Taylor and I saw what Mad Dog wrote, I was completely fucking destroyed beyond recognition."

Julian's mind spun until it threatened to fly out of his skull and into some crazy, paranoid alternate universe. The universe he thought he and Taylor had escaped. "What did the message say?"

Tim paled, flinched. "They see you. You've got candy."

"Candy?"

"It's code. For shifter babies."

Julian's stomach cramped. Poisonous bile surged up his throat. He held Mal a little tighter, more determined than ever to end these twisted freaks who'd stolen his child. Parts snapped into place with a numb logic. "They've been monitoring us because we have something they want. Surveillance. That much is clear. But I'm betting it's a more sophisticated system than the Internet. Satellites. Nanotech. Whatever is in Taylor's body."

"Drones, heat sensors, artificial intelligence spies travelling through the Internet or online devices, cutting-edge motion detection. Some or all of those. All possibilities are on the table, but yeah. Next-level sophistication." Tim's expression was exhaustion packaged in a resigned scowl. "My firewalls apparently aren't doing shit. I unplugged the computer as soon as Taylor walked out that door, but who knows. I feel like I led them to us, to Luna. I wish that I had more to offer besides another useless apology."

Lashing out in blame wasn't productive despite the temptation of catharsis. "You did your best," Julian managed. "But I don't think that anyone should be online anymore."

Tim gestured to the dining table, where folks were still lost to the joys of food, revelry, and blissful ignorance. "If I ban Internet here, we'll be looking at a revolt. Mutiny. Anarchy within days. And I wouldn't blame them. These folks signed up for communal living in a good society, not an authoritarian regime subject to the whims of a dictator. You see how I'm hamstrung. I can't pull a bait and switch."

Julian paced, the movement serving the dual purpose of keeping Mal calm and helping Julian brainstorm. "If Taylor seals the portal, at least that buys us time. They can watch and monitor us all day long, but as long as they're barred from executing any more abductions, it's no worse than being looked at through a peephole. Creepy, but the community is safe."

Tim tapped a foot, moving his head side to side as if swayed by Julian's persuasion. "Unless they adapt. Which I'm sure they're always doing. They might find a way to negate the portal seal or open a new doorway."

"They might do a lot of things. But I'm not going to roll over and give in to them. Not now, not ever. And you didn't answer me initially. Why the apprehension about us going after them?"

Tim's Adam's apple bobbed on the heels of a big, grave swallow. He picked up a dishrag and wrung it hard, using the frayed cloth as a stress ball. "I love you guys, and I don't want them to lure you to where they are, to where any number of their agents are stationed. They tried this last year, remember? They *want* you to go after them. Draw you into their ritual."

"Yeah, well, they *tried* that last year, like you said. Tried and failed. Why don't you have faith that we'll stop them again?"

"The zodiac calendar. Last year, we had a head start. Of several days. Now, there's a distinct possibility that they planned that too, that they wanted Taylor there on day one to perform the extraction. But regardless, we got the drop on them. They were weakened, as they lacked the power boost of ritual-generated energy to draw from."

Blood drained from Julian's face. The point emerged. "Not the case now."

"Nope. They caught us off guard. Abducting a baby means that they're around a week in."

"A week into what?" Julian sucked his teeth in preparation. He didn't want to know, but what he wanted didn't matter. Only rescuing Luna did.

Kathleen doddered up to the sink, the hem of her patchwork skirt swirling right above her sandaled feet, and set her cup and bowl in the basin. The white-haired elder smiled at Tim, then shifted her attention to Mal.

"Look at this beautiful little boy," she whispered, leaning in for a closer look, the wrinkles crossing her face carving deep grooves as she smiled. "Such a proud papa." She squeezed Julian's arm, her papery, cool touch surprisingly strong for her age.

He waited patiently for the innocent old woman to finish cooing, his mind fixed on returning to the conversation with Tim even as he preserved the veneer of normalcy, politeness, and order for the sake of the others.

Tim held tense, eternal silence. He lobbed Kathleen an affable but sharp smile, a message that she was interrupting an important conversation and ought to go away.

She must've registered the signal, because she winked at Tim and said, "Perfect meal today," in her rickety voice before ambling back to her spot.

To the thumping soundtrack of his elevated pulse, Julian waved his hand in the "come on" gesture.

"It's called the Song of Virgo. Their inversion of our autumnal equinox ritual. We went over it last year. What their practice entails."

Awash in grim memories of an unspeakable conversation, Julian nodded. Torture, murder, canned hunts. Sacrificing shifters, bathing in their blood, and dancing through desecrated chambers while adorned in their skins.

A slow, creeping sense of anger at his own stupidity engulfed him whole. "I can't believe that we didn't prepare for this. Anticipate them making another move this time of year."

Tim puffed out his cheeks and blew out a loud breath. "Yeah, I know, but I think we were all just wishing and praying that it was over. And honestly? When we got through the sabbats and solstices, the other equinox without any disturbances, I lulled myself into a false sense of security. Let myself believe that they'd given up on us. I didn't want to overreact or alarm anyone; be a fear monger." Tim rubbed his frown-creased forehead. "And here we are."

Julian timed a long inhale and even longer exhale in hopes of loosening the tightness squeezing his chest. Lots of new information about seasonal milestones, likely none of it good. "We're a week into the Song of Virgo. What does that mean?"

"The equinox that we're approaching marks the onset of autumn and ushers in the shadowy half of the year. Their darkest practices occur starting now, and ease up at the spring equinox, the Ballad of Pisces. God knows what they do then, but that really doesn't concern us now."

A cloud surfaced at the forefront of Julian's thoughts, a somber epiphany of the grimmest sort. "They're going to sacrifice Luna." The floor seemed to crumble beneath him as he battled an urge to vomit. His head spun, and dizziness took over, but he had to be strong and put up a show of composure and confidence.

Tim flinched, his face contorting like he could barely spit out the awful truths. "Yeah. Their season of sacrifice begins soon and continues until the next equinox. Three more events occur after this one, two sabbats and the winter solstice. From what I can tell, they believe that they can harvest the fear and other negative emotions generated and funnel that energy into whatever evil projects they have underway. Then they spend the so-called light half of the year working on those initiatives. It's a bastardization of paganism, you know? Like presenting a burnt offering to the gods in exchange for a bountiful harvest. Reaping and sowing. Shifter babies supposedly carry a higher magical charge."

Julian scrubbed a hand over his face, the nausea roiling his guts worsening with each passing second of this abhorrent conversation. In his brain, a ticking clock marched on without mercy. The time to stop plotting and start moving had passed. "Any clues from the board how we should get into the park, anything?"

Tim parted his lips and made a clipped sound before laying a hand at Julian's forearm. "This will be the last time I warn you, but they've been preparing for their ceremony for an entire week now and probably have a contingency in place if you pursue them. The wind is at their backs, magically and energetically speaking. Hold your hope, but know there is a strong possibility of this being a fool's errand. A deadly one."

Julian held the other man's stare right along with his hope. "This is my daughter, and I'm going to do whatever it takes even if I die trying. Do I make myself clear?"

"Yeah." Tim took his hand away. "Your instinct to start at the Florida park, the feminine one, makes sense."

Florida it was. Time to find Taylor and set the plan into motion. Julian took off walking, leaving the cafeteria. A forgettable day in the jungle lay beyond those eatery walls, the atmosphere balmy and overcast.

He quick-stepped to the cabin he shared with Taylor, Tim catching up to walk at his side, and found their home empty. A panoramic glance at the dirt hinted at her whereabouts.

While no expert tracker, he recognized the small footprints left by her tennis shoes.

They'd joked about the pattern on the bottom of those shoes, indulged in a shared, juvenile laugh about how the rubber molding near the soles left behind stamps in the shape of penises. Days spent deep in the rainforest got boring at times, a mundane routine broken up by goofy humor.

His protective arm securing Mal in his wrap, Julian followed the trail. "I bet she went to the creek."

"Water magic. Checks out," Tim said.

Hasty passage through some scruffy underbrush soon opened into a clearing, largely forgotten space inhabited by a crumbling storage shed and an outhouse that got abandoned once the community amassed enough money and expertise to build compost toilets and simple plumbing.

Beyond the patch of green space, the creek flowed, beckoning visitors with a liquid melody purring from the bottom of an earth gash that wound through wild land. A fat log slung over the groove made a makeshift bridge, one jagged end stopping at a tree whose roots speared coal-black layers of mud.

Julian approached the precipice and glanced down to the ripples. Nobody in sight. Clear water glossed rocks and sticks as the stream slid by in a jaunty flow. "Taylor? You around, babe?" he called out, voice raised enough to penetrate the jungle mass, but all he got back were the haunting sounds of his own words returned as a slight echo.

Tim held up his hand like a visor and looked in both directions. "She went deeper than this. Probably didn't want to be disturbed."

If they marched east, they'd traverse a path marked by big swaths of jungle before curving around to end up back at the residential cabins. The westward trajectory led to the river, with the creek getting fuller and wider as the Amazon approached. His intuition pinged, and he tipped his head to the west.

Tim nodded, the gesture spurring Julian to move. The pair trekked down a trodden path popular among those seeking a light hike to the tune of running water.

After ten paces, the creek widened and deepened, water now too murky to see to the bottom. Julian kicked a large stick out of his path as a strange, eerie feeling settled over him.

The sensation was a creeping one, stillness pregnant with chaos, like in an apocalypse movie where a character confronts calmness before being rushed by the first pack of zombies.

Weird energy vibrated off Tim too, some force field passing between them. They didn't discuss it as they walked in tandem, sticks crunching underfoot.

"Taylor," Julian shouted into the trees. His own voice boomeranged again, the effect toeing the edge of a taunt thrown his way by some mocking nature spirit.

They'd ventured deeper still, until Tim said, "Let's check the eastern route," when an impossible image trespassed into Julian's field of vision and shredded his sense of reason.

On the same side of the creek where he and Tim hiked, two sneaker-clad feet, toes pointed down, levitated amidst tree branches. He halted his steps and glanced up, squinting against the shards of sunlight filtering through leaves.

Shoes led to jeans, then a familiar sweatshirt with a sports team logo on the front. Taylor, floating in midair.

His senses careened into free fall. Logic charged out of the gate first, getting in front of crazy speculation as logic often did, and the heinous possibility she'd been hanged from a tree ambushed his thoughts.

The next thing he saw assured him that an entirely different scenario was unfolding.

Her book levitated in front of her, open. The effect was uncanny, imbuing the inanimate object with an aura of sentience.

When the first notes of her speech struck his ears, flatter and lower in pitch than her normal timbre, he lost the capacity to do anything but listen while riding the icy-hot waves of shock pulsing in him, over him, all around him.

To say that magic—*dark* magic—loomed, well, that was a massive understatement.

His wife spoke a clear directive in chilling monotone, the sound of her speech so foreign another person could have uttered the statement. "May every molecule of your body merge with the energetic intentions of those who love us not. Go, now, to those places corrupted by the evil energies of chaos mongers and those who tarry with Other Ones. Bind with their spells and muddy their intentions. Dissolve their powers in your mighty solvent."

"She's sealing the portal. This is good." Tim no doubt sensed Julian's unmoored trepidation that the unfolding scene wasn't good at all. His insistent whisper tried too hard to reassure.

Pages flipped in the book, deliberate turns not simply dashed by the wind, stopping when a large portion of the text lay to the left. A lone tendril of gray smoke curled upward from those pages near the end and drifted into Taylor's nostrils.

A slow smirk tugged one side of her face upward. "Let the reaping commence." She floated downward and gasped when her soles hit the ground.

FIVE

Recent circumstances had turned Taylor's brain into a pliable organ. This insight only became possible by the highlighting powers of contrast.

Though she continued to reel, dizzy and spaced out from working with magic, she grasped enough of her environment to enjoy a novel *wow* factor in the familiar.

From the creek flowing like liquid glass to a panorama of jungle greenery sprayed with drops of sunlit humidity, the surroundings enveloped her in sparkle. Moist air smelled of sweet, exotic flowers, and she breathed in as much of the natural fragrance as her lungs would hold.

A precise, carved character to her mind mirrored the glittery freshness surrounding her.

She was clear now. Poised. Clean. Revitalized and ready.

She shifted her weight on her feet, circling her ankle until the joint cracked and she felt sufficiently grounded.

Some voices that were not her own murmured in the back of her mind, but it was okay. They said they were here to help, and she chose to believe them. Believing them felt good and right and true.

Her vision blurred when she looked past the vantage point upon which she'd fixed, sight wobbly and watery as if loaded with gelatinous tears. A headache pinched behind the inside of her left eye. Other than those minor symptoms, she'd weathered her experiment and returned to normal.

Except for the voices. But they were here to help.

As her vision began to clear and the outlines of two fuzzy figures swam before her, she nodded, chalking up her first practiced effort at spell casting to a success.

"Babe. Talk to me. Are you alright?" Julian's deep tone floated to her ears with a faraway, dreamy quality that comforted her.

"Yeah." The heavy word stumbled off a clumsy tongue trapped in her dry, hot mouth, awkwardness of speech making it difficult to voice a more articulate answer. Her body hadn't yet caught up to her mind. She knew she ought to be reassuring Julian, but remaining upright and alert demanded her attention. Queasiness washed over her as she organized her thoughts. "Let's go check the portal."

Mention of the doorway in space prompted her to crouch, swallowing a particularly vicious bolt of nausea. She lifted the book and stood.

An unpleasant awareness, like being watched by invisible beings, nagged from some murky place where thoughts weren't easily identified or named. The feeling was totally foreign, unsettling yet too obscure to count as scary.

Only Julian, Mal, and Tim faced her, though, her husband's expression one of concern shot through with awe. Tim's face was tougher to read, his eyes narrowed, and his head drawn back in skepticism or suspicion. What was wrong with him?

With as much nonchalance as the situation would allow, she glanced over each of her shoulders, mustering a friendly smile when she saw nothing but the typical browns and greens painting the jungle landscape. No monsters lurked behind her. She was a little destabilized and freaked out by the magical immersion was all.

"Suppose you weren't expecting to see me hanging out in the air, huh?" She threw her levity at Tim's scowl. When the leader acted like this, reticent and walled with a penchant for keeping to himself, it meant he harbored some grievance.

Tim shook his head and muttered a couple of indecipherable words.

She chose not to press the issue. He'd get over whatever was bothering him eventually or share if he deemed fit.

Julian placed his palm on her forehead, the sensation of his warm, callused skin delivering a taste of respite. "I know that I wasn't. Sounds like you made progress."

She slid his hand to her mouth and kissed the spot where a palmist would read lines before interlacing their fingers and starting back to the camp. "Yeah. I'm confident. We should check the portal, then circle back to the message board for clues."

Taylor glanced at a sleeping Mal, his tiny fistful of doll fingers balled near his dimpled chin. A pang of hollow pain, the ache in her heart where Luna ought to be, lanced her, but she staved off impending sorrow. She'd made major gains and had to stay strong as they advanced to the next phase of the rescue.

Tim cleared his throat. "Do you remember what you said while you were casting the spell?" He asked the question casually, his inquiry sounding more pointed and accusatory than he likely intended.

Jumbled syllables of spoken incantations and the fading, phantom recollections of intense sensations surfaced from her memory, dissolving as quickly as they arrived. Déjà vu bent her attempts to think into a trippy Mobius Strip of dreams, daydreams, and reality until past merged with present, then blended into future. She had no idea if that was expected and chose honesty in an attempt to allay whatever suspicion he harbored. "Not really, no. The harder I try to, the more weirded out I get."

Let the reaping commence. The voice in her head, androgynous and undeniably other, drifted through her mind the same as an evil wind. She clutched Julian's hand a little tighter. That voice, one of many, rose above the other helper spirits. Why would helper spirits talk about reaping?

"You sure you're alright?" her husband asked.

"I'm fine." She concentrated on putting one foot in front of the other and appreciating the sights of Julian's handsome profile and their slumbering bundle of love.

It didn't do anyone any good to start obsessing. She'd launched the spell. It was done. The die was cast, the effects set into motion. The back of her neck prickled, a sensation she ignored as best she could.

"Not a single memory?" Tim's brown eyes seared into hers. A muscle near his throat feathered. "A sound? Singing or chanting? Voices?"

The way he said "voices" struck a troublesome chord. Like he knew she had heard them, had some experience with this topic that he wasn't admitting for whatever guarded, typical Tim reason.

"Leave her be, man. She's been through enough," Julian delivered with firm authority.

"Well, if you remember anything," Tim pressed, "I'd write it down. Might prove useful to us later."

She saluted him with enough of self-awareness to indicate that the subject was closed for now. "Sure thing." She patted the book. "I'll write it in here. Everyone else and their mom has written in this thing."

Tim pursed his lips like he wanted to speak more but found the resolve not to.

Soon, they reached Julian and Taylor's cabin. She glanced around, taking in hazy skies and fluttering leaves, the sights and sounds of people milling about.

A man hauled a glistening, pink side of meat to the shed where the community hunters processed the bountiful fruits of nature, waving hello to lesbian couple canoodling in a hammock stretched between two trees.

A group of five kids playing hopscotch, skipping through chalked squares on nimble feet, chatted and laughed. Another day filled with everyday activity and enjoyable pastimes. Yet an ineffable, insidious force saturated the atmosphere.

Taylor unlocked the front door with the click of her key, shutting down her overactive imagination. "Stands to reason that this portal they used must be in our home."

"Otherwise, we would have heard them break in," Julian supplied the unspoken piece of logic, ducking to clear the doorway as he stepped over the threshold.

"Valid hypothesis." Tim brought up the rear. "Assuming that the portal is limited to one location and can't be moved or relocated once a target is identified."

If Tim was right, she'd have no way to verify whether her magic had sealed the entry point. Scarab could have taken Luna and moved their portal to Tibet, Wyoming, or Pakistan in search of their next innocent target.

She walked to the desk in the corner where she'd finished her classes online and sat, battling a rush of dizziness as an unpleasant, fluttery tightness constricted her chest. Lack of sleep was wearing her down, with magic surely exacerbating her weakened state, but it wasn't time to rest yet. After a futile attempt to salve her anxiety with mindful breaths, she logged on to the message board and clicked on Mad_Dog_Margarita's profile. "I'll see if I can pull anything else useful out of him," she said while typing up a follow-up inquiry. "A few more details before we get moving would be great."

Julian's hand on her shoulder stopped her before she hit send.

She looked at her man with confusion, registering with dread the somber look on his face. "Why don't you want me to contact him again?"

"Because I want to save us every minute I can at this point." He squeezed, a firm yet grasping hold that somehow both instilled security in her and clung tight for stability. The pain behind his eyes shone stark and horrifying.

"What do you know?" Her mouth went to cotton again, her head fuzzy even as she scooted to the end of her seat, desperate to accrue more information.

Julian looked at Tim, who clenched his jaw, the silent, conspiratorial exchange worrying Taylor, angering her. She ought to be in every loop there was, never frozen out on what was happening with her baby.

"Tell me." Her words squeaked out through a closing throat. Abject images dredged from the darkest recesses of a mother's mind emerged. "Fucking tell me."

Time ceased to exist in the lapse between when Julian's lips parted, and the words came. From that point on, she caught snatches, unspeakable concepts delivered in glum reports punctuated by deep, pounding blank spots that bloomed when her mind refused to process.

One week. One week to save Luna before she became the sacrifice in some twisted, evil ritual of hate and malice. Taylor pulled at her short hair, a poor substitute for a tangible plan to hold onto. "You knew," she looked to Tim as the accusation spread through her and outward.

"I've been monitoring them for awhile. Keeping tabs." A

straightforward explanation collected an apology in the rise and fall of consonants and vowels.

Caught at the crossroads of fury and terror, Taylor sprung from her seat and got in Tim's face. He had several inches of muscled, male body on her, but he startled all the same. Good. If he had something to be sorry for, she'd make him regret it. "You *knew*. And you didn't warn us. Or prepare us. Or tell us what to expect. Why?"

Paranoia ate into her rational capacity in an acidic frenzy of speculation. Was Tim a spy, a plant, bribed to facilitate the kidnapping of Luna? She shoved his chest, meeting stalwart resistance in a solid wall. "Why, why, why?" Demands morphed to laments as tears stung her ducts and hysteria threatened to shred the vestiges of her dignity and composure.

"It isn't his fault." With a gentle tug above her elbow, Julian pulled her a foot away from Tim.

She was shaking now, spinning. "No." Taylor made her eyes into slits, narrow apertures aiming lasers at Tim. "He's to blame. You are, aren't you? Admit it."

Tim let out a sharp, keening sob. "They were monitoring us, and I didn't know it. The more I researched, the more footprints I left, the easier it was for them to track Luna. There's new tech in your body, or a chemical agent, possibly, to assist the tracking. I realize that my apology's worthless at this point, but I was trying to protect us. But they got out in front of me."

Taylor's knees wobbled. She fought the onslaught of incoming information. A baleful eureka sprung from the cracks in her fractured psyche. "They put more chips or nanoparticles in me on Scarab Island. When they tried to extract Mal and Luna. The cause of my pain is whatever new shit is in me. It has to be."

But why? No leads, clues, or answers. No safety net or assurance. On the verge of beaten, Taylor clutched her violated midsection. She sat and buried her face in the crook of her other elbow as utter despair crushed her spirit.

Luna was gone, and instead of a path forward, they faced a discombobulating maze where every route led to another minotaur.

"Taylor." Julian's soft rumble of a whisper came to her like a cord of steel to grab.

She lifted her chin to face him, angling toward one ray of hope, and allowed herself to find an anchor in his dark eyes. "Promise me this isn't hopeless. Even if you have to lie, promise me."

"I can't make promises, and I won't condescend to you. You're too smart for that. But I won't give up, and I won't let you give up. Starting tomorrow morning, we're going to go after Luna and fight like hell to get her back. We'll plot our course as strategically as we can and chase every lead there is. Stay with me here, babe."

Taylor reined in all her scattered parts. She assessed the weapons in her arsenal. Her magic. Her book. Her determination, the unmatched ferocity of a mother intent on saving her child. These would be her fire.

Her husband would be her strength. Julian was her rock, always and forever. There was nobody but him, the love of her life and her fate-bound mate, that she'd pick to go to war with.

No more going crazy, no more flailing in search of scapegoats.

She brushed the backs of her fingers against Mal's silken cheek and leaned in close enough to savor his baby smell. "We can't take him with us."

Her battered heart broke into even smaller pieces. She'd be separated from both of her children soon, but no way in hell would she subject her remaining infant to mortal danger.

"I'll call a meeting in the morning," Tim put in. "And we'll decide collectively who is best suited to take on the responsibility of his care while you two are gone."

She exhaled deeply, getting rid of the lingering remnants of her resentment and distrust of Tim. He'd made a mistake, an awful though unintended misstep, and rejecting him would not help. "Yeah. Okay. Our passports don't expire for another year."

"We'll fly to Florida in the morning." Julian grabbed the laptop and brought up an airfare website. "And hope like hell that's the right park."

Taylor cracked her book, eyes growing achy as she read. "I'll look through this for a spell. Maybe I can do divination or access visions—see through time and space."

That didn't sound right. Not like a water magic thing. Collaborating with other witches *had* come up in the book. Maybe there was a possibility of combining her water magic with one of the other types to obtain a mixed result. She flipped the thin pages with gusto, in pursuit of a hunch.

"Alright, we're booked for the flights." Keys clicked in a steady pattern of taps. "I say we buy day passes to the park and go in there as tourists. You can continue to research your magic on the plane while I see if I can get any more out of Mad Dog. Once we're on the ground, we'll hopefully have more leads to work from and tools to use."

Julian's plan ordered the worst of the chaos. She cut to the collaboration section. Her pulse banged as dampness kissed her palms, perspiration slicking the back of her neck. When her gaze landed on the section she sought, triumph juiced her pulse.

"Here." She stabbed her finger against paper with a dull thump. She read a chunk to herself first, then reread for confirmation, before reading aloud a paragraph of text on collaboration with spirit element. "Water and spirit collaboration yields unique opportunities for movement of energy. Where water witchery excels in the manipulation of physical bodily functions, mimicry of disease, and marshaling the natural resource in question to suit the practitioner's will, spirit's talents lay in the domain of the mind. If applied to the witch's own mind, this force facilitates astral travel, remote viewing, teleportation, and moving one's body through walls and other solid masses. When used on others' minds, especially in collaboration with chaos witchery, a spirit practitioner may be able to construct and apply mind control programs, wipe memories, or install false ones, or even hack the consciousness of another to achieve a secondary form of possession [Folly/Skull]."

Taylor read on, devouring words in an insatiable information binge. Parts snapped together neatly to assume the shape of a fearsome, occult weapon. *Watch out, kidnappers.*

In her peripheral vision, Julian stepped closer. Tim followed suit until each man's face hovered over one of her shoulders.

Her heartbeat slammed, excitement a magnetic field drawing opportunity into its orbit. She had power here, real power. Power to save Luna.

She'd use her power to its fullest extent and call upon her might to plunge her captors into a world of misery. But they weren't there yet.

Following an extended pause, Julian offered a reply. "Sounds like a ton of potential for all kinds of action there. I'm not hearing or seeing how any of it gets us closer to Luna."

"Agreed," Tim said. "While those are badass spells and all, if there's a connection between disease mimicry or mind control and nailing down specs on Luna's location, it's not obvious to me. At all."

For the first time since the nightmare begun, Taylor smiled. "That's because I haven't read the best part. Check it." She began at the top of the following page. "With the assistance of spirit, a water witch can harness the ability to send her consciousness into and through water, using the substance as a psychic medium. From there, if her wits are focused and trained, she may travel in the direction of targets by establishing energetic communion with others' emotions, auras, and desires."

Taylor paused to let the words sink in, infusing them with potential. She focused on the outcome she wished to manifest: demolishing blockage, opening doors. Below the portion she'd read, someone had scribbled an incantation and some directions. Details to deal with later. For now, she'd celebrate the breakthrough.

"Damn." Julian sounded hella impressed, rightfully. This was awesome stuff, sweet nectar ripe with possibility. "You've got a magical Coast Guard mission in mind."

"Search and rescue." Taylor closed her book with pride. "Now let's go save Luna."

All she had to do was quickly locate a spirit witch and, in short order, convince the total stranger to participate in collaborative spell work in the service of a high-stakes, dangerous rescue.

Challenging? Sure. But Taylor had beaten plenty of challenges and wasn't about to quit on the biggest and most important one of her life.

SIX

WITH PURPOSEFUL FOCUS, JULIAN BLAZED A PATH ACROSS THE SMALL kitchen's tile floor and opened the refrigerator. A few of bottles stared back at him, backup filled with Taylor's breast milk. More milk packed the freezer.

He allowed the visual evidence of their fastidious planning to salve some of his anxiety.

Taylor had been saving her surplus flow for an emergency, and the emergency was now.

He pulled a pencil from behind his ear and drew a line through the first item on the list, then turned to Crystal and Sasha.

Following a rigorous process of application, interviewing, full debriefing, community popular vote, and final approval by Taylor and Julian, they'd landed the job. Much deserved. Mal was in expert, loving hands. "Plenty of milk to start. There's two months' worth of formula and filtered water in the cupboards and pantry too." He sunk his teeth into the pencil and chewed the soft wood. "Did I show you where to find the supplies to clean and sanitize the bottles?"

Crystal, a plump thirty-year-old with curly black hair and skin the color of sand, approached Julian and touched his wrist before he could launch into a spiel about diaper changing. "Yes. We'll be fine. Sash and I babysat the twins when you two took that overnight trip into town, remember? We've got this."

Sasha, silver bracelets tinkling, took her place at Crystal's side. "We'll be more than fine. We're thrilled. In fact, this is good practice for us."

The women's rapport put Julian at ease, a more authentic sense of calm than the false one he tried to create by being in control. They were good, kind people, a beautiful couple whose maturity and competence made them ideal caretakers. They'd taken the news as well as anyone could have, expressing their sympathies while remaining calm and optimistic. Morning sunlight framed one blond and one brunette head, ringing each with an appropriately angelic halo.

"I concur," Crystal said.

Sasha turned a serious, blue-eyed gaze to Julian. "You guys better get moving."

A few feet away, a toilet flushed, then the water came on as Taylor washed her hands.

Julian took in a long look at his son, innocent as he slept in the crib, and cleared his throat as he prepared to say some difficult yet important parting words. Words he didn't want his wife to hear—she'd endured enough trauma. "I want the two of you to be godmothers to Malcom. Luna too. In case anything happens to Taylor and I."

"Of course," Sasha said, pressing a hand to her heart. "We'd be honored."

Crystal's chin trembled. She turned her head and pretended to sneeze. "Absolutely. But nothing is going to happen to you guys. You'll be back here with Luna and reunited with Mal in no time."

He heard the doubt in her voice, upswing dampened with unshed tears, and didn't blame her. His confidence in a successful rescue ebbed and flowed. The operation was dangerous and scary, with a lot of moving parts. "I amended my will." Julian lowered his voice as the bathroom door clicked and Taylor came into view. "Everything is in writing."

Sasha pursed her lips and nodded, two slow and solemn bobs of her head.

"Okay," Crystal whispered. "Sounds good."

Taylor peeked at Julian's checklist. "What sounds good?"

"Just ironing out those last few details." For emphasis, he marked a couple of completed, inconsequential items off the to-do list. He'd broach the subject of Mal's guardianship with Taylor and hear out any objections she had once they were in private, but for peace of mind, he had to handle the matter before they left. What if the plane crashed? "Are we ready?"

Taylor slapped the sides of her jean-clad thighs and looked around, a somber pall hanging over her pretty pixie features. "Yeah."

Seeming to grasp an unspoken emotion, Crystal tugged on Sasha's arm. "We'll wait outside. Take as long as you need."

"Thank you." He thanked her for not adding a phrase about goodbyes as much as for her courtesy. Concerns about not returning were real, but gloom and doom didn't serve anyone.

Two tears rolled down his cheeks as he watched his boy sleep. "I'll be back for you, with your sister." A crack in Julian's voice broke through his whisper, shattering his attempt to be strong. "You're in the best hands."

Breathing shakily, Taylor clutched the side of the crib. "I love you, Mal. Mama loves you." She turned away and whimpered quietly, the swallowed sobs of a person barely keeping it together. He and Taylor performed their strength in similar ways, one especially potent feature of their attraction and bond.

Julian held his wife. Even the strongest people needed to be vulnerable sometimes, and he did his best to care for and caress her in her time of need. "We're going to win," he said with as much surety as possible.

She tensed on an inhale and stepped back, still gripping his hands, the look in her dark-blue eyes stoic, though bloodshot evidence of her emotions painted the whites red. "You asked Crystal and Sasha to adopt Malcom if we don't return, didn't you?"

"Yes. I'm sorry I didn't consult you first. I didn't want to upset you with that kind of talk. Did I screw up?"

She closed her eyes, those pale lashes he loved serrated by tears. "I should be upset, I guess, but this isn't the time for conflict. No, I take that back. You did the right thing. I trust Sasha and Crystal implicitly." She tightened her grasp, punctuating her statement with an assuring squeeze. "Thank you for taking the lead."

Without another word or a torturous backwards glance at what he was leaving behind, Julian led his wife through the front door before he second-guessed his decision.

Talking softly to her partner, Sasha acknowledged the handoff with a curt tip of the chin, and both women walked into Julian and Taylor's cabin and locked the door behind them. Conscientious and safe from the get-go. Off to a solid start.

Both heaviness and jitters consumed him as he stepped into a sunny morning brisk with notes of fall and the ubiquitous Iquitos smell of burning wood cooking fish, yucca, and plantains. The two of them were about to leave their home; trade quaint, pleasantly familiar rural tidings for a journey into a sinister maw of unknown depravities.

Mission engaged.

The cranking grind of a shot-out engine broke his train of thought. He clutched his plastic suitcase handle in one hand and Taylor's slender fingers in the other, clenching lifelines to home when a motorcycle pulling a yellow riding car drove up and idled. The driver, short and dark, pinched the wide brim of his sun hat and tipped it to greet his customers.

With a long and purposeful stride, Taylor stepped out first, slid her bag to the end of the bench, and boarded the uncovered buggy. Julian joined her and laid his head on her shoulder.

He'd find strength and courage in her, as she would from him. There was no other way.

In confirmation of the promise forged in their fate-bond, she rested her hand above his knee. They rode like that, silent, captured by a sensorium of hair-whipping breezes, the one-note moan of an old engine, and petroleum exhaust fumes that cancelled any temptation to speak. She gave no indication of any pain, and he accepted the blessing as a good tiding.

Parking lot, airport, check-in, security. They didn't speak until settled on the plane in seats purposefully chosen near the back of the small aircraft. At least that way there were no passengers behind them to peer forward with spying eyes or curious ears.

Taylor wasted no time after the flight attendant's safety check protocol and the captain's greeting to haul out her book. Once final crew checks wrapped up, she splayed the magic tome open on her lap. He understood why they needed to deal with the book, yet the sight of it bothered him considering the disturbing events of the jungle.

Really, he low-key hated that book; its ponderous bulk, and ugly, haphazard script. Doozy of a thing, authentic and creepy with all those esoteric symbols and writings of people from unknown times and places. Were those people alive, dead, watching and listening now? *Let the reaping commence.* He suppressed a squirm and initiated conversation instead. "Is step one still to call Eve once we get to the hotel?"

Eve. Now there was an exceptionally strange person in a cast of characters where strangeness was the baseline. The haunted woman and her vampire partner had brought a lot of tumult to the jungle last year in their search for cures to their afflictions, but they'd seemed like decent enough people who deserved the peace they sought.

"Yeah. It was." Taylor scrunched her brows and leaned in to get a better look at her pages, mouthing words as her expression slid into puzzlement.

Liftoff sent the plane soaring, and Julian's ears popped as his stomach jumped from the weightless sensation of flight. He didn't mind flying, but that initial unmoored feeling never failed to deliver a slight shock. He pinched his nose and sucked in air, correcting his internal pressure before following up with his wife. "Was? Your plan changed?"

She backtracked a few pages then returned to her original spot. "There's a numeric pattern in here. I think it's geographic coordinates."

They'd done this dance before, but back then the captured shifters had been able to hack Taylor's technological programming implants to communicate their location. "As in there's a chance that they hid a clue to Luna's location in the book?"

Taylor grumbled a skeptical noise. "I suppose that idea supports the theory that they want to lead the owners of the book to their ritual zone."

"Based on this hypothesis someone planted a clue to lure you."

A scowl knotted her features. "Yeah, but that doesn't sound quite right. I mean, who, and how? Feels like too long of a game, you know? That's a lot of steps, to acquire or steal the book somehow after already having the ritual plotted out, then slip in a bread crumb. You'd think there'd be an easier way to bait us."

"We should keep the option on the table. As soon as we land, we'll look up the coordinates." He glanced out the window, where a slab of gray ocean pockmarked by an occasional crest of white wave stretched to the horizon. They wouldn't land for awhile. "Any other clues or details give you pause?"

"Uh-huh." She scratched the side of her head. "The pattern is in the spirit witch's section. I noticed it when I was studying for more information on spirit-water combo spells."

A bright light flickered on the surface of his awareness, the pleasurable sensation of making a good guess. "Possible location of the spirit witch."

"Possibly," she confirmed, her head bowed as she flipped pages. "I can't be sure."

"The spirit witch might be Eve."

"No, her element was earth."

A disturbing conversation drifted out of a compartment in his mind. "We need to be careful about any messages we see, hear, or read pertaining to this."

Was it safe, even, to look at that stuff? Pages and pages of occult weirdness? Even if it was meant for Taylor's eyes, was it safe for his? What if merely looking at it, absorbing the content, initiated some sort of programming? Like opening Pandora's Box.

Let the reaping commence.

Let the reaping commence.

Let the reaping commence.

His skin crawled, heart accelerating to an elevated tempo. The book was doing it to him right now. Goddamn it, no it wasn't. Now he was freaking himself out for no reason.

Taylor glanced at him sidelong. "Why should we be careful?"

"Would you like anything to drink, sir? Complimentary biscuits or crackers?" The sudden intrusion of the stranger's cheerful voice jarred him from the paranoid machinations of his thoughts and made him jerk.

"No, thank you." He managed to smile at a uniformed stewardess. She looked at him with an unwanted combo of confusion and pity before fussing with creamer packets on her refreshment cart in a likely excuse to break eye contact.

"Sorry to startle you," she said, tapping the toe of her navy pump into the serving cart's wheel. "The noise this one makes bothers me too. Needs some new parts or at least a good greasing." The flight attendant aimed a practiced, toothy smile at Taylor. "Miss? Something to drink? Complimentary biscuits or crackers?"

"No thanks," Taylor said in a bemused tone.

Steps fast, the flight attendant assumed a place at the end of her cart and made haste up the aisle. Now, of course, the shrill, metallic squeak of the wheel grated on him until he clenched his jaw.

"What was that about?" Taylor asked on an awkward laugh.

Julian drew in a heavy gulp of oxygen, commanding his pulse to slow on the exhale before inhaling again. Once soothed by the balm of breath work, he circled back to his original point. "A conversation that I had with Tim really freaked me out. Obviously."

The leader himself seemed spooked as hell, and anxiety and fear were infectious diseases.

"Why?" A frown rippled his wife's brow.

Julian peered down the aisle. The flight attendant had moved along twenty feet and was dealing with a customer, too distracted and busy to eavesdrop. "He told me about a rabbit hole he fell down while doing research and said that he got really scared. There was a video he watched that bothered him. All he said was that he got extremely disturbed while watching it, an uncanny feeling that he couldn't name." Wishing that he'd accepted the flight attendant's offer of a beverage, Julian swallowed. He glanced at the call button but nixed the idea of summoning her. The woman irrationally unnerved him, with her red-lipped mouth full of porcelain teeth delivering canned lines in a robotic voice. Like a drone or clone. "He said that it felt like mind control. That someone or something had led him to the video and was using it to mind control him."

Taylor cocked her head. "Something?"

"Spirit force, entity, artificial intelligence, etcetera." Even discussing the matter felt like a violation of some ancient taboo.

"Mind controlled him into doing what?"

"He didn't get that far. He described it as more of an initial feeling. That watching the video felt like consenting to have a programming script uploaded into his mind. Got me thinking about the book having a similar ability."

Pursing her lips, Taylor murmured a *hum* sound. "I don't feel good about making any major decisions on anything based on Tim's single anecdote about spooking himself during a late-night binge on the conspiracy sub-Reddit."

Julian clucked his tongue at himself, feeling like a fool. "Yeah, the entire thing sounds absurd when you break it down out loud like that."

"I'm not saying that we should rule out any hypothesis at this point either." Yet he detected mild dismissal in her tone. She'd deemed the mind control concern a crock, and was probably right.

"Grain of salt and all." He ordered himself to calm down, though he damn near jumped when a fellow passenger aboard their claustrophobic tin can guffawed at some movie he was watching. Aiming for a casual segue, he pivoted to an equally nagging and not unrelated topic. "Does the phrase 'let the reaping commence' mean anything to you?"

Taylor's face blanked into an indecipherable tabula rasa devoid of emotion. She rode the pause a little too long, her odd reaction setting off a fresh spurt of discomfiture. "No."

"But you had to think about it." He hoped the neutral statement didn't sound accusatory. It wasn't meant to. They were in this together, exploring relevant facts. "Don't you remember chanting it when you were floating?"

"No, I..." After trailing off, she rubbed her temples. "I'm not feeling well all of a sudden. Pain flare. I'm going to try for a little rest before we're on the ground."

He couldn't argue with any of that. The entire point, perhaps, being to shut down the subject. Interrogating his wife about a matter that made her uncomfortable would make him an asshole in addition to a lunatic. He accepted his only choice and dropped the matter. His brain needed a break anyway. "Me too."

After dropping a kiss to his cheek, she closed the book, rested her hands on the leather cover, and shut her eyes.

Julian stared at that gross book cover for awhile. Dried, puckered flesh the color of dirt and crowded with symbolism beckoned the reader to enter buried mystery worlds of power and danger. Worlds perhaps best left alone.

How convenient, how Taylor had splayed her palms flat over the volume in an obvious posture of protection. No way could he slip it away without waking her and outing himself as a shifty jerk with no qualms about violating her privacy.

Well played, babe. The bitter thought dripped with sarcasm and even animosity.

"Stop," he hissed at himself upon realizing that he was suspecting his wife of...what, exactly? He was going nuts and needed to get a grip.

Desperate for distraction, Julian tugged a Sky Mall catalogue from the seat back. He'd almost lost himself to amusement in the ridiculous extremes of consumerism when wheels squeaked, sending his muscles into lockdown in embarrassing testimony to the power of classical conditioning. What the hell was his problem with this poor flight attendant?

He gritted his teeth and stared at a photograph of a life-sized, bronze Bigfoot statue.

Perfect for any garden. Will surely entertain your houseguests!

Squeak, squeak, squeak. Goosebumps flared on his arms as she approached. He smelled his own sweat and chastised his idiocy. Reactive, rabbit behavior like this wasn't doing Luna the justice she deserved. She needed her father to remain focused, collected, in control.

The cart passed him, trademark metal-on-metal whine ceasing as she presumably docked her serving station in the back.

See? He told Bigfoot telepathically. *Quit acting like a damn fool.*

Before he found mindless escape, four awful words in the flight attendant's voice stormed his mind like a curse straight from hell: "Let the reaping commence."

Too stunned to scream, he turned to the narrow aisle, where of course she stood behind her stupid cart. Her face was empty, uncanny, her soul aborted and replaced with the vacuum of trance. She stretched her mouth into a gaping red ring and pointed a finger at sleeping Taylor.

A flash of movement to the right caught Julian's attention. Brain tenderized with shock, he whipped his head to Taylor's seat. His wife stood now, her posture and face identical to the other woman's as they pointed at each other.

The flight attendant's lips didn't budge when she spoke next, an abject horror spectacle of words spilling forth from somewhere *else*. "Other Places house Other Ones, beings attracted to the sticky dark residue produced by Chaos magic in their drive to mate with Folly." Her next words came with gasping, hushed urgency as they ran together. "Folly into skull, level ten possession. Let the reaping commence. Letthereapingcommence." And so on.

To his utter dismay, Taylor mimicked the incantation word for word, "Other Places house Other Ones, beings attracted to the sticky dark residue produced by Chaos magic in their drive to mate with Folly. Folly into skull, level ten possession. Let the reaping commence. Letthereapingcommence."

Letthereapingcommence. The chant invaded his head, distinct words blending into sinister, head-exploding babble. He jumped to his feet and shook Taylor by the shoulders. "Babe. Wake up. Come on. This isn't you."

Instead of rousing Taylor, Julian zapped out of consciousness and awoke on the deck of a large boat with battered wooden floors, bobbing in tune with restless water.

He was too shocked to panic, capable only of processing a simple, chilling realization.

He'd gone through a portal. Been zapped somewhere else. Tamping down terror to the extent he was able, he took stock.

He sat on a kitchen chair, the witchcraft book open on his lap. Midday skies and rough seas surrounded the vessel in every direction while stormy wind whipped his hair into a maelstrom until strands stuck to his face like slices of black tape.

"Taylor," he shouted over the persistent, whistling blasts, standing and allowing the book to drop with a *thud*. Pages tore themselves loose and shot upward in whirlpools of paper. "Babe, are you here?"

He knew in his marrow, however, that he was alone. Yet not. Evil encroached unseen.

Overcome by a sudden, soporific daze accompanied by a humming in his skull, Julian gazed out over the ocean. Though the wind raged unabated, demolishing the book and scattering its sheets over the liquid expanse, the waters relaxed to impossible, unnatural stillness.

The sheet of liquid was serene enough for him to see three cords of sinuous, serpentine movement, each fat as a tree trunk and coming right for him.

Let the reaping commence. In his head, but a blend of other voices.

He'd transcended fear and made the jump to morbid curiosity when a creature burst from the ocean in all of its terrible, ancient splendor. As huge as a skyscraper, the monster flapped black dragon's wings attached to a scaly, reptilian body.

A mess of writhing tentacles spilled from the beast's mouth as it fixed Julian in a bottomless stare as red as the river Styx. After a few torturous seconds, the abomination spoke in a low, smooth male voice fit for an angel, "Let the reaping commence."

Julian awoke with a gasp, bathed in cold sweat. His heart bashed against his ribcage as sizzling rushes of cortisol poisoned his blood. Disoriented and spinning, he looked around. The plane. He sat on the plane, now making its initial descent into the grayscale urban sprawl of Miami.

"Babe, are you okay?" Beside him, Taylor was normal and spoke with concern.

"Yeah." He did his best to purge the dregs of a nightmare he'd surely never forget. "Bad dream."

But while fantastical dissolved into everyday, people lurching as the aircraft applied its brakes, then springing up, eager to deplane, he took no solace in his rationalizing minimizations.

"You sure?" She rubbed his upper arm, looking on with a hint of worry.

No, but that didn't matter. This wasn't about him. "Yeah." He yanked his suitcase from the overhead compartment, closure marking the start of the next phase of their journey. "Now let's find Luna and bring her home."

SEVEN

A CRAMP TWISTED TAYLOR'S GUTS AS SHE LIFTED HER SUITCASE, forcing her to bend over to counteract the advance of her enemy. She leaned on the hotel bed and breathed with intention, balanced on a spike of agony, focusing on one of the wall hangings. The trip from airport to hotel had gone smoothly, but travel fatigue surely wasn't helping her pain issues.

A black-and-white photo of a woman in twenties garb stood with her arms in the air, expression jubilant. Taylor might never again wear the carefree, unbothered expression of the flapper, but at least she was sort of getting used to repeated stabs coming at seemingly random intervals. Yay positivity.

"Ah, babe, I'm sorry." Julian was at her side in seconds, lifting her gently to ease her into a reclined position on the mattress.

"Thank you." She pushed into a throbbing area below her navel and applied gentle pressure, a technique which sometimes worked. "Can you hand me my spell book?"

He sat on the edge of the bed and stroked her hair. "Are you sure that's a good idea?"

Despite the pain clouding her thoughts, she connected another few dots in a hypothesis that began to form on the plane, the time when

Julian started acting weird. "You think the book is doing things to us. Maybe even caused this." She patted her stomach for emphasis, projecting mild sarcasm as some final defense against realizing that he might be right. Her symptoms had showed up shortly after she'd acquired the manual.

"Do you?" A kind but firm prompt, as if he'd read her mind.

Taylor found some relief when she shifted to her side. Looking up at her husband, she reviewed options. "I think it doesn't matter. This is the only chance we have to save Luna."

"It matters if the book takes control of you."

She toed off her sandals, the spasm inside mocking her as it worsened. She'd obviously acted bizarre during the sealing spell, and just because she didn't remember her behavior didn't mean the incident hadn't happened. "You're big on this possession and mind control kick, aren't you?" Snark failed to negate terror and helplessness.

Experimenting with dark powers that one didn't understand was a classic recipe for disaster if countless fictional cautionary tales on the subject held a shred of truth.

"What concerns me is the pattern of incidents. You saying words you don't remember. Tim's run-in with the video." A heavy shadow passed across his stare, hinting at additional concerns not voiced.

"Is there more? Two incidents isn't quite a pattern."

"My dreams. I hesitate to even bring this up."

A chill swept over her as deep intuition bloomed. Julian had undergone an experience that he couldn't explain. "I feel like we'd better put everything on the table right now. We don't have a lot of time, and ignorance isn't our friend."

"True." His Adam's apple bobbed when he swallowed, every small motion of his body heightening her state of anticipation.

She scooted closer to him as if proximity enhanced her concentration. "You were saying?"

"People in my dreams spoke this very specific, memorable verbiage with occult overtones. One person said, 'Other Places house Other Ones.' There was stuff about chaos magic, some chant about Folly into skull and possession. Is any of that meaningful to you?"

Taylor adjusted her position, a firm mattress and snow plane of pristine bedding the only things anchoring her to physical reality. Occam's Razor had to apply, meaning that a simple explanation was likely true. "You read through the book."

He fixed her in a serious, earnest stare. "No, babe, I didn't. I take it the phrases I quoted came from those pages?"

Her mind spun in looping swirls. She sat up, looking to an upright position for more control. With cruel irony, pain pinched her side as she re-oriented. "Yes. Meaning the book might have infiltrated you through me. Put messages inside both of us for whatever reason. Fuck." A realization hit. She reclined in a posture of defeat. "This book is dangerous to use. But I need that spirit combo spell to track Luna."

"Unless we don't. Let's try Mad Dog again. Or how about we visit the park as guests and scope it out for secret entrances to hidden chambers."

She sighed, the idea of wandering around a theme park in aimless pursuit of murky goals making her impatient. "Good call on Mad Dog. I'm gonna message Eve. I don't want to hit up that park until we have more information to work with. We can't afford to waste time or run down any blind alleys."

"Eve." He spoke her name like a warning and cast a baleful glance toward the door.

"I know you're not crazy about her, but she has one of these books too, meaning she's an asset. What if she's been through mind control and has tips for counteracting it? Or lends insights into the coordinate phenomenon will that save me from having to look through pages anymore?"

"Yeah. That's fair. You take Eve, and I'll reach out to Mad Dog again." After handing Taylor her laptop, he got out his own computer and set up at the glossy, generic desk beside the dresser, soft clicks issuing from his fast-moving fingers.

Taylor set up the Wi-Fi and messaged Eve on social media. *Hi. I need to talk to you. Emergency. Please call me ASAP.*

She typed out her phone number and pushed the computer off to the side in case Eve followed up with a question on social media. With any luck she'd call. A phone call was more secure, in theory, less vulnerable to compromise. "I'm getting more paranoid by the hour."

The sounds from Julian's station ceased, and he joined her on the bed. "I'd say you're justified."

Finding a measure of assurance in her husband's presence, she laid a hand on his stomach and rested her head against the solidity of his chest.

Here they were in their corporate-nice hotel room, surrounded by a tasteful medley of beiges and blacks and a room service menu bound in faux leather. Four-star trappings mocked their fiendish problem with a façade of escape. In some alternate timeline, they might be enjoying a weekend getaway amid these spoils of affordable luxury. "Are you scared?"

"I can't afford to panic. It messes up my thinking," he said.

Crisp, processed air grew heavy, choked by a clash of cleaning products and air freshener that undoubtedly had a name like "clean linen." The flapper looked on, beside herself in a fit of incongruous, anachronistic ecstasy. How dare the machinations of the normal world keep turning when Taylor's baby had been kidnapped by demonic psychopaths? "That's not what I asked."

"Yeah," he said in a quiet, sad drawl that counterbalanced her burst of irrational anger. "Terrified."

"Same." Awful thoughts threatened, but Taylor stuffed them before they formed into images. Compartmentalization saved her from falling apart, staved off madness. "At least we have each other."

"Sasha texted. Mal's doing fine. She sent a smiley face and a heart emoji."

"I miss him." Her throat swelled as bitter tides of hot emotions ebbed to the cool waters of grief, sorrow, and yearning.

"I do too. We'll get Luna and go back to him soon. I feel it. I promise."

Taylor gazed up at her husband, those dark features and robust bone structure imbuing him with a godlike, powerful aura. Gratitude swelled her heart, elusive feelings of true positivity resurging. "I love you."

He brushed a lingering kiss to her temple, and in response she closed her eyes and savored the warm affection of his touch.

"I love you too."

A sudden cacophony of vibrational buzzes in tandem with her cheerful ringtone startled her out of her reverie. She snatched her cell and answered, "Hello?" The desperate upswing in her tone would have embarrassed her had she not long ago surpassed the point of caring about downplaying her desperation.

"Hi, it's Eve. What's going on?" Curt, polite; not warm.

Taylor didn't blame Eve for her apprehension. The woman was smart and probably sensed the vicinity of the catastrophe well enough to guess bad magical juju was afoot and threatening to rope her in. Why else would Taylor reach out after almost a year without contact? "My daughter's been kidnapped through a portal. We think it's Scarab resurfacing to launch some new shadow initiative."

A click followed by a scratchy static noise trespassed into the air space, the disturbing invasion vanishing as suddenly as it arrived. Or was Taylor imagining things?

"I'm sorry. How can I help?"

Since Eve didn't mention the intrusive noise, Taylor halfway convinced herself that her ears were playing tricks even as she reconsidered how much she ought to divulge over the line. Too bad there wasn't a plan B. She'd have to take her chances with faceless spooks listening in. "That's what I'm trying to figure out. I've made some progress with my book, and we have another contact we're working with, but before I do any more work with it, I wanted to reach out to you and compare accounts."

No immediate reply from Eve, and in the absence of human voice the drone of white noise became ominous. Taylor bobbed a restless leg, trying not to listen too carefully for unauthorized personnel dropping messages in the fuzz.

"Okay, but I need to ask you not to repeat anything specific you may have read in the book. The final section in particular. None of us are supposed to be even looking at it, let alone reciting from it."

Taylor's blood went arctic. Spots flared in her vision as she stared at a random tear on the otherwise perfect comforter. She'd read a whole lot from the final section. "Why not?"

Eve muttered something indecipherable. "Keep in mind this is secondhand, and hearsay. Take what I'm about to say with a grain of salt."

"Just spit it out." She hadn't meant to sound snippy. Mostly she was mad at herself and dying from the torturous anticipation of bad news.

"It's a path to possession, a conduit or doorway to other dimensions. Once a witch is possessed, her master can use her as a tool to carry out whatever tasks they want, accomplished through a human vessel. Supposedly. Look, I don't fully understand this stuff. And I don't want to. All I want to do is help the souls of the dead pass over, like I've always done. But you're my coven sister. I won't desert you."

Did the universe tumble into the actual pits of hell? Taylor pinched the inner corners of her eyes and called herself a bunch of names, none of them nice. "Possessed by what?"

An F-word suddenly much filthier than "fuck" bobbed up from the murky bog of Taylor's subconscious, a proper noun she'd read all over the pages of that final section. Folly. Possession. It was underway. The gears were turning, the stage set.

Shit, shit. She ought to have read those footnotes. Acted with more caution.

"I can't say the name out loud. None of us are supposed to."

"I know what it is." There was, however, a dimly flickering bright spot illuminating a possible exit from the pit. Eve's talk of secondhand hearsay and a group of "us" banned from uttering the forbidden name hinted at the involvement of additional people who might have more answers. "Who told you all of this secondhand? Do you talk to the other four witches?"

"Yeah. I know one of the witches. Her mentor is the person who gave the warning about the final section, and Helen subsequently relayed it to me. Like I said, secondhand."

Jesus fucking Christ, could Taylor have a mentor, pretty please? What did a witch have to do to get a hookup like that? "What's her element?"

"Spirit. Why?"

Taylor gasped and leapt out of bed. Jackpot! Bingo! "I need her. I need you to put me in touch with her." Intel on the spirit witch. Finally, a crumb of good news, the first morsel in awhile. The possibility of a combo spell with real potential to track Luna lay within her reach.

Taylor gave Julian a thumbs up, but he was engrossed in his screen and didn't notice.

"Normally, I'd say not before I asked her permission, but like you said this is a major emergency. I'm sure that she'll be willing to help. Make sure that you mention that I referred you. That way she knows this is legitimate."

"Of course. Yes, absolutely. Thank you, Eve."

"You have something to write with, or do you want me to text it?"

Taylor dumped the contents of her purse onto the bed and pawed through junk, offering up her kingdom for a pen. A text could get lost in the ether of cyberspace or fall victim to a typo. "Both. Please."

"Okay. You ready?"

She shook out the pages of her day planner. Nope. She closed her hand in triumph around a smooth, cylindrical object only to face the taunt of a useless nail clipper. "Shit. Seriously?" At long last, she pawed a luscious blue ballpoint out from under her wallet. "Yes! I knew I had one. Go for it."

"Look, I don't know what you're hoping to accomplish, and I won't ask because it's none of my business, but try not to get your hopes way up over this. Helen's had her own bad experiences with magic, and I can't guarantee that she'll cooperate with whatever it is you want from her."

How about you let her speak for herself. Taylor bit down on her tongue until the urge to fire off a comeback passed. No way would she allow poor impulse control to provoke Eve into hanging up the phone and ghosting. She ripped off the pointed cap and poised the tip of her instrument against a page near the end of her planner. "I understand."

"I hope so." Eve rattled off a string of digits while Taylor scribbled as fast as possible.

"Can you text it to me also?" The victorious line of numbers, strung together by dashes leading to salvation, held promise. Like a rope thrown into an abandoned well. "I can't thank you enough. Working with her is going to be a game changer, I can feel it."

"Yeah. Just out of curiosity, have you ever tried a combo spell before?"

"I didn't say anything about a combo spell."

"But I'm right, aren't I? About why you want to connect with another one of us?"

Taylor drew stars around the phone number. Lying struck her as pointless at best. "Yeah. I think I have a lead on one that might get me somewhere."

"I'd be lying if I said I wasn't apprehensive. But I won't try to stop you. I hope that Helen can be a resource. Good luck." Eve's demeanor was a little off-putting, deliberately disengaged as if she made a conscious effort not to invest much stake in Taylor's outcome.

Because she believed it to be doomed? Whatever. There wasn't room for any more second-guessing, for any stalling. For anything but moving forward with purpose. "Thank you."

"Keep me posted." Rumblings followed. They weren't at a closure point yet. "Don't hesitate to reach out to me again if there's any way I can be of service."

Now there was a pleasant surprise. She wasn't expecting that turnaround from Eve. "I appreciate it."

"You were there for me when I needed help. You didn't have to be, but you were. I owe you. In fact, tell Helen that. Tell her Eve owed you a favor."

"I sure will. And yeah, I'll be in touch."

"I'm glad you called. Take care."

"Yeah. Same. Bye."

Overcome by mind-clearing gusts of relief, Taylor added her phone to the pile of purse debris and went to stand at Julian's side. He hadn't budged since she'd picked up the phone, apparently rapt in his own part of the fact-finding mission.

Taylor peeked through a crack between the blackout curtains, her line of sight travelling to where a sunset parfait spilled golden-red light over a kiddie pool-sized pond at the edge of the hotel grounds. Plenty of time to call Helen before it became rudely late. "Not sure what all you caught, but I made serious progress. Any leads?" Over his shoulder, a convoluted image overtook the screen. A crudely drawn map.

"What time did Eve call?" Posture hunched and crunched, he leaned in closer, totally absorbed.

Intrigued and on a high-vibe roll from taking forward steps, Taylor retrieved her cell and checked. "Seven thirty-four. Why, does that matter to what we're looking at here? Which is what, by the way?"

"When I got online to write to Mad Dog, there was some odd interference in the beginning. Like I was looking at someone else's browser tabs. At first, I thought it was pop-up adware, but then the cursor started moving on its own."

"Were you able to grab a screenshot?"

"No. My entire desktop froze. By the time I got the keyboard commands for a screenshot ready, the computer was normal again. I went to the message board as planned, then I saw a user had posted this. But my hunch was wrong. The times of when I saw the post and when Eve called don't match."

Taylor crouched for a better look. The time stamp read seven thirty-*five*. She sucked her teeth as her neck hairs lifted. "I heard a noise on the line around then. Like someone jumped on to listen in then left. What's this a map of?"

Julian pointed at the headline: *Leaked Doc of Scarab Ritual Sacrifice Lair*, posted by username Gods_of_War3819877.

She shook her head. "Something isn't right. This is too obvious, too easy. It's a disinformation trap."

"I had that thought. But it seems odd for Scarab to toss out such a clear red herring. They've never operated through trickery before. They're too powerful. I wondered if this new user was Mad Dog posting under a new identity, deliberately hidden."

"Which doesn't explain the other person's desktop or the click on the line. We're clearly being watched and monitored."

"None of it squares up. There's no need to throw us off the scent before we're even on a trail in the first place. And if they wanted to lure us, I have to believe that their method would be smarter." He waved a dismissive hand at the screen. "This seems basic. They'd know we'd see through it and have this exact discussion."

She raked both hands through her hair, refusing to be checkmated even as she came up without a move. The map was bare bones but delineated into sections, like the floor plan of a house.

Cylindrical etchings snaked through the lower part of the page, marked with the scary yet simple word "tunnels." A compass sat in the lower-right hand corner of the frame, a name stamped above each directional point like at a train station.

A switch of recognition flicked to "on" when Taylor laid eyes on the north coordinate. "Pennyweather Avenue Entrance. That's definitely the Florida park. I remember it from when I went there as a kid."

Julian turned to her, his mouth open, when two knocks struck the door in a calm, evenly spaced pattern. Maid service had been in before they'd arrived, judging by the state of the room, and cleaning staff never showed up this late. Fixing her husband with a knowing stare, she called out, "Can I help you?"

"Yes," a male voice replied with unnerving, calculated smoothness. "And likewise, I can help you."

EIGHT

As a teenage boy growing up on the rez and accustomed to poverty, Julian used to daydream about meeting a beautiful woman and taking her to a fancy hotel with room service and free shampoo. They'd kiss on a pristine bed fit for royalty; their sheets scented by a soft floral fragrance to encourage a sensual mood.

Now, though he'd fallen in love with a beautiful woman and taken her to the fancy hotel, all he was thinking about was whether he was an idiot for not bringing a gun. Irony was a sick jerk.

He stepped in front of his wife and tuned in to his shifting wavelength. Facing a black wolf baring a full set of sharp teeth might startle this visitor if he turned out to be hostile, buying a few precious seconds. "I'm gonna need more than that. Who are you and why are you here?"

"Don't be *mad*. I'm just a scrappy old *dog* like you."

The emphasized words of the unseen male behind the door told Julian what he needed to know. Still, he exchanged a look of disbelief with Taylor. She stood in an aggressive stance, her fists raised in the air. "Give me one reason to believe that this isn't a setup," Julian pressed.

For all he knew, the stranger was armed with a syringe full of some knockout drug designed for assassination, tasked by Scarab with subtracting Taylor and Julian from the equation.

Seconds passed, they passed like a molasses flow, until Julian clenched his teeth and hissed a self-recrimination. He'd played his move wrong, misfired thanks to not knowing the nature or rules of the game he found himself engaged in, and somehow had driven the man away.

Julian had all but given up when a yellow rectangle of paper the size of a standard envelope slid under the door. The bright voltage of it violated the room, almost obscene, carrying promises to deliver sinister secrets once unfolded.

His heart in his throat, adrenaline ready to catapult him into fight mode, he swiped the thin slice torn from a legal pad and read:

Don't speak one more word aloud. Sweep your room for everything with a recording capacity—phones, computers, electronic watches, any smart devices. If you have opaque tape, put some over each camera. If not, wrap the tech in towels and put them in the bathtub. Unplug the hotel television, modem, coffee pot, and phone, and put fabric over those as well. When you are done, give two knocks on the door, wait for my signal, then let me in.

Julian didn't legitimately entertain the notion that he might be having a nervous breakdown until he found himself shrouding the cheap coffee maker in a hand towel while inspecting the filtration bowl for bugs, wires, or other nefarious devices.

In addition to the Navajo Nation and the United States, go ahead and register him as a card-carrying member of the Tin Foil Hat Republic. Yet he forged ahead, toweling the tech for a shot at saving his baby girl.

Beside him, Taylor wrapped the television. Swaddled in a bed sheet stretched as taut as plastic covering, the plasma screen looked fit for FBI confiscation. She gave him a thumbs up, pupils dilated and sheen of sweat glistening on her brow. His wife was right. At least they were in this together, riding the crazy train as a team.

He scanned their freshly secured surveillance nest and nodded at her. Once she returned the gesture, he walked over and did the knock as directed.

Another piece of paper sailed through the crack separating door and floor, coming to rest between Julian's feet.

Don't scream when you see me.

The whooshing noise of Taylor sucking down a breath filled otherwise dead air. He squeezed support into her shoulder, and once he felt confident that they'd both be able to cope, he wrapped his fingers around the hardness of the metal handle and opened the room to their guest. His next thought was a plunge into the abyss: *Here goes.*

The man in the hallway was shorter than Julian pictured; apparently, he'd chosen to cast some thuggish, man-in-black giant in the foreboding role of shadowy informant.

But no; there stood a remarkably average human male in department store jeans and a tucked-in, button down shirt the color of rust. He clutched the legal pad in one hand and a pen in the other.

Julian only partially made sense of the "scream" business once he studied the man's face and noticed details that were off. He wore voids of sunglasses paired with an outdoorsy hat, its brim wide enough to cast a shadow on his face. A casual observer would have to do a double take to catalog his features, especially if he was moving, and by that time the man would be gone.

Then there was his hair—thick brown pieces long enough to graze his shoulders and further hide his identity. The texture of the strands looked synthetic and hung cockeyed. Though no fashion snob, Julian marked the tells of a cheap wig. Clearly, disguise was paramount to this guy. But who was he running from, and why? The entire thing was dubious.

Still, Julian beckoned him in with a swoop of his hand. No turning back now.

The man walked in at a fast clip, froze, then shook all over. The seizure passed, and he sat on the edge of the bed.

Taylor scribbled in her journal and showed it to him: *Can we help?*

Their visitor wrote on his pad and held it up to reveal one word etched in sad, squiggly penmanship bungled by an unsteady hand: *Water.*

Julian bolted to the bathroom, filled a glass from the tap, and brought it over. Helping was the ethical thing to do. Plus, if the man was enslaved by physical needs, it meant leverage.

The poor man guzzled like he'd wandered through a desert for days.

Perplexed, Julian sat beside his wife, held her hand, and waited. He wasn't scared of this person anymore. He hurt with sympathy for him.

Maybe his healing magic could provide relief, but they hadn't reached an appropriate moment to discuss such an offer.

More writing on the pad, this time yielding more words:

Scarab did this to me. I drink and drink, but I can't get hydrated. Just piss all day long. I'm either chugging, pissing, or shaking. If I get lucky, all three at once. No employer will put up with all of that, let alone any woman.

How awful. Julian couldn't imagine the helplessness and defeat involved in losing near-total control over one's body. With as much tact as he could muster, he penned a follow-up question in Taylor's journal.

I'm sorry. Were you kidnapped and administered these modifications against your will?

Determining precisely where the guy stood helped Julian pinpoint his motivations and map his dominant emotional state. If they were to work with him, he needed to understand what drove him.

I wish that I had the moral high ground. But nah, I did it for money. I went broke from some bad investments and saw their ad in a university newspaper asking for medical test subjects. I'm not a victim, just a dope and an idiot.

Julian: *Nah, man, you're still a victim. You were grossly misled. Tell me if I've got this right. You tracked us down and put surveillance on us because you want our help in taking out Scarab. You want revenge.*

Synthetic brown hair fell in the visitor's face as he wrote his reply, pen scratching against paper. *Basically. Revenge and an antidote to this hell I live in. I know they've got miracle meds squirreled away in their underground bunkers.*

Taylor wrote: *How did you find us?*

I still have my Scarab scout tech, which allows me to interface with various cellular networks and use keywords to identify the locations of parties interested in Scarab's activities. I hop on and off, like when normies surf the web, but all I'm using is the meat in my skull. Cool, huh? That conspiracy board is a hotbed. I get an alert, a little ding in my head, when someone says Scarab over the phone. Like you.

The Scarab victim pointed a trembling finger at Taylor, who was already writing again. *Scarab tech has gotten more sophisticated. I was outfitted against my will last year.*

The guy nodded and returned to his pad. *They sure have. They've ramped up their scale. Me, and those like me, were never supposed to have escaped.*

We were code name Mad Dog, all branded with the same label, devoid of individual identity. You know what's supposed to happen to mad dogs.

Julian bunched his brow as a problematic aspect of the tale bothered him. He voiced his issue via Taylor's notebook. *Why do you identify yourself blatantly on the sub? Isn't that leading them right to you?*

The first sound during the tense encounter was a dry, humorless chuckle from the mystery man. The novel rupture of his voice, sourness and suffering raked across gravel, lingered in the perfumed room long after he'd quieted. He chewed on his pen, a theatrical riding of the pause, perhaps before contributing:

Let them try. I've got encryptions upon encryptions going. If we out ourselves, though, we can find each other and collaborate quicker with other accomplices in the know. A bunch of us share various Mad Dog usernames and have our IPs scrambled real good. It's too much work, not worthwhile for their foot soldiers to hunt us. Above their pay grade, ya know?

It struck Julian how badly this man clearly wanted to be heard, itched to get his story of injustice out. Valid, and more importantly additional leverage. They had this dude for however they wanted to use him as long as they came to the table with sympathy and a genuine desire to help.

Taylor snatched the journal. *What's with the God of War identity? I'm assuming that was also you, showing us the map?*

Yes. That identity is code within code. It doesn't concern you. But the map does.

Fair enough. Satisfied with the explanation Taylor asked for, Julian formed another inquiry. He still didn't have the best sense of what Scarab had done to this guy and for what reasons, or how other people were involved. Having a sense of all facts would help him proceed with confidence and clear eyes. He wrote:

What did they do to you, exactly? You and the other Mad Dogs? And why?

This time, the odd man paused with his legal tablet in his lap before writing a response.

Though Julian couldn't see his eyes under the shades, he appeared to be looking off into the distance in contemplation. Following an extended beat, he wrote extensively before displaying his tablet:

Experiments in meta-humanism. Making cyborgs, people who can synchronize with various cellular-powered satellite networks and receive programming from artificial intelligence and other centralized smart computers. You can see the endgame if you wake up and look. Mind control, hybridization of human and robot to maximize efficiency and promote automation. We Mad Dogs were meant to be versatile, available for use as spies, hackers, trade secret couriers, and even hit men activated by the push of a button. They put all sorts of programs in us, scripts for them to access and activate. Sex slaves, mindless consumer drones to stimulate the economy, free labor for various projects. No limits. Screwed up our DNA, mutated our cells. Hence the shakes. Can I have some more water?

Wild confessions. Water was the least that Julian could offer as payment for what had to be highly classified intel. Not exactly front-page news on the mainstream media sources. By the time Julian returned from his second trip to the bathroom, the poor fellow was lost to the grips of a violent spasm, twitching on the bed and foaming at the mouth.

Taylor looked at the floor, tears in her eyes, biting the knuckle of one balled hand. Poor, beautiful, brilliant Taylor. She knew the stranger's pain far too well—intimately.

Julian held his wife for a good long while. She'd been monstrously violated by Scarab tech, suffered bodily indignities and traumas because of their projects, and deserved time to mourn.

Once his jerking ceased long enough for him to write, the visitor followed up: *They have a cure for your condition in their bunker, Taylor. You don't need to live like this, with your insides ruined. Neither of us do.*

She responded: *How can you know the details of my condition?*

Mad Dog flipped a page, used sheets hanging down like yellow tongues as he reached the end of his pad. *You were a victim of the Eyes project, an initiative launched to both mutate humans and use them to lure animal shifters to secret Scarab bases for trafficking and experimentation. Did I get the gist?*

Taylor paled.

Julian stroked her arm, horizon contracting to the tense exchange unfolding.

She wrote: *Close enough.*

When they put their hi-tech gizmos in us, we suffer side effects. Eyes, Mad Dogs, you name it. But like I told you, they've got cures hoarded down there. I want that good shit. Trust me, you do too. And you want your daughter. We work together to get what we want. Sound like a plan?

Taylor looked at Julian. Julian looked at Mad Dog, then at Taylor again, on the verge of pulling the trigger even as an unresolved facet of the encounter chewed at the back of his head. He scribbled a final query to Mad Dog: *Why did you tell me not to scream when I saw you? All I see is a regular guy in a cheap disguise.*

A soft, papery whooshing sound as a page sailed forward to land amidst its used brethren.

I'm ugly underneath this. Really ugly—a monster. They tried to mutate me for use in something called Operation Gorgon, but it didn't stick. They were gonna off me and throw my carcass in the incinerator they use for botched experiments. Wanna see?

It wasn't a want but a drive to understand, to amass every piece of information imaginable, as if going in armed with knowledge would assure success, predict outcomes. Julian didn't fair well with secrets or hidden agendas. Subterfuge had been used against him all too often.

Julian chanced a glance to Taylor, requesting her consent with his look. She tipped her chin down in the smallest nod.

Maybe morbid curiosity had seduced both into its thrall, because an odd, wild heat passed between their eyes like a signal flare. His elevated heartbeat a thudding soundtrack against external silence, he jotted one big word: *Yes.*

Mad Dog reached for his hat, then took it off. Followed by the wig.

The cliché about time moving in slow motion wasn't quite accurate to describe the changes when one is actively witnessing an epic event contoured by sheer horror.

He could only describe the phenomenon as sense details gulped down whole by the progression of seconds. Like a cosmic serpent swallowing the world and vomiting existence into an alternate timeline.

Speaking of serpents, Julian's body hardened to cold, grave-dead stone as he sat and stared. His mama taught him that staring at folks who were different was rude, but all he could do was stare. Concrete oozed through his arteries before stiffening into rock.

The man's head was bald, and above his left ear, a dusting of black-and-tan scales was most concentrated, tapering into sparse flecks as they spread outward to mar his eyelid, forehead, and temple with the trappings of reptilian skin.

That wasn't the worst part. A lance-shaped snake head, the face of a

Western Diamondback Rattlesnake like the ones Julian had dodged in the Arizona deserts and Texas prairies, jutted from a spot near the guy's hairline. Its eyes were open, sentient, and alive. The creature looked around.

A forked tongue the color of soot tasted the air. Acrid heat bolted up Julian's throat, but he managed to force it down when he heard the tell-tale sound of a rattle. That's when he noticed the tail tip, shaking until it became a fuzzy blur, sticking out of Mad Dog's ear.

That wasn't even the worst part. The worst part was the pain behind the poor man's jaundiced, hazel eyes, ringed by circles so dark it looked like he hadn't slept in years.

A stifled cry erupted from Taylor.

Julian's suspicion and skepticism dissolved the longer he looked into those suffering eyes. He wrote a message: *I have healing magic. Can I try it on you?*

Won't work. Been there, tried that. Thanks though. You know that feeling in your body, like everything started turning to stone when you looked at me?

Julian nodded, but he couldn't say for sure if his head obeyed his neural command to move. Was shock setting in?

An answer came fast: *Intentional outcome of the bioweapon. The first round of Gorgon subjects turned out to be duds. Otherwise, you'd be dead, Medusa-style, overcome by a spontaneous heart attack and instantaneous rigor mortis. They can only get the results they want from female Gorgons and male victims, in line with the mythological origins. But don't worry. They're working every day to solve that problem.*

Mad Dog put his accessories back on, and in an instant Julian's muscles loosened, his perception returning to relative normal. Mad Dog had to be telling the truth about being in possession of low-grade, ineffective magic that caused spectators to go stiff. But not stiff enough.

Julian wrote the only response that seemed adequate: *Let us know how we can help. We're in this together.*

Mad Dog penned on the cardboard backing of his tablet. *Good deal. I need more time to study the map and consult with a couple of my contacts about strategy. It's a maze, basically. Taylor, I suggest that you continue to work on tracking down the spirit witch and augmenting both your individual and collaborative magic. Think max firepower.*

Quick on the draw, Taylor replied: *But you said that all our communication is compromised.*

You got that right. Your best bet is to go the magical route to circumvent technology, use telepathy if you have it. If not, learn it. Can you do that with him? Mind-melding communion type stuff? Mad Dog gestured to Julian.

Although they hadn't practiced in awhile, Julian and Taylor could talk with their minds when both were in wolf form. Looked as if some shifting was in their future.

Yes, Taylor said. *It's your opinion that we'll still need to draw from magic, even though we have this map now?*

Yeah. Definitely. From what I can surmise, they have their own magic users down there, maybe even the chaos witch of the sextet, possessed by F—ly. Meaning they'll be using magical tactics to subvert, confuse, and stymie us at every turn. We need strength in numbers. Which is why I reached out to you.

Fair point. Mad Dog wanted to link up with Taylor and Julian because they had magic, powers that increased everyone's chances of success. Pretty clear what was motivating him.

You've studied, I see, Taylor replied.

Oh yeah. The coven daughter prophecy and Scarab are two of the hottest topics on the board. I got a thousand up votes in a few minutes for that map post. Can't say that I'm not developing a taste for Internet fame. Anyway, Scarab's gonna burn, but not unless we get busy.

On that note, Julian responded: *We need to get down there soon. There are a few days left before our daughter's life is a lost cause. It's impossible to say how quickly we'll be able to get in and out. Meaning we need to secure food and water, solutions for bathrooms, and reliable communications in case the three of us get separated. Weapons too.*

Taylor countered, *Unless we locate a portal point in the bunker that leads to somewhere near civilization, but I wouldn't bet on it.* She wrote more and aimed her journal at Mad Dog. *You study your map. I'll work on my contact while Julian handles logistics. We'll reconvene in the morning.*

I'm in. See you tomorrow. Mad Dog left, an unceremonious exit given the outlandish circumstances.

On a deep breath, Julian drew his awareness inward to activate his shift. Far away, on some distant horizon of his consciousness, the wolf howled. With calm energy and coaxing, Julian shepherded him to the surface until his change began.

A round of queasiness, followed by the whole-body drop of his center of gravity plummeting and chased by a mild bout of organ pain, ended with him standing on all fours.

He faced Taylor, his sapphire-eyed queen of a white wolf, and prepared to voice the concerns that arose during the meeting with Mad Dog. He pushed out his thoughts using the focus technique required to make them audible in both his and Taylor's heads. "We need to talk this over. There are things about Mad Dog's story that don't sit right with me."

NINE

USING THE FLESHY PADS ON THE BOTTOM OF HER PAW FOR TRACTION, Taylor turned a page in her spell book and mulled over Julian's concern about Mad Dog. She glanced up from pages full of runes interspersed with text, noting the pensive cast to his eyes, a storminess underlying wolfish vigor.

"What are you thinking? That he's still loyal to Scarab and at risk of double-crossing us?" Her telepathic thoughts came out stuttered and slow, thick as peanut butter. They really needed to practice talking with their minds more often. Mastering the psychic skill wasn't like riding a bike.

Julian swiped his pink tongue over the black fur ringing his mouth. "He was too eager to team up with us. And effusive about everything he knew. Makes me wonder if he's motivated by something stronger than revenge. Something he's not telling us. Stands to reason that he's heard all of our conversations and everything that entails."

She looked into her husband's dark brown eyes, his keen intellect and gift for strategic thinking shining through, the depth of human self-awareness uncanny within an animal's shape. Despite how stressful and weird their circumstances grew, she never ceased to treasure the unique bond they shared. "Like what? Money?"

His bushy tail flicked back and forth against the carpet in agitated twitches. "Sure. I'd hate to rule it out. The guy's obviously desperate for cash. Like he said, he can't find work. What if there's a hit out on us, and he's the hunter? Like he said, part of his programming was as a hit man."

Compassion and sympathy for Mad Dog weighed on her as she considered the points. Julian's logical reasons pushed against her drive to help. Once upon a time, Taylor lacked compassion to spare, but dealing with Scarab had changed that. "Babe, you saw him. He wants to take down Scarab for obvious reasons."

A muted growl rumbled from Julian's throat, the noise he made when feeling contemplative as the wolf. "All I'm saying is that pity can be a clouding emotion, and we should keep our judgment sharp. Good Samaritans get duped and die."

For the first time, Taylor entertained the possibility she'd swung too far in the opposite direction of her formerly ruthless self and acquired a surplus of tender emotions that had softened her head along with her heart. "Fair enough. But I didn't pick up the vibes that you did. All I saw was a pathetic, disfigured man desperate to reclaim a shred of his dignity through justice."

Julian laid on his belly and rested his chin on his paws, gazing up at Taylor with eyes the color of oak. "I'm supposed to be the healer, yet here you are with the great big heart."

Her chuckle came out as three staccato yaps. She nuzzled the fur near her husband's neck, breathing in his animal smell, and licked the side of his face. "Yeah. Only my body is broken now. On the plus side, I don't lay awake at night anymore wondering if I'm a sociopath."

His breath puffed hot against her ear. "Your body isn't broken. But I hope this can bring an end to your suffering. Bring us answers along with Luna. Back in our arms where she belongs."

Uncomfortable with being fussed over when they had work to do, she backed away a foot and returned to reading while Julian looked on. It was getting late, and they needed to try for a decent night's sleep, but there was work to do first.

A half-page footnote in the Oceans and Creature Work section eventually made her sit up on her haunches and take notice. Her heart raced while she digested the information. She tapped Julian's onyx paw with her ivory one and said, "Are you reading this?"

"You bet. Reads like opportunity."

If she was reading the passage right, the incantations might help her travel to Helen the spirit witch.

Just to be sure, she re-read:

Familiar creature bonds can be tapped by any witch who shares mind-flow, psychic connection, or enhanced empathy with an animal or human with an animal aspect. Once the familiar creature is identified, a witch may leverage her bond with said creature to draw from a sister witch's element.

Taylor swatted her paw over chunks of pages at a time, nails scratching paper that flapped at a rapid clip until she settled on the clue she sought. Electric with triumph, she stabbed the hooked point of her claw against a paragraph in the spirit section. "Teleportation is a spirit witch power. If I can pull off the familiar bond with you, I might be able to access it."

"Check this out." Julian butted his snout into a marginal note written in cursive and read the scrawl. "The bonded familiar or animal aspect may enjoy augmentation as well if they are gifted. Suggested course: explore opportunities for bonded familiar or animal aspect to enhance for maximum power gain." He hummed, rubbing a canine foot against parchment. "It's like a chain reaction, this spell. When we cast it, you draw powers from spirit, which in turn allows me to draw power from somewhere."

"The question is, from where?" Taylor perused the spirit witch section, came up empty, and returned to the water witch's part. "But yes. You're correct. And this collaborative aspect of the work answers my questions about why there are sections for other witches in the book. We were meant to work together and with familiars."

"Meant by who?"

Now there was a question. Déjà vu hit her hard, jettisoning her into a wonky, time-warp state until she gathered her wits and escaped the matrix. "Mad Dog mentioned the coven daughters' prophecy. Does this feel prophetic to you?"

"I don't know how to answer that. As in Biblical, or in some other religious sense?"

She sighed, messes of strange words and symbols blurring together. A couple of big blinks cleared up her vision. "I don't know. Maybe. Or maybe I'm going crazy."

"No, you aren't. This is insane stuff. I still can't believe it's real." Julian laid a paw in the crease of the book, his coarse black fur juxtaposed against blanched paper. "Familiar pulls from unused opposition adjacent proxy element." He looked at Taylor, head cocked at a sharp angle. "On my read, if you're calling upon me to access your opposition element, spirit, then I pull from spirit's other neighbor. Whatever's on the other side."

"A chain reaction, like you said." Troublesome. If Julian pulled from spirit's other opposing element, and that opposing element pulled from somewhere else, someone would eventually end up pulling from chaos. Would that activate the evil one?

She growled. "This is complicated." To un-complicate matters, she skipped to the glossary at the end of the tome, being mindful not to look at the sixth section.

On one of the final pages, she came upon a simple hexagon drawn in watery blue ink and large enough to encompass most of the paper. The name of each element in round, feminine cursive, marked a junction of two lines. earth and spirit flanked water, while spirit's non-water neighbor was fire.

An X made up of two diagonal lines connected Water to Chaos on one axis and Spirit to Air on the other, with a square in the middle of the hexagon marking the spot where the diagonal trajectories met. Who knew what that was all about? They'd have to reserve cracking that conundrum for another day. One step at a time, triaged according to relevance and urgency.

"Looks like it's time for me to learn all about fire magic," Julian said with a touch of levity that made her smile. Hey, if they were going to be opening Pandora's Box, might as well enjoy the process to the extent possible.

After thirty more seconds of reading, Taylor was rapt. "This familiar work magic is legit. Two birds, meet stone." She stared at her man while digesting the information in front of her. "We can make a literal firewall against mind-control magic and other invasions into our thoughts. You think it works with technology, the phone tapping and such that Mad Dog talked about?"

"I think it's our best bet to shield us against eavesdropping by Scarab spies, which will come in handy once we're down in the tunnels and at risk of them tracking us. Tossing up this firewall might keep Mad Dog out of our heads and networks. Bonus bit of protection in case he's up to anything underhanded."

Julian wasn't ready to let the Mad Dog as double agent theory go, a theory that Taylor didn't see much purpose in clinging to, but she also didn't feel inclined to press the issue. If the mutated man lost his ability to run surveillance and ghosted them, then he'd show his true colors. "Let's try it."

She read the directions for launching a familiar creature bond spell.

Sit with your familiar until both parties establish communion. Once a telepathic or emotional bond is achieved, recite the opposition-adjacent spell you wish to cast while the familiar meditates on the essence of the element from which they will take. After the witch takes from her opponent to cast desired spell, the familiar takes to cast theirs.

A heavy current coursed through wherever the tributaries of their subconscious minds intersected.

"There's a lot of taking involved in this system," Julian finally muttered. "Which gives me a pause. Considering what's already happened."

His apprehension and careful, roundabout language evoked the possibly dormant but unresolved possession issue, spiking her with resentment dipped in shame. "Do you have a plan B for saving Luna? We can't exactly just rush the tunnels and hope for the best."

His eyes became stormy. "No, but I'm real worried that we won't come out of this the same. You must share that worry."

Sharp heat pierced her chest, like her heart had been crusted in broken glass. "I'm not going to let our daughter die, Julian. I don't care if I come out of this possessed, we are going to save Luna. You shouldn't care what we have to sacrifice either. Whatever it takes."

"Absolutely whatever it takes." He laid his paw over hers, their fur swirling into a yin yang pattern, opposite but complementary. "I love you, babe. I don't want the sacrifice to be you."

She held his stare for a long time, two alphas and a pair of mates locked into the other's wavelength, and entertained an awful scenario. "It might come to that. And if it does, if whatever is happening gets to a point where I'm not myself anymore, where I'm a danger to you or Malcom or Luna, or a liability against saving Luna, I need your assurance that you'll be willing and able to take care of it. Solve the problem."

He whined, baring his teeth in a grimace, lips pulled back to reveal rows of pointed incisors, the adverse reaction indicating that he'd gotten the grim, indirect order to put her down if circumstances demanded that severe measures apply. "Don't talk like that."

"It's the truth."

"For now, we concentrate on the task at hand."

"Promise me, Julian, that you'll do what it takes to protect yourself and our babies if I become a threat."

A stare down steeped in unspeakable silence claimed several seconds, with Julian finally breaking it. "Yes."

"Good." Satisfied, as Julian was a man of his word, Taylor travelled again to the spirit section. "If the teleport works, we need to make sure that I'm able to teleport back to this room without you physically present beside me. Otherwise, I'm stranded, and we lose precious hours or even days."

"Just spitballing here, but my thought is that we want a spell where I act like an anchor, or that my presence is with you even while my body stays here."

"Smart thinking," she muttered, pages crinkling softly as she swatted one after the other. "We make a good team."

He pushed his nose into her throat, whimpered, then backed off. His gesture kindled a pang of sadness, as he was likely ruminating over the grisly scenario broached earlier.

He'd cope if he had to.

Both read, spending serious time with the book and hitting multiple dead ends at the terminus of blind alleys. A solution presented at last.

"Personal charms or talismans," Julian affirmed, reading a typed segment in the spirit section. "There's wording exactly like this in the fire part."

"Meaning there's a good chance it's a universal feature of this magic system." Tension unfurled beneath her ribs, a knotted ribbon smoothing into a forward path. "Consistency comforts me. I don't know how rational that is, but I'm sticking with it."

He barked, a good-natured chuckle. "I think we've left the realm of rational." Julian shifted into a person, lengthening, and morphing in a series of fluid transformations. He grabbed his wallet off the nightstand, handed Taylor a two-inch portrait photo of the twins, and changed back to the wolf. "This has to be charged with the good energy that we need right now."

Her breasts ached with pressure, filling with longing, grief, and the ferocity of a mother's love. She laid a paw over the snapshot of her babies before gazing at their cherubic, innocent faces peeking out of crocheted blankets.

I will come back to you, my loves. I will save you, Luna. "Perfect." Her thought-word tumbled out as a saturated, beating life-form, drenched in the richest rivulets of her heart's blood.

Julian laid one of his front legs over her back, and they cuddled and cried as one until composure and logic once more took center stage.

Taylor changed to a person, pumped her breasts to relieve the painful engorging of fluid, and became animal once more.

A fizzy, carbonated bubbling going off in her belly, she reviewed the relevant notes.

Personal charms or talismans can be used to anchor a witch as she undertakes astral travel or works with a proxy. Concentrate on charm or talisman in lieu of proxy involvement, or to escape astral plane and seek earthly grounding.

She blew out a breath, the hotel room lamp light casting sharp glares on the words though the wattage was soft. Must've been her nerves, making her surroundings hot and bright. "If I'm reading this right, I basically turn to the picture as a stand in for you once I choose to teleport back here. Then I say my spirit teleportation spell and hope for the best."

Her pulse thrummed in her neck. She'd need lots of hope and faith to pull this off.

Preferably divine intervention. Too bad her college theology classes had left her on the side of agnosticism.

"You will absolutely pull this off. I feel it down to my marrow. And remember, I have the book here. If things get hairy, I'll look for an emergency spell to get to you. Or reach out to Mad Dog if I must."

"Okay." Her word contracted into purpose, collapsed into a laser beam. Sync up with Julian. Cast fire spell to block interlopers. Cast Spirit spell, zap self to Helen's coordinates. Find Helen, plead and persuade for help, insight, information. Concentrate on twins' picture to return to hotel room. She blew out a ragged, heavy breath. "It's highly involved."

"Good thing you're the smartest person I know."

"Let's hope luck is on our side."

"It is."

His confidence enriched hers, and she urged herself back into the human suit, muscles burning as they stretched, toughing out uncomfortable shortness of breath and queasiness until she stood upright. Julian followed. As a final act of assurance, she kissed each of her children on the glossy, printed versions of their foreheads and stuck the photo in her back pocket.

They sat cross-legged on the floor and pressed palms together. The feel of his callused warmth centered her, stitching their gazes into unity until reality swung left to right like a lazy pendulum and time lost meaning.

Irises blended like paint on one of Julian's palates, brown and blue swirling to make a new shade. Seduced by the bleed of color across joined brains, neither was sure anymore where one person ended and the other began.

He moved through the black hole portal of her pupil, wrapping himself in the protective cloak of her aura as he accessed her memories. She'd bicycled through sand once with her sister Chloe during a beach vacation when the girls were preteens, laughing at how the tires wouldn't move, slurping ice cream. Tall grass sprouting from sloping sand dunes swayed in the lazy breeze to meet sheets of blue-gray sea and sky that rolled to the edge of the world. Pure heaven.

Julian smiled, inhaling salty ocean air and riding the cresting caw of a seagull, appreciating the memory as if it was his own.

Then there were the more painful memories, like when Taylor got teased in middle school for having pink braces and an unfortunate haircut. Karen Baker called her ugly every day, only stopping when Taylor let Karen "borrow" her favorite Guess jean jacket.

In turn she entered the space of his existence and opened doors leading to his past.

In Julian's teenage skin, she sat with his mama while she wove at the loom of their desert home, admiring her dedication to her craft, her focus and resolve, in addition to the copious business savvy required to make a profit selling the wares at the trading post. He'd picked up many skills from her and drawn from them throughout his successful artistic career.

She slipped her hand underneath a basketball to scoop it up, orange skin leathery in her palm, and enjoyed the juicy thwacks it made as it smacked concrete. After a competitive game of pickup with some other kids, she trekked the dirt road home, then munched on a taco while watching television with the family. What a good day.

Before she got too lost in Julian, and vice versa, Taylor snapped herself into relative lucidity and, with three blinks, gave him the signal to move forward.

He recited the firewall spell, and soon after the sensation-sound of a humming forcefield took shape around her outline. The feeling was one of safety, security.

Go time. She slurped down a mega breath and recited her part. "Sister Spirit, I, a water born, humbly request your assistance. I must deliver myself to another location with the purpose of contacting one of my dear coven sisters. This is a matter of much urgency and exigent circumstance."

Her sense of self melted further, until she was little more than putty, viscous streams of color and light sprinkled with stardust. Movement propelled Taylor upward and down, forward and back, her being obliterated and reformed before she awoke with a gasp ejected through red-hot lungs.

Her palms were on solid ground, dirt and grass, a mass of equal hardness supporting her knees. The air was crisp with earth, moisture, and decaying leaves. She hacked a dry cough, heaving and burning.

The world spun in a blurry swirl of color patches, gradually coalescing into a comprehensible landscape of trees shedding their red-and-orange autumnal leaves. Her blood spiked with fear—was she in wilderness? The middle of nowhere?

But the worry was soon allayed when she spotted two-story redbrick buildings on either side of the green space and heard car engines close by. Blurry blobs sharpened into the shapes of moving cars traveling down a populated street. Civilization, good. But where was Helen?

After several clumsy attempts, one ending in a face plant and a taste of dirt, Taylor staggered to stand on wobbly knees. She was about to start walking when a woman screamed.

TEN

THE SHRIEKING, TWENTY-SOMETHING WHITE WOMAN WORE fashionable jeans that sheathed her shaky legs and dark hair piled in a messy bun. More importantly, her sweatshirt bore the visage of a smiling gopher on the front, with the words "University of Minnesota" etched beneath. A good sign.

Kneeling, Taylor faced her palms outward in the "don't shoot" position. A couple of license plates on nearby cars had a state outline that confirmed her hunch. Minnesota plates, and the main university was in Minneapolis. She'd stuck her landing.

Whew. Terrific news. Go witchcraft. The bad news was that the woman kept screaming and pointing, and her histrionics were drawing a steadily increasing crowd of gawkers who clustered in a semi-circle where grass met sidewalk.

"She materialized out of nowhere!" the screamer shouted to a bewildered-looking black man also dressed in collegiate apparel. "Did anyone else see that? One minute nobody was there, and the next, poof! This girl is facedown on the ground."

"I don't have time to explain, but I'm harmless." Bracing her hand on a tree trunk, Taylor staggered to her feet and advanced upon the gaggle of about ten college kids. As expected, they gaped or backed away. Might be a challenge to get information out of the panicked crew, but she'd damn sure try. "I'm looking for a woman named Helen Schrader. She might work as a psychic, or a medium. Maybe a tarot card reader. Something like that. Anyone know her?"

The screamer, green eyes stretched to saucer-like width, finally ceased her battle cries. "Are you an alien?" she eked out in a shaky whisper. "Like that guy on *Star Trek*?"

This all would have been funny if Taylor wasn't focused on her mission, poised to swat distractions like flies. Not that she blamed the screamer. She'd had plenty of meltdowns upon discovering that the world wasn't as normal as it seemed. "No. I'm a person like you guys. Well, basically. Long story. I went to the University of Texas and studied economics, wrote out finals and bought overpriced textbooks like a typical college student. But I really need to find Helen. It's an emergency. My child is in danger. Anyone know of her?"

Several of the campus-goers shook their heads. The question seemed like a dead end until a petite goth in fishnets and leather pointed a black tipped thumb nail in the direction of a popular burger chain's golden arches. "There's an arcane magic shop over there. Cross University Avenue and head west on Third for a couple of blocks. They might know local fortune tellers or whatever."

"Thank you." Taylor took off in a sprint, the crowd affording her a wide berth, and followed the directions. A car honked at her when she crossed on a red light, but she kept moving like a heat-seeking missile.

She passed a mishmash of retail shops with trendy clothes in their windows, a bubble tea place, and a couple of chain eateries. The sidewalks were populated with college kids walking and hanging out on outdoor patios.

Judging by the position of the sun and the numbers of people flowing into bars, the time had to be nearing midafternoon. Meaning she'd better do her best to make this quick, find Helen and accumulate information, and get back to Florida with enough time to steal a few hours of sleep before Mad Dog showed up with his part of the plan.

A yellow sign above a glass storefront grabbed her attention. Magus Books, read the name in black lettering. Victory rushing over her skin in bursts, she bounded down wide, carpeted stairs, the walls on either side displaying fliers for chakra healers and specialists in past life regression therapy. She had to be in the right place.

After pausing to scan for Helen's info and not seeing it, she continued her descent into a basement establishment that smelled of incense and promised authenticity. Taylor bypassed shelves of books and a table covered in assorted candles, approaching a glass display of elaborate crystal balls and jeweled necklaces stuffed with fat gems. A heavyset blond woman well into middle age paused from refilling clear jars with herbs and looked over her shoulder, the smile on her pale face hospitable. "May I help you?"

"I hope." Thankfully, Taylor hit her target of projecting assertive calmness. If she came off as as desperate or loony, she risked getting kicked out and blowing her shot. Too casual, and the woman might dismiss her or pawn her off on someone else. "A friend of mine bought me a gift certificate for a professional service, but I lost it and can't contact the provider."

The shop woman's smile bent into a lopsided, sly smirk. "Might I suggest an herbal concoction to improve memory function?"

Taylor balled a fist and exhaled deeply until the urge to pop off a smartass remark passed. She had no time for games.

Her bangles tinkling as she waved a hand in front of her face, the clerk said, "I apologize. Do you remember her name?"

"Helen Schrader."

The cashier's brow scrunched in a frown as she scratched her head. "What services does she offer?"

Surely, a legitimate witch would leverage her skill set in the marketplace. Best to go for plausible yet generic while covering a lot of bases. "Energy work."

The blonde's eyes sparkled. "Oh, yeah. I know who that is. She did a workshop here awhile back. Total sweetheart. Hold on, I think she left some business cards." She walked to a small end table on the outside edge of the display case and returned with a paper rectangle the shade of a robin's egg.

In the moment, Taylor was sure she'd never seen anything as beautiful as that little card; its dreamy, graceful hue of pastel promise.

She ran the pad of her thumb over the glossy finish, savoring her victory with a silent prayer of thanks before reading the text.

Bingo. Helen Schrader, yoga teacher and studio owner of a place called Light & Enlightened. Complete with an address and phone number different than the one Eve gave her.

Taylor bit the inside of her cheek. Had Eve lied to her, given out the incorrect number on purpose? Why?

"Everything okay? You get what you need, hon?" The shopkeeper went back to work, sticking a metal scoop in a plastic bag and pouring some dusty green substance in the jar.

"Perfect. Thanks for your help. I'll take ten dollars worth of those memory herbs." The polite thing to do was buy something as a gesture of appreciation, and memory-boosting medicinal plants sounded useful.

The clerk lit up. "They're best when strained in hot water, made into a tea." The shopkeeper filled a sealable bag no larger than Helen's business card. Geez, that was ten dollars' worth? Those herbs better work.

"Do they prevent dementia in old age?" Taylor slipped a credit card out of her wallet.

The lady placed the bag of herbs in a larger paper bag along with a pink stone, her gray eyes glittering as she ran the sale. Her entire expression was somehow one big wink. "For those of us with the gift, they expand our minds in truly remarkable ways. I know you're skeptical about the price but trust me." She slipped a business card like Helen's in the sack. "Call when you need a refill and ask for Shauna. I ship worldwide." A pause before the impact landed. "Including to South America."

The raw, naked feeling of being exposed stole over Taylor. Given everything going on with Mad Dog, Scarab, and surveillance, Shauna's comment made her skin tighten. Accepting the bag in a dampening hand, she stared at Shauna like those college kids had gawked at her. "How did you know that about me?"

Shauna tapped her temple. "Take your herbs and study your craft, and soon you'll recognize your coven sisters, mothers, aunties, and someday daughters on sight too. The road ahead is long and fraught with pain, but fruitful and glorious."

Who knew what that meant, but she'd have to postpone soul-searching and connecting with her witchy community for another day. "Okay. Thanks."

Doing her best to appear unbothered, Taylor forced her feet to ascend the stairs at a normal clip, though her footfalls came out as heavy clomps even against the carpet. She nixed the temptation to look back, but she felt Shauna's eyes on her.

Not a moment too soon did she exit to a lively street. Robust fall breezes cooled her face and arms, and for the first time, she noticed that she'd overheated. What a day already.

Taylor walked ten feet and ducked around the side of a corner building, a safe distance away from Magus and out of Shauna's line of sight. She texted Julian: *Made it and got a different number. How are you holding up?*

Seconds later: *I'm fine. About to go shopping for supplies. Going to try and unwind with some silly movie after. Miss you. Love you.*

Exchanging words with Julian balanced her unease with reassuring normalcy and positive emotion. Her muscles loosened as she unclenched a bundle of tension. *Miss you. Love you. I'll keep you posted.*

He texted three heart emojis, and she pressed her phone to her chest and closed her eyes for a beat. Thank God for Julian, their relationship. A precious gift to cradle with gratitude. Redirecting, she turned on data, tapped the icon on her phone to summon a car, and entered Helen's address as the starting point. GPS knew her current location and filled that in, and within seconds the little black icon for her ride scooted down the route, tracing a blue line on the digital map.

Waiting for the car, she thought of Mad Dog's wild confessions about nanotechnology and Scarab synching him to a mainframe with smart dust, not that different from her own ordeal with tracking and DNA modification chips inserted under her skin, the process that had turned her into a human camera.

Technological innovation could be wondrously convenient and downright magical in its brilliance, but the sheer sorcery of those genius innovations sure had their dystopian dark sides.

A white whale of a pickup truck with both pink and black ride service logos on the front windshield pulled up before she could continue philosophizing.

The chemically pleasant fragrance of new car smell grounded her as she climbed into a pristine back seat. Piloting the behemoth was a stocky man with a full moustache, around sixty judging by the lines on his face. He greeted her with an affable wave. The drive took them past a popular upmarket grocery store before crossing a towering bridge stretching across the Mississippi River.

High-rise buildings gave way to an art museum, a nest of cafes, and three restaurants with funky hipster names before pulling up in front of a bungalow home.

The house's curb appeal was inviting, with a cream façade and a door painted the same dreamy, pastel blue as the business card. A sign near the sidewalk, distressed wood frosted with lavender paint, signaled that they'd come to the right place. Helen had good taste. At least Taylor had something to slot in the positive first impressions category.

She got out and pushed a button on the app to tip the driver. Transaction completed, Taylor put her phone away and marched up the slight incline of a paved walkway leading to Light and Enlightened.

She reached the door of an enclosed porch, where a hand-written sign spelled the word "open" in black cursive lettering painted on what looked like upcycled driftwood hanging from a string of twine. The cockeyed angle from which it hung somehow made the place appear more welcoming, real, like a good friend's house.

Helen had come across as an earnest, genuine person. Made the fake number an even weirder loose end.

Upon finding the porch unlocked and taking that and the sign as an invitation to enter, Taylor walked into a cozy vestibule, wind chimes tinkling in announcement of her presence.

The sitting area was stocked with lush, healthy ferns and a Mad Hatter's collection of chairs upholstered in velvet and other sumptuous cloths in a fun jumble of jeweled tones and curious patterns. Short, filled bookshelves and a coffee table decorated with a neatly presented fan of yoga and meditation magazines rounded out the nook. Perfumed a bit like Magus, incense smoke brushed with floral kisses, this was a place where you wanted to have a seat and stay for awhile.

Taylor poked her finger into the pearlescent disc of a doorbell button, rocking on her feet as anticipation nudged her to an edge. Inside, flooring squeaked against footsteps, prompting Taylor to mentally rehearse her opening lines.

One first impression, crucial even by baseline first impression standards, awaited.

She'd picked an opener she'd once heard Madeline Albright mention on a podcast, while discussing how she initiated conversations with foreign leaders in her role as Secretary of State.

I've come a long way, so I'm going to get right down to business.

The door opened wide, giving way to a petite Asian woman in cat-eye glasses and a bob haircut. Dressed in black leggings and a cropped hoodie, she projected a confident air of ownership over the territory. Taylor could barely see past the cut of her perfect posture, catching fragmented glimpses of a tidy desk with a computer on it and a beaded curtain to the left of the main room's hardwood flooring.

"Hi. Are you here for the six-fifteen Vinyasa?" the woman asked with a touch of confusion. It wasn't even five, and Taylor wore street clothes that were likely dirtied and wrinkled by the debacle on the university's lawn.

She hadn't even thought to check her face for smudges of soil or grass. She probably looked like an unmade bed at best, at worst a vagrant.

She tried to snag a discreet glimpse of herself in the window beside the doorway, then stopped. Peeping around corners made her look like a shifty person casing the place. "No. Are you Helen?"

The woman drew back in a gesture of distancing. "I'm Lisa. The other owner. May I help you?" Lisa moved a hand out of sight, to the unseen side of the doorway. Possibly preparing to activate a security system, meaning Taylor had no other way to play this than carefully.

She looked Lisa dead in the eye, softening her features as much as she could and even deploying an old tactic from drama class to conjure bogus tears. "I really need to find Helen and talk to her. Please. I don't know how to explain this, but we have a connection from way back. There's an emergency, and I need her help."

Came out pretty sketchy. Forget being a badass like Madeline Albright. Taylor waited for the door to slam in her face.

But Lisa pursed her unpainted lips and dropped the hand she'd moved to her side. "I know what you're getting at."

"Then you know how serious this is. Can you help me contact her?"

"Are you in danger?" From the pitch to the fixed stare that came with it, every single element of Lisa's question sliced to the bone. Taylor was dealing with a fellow no-nonsense person here. Good. Straightforward types she could deal with, it was small talk and between-the-lines circumspection that damn near made her break out in hives.

"Life and death," Taylor said, a little cooler and more Madeline-y this time.

Lisa's posture stiffened. Her exacting gaze bounced to a couple of spots over each of Taylor's shoulders. "Is there anyone or any*thing* with you, following you, or attached to you?"

Any*thing*. Attached to you. Lisa was on the level. Taylor toyed with the idea of mentioning the possession in the interests of full disclosure, but since that subject hadn't posed a problem in awhile, she nixed the idea. Why scare Lisa over what might be a false alarm? "No. Not that I know of."

"Come in, I suppose." Lisa's words were formal to the point of unfriendly, like she didn't actually want Taylor in her business but her conscience demanded that she help. Good enough.

"Thank you."

The business owner stepped aside, watching Taylor in manner both mercilessly guarded and cautiously curious. What had the studio co-owner witnessed? Ideally, they'd build enough trust to where Taylor could initiate an honest conversation with her.

"Welcome," Lisa said.

The entry area of the house matched the porch in its cozy energy and neatness. A wall mounted corkboard advertised restaurants, massage therapists, and more. Taylor took a seat on a padded bench and picked up a glittery cobalt throw pillow, admiring how each of the sequins caught glimmers of sunset to sparkle in a dynamic play of natural light on reflective color.

She bumped the pads of her fingers over the sharp ridges of thin plastic and cracked a smile. "You have a beautiful studio. How long have you been here?"

The interest and compliment was genuine. L&E struck Taylor as the kind of place where you could get a good workout in a non-judgmental atmosphere while connecting to spiritual concepts.

Lisa sat stationed at the front desk now, fingers flying over a keyboard as she wrote out a message or worked on a document in a series of click click clicks.

"Coming up on five years. I can hardly believe it. There's tea service and a sink for water if you'd like a cup." Lisa pointed to a varied assortment of mugs drying on a dish towel. Beside an electric kettle, a wooden box the size of a textbook held tea pouches in various colors. In the windowsill above, three potted plants no larger than dandelions thrived.

Taylor leaned back in her seat, relaxing despite Lisa's crispness. She liked this woman, how she was tart but kind in her own way. Before she could take Lisa up on her offer and ask another question to keep the conversation moving, the wind chimes tinkled as the front door creaked.

A curvaceous brunette in yoga pants and a tee shirt that said "I'm Not Flaky, I'm A Pisces" on the front held a reusable shopping bag to her ample chest. Her mouth made an "O" as she processed Taylor's existence. "No. Fucking. Way."

Oh boy. Taylor set the pillow down and schooled her face into a serious expression designed to both address Helen's shock and mitigate it.

I've come a long way, so I'm going to get right down to business.

ELEVEN

JULIAN SLID THE THREE SOFT RIFLE CASES ACROSS THE GUN STORE'S counter and slung his haul over his shoulder, the weight and heft of the weapons burning off some inner stress. Luna's angel face, her enormous brown eyes, played through his mind. *Daddy's coming, my sweet baby girl.*

While he was no firearm nut, no way was he going to lead Taylor into the dungeon with nothing more than his fists to protect them and Luna. His papa had taught him how to hunt and shoot, skills likely to come in useful during the rescue.

The employee, a bearded, ginger behemoth in a patriotic tee shirt, handed Julian his change. "What are you fixin' to do with an arsenal like this?" He set the rest of Julian's purchases between them, a plastic bag containing two handguns and plenty of ammunition.

"Protect my family." Julian counted out several twenties and eyed the wall of weapons behind the man, rows of shotguns giving way to bladed instruments of death. "I'll take two hunting knives as well."

"Second Amendment, man. I feel ya." Nodding, the big bubba poked keys on his computer with meaty fingers, the pinky on one hand amputated at the first knuckle.

The Second Amendment had little to do with amassing a personal weaponry collection, but Julian hadn't walked into the Florida gun store to debate the finer points of the Constitution. "We live in strange times." Noncommittal, and scrubbed of either agreement or disagreement.

"Yeah. Shit's weird these days." While wrapping the sheathed knives in paper, the clerk segued into some story about a protest that Julian lacked the interest to follow.

His mind wandered, and with it his attention drifted behind the counter, where a second man, reed-thin with stringy hair, stared at a tablet clenched in his pale hands.

From the angle that the man stood, Julian managed to steal glimpses of the screen. The guy watched what looked like a documentary film, judging by the editing together of news clips and footage overlaid with digital graphics. Fast-moving imagery reflected in his glazed eyes.

Something about the movie prompted Julian to keep looking, perhaps the sheer variety of seemingly disparate content popping up on the viewer. A laboratory where scientists in white lab coats peered into test tubes, followed by two women looking into the camera and speaking as if delivering testimony. Then, a shot of a grim reaper-type thing, skeleton head peeking out from beneath a black cloak.

How did all the content fit together? Rapt, Julian squinted for a better view.

The scene cut to what looked like a shot of several people traipsing through a cave, their puny flashlight beams scratching patches of light over rock. Words appeared at the bottom of the frame. As Julian read, chilling text stabbed hooks of intrigue into him. He thanked his ancestors for passing down twenty-twenty vision.

Part Two: Magic Meets Science, A Corporate Agenda Exposed.

"Well, have you?" The original guy asked, tone piqued, and hands planted on hips as wide as a gorilla's.

Julian tore his stare away from the computer and made an effort to be cordial as he grabbed his bag, committing the text from the documentary to memory. "Sorry, man, I got distracted. Have I ever what?"

"Served in the armed forces."

"No, but my dad did." His papa walked the great road beyond now, but with any luck he'd send Julian and Taylor guidance. Because now, stocked up on weapons as he faced down the eve of the most dangerous mission of his life, Julian could use some wisdom. "Marines."

"Well, thank him for his service on my behalf."

The front door creaked as a couple of women walked in, one rough-looking and the other as made up as a model, both clad in dominatrix heels and denim jackets patterned to look like the American flag. The clerk jutted his chin at them to acknowledge their presence. The pair settled right behind Julian to form a line, engulfing him in a fog of spicy barfly perfumes, but he wasn't quite ready to take his cue to leave yet.

"I'll thank him in my nightly prayers." This elicited a tender look of sympathy from the salesman. Julian leveraged the goodwill he'd accrued and advanced with a nosy question. "Have you seen the film he's watching?" Julian tipped his head in the direction of the transfixed, skinny man.

The beefy ginger snorted. "He's a conspiracy freak."

The taunt must've snagged the scrawny one's attention because he whipped his head in the direction of the register, nostrils of his crooked nose flaring. He shot back a retort in a fast-paced, nasal twang. "It's all true, asshole. I know the guys who made it. You're just too damn scared to face the truth."

Julian made eye contact with the thin man, stepping aside to allow the big one space to help the women. "Oh yeah? They pretty good researchers?"

"Mmm hmm. Monty lives right over there on Flamingo Drive. He's spent the last five years studying this stuff. Explosive."

Gears turned in Julian's brain. If he rounded up a few more facts from Monty or his colleagues, he could cross-reference it against Mad Dog's claims, possibly adding more actionable info to his figurative arsenal before they hit the park in the morning. Weed out any bad facts and keep the good, cull chaff from wheat. Knowledge was power. "You have a phone number or social media account for him?"

A throaty, feminine guffaw entered the chat in a thunderously unapologetic peal. "You don't need one. Just drive over to Flamingo and look for a house where the Unabomber would hang out. Blacked out windows and shit. Fuckin' junked out tractor in the yard." She spoke in a sultry voice laced with an accent like the thin man's, probably leftovers of Creole roots.

Julian turned to the women. Each now held an obsidian demon of an assault weapon, petting the contraptions with lust in their eyes. He was more than ready to get away from all these guns and the people who loved them. But not before raking in a bit more detail. "He's notorious, or what?"

The glamor girl flipped glossy curls the color of ermine, running manicured red claws over the barrel of her piece. "Yeah, he's always turning up at The Alibi or Alligator's Den, ranting and raving about aliens or 9/11 or whatever. He loves talkin' to people, to anyone who will listen. He can be real funny, if you're bored and want some entertainment value."

"Are those names of bars?" Approaching him in public might work better than going to his home.

The second woman, split ends crispy and face a topographical map of grooves and pockmarks, flashed bad teeth and rested her gun against her bosom. "Yeah. Brenda's right. Monty's the damn town crier. He'll talk to any crackpot reporter who'll have him. He makes pamphlets and shit. He has a basement full of equipment and footage he shot. A real hoot."

Both women cackled uproariously while the red-haired clerk chuckled and flipped through a magazine about doomsday preparation strategies. All Julian kept thinking about during the laugh-fest was how he'd love to get a look at this "footage." Maybe he had a snowball's chance in hell of establishing enough trust with Monty to make that happen. A long shot but might as well try. With any luck, everyone in this town was as chatty as Brenda and her pal.

A poisonous aura radiating off the thin man, he popped earbuds in and returned to his program. "One day you fuckers will all see the truth."

One day might come sooner than anyone in the store thought if Julian, Taylor, and Mad Dog escaped the pit with Luna in tow and lived to tell. Speaking of Taylor, it was time to check in. "Thanks, man," he said to the salesman.

"You bet. God bless." He saluted Julian before addressing the women. "You ladies let me know if you have any questions."

Julian exited to a muggy, overcast day. He laid his purchases in the trunk of the rental car, slammed the door, and set off for the hotel, where he'd stash the guns before making a pit stop at The Alibi and Alligator's Den. Then he'd reconnected with Taylor armed with, hopefully, new developments as well as guns.

He drove away from the dingy commercial neighborhood and merged onto the palm tree-flanked freeway. Those Scarab fuckers were about to get clobbered.

✳

"I've come a long way, so I'm going to—"

"Why are you here?" Helen set her grocery bag and a big purse on the bench and moved with speedy determination into Taylor's personal space bubble.

Before Taylor had a chance to answer, Helen was guiding them both, her hand clamped around Taylor's upper arm in the type of hold intended to prevent escape.

The pace of her steps brisk with urgency, she ushered Taylor through the beaded curtain, leading the pair into a sunny room with hardwood floors and no furniture.

Though a slight tremor shook Helen's arms, the studio owner strode across the airy, perfumed yoga floor with gusto. She grabbed two bolsters from a rack stocked with soft bricks and other props and threw the cushions on the floor. "Wait. Don't tell me. It's bad, isn't it?" The yoga teacher sat on her pillow and cradled her head in her hands.

"Um, I can't tell if you want me to tell you what's going on or not." Taylor lowered herself onto the corresponding prop.

"I do. Yeah, I do. I don't want to know, but I need to know." Helen rested her head against a lime-hued wall and slid Taylor a sidelong glance steeped in apprehension. "It's bad, but I need to know. Can't stick my head in the sand and pretend it's not happening, right?"

"Right. Bad, but not hopeless. But before we get into all of that, can I ask how you know who I am?"

As if a wave of history and memories crashed over Helen's mind, her wholesome features redrew themselves into a weary, wise cast.

Taylor felt guilt for heaping the drama at Helen's feet. Unfortunate that she had to put her shit on other people, but this was her daughter's life. No limits.

Helen said, "Eve showed me your profile on social media. I've been keeping tabs on you a little bit since then, on and off. Stalkerish, I realize. But I knew it in my gut all along."

Kinship blossomed in the eye contact that followed, a grim sort of bond. "I knew that we were alike." If there was any way to recruit Helen as an ally, and do it quickly, Taylor staked her bet on blunt truth, making them a "we" in the process.

"Yeah." Helen rubbed her knees in fast, repetitive motions that seemed like a nervous tic. "I didn't want you to be like me, not after Eve, because it felt like inviting things to start up all over again." A laugh devoid of humor came on the heels of frank, flat speech. "I have to admit I was getting used to the peace and quiet around here. But I suppose in trying to push away what I didn't want, I attracted it."

"Is that why you gave Eve a fake phone number to give to me?"

Helen pursed her full lips and pulled a lose thread on her shirt until a line of fabric unraveled. "No. I've changed my number since I last spoke to Eve."

"Can I ask why?"

Her mouth quirked, and a dry, lopsided smile paired with narrowed eyes reshaped her features. "Because evil started following me again. Right after Eve reached out was when my phone started making noises at night. I'd wake up to, like, screeches of cats hissing and meowing coming from the speaker. Then it started ringing, and when I answered it, I decided that what I heard on the other line wasn't something I wanted to hear ever again. I got a new phone and changed my number and ghosted Eve like an asshole. I should have known that running wouldn't fix anything. It never does." Helen hugged herself.

Sensing an inroad, Taylor went for broke. "They're tracking us, manipulating us. I can't figure out if it's psychological warfare or if they want to keep us apart. Or bring us together. But they've been after me too, and I think they used technology to launch their attack. Which is why I'm here."

Helen looked on with a blend of suspicion and interest, stilling her hand motions and affording Taylor her full attention. "Who's 'they'?"

"Ever heard of Scarab?"

"The medical company? Yeah. Eve mentioned the name." She shook her head, her jaw set. "I wish I would have put in the work to build a stronger relationship with her."

"They're involved in more than medical. Way more. It's not too late. Actually, I think we can stop them if we work together."

"I can't throw myself in to magic again. When I started, it was so much, so fast. Taking on all that power drained me. I've spent the last several months regaining my strength and reining in my mind. It's hard to explain, but this stuff can take hold of you. Take pieces of you. And it happens insidiously, bit by bit, until one day you wake up and realize that you haven't felt like yourself for weeks. This was after I quit, mind you."

Taylor looked her fellow witch in the eye. "Which is exactly why I need your help. I'm in over my head already, and I can't do this alone. But I need my magic. I need to practice and develop it until those powers are reliable, and I'm able to wield them with confidence. Like a second nature."

Helen glanced away, tendrils of loose hair tumbling over her cheeks. "I hear it in your voice, the obsession taking hold. It might seem like going all in with magic is the only way, but I promise there are other solutions. Better ones."

"Scarab kidnapped my daughter through a portal. They stole my baby girl and have taken her to some dungeon where they're preparing to use her in a dark magic ritual. Sacrifice."

The atmosphere changed in such a drastic, immediate shift. In the span of a second, the air fled the room and a shift of unseen particles replaced oxygen with a fog of vaporized horror. The miasma engulfing them teemed, breathed, a creepy hybrid of smell and sound that lifted Taylor's neck hairs.

All that remained in the space were Taylor's desperation and Helen's dark eyes, blazing with recognition of a force larger than the two of them, more evil than imaginable, and impossible to understand. Time and space stretched to a taut, endless wire, vanishing into the endpoint that each woman scrabbled for in the other's bottomless gaze.

"I know all about dark magic sacrifices. Oh, I'm intimately familiar." Sarcasm as viscous as tar dripped from Helen's words. Black smoke seemed to saturate her irises, darkening them from mahogany to blood-soaked earth.

"Tell me what you mean," Taylor whispered, her soft words so heavy that they seemed to land like thunder. "Tell me everything you know."

"That's why I started studying magic in the first place, cracked my book, and self-enrolled in the crash course. I put a spell on someone by mistake. It's hard to explain what happened next, but the best I can summarize is that the negative energy, the curse, got out. It broke free. These other cultists got ahold of the curse and tried to manipulate it for their own agenda."

Taylor's blood was cold, and her stomach knotted. She hated being here, in this strange place, talking about curses and evil when her daughter was missing. But Helen was in this situation now, a part of the whole. "Their agenda was sacrificing someone, wasn't it?"

"Yeah." Helen's voice shook. She bit a nail and clawed fingers through her hair in a hard slash, messing up her bun. "The person I accidentally ensnared. He was already on their radar somehow, primed. Maybe the magic was manipulating everyone to get the sacrifice it wanted. Maybe the magic was the only player in the game with any agency. I still don't get it." The glance she lobbed Taylor pinned her in place. "And I don't want to."

"I think we have to understand. Together. Because Scarab isn't stopping. They won't stop. I agree that they want us, that they're using us, but we can't let them. We're stronger together."

Helen shook her head. "You don't know that."

"I do know that. It's obvious. Why else are there combination spells in my book? Opposition elements and partner work? We're meant to be together, working and practicing. As a coven. You have a mentor. Doesn't she tell you all this herself?"

Helen sighed, the gust of her exhale sending a stray piece of her hair to flutter in the wind. "Like I said, I've pulled away from it all. The last time I talked to her was on her birthday two months ago."

"You've met Eve and now me. There's three more of us out there. Do you have any idea of who they might be?"

Helen looked to the upper-right as if accessing a recollection.

"Maybe. Thom was enamored with this paranormal investigator a little while back, and I had a hunch about her. But they lost touch."

"Who's Thom?"

"He's the bass player in Brian's band, Brian my fiancé, that is. The person I accidentally hexed."

Recognition of the band in question clicked. "It can't be a coincidence that two of us witches ended up with two of them."

"Three," Helen said on an exhale. "Eve met Jonnie, the other guitarist, through some seemingly random occurrence, and now they're an item."

"Three, then. What do you suppose that means?"

"That rock stars dig witches because we bring with us a sexy element of danger and taboo?"

The surprising turn to irreverence startled a laugh out of Taylor, and it pleased her to see Helen smile in reply. Maybe some semblance of a friendship was possible, eventually. "It has to be more than that."

"If you crack the code, let me know."

Timing was everything, and Taylor seized a moment. "Do spell work with me. Help me enhance my powers and boost your own. We'll crack all sorts of codes."

She didn't answer right away, but neither did she rise when the front door chimes tinkled their gentle, fairy-like greeting. Taylor considered the latter to be a good sign. "My mentor is out of the country for a couple of days. I can consult her when she's back in town."

"Not enough time."

Helen pointed a finger, her voice tightening as it dropped in pitch. "This is exactly what I'm talking about. *Such* a red flag, this insistence on right now. And I should know. Impatience with magic got me into deep shit. People almost died—at least one person *did* die—because I couldn't wait."

Taylor leaned forward, closing some space to counterattack. "My baby is about to die, Helen. My baby and who knows who else. I need you. I need your spirit magic, and I need us to move forward and balance speed with preparation as best we can. But I need us to move."

Helen gritted her teeth. "Did you bring your book?"

"No. I teleported. The book's in my hotel room in Florida."

That got Helen's attention. Her lips parted. She bolted upright. "You're already advanced enough to teleport?"

"What can I say, I'm a quick study."

Helen snorted. "Where have I heard that before? Oh yeah, out of my own mouth."

Lisa called from the other room, "Are you about ready for Vinyasa? Trevor and Wei Lin signed in, but I told them you needed a minute. You know how they like to set up early."

Helen didn't take her eyes off Taylor as she responded to Lisa. "Can you sub for me?"

"Do I even want to know why?" Lisa deadpanned.

"Probably not." While Helen sprung to her feet and picked up her purse, Taylor suppressed the drive to shake a victory fist.

"Fine. You owe me," Lisa said.

Taylor had barely finished standing when Helen said, "We'll go to my place and get my book. I'm pretty solid on teleportation. Barring a disaster, we can launch from there. Once we're in Florida, we can compare books."

Though Taylor would be remiss to dismiss the possibility of disaster, she put the latest development in the win category and followed Helen out of the house. One step closer.

TWELVE

Seated on the carpeted floor of Helen's apartment, facing her sister witch's split magical tome, Taylor tried to ignore the pinch needling deep in her abdomen. The particular sensation often signaled the onset of a bad pain flare, but in this case it had to be triggered by stress.

Or teleporting. Or maybe it was just gas.

She pressed into her abdomen, felt hardness, and rode a crest of panic at the thought that she'd worsened the problem by messing with her body.

Instead of fixating on pain, she concentrated on the seductive, vaguely lurid sight of yellowed pages stuffed with script and graphs. Similar style and format as her book and clearly born from the contribution of many hands yet alluring in its subtle differences. Interest uncurled in her like a glossy ribbon.

Maybe cultivating positivity would counteract the unpleasantness. After all, she sat in the den of a bona fide hippie witch, if appearances were any indication. An array of sparkling crystals topped a non-operational fireplace retooled to house a wrought-iron candelabra. The centerpiece occupying the belly of the chimney's opening supported three lit candles that produced a relaxing vanilla fragrance. Several bookshelves showed off texts about subjects ranging from meditation to witchcraft to philosophy. Paying a compliment couldn't hurt to establish rapport. "You have a lovely home."

Crouching as she arranged assorted crystals in various shapes and colors in a circle around where she and Taylor sat on an area rug, Helen paused her task. The soft glow of a shaded lamp and the candle flames cast a shadow on her face that highlighted the frown grooving her forehead. "Thanks. Are you okay?"

"Of course. Absolutely." As she exhaled her words along with an unspoken prayer for relief, the cramp deepened enough to spur a wince.

Another subtle massage technique worsened the hurt. Damn it. Self-palpating typically promised decent success odds. Why was the pain reaction happening now, and persisting stubbornly? The last thing she wanted was to come across as weak and sow doubts in Helen.

Fortunately, Helen took her seat across from Taylor, folded her legs crisscross, and didn't force the issue. "I think I found an incantation that has both short and long-term applications. We can bind our essences for this specific purpose and open the door for ongoing collaboration. Have you ever done partner work before?" She rubbed her hands together in what Taylor recognized as a nervous tell, anxiety she hid behind charm.

The glimpse of Helen's vulnerability helped Taylor loosen some of the grip on her own. They were in this together, two women trying to hack mysteries larger than the both of them combined. She leaned against the back of Helen's sofa to find a more comfortable position. "No. Never. I guess I'm a little anxious about it because my stomach's upset. I've, well, I've been dealing with chronic pain since my twins were born."

Compassion shone through Helen's eyes. "Can I get you an antacid or pain pill? Herbal tea for nausea? I have a heating pad that I use for menstrual cramps."

She'd tried every conceivable relief method to no avail, but the kindness didn't fly by unappreciated. "No, thank you. Have you done partner work?"

Helen pulled up and down on the strings of her hoodie, like she was milking a cow, and puffed out her cheeks. "I have not. Eve and I looked at my book together and talked about some concepts, but we didn't get farther than that. I'd love to get a look at yours. Two books in the same room would represent a major breakthrough."

Taylor tried a different tactic on the sore area, kneading until the worst of the discomfort ebbed. She didn't feel a foreign object in there, and the doctor who'd removed her IUD was an expert who performed the procedure safely and without any of the common complications. Every now and again she wondered if she'd been poisoned, but without any evidence or a motive it made no sense to speculate. "A breakthrough would be excellent."

Helen threw her shoulders back and closed her thumb and forefinger into a circle with the backs of her hands rested against her thighs. Even in the hoodie and cloth shorts, she for sure looked the part of the wise yogi in contemplation, which Taylor had to hope mattered.

"Let's do this." Helen dipped her head, loose brown waves falling like a curtain over her face and began to read. "Sister Spirit, I, a spirit born, humbly call upon your guidance. Sister Water, I, a spirit born, humbly request your assistance as an accomplice. My coven sister, a water born, suffers and needs healing. Please yoke our essences and allow me to travel with her through the astral farther, so that I may be of duty and service."

As Helen spoke, it occurred to Taylor that Fol—*the bad sister*, was the only one who didn't match up with her element, chaos, as spirit and water and the rest did. That had to be significant somehow, but now wasn't the time to introduce a new conundrum, not when they'd just gotten into the flow.

Face still obscured, Helen held up her hands, palms out.

Taylor mirrored the gesture, swallowing a lump of nerves as she pressed the undersides of her own hands into Helen's smooth, warm ones.

Helen continued, "Where water flows, spirit goes. Into the molecules of ocean and blood, I infuse sentience and sight. A stream made of eyes shall branch both above and below, casting us across land and beneath earth. May we move fluidly, with adaptability and good measure, as we search and seek as one mighty element that draws the strongest from each of us."

Taylor's head began to hum, an all-encompassing buzzing that set her brain alive and squirming. Sweat dampened her collar and beaded her brow, hairline, and neck until warm wetness sluiced down her face. Gravity seemed to relax its pull because she lightened enough to float.

Though her vision went foggy, she could, paradoxically, read Helen's book clearly. It was as if the words rose from the pages and hung in the air like juicy, teasing talismans begging her to reach out and touch.

Taylor's whole body swelled, too big and too much for any shell to contain, every nerve ending awakened to hypersensitivity. Candle flames licked her all over with their orange tongues made of warmed honey. The energy was sexual, almost. Primal.

Hot all over and with an unspeakable force swelling her organs and pushing against her skin from inside, she gaped at those levitating words. They surrounded her, dancing in circles like crazed elves in some enchanted forest, until all she heard was feral panting.

"What is this?" Helen asked in a stunned stage whisper.

Despite her stupor, Taylor knew. She was shifting, involuntarily for the first time since she'd first suffered the effects of the modification chip that had mutated her. Before Helen freaked out and pulled the plug on the ceremony, Taylor read the words as they scrolled past her in their Mobius strip of animation.

"Wind of my song, breath of my fire. Hydrogen, oxygen, fecund with desire. Of what breeds in this soil, Eve's sin and Adam's toil, may we tarry with a chaos foil. Spirit and water, sisters of ancient coven. Water and spirit, lay burnt offerings in the oven. We permeate matter, ripe in excess, too much and not enough. Spirit witch, light and wise. Spirit witch, on a throne made of eyes. Water to clean, water is pure. Mud to lotus, a blossom out of manure. Spirit in water washes out lies. Water floats spirit, we bind our ties. I bind you, spirit witch, bind your magic to mind in both still seas and rough. I bind me to you, my essence, my life. I hand you my power and declare you coven wife."

Taylor's intuition took over, roaring internal currents directing her next move. She gripped Helen's hands as tightly as she could until she lost track of where one witch ended and the other began. Then, she howled. Full belly, unbridled from the pit, like a full moon, engorged to bursting, penetrated velvet skies.

Shocks ripped through her in a fast succession, reverberations of electric pain that nullified her vision and sent her spiraling into total disorientation.

The next thing she saw was a slab of white, which immediately began to spin in the most hideous way, plunging her into the whirlpool of sadistic nausea.

She tried to cry out, found her voice gone, and moaned like a wounded animal instead.

Once she reclaimed the ability to move, she rolled to her side and voided the meager contents of her stomach with a single, pathetic retch.

Am I in Hell? Why did Hell feel scratchy against her cheek and smell chemical-sweet, like rug shampoo?

She was regaining her alignment. Taylor squeezed her eyes shut and opened them. The blissful flapper gazed down at her like a pagan goddess in a bob haircut and pearls while Taylor writhed on the floor of a room that became more familiar every second.

She sat up, head swimming, and patted her back pockets. Her phone and cards were still there, at least they hadn't dematerialized when she'd teleported back to the hotel. Teleported alone, from the looks of things. "Helen?" Maybe she'd gotten sick in the journey, too, and run to the toilet. But nobody answered.

"Helen, did you make it?" Using the bed for leverage, Taylor dragged herself upright, staggered to the bathroom, and fumbled for the handle until she managed to push open the door.

Nobody there, just blue-and-white floor tile and an artfully arranged assortment of washcloths arranged alongside miniature toiletry bottles.

She pulled open the glass door to the shower and checked just in case, and upon finding it empty, sat on the toilet to decompress. "Crap." She slapped the wall.

Mission failure. She worked her phone free from the pocket and texted Helen, mindful to keep the communication vague in case surveillance managed to crack the firewall. *Hey. Obvs that went sideways. Are you okay?*

Fine overall, but I don't think that collaboration is a good idea right now since we clearly can't control our outcomes. I'll try to find alternative ways to help and reach out if I come up with something.

Taylor's heart sank. How was she supposed to find Luna without the help of the spirit witch? She re-read the message a few times, about to argue before rethinking the instinct. The right thing to do was honor Helen's request, and respecting her wishes was the clearer course to keeping her around in case an opportunity arose to reexamine the collaboration strategy. *I appreciate it.*

She'd taken a big gamble on Helen, and it sucked hardcore that her plan hadn't worked out. No time to mope. Time to explore alternative plans. She called Julian.

One ring later, "How's it going, babe? You okay?" A whoosh came through the line, an outdoor element like a breeze or passing car.

"Yeah, I'm alright. Minneapolis was a bust. I tried to bring Helen back with me, but our plan didn't work. Gotta figure something else out. What's going on with you?"

"I found someone who might be able to help us. Or at least has information to take under advisement. If I give you and address, can you come meet me at the person's place?"

She peeled the phone away from her ear and checked the time. After seven now, but she wasn't in a mood to sit in the room and watch television, and no way was Julian ready to veg out either. They needed all the help they could get. "Yeah. Okay."

"I'm glad you're back safe. I love you."

She touched her heart and midsection, thankful at least that the botched spell hadn't plunged her or Helen into some nightmare dimension. Plus, her pain had let up, whatever that meant. "I love you too."

Taylor swiped her screen to the little black box that would summon a car and tapped the ride share icon that was getting a workout lately.

An unremarkable Uber experience landed her at the doorstep of a one-story shack with drawn curtains blocking curious spectators from peeking in the windows. A minimal front yard thirsted for water and grass seeds. Dodging shards of broken brown glass sprayed on the sidewalk, she walked through the door of a chain-link fence and texted

Julian from the stoop, firing off the address. He confirmed she'd come to the right home.

"Come in," a low, clear male voice called from inside, the tone pleasant and inviting. "It's unlocked."

Julian had endorsed whoever this was, and she trusted him implicitly.

She entered, venturing into a poorly lit but neat living room, sparsely furnished with a single leather recliner. Books stacked against the wall in columns reached halfway to the moulding. She took the collection as an indication that their host was alright. Folks who read a lot tended to have good qualities like critical thinking skills and a honed sense of logic.

"Hello?" To her left, a minimalist kitchen scrubbed to floor-eating cleanliness was bereft of people. "Julian?"

"We're in the spare bedroom," her husband called. "Come on back."

He sounded weirdly energized, enthusiastic even, and she set off with curiosity down a short hallway. After the magical nosedive in Minneapolis, she was eager for positive developments.

The walkway bottomed out quickly, ending in a closed door. Another shut one sat to the right. The lone open area must've been the spare bedroom, and Taylor came upon what was, in her best estimation, a makeshift recording studio. A chaotic anomaly in the otherwise maintained home, the equipment room was lined with bookshelves, nearly every surface occupied by a camcorder, VCR, wires and other gizmo guts, or some gadget Taylor didn't recognize.

Julian sat at a picnic table, hunched over what looked like one of the ancient microfiche machines stashed in the bowels of the old library where they'd met. He looked up and beckoned her with a tip of his chin. "I'm glad you're here. You have got to see this."

His presence was a soothing familiarity amidst upheaval, and she walked over and placed her hand on his shoulder. "What are we looking at here?"

"Answers, I hope." Julian's hope was raw, right there on the surface.

Someone else entered the picture, slipping out of a supply closet. The third party, a looming scarecrow with noodle arms and endless legs, ducked to clear the doorway and strode to her in fluid movements.

A slip of a fellow stood before her, too tall and naturally reedy, like a blade of grass in human form. He wore jeans and a tee shirt, both garments tight enough to emphasize his extreme thinness, an aesthetic choice plausibly made to disturb or unnerve. Only those with the most peculiar of taste would call him attractive.

"Monty W. Cooper. Welcome to my home, kindred spirit." The timbre of his speech was booming while breathy, a soporific style fit for a cult leader. Monty extended a hand defined by a stunning finger-to-palm ratio.

She braced for a moist and fishy shake, but he defied expectations with a businessman's clasp. Their eye contact was chilling, but not disturbing or even awkward. The creepy factor came from around him, a forcefield orbiting him, rather than from within. She placed his age at around forty but couldn't be sure. He had an ageless baby face and only a few wisps of pale hair.

Monty looked like an elderly child while not really resembling either a geriatric man or a young boy. Just *strange*. Paradoxes all the way around.

"Taylor McClure. Has Julian filled you in?"

Monty traversed the room, the grace and determination in his strides inspiring confidence. He knew what he was doing, whatever that was. He returned from the bookcase and presented her with a flash drive, one little black pill enthroned on open palm. "Yes. Extensively. The contents of this drive are classified and not for dissemination or consumption by any individuals outside of this room, a directive with which I trust you will comply. Watch at your own risk and at your leisure."

Of course, he pronounced the final word *leh-sure*. As seconds ticked by, she began to feel weird. Uncanny and impersonal, like Monty was a robot and his house was a projection or animation. She slipped beside herself, acutely aware of the presence of someone else inside of her, watching through her eyes. Stunned, she turned her head in either direction, and the observer moved with her. Taylor's body was a hollow shell, manipulated by a puppet master.

"Are you okay?" Monty asked, his keen eyes burrowing into her soul like he could see her entire episode unfolding.

She felt like she was in *The Matrix*, but it wasn't smart to project weakness to this stranger when she needed his cooperation. He might think she was compromised. Taylor pinched the hunk of tech between two fingers. "Fine. What's your stake in this?"

"True whistleblowers are driven by an inherent call to justice and the urge to see good triumph over evil. The more dubious actors, on the other hand, come to the table corrupted. Personal vendettas, you see, poison the palate with a taste for vengeance. Some of these operatives are so deep undercover they forget which master they serve. Stay on high alert at all times."

His scalpel stare cut through flesh to bone. A hole opened inside of her. She connected dots. "You're warning us about Mad Dog."

"Precisely."

A bitter film congealing on her tongue, she asked, "Why?"

"It's the right thing to do."

"What do you want?"

"Order. Harmony. Evil to perish in a noble and prophetic fashion. Scarab, as I'm sure you're aware, is the evil in this scenario."

"This is a spiritual warfare thing for you?"

Julian interjected from the machine, "Come read."

Welcoming a break from Monty, she took her place at Julian's side. He moved to give her access to the viewer.

Taylor looked through magnifying goggles at enlarged newsprint copy from decades ago. Before delving into the content, she took note of the layout, style, graphics. Same paper as the one she'd seen Julian reading in the library the day they'd met, the one that first introduced to her the possibility that shifters and other paranormal creatures were as real as the stars and sun.

"Is this your publication?" she asked Monty as a hypothetical scenario bounced into her head.

Had he disseminated his writings in a targeted fashion with the goal of bringing Taylor and Julian together? Why? Monty was twice as enigmatic as Mad Dog and jumbled the pieces even more by casting the two anti-Scarab crusaders in tension.

"Yes." He matched her lack of affect with his own vocal flatness. "And yes to your earlier question about spiritual warfare."

Hard, rubber rings surrounding the eye pieces pushed into her orbital plates. She adjusted the focus for a better look. Skepticism sat on one of her shoulders, a raging desire for answers perched on the other. They warred for control of her brain.

An all-caps headline screamed at her: MIND CONTROL VIRUS PLOT EXPOSED.

Reading on, she tried to visualize her blood, cells, organs. Tried to grasp the plausibility of the words before her eyes.

Was the claim true? If it was, she hadn't been poisoned, injured, or implanted with any more microchips or other foreign objects.

Her internal antagonist was viral, some substance called black goo. She'd been *infected*.

THIRTEEN

JULIAN URGED HIS WIFE TO SIT ON THE EDGE OF THE HOTEL ROOM BED by gently tugging on her arm, his chest aching for her plight. Identifying the cause of her duress mattered for closure, of course, but learning as much as possible before going in did as well. Anxiety skipped over his chest when he thought about how little time remained and whether they'd prepared enough.

Behind them, the laptop now populated with Monty's archive of classified shadow documents emitted an icy, watchful glow. The thumb drive jutted out of the machine like an impish black tongue poisoned by corruption.

Her fists balled at her side, she resisted his pull. "I can't look any more. I can't. It's too sickening. I'm too tired."

"I understand, but we need to. We're close, babe, and every piece we gather before going into those tunnels is like insurance."

Taylor cast a baleful glance over her shoulder before taking a seat, slouching as she braced her elbows on her knees. "I just can't understand the motive for giving me a degenerative disease. What if the papers are faked?"

As far as he'd surmised from his visit to Monty's place and subsequent crash course in Scarab moral bankruptcy, the incentive was to study the effect of some new lab-created super virus in shifter hybrids like Taylor. That plan had fallen through when she'd cut out her chips and halted the operation, though a panoply of second-order complications remained.

He rubbed her neck and shoulders, staying the course of empathy even as he hoped she'd marshal her fortitude. They were on the verge of having enough clues to make a pattern. "I don't see why they'd be falsified, do you? Who stands to profit, financially or otherwise, from fabricating those papers? That's an honest question, and if you have an answer, I swear I will listen."

Yet he doubted she'd front a hypothesis for discrediting Monty. He was a citizen journalist to his bones and had had no discernable life outside of researching Scarab. Nor was it in his best interests to lie or forge evidence. Julian prided himself on being an excellent judge of character, first impressions especially, and not one shred of data pointed in the direction of Monty being duplicitous. Mad Dog, however, was a potential loose cannon. But the disgruntled mutation victim was a problem for another time.

"No." She rubbed her face until it reddened. "I don't have an answer. But the more of these theories I entertain, the more I ask, 'what if?' I feel like I'm running into dark holes. Holes that never end or open up into light. They just go deeper and deeper into the cave. Into the fucking underworld."

He resurrected what he'd read at Monty's, subjecting the claims to another round of critical thinking. Monty's assertions hadn't yet stuck with total tenacity, but they held merit. They had data to cross-reference, material right in front of them, and ought to stay with their study. But Taylor needed time to process, meaning the right thing to do was be patient.

He said, "Well, let's go back to what we read. If we take that story as true and compare it to the flash drive documents, then the virus was supposed to stay dormant in you for awhile, making you a carrier until you could be brought in for more experiments."

"They wanted to pull me into the lab, inject me with a booster, and use me for virology experimentation," she supplied with a palpable note of bitterness. She did understand the motive, she just hadn't wanted to acknowledge it. Likely because her own father had been involved in the cruel violations.

"Yes, unfortunately. Instead, though, you're presenting symptoms. They also didn't count on you getting pregnant with shifter babies, but once you did, those babies became exactly what they wanted. Somewhere along the way, the goalposts moved."

Her gaze was savvy but exhausted. "This has to do with my magic. It has to. They found out I had it through the spying and surveillance program; they knew before I did, and once that was in the mix, I became more valuable than just a lab rat to pull cell lines from to tinker with for manmade viruses and bioweapons." A flare of awareness lit up her blue eyes. "What if Luna has my magic? Or some new magic that they're after? Either might pass to female children, explaining why they grabbed her instead of Mal."

"Plausible." He glanced at the laptop, its face now a black square thanks to the screen saver. "I think we'd better read on."

"Yeah." He heard the revulsion in her voice, the aversion to learning more terrible things, and pulled her close.

"I'm sorry you're going through this." Stroking her arm, he spoke into her soft and fragrant hair. "We'll set things right. I promise."

"You can't promise that, Julian."

"Yes, I can." Though he projected enough confidence and strength for both of them, he took her point.

Scarab was always a step ahead, out in front, forcing them to chase a moving target. Once he and Taylor got close to what seemed like the center, their opponent moved up, down, or to the margins. Tough to level the playing field when the rules of engagement and terrain never stopped changing.

Julian grabbed the lightweight laptop, the sole bastion of solid leads. He handed the machine to Taylor, who plugged in her password.

They picked up where they'd left off, facing down a heavily redacted internal memo full of black bars that darkened out text. The effect of those bars, marching down the page in tidy lockstep, was esoteric in its sadistic, bloodless proficiency. Bureaucratic technology protocols keyed in by bored people concealed sinister secrets, making quite the blend of mechanical and monstrous.

"Where do you suppose he got all this?" Taylor nudged her fingers down the track pad to scroll through limited words.

Monty had been circumspect and elusive, but Julian had formed a theory. The guy, in his estimation, was a mid-level employee who used his security clearance to smuggle out trade secrets in hopes of parlaying his cache into a journalism or filmmaking career. "I think he was about to quit or got fired, and before that happened, he grabbed everything he could carry from the computers and offices he had access to. See how some of these look scanned?" Julian pointed to a paper with the slightly blurred look and smudgy edges made by a copier.

"Yeah." Taylor's fingers brushed the pad faster as she continued to read. "Essentially, we're in possession of stolen property right now."

"Correct. However, I'd argue that's the least of our worries."

Silence stretched between them. Julian irrationally listened for odd noises beyond the hotel room and staved off the temptation to twitch. They were living in a spy movie. Maybe they had been since the day they met.

Finally, she said the quiet part out loud with a welcome touch of dry humor. "I keep expecting for there to be another knock on that door, then we open it to a maid pointing a gun outfitted with a silencer at us."

He got out a chuckle to break the height of the tension, but unease swept through him.

She wasn't wrong. They were putting themselves at risk by looking at the memos, and there was no guarantee that Monty wasn't a plant who'd called his handler the second Julian and Taylor left his home. When Taylor wasn't watching, he looked at the window to outdoor nighttime, both spooked and feeling silly for being spooked. "All the more reason to get what we need and get into that park."

Taylor brought up a different PDF of similar appearance, largely censored and with the words INTERNAL MEMO typed in the upper-right header. "This is meaningful." She drew an air circle over a portion of the document and read, "Preliminary tests have shown that shifters, both naturally occurring and lab-created, possess latent magic. Early trials suggest that the chemical compound enabling magical manipulation of the environment can be extracted from young shifters, females in particular. Chances of success fall twenty percent after age five, decrease sharply with each passing year after puberty, and finally become null at adulthood."

"You were right, they want to pull a substance from Luna." The vile thought of his daughter subjected to such cruel, callous perversions made Julian's stomach tighten with rage and revulsion. They had to stop these monsters. He scanned for more details but hit abyss after abyss in those maddening, symmetrical black bars. "What you read is what they're comfortable letting out to wider circles. What the hell is redacted?"

"Yeah, really makes you wonder, doesn't it?" She returned to the original doc, a quick alteration of the settings making both papers visible at once. "We know also that this isn't pure science. They want to perform this extraction in a ritualistic manner. The question is why, and what they plan to do with the output."

Fatigued on strategizing the reasoning behind evil, Julian drew inward and went contemplative. "There's a part of me that wonders if it doesn't even matter. The 'why' question."

"Why do you say that?" Though she met him with a challenge in her tone, she pushed the laptop a few inches away.

"We know their reasons are depraved and malevolent. That's all I need to know. I don't even want to go far into their psychology or philosophy; I just want Luna back. I want to get these sick fucks out of our lives once and for all and get back to being a family."

"Can we look at the pictures of Mal that Crystal and Sasha sent?"

He couldn't get to his phone fast enough. Nothing mattered more than sinking into this brief, sweet moment of respite with Taylor. He snatched it from the dresser and poked the text icon, calling up the message that came in while he was researching at Monty's.

In the thumbnail, Mal directed loving eyes at Sasha or Crystal, resting on his back with his chubby arms and legs pointed at the ceiling like a wiggly little bug. The familiar pattern of his crib sheets and a hint of the animal mobile sneaking into the frame comforted Julian while breaking his heart. Their boy, at least, was happy and safe.

Taylor covered her mouth with the back of her hand and eked out a peep of a laugh turgid with tears. "He's too damn cute. I miss him. Both of them." In a fast motion, she vaulted toward Julian until their bellies were flush and her nose brushed against his throat. "I feel like one of my organs has been ripped out, and all I have now is a big bloody hole." Whimpers deepened to wracked sobs as her body convulsed. "I can't take it. I can't. It hurts too much."

He rocked her, laying soothing hands on her arms and shoulders while she wept the lost soul wails of a suffering, aggrieved mother.

His emotions erupted into a chaotic melee where love for Taylor and the babies, his own loss, and the murderous drive to utterly decimate the demons responsible for this heinous crime laid mayhem upon him.

"I know you can be strong for her. I know you can hold on and be strong for her." He held her as tightly as he could, swaddling and anchoring like he'd done when she'd first learned what had been done to her. "Because there will come a time where you will need to be strong for me, and when we'll have nothing to hold on to but each other."

She broke away and stared up at him, the whites of her eyes red with the blood stains of sorrow. "Make love to me."

Tears streaked her face, her proud chin tipped up in a suppliant's submission. She stared, expectant, asking him with her yielding expression, with the intimate press of her soft form, to ease her pain. To make her forget and help her remember. Escapism seemed wrong. Selfish and decadent.

Of course, his body rebelled against his chastising superego, the dumb male organ plumping up with hunger for his gorgeous, sexy wife coming to him in her time of need, as pliant as the star of a fantasy.

He could forget, just for the time it took to lose himself with her, in her, and transport to that erotic dimension of hedonistic delights where the only concern was passion.

He forced reason and good sense to prevail. "I don't want to take advantage of you when you're upset."

"Take advantage of me? You've got to be kidding. Since when has that ever happened?" They reclined together. She slung her leg over his hip, bringing their pelvises in consort, and began to grind against his hardening cock. She stared into his eyes while she gyrated, watching his reaction as if the sight of his pleasurable torment turned her on.

"We should be escaping *with* one another, not *to* each other. It feels exploitative, turning to sex to blot out pain." And yet, he longed to do exactly what he'd spoken against, making him the most tedious sort of hypocrite. The bulge between his legs reminded him with every jerk and pulse how much he wanted her, how empty his spoken words rang.

The pace of her motions increased, sweet friction both stymied and enhanced by the rapidly heating denim barriers separating them. "I think the right thing to do is enjoy each other. Practice gratitude for what we have left."

She moaned, and her lips skated over the tender spot beneath his jaw, crumbling the last of his restraint into sand grains that slipped through his fingers. Though he remained powerless in many ways, big ways, he still held the power to deliver both of them pleasure, touch, intimacy. Ease their worried minds.

In concession to her final comment, he pulled her shirt over her head, revealing one of her white cotton bras that drove him wild. Simple and utilitarian, her taste in undergarments, a hot misdirection from the vixen underneath.

Eager now, body taking over as mind dropped into the background, he snapped the latch and cast her covering aside.

Pert, round breasts topped by pink nipples rose against an expanse of pale skin unmarked by tattoos. The blank canvas of her flesh aroused him every time and made him want to tattoo his name on her ass or right above her pussy lips.

Not that he'd ever actually make the coarse request, but his dick loved the thought.

Though she usually took part in undressing herself, as ready to get to the action as he often was, this time Taylor was still, looking up with her big eyes as she played this new, submissive character that admittedly got his blood boiling. Like role-playing.

He angled the button of her jeans and pressed the copper disc through the slit, purposefully slowing their pace down even as his urges protested.

She raised her hips in assistance, and he slid off the pants, getting rid of her socks along the way before tossing all garments to the floor.

The flurry of movement ended with her legs parted, and he sucked his bottom lip between his teeth while gawking at the prize between them. A thin curtain of white fabric hid a feast of wet, pink goodness, the hint of hay-colored curls visible beneath damp cotton.

Funny thing was, Julian hadn't always been such a visual guy when it came to sex. He'd never really watched porn. But when Taylor started undressing, he turned into an absolute dog, sniffing out a female in heat as if semen saturated his brain. Ah, well. He *was* a wolf-shifter.

Watching him watch with hungry eyes of her own, she played with her engorged nipples, rolling two buds as stiff as pencil erasers between both pairs of fingers. "Stop staring and take your dick out."

She gave him permission to be a little coarse because she liked acting nasty. He fumbled with the fastener of his jeans. The zing of a zipper followed by a faint scratch of fabric against his sensitive skin—every step along the way made him ravenous with anticipation of what was ahead. He shoved his pants halfway down his thighs in a symbol of crude impatience and freed the fully hard extent of his cock.

"Oh, yeah," Taylor whispered, giving her tits a little squeeze and jiggle. "Play with yourself."

The request was redundant, for the act came naturally, his hand gliding up and down his length to squeeze the swollen crown. The wet spot on her panties spread, offering a greater glimpse of her juicy folds. He groaned. There wasn't much more of this teasing that he could take.

She hooked the elastic band of her panties with her thumbs and pulled them down low enough to give him a glimpse of blond trim. "Is this what you want?"

"Yes," he gritted out, forcing himself not to stroke too fast as the urge for release built and built, tightening to carnivorous lust. "Show me."

It felt like forever before she worked the fabric past her mound.

"Oh, fuck." He treated himself to a few quick pumps when he first spotted that perfect pink clamp of hers. "I want you."

Her smirk was devilish, everything about the expression saying *yeah, I know big boy*. She threw her legs in the air, feet crossed at the ankles, giving him a different perspective of her snatch. Outer lips pushed out, pouting at him from the juncture of her thighs. He even stole a peek of her asshole, that little star winking with the promise of dirty adventure.

They'd never tried *that*. His fist jacked like a piston now, taking on a greedy mind of its own.

A wave surged in him, settling against the root of his sex with hot, dense pressure. He was close. "Oh, fuck, Taylor, I'm right there." He choked the base in a tight fist to stave off orgasm as long as possible. "Tell me how you want to get off." Cause he'd be a goddamn second behind.

She yanked the underwear over her ankles and finally ditched that loathsome piece of cloth, his sole impediment to satisfaction. Triumph swelled his dick even bigger as he pinned his stare to her ripe pussy. His, all his, to have.

"Rub your dick over my clit to start." Her words came out breathy on the exhale, her chest heaving as she spoke.

She was as horny as he was, overcome by urgency. The flush on her cheeks and glaze clouding her hooded eyes also gave away her spiked arousal.

Beside himself, too far gone to banter or tease or dirty talk, Julian lowered himself until his shaft rested in her warm, slippery seam. He started stroking and nearly burst at the intoxicating sensation, his cock coated with her excitement after a few up-and-down glides. "I want your ass next time," he blurted out the crass demand before he could stop himself, all delicacy and gentleman's romanticism losing out to instinct and whatever unwholesome idea popped into his head in service of getting off as fast as possible.

"You want to fuck me in the ass?" she gasped, her muscles locking up, breasts and stomach sticking sweaty to the shirt he'd never bothered to lose.

"Balls-deep." He punched his hips fast, faster, sliding his tender crown through the juicy track of her lubed lips in a race to climax. "I'd fuck your ass good."

With that, she was a goner, howling and moaning as she jerked through a round of orgasmic convulsions. Her short nails dug into his shoulders, legs locking around his hips like she wanted to pull him near until they merged into one ecstatic body of bliss.

Her deep, throaty cries tapered to pants and keening moans, but before she finished completely, he submitted to his own demand. He pushed up on his elbows, enough to create a few inches of space between their bodies and provide him with a show and let loose.

Julian shot, exploding, and gaped in wonder as two streams of milky seed shot up the length of her glistening belly to land on her breasts, neck, chin.

She rubbed the semen into her skin like lotion, a spectacle he enjoyed to the fullest until his quakes died to aftershocks, and he reclaimed his functioning mind and civilized comportment.

Julian flopped to his side and cuddled his wife, who returned the gesture by stroking his chest and nestling into a nook under his shoulder. Even as they laid like that, in a pose that had many times before been a blissful afterglow, a terrible feeling returned to settle beneath his ribs.

Their good time had been temporary, fleeting and incapable of providing sustainable happiness, and in a few short hours the descent would commence. Even that word he'd thought—commence—worsened his creeping dread. He'd heard it before, on the lips of the woman he loved, in a terrible way.

Taylor kissed his collarbone.

He repaid her kiss by dropping one of his own near her eyebrow. Usually, they talked and laughed after sex, but now their ordeal had stolen that precious, private ritual along with everything else. Once the sun rose, they'd have another chance to fight for Luna before their daughter became a lost cause.

FOURTEEN

THE HOTEL ROOM COFFEE WENT DOWN SHARP, DISGUSTINGLY SLUDGY, but Taylor drained the dregs of her cup anyway. In a perverse way, she welcomed the acidic burn of the liquid when it settled in the pit of her stomach. Reminded her that she was alive, present. A bitter brew to counteract numbness, especially when she lost herself and could only observe the observer.

She told herself that the lapses of personhood were caused by stress and trauma, halfway believing her rationalization of the weird new phenomenon that'd shown up at Monty's.

Java jitters worsened by the ticking of the clock, she surveyed the cache. Supplies crowded both queen beds, objects lined up like soldiers at the ready: a rifle and handgun for each of them plus a spare shotgun. Twin hunting knives. Several handfuls of energy bars and many packages of nutrition gel. Julian had also scored three hydration backpacks, signal flares, walkie talkies, flashlight headlamps and batteries, a compass, and more.

A seemingly never-ending string of logistics, contingencies to remain mindful of as they prepared to be underground for who knew how long.

The plastic was thin and smooth between her fingers, designed for a school lunch or similar, an ordinary object discordant with their predicament. The weirdest and most random moments challenged her resolve.

Julian filled his hiking pack with his share of the supplies, holstering the smaller weapon to his hip. "Once Mad Dog gets here, we'll review the maps and try the first secret entrance."

His matter-of-fact assessment snapped her out of her musings and into preparation mode.

She transferred provisions into her one backpack as he had, holstered up, and donned the wearable canteen and second, hiking pack. Proper fit established, she took them off and quickly swept the room for forgotten phone chargers or other essentials.

Her laptop, conspicuously laid on the dresser by the television, was designated collateral damage. She'd backed up her important files elsewhere and wiped the machine clean, and if they made it out of the dungeon alive, she'd buy a new one. Not that she cared about a computer. Bigger fish.

She patted the firearm at her hip. "I hope the first entrance is a go, because we're conspicuous. If there's any park security hanging around, they'll know in a second that we aren't there to get our faces painted and ride the Cupcake Express."

Despite her attempt at wit, Julian grumbled. "We may have to prepare to subdue any interlopers with non-lethal force. I'm not going to let anyone stop us. You know that, right?" A fire burned in his dark eyes, ablaze with resolve.

She caught his fingers and squeezed. "Yeah. I know." The bigger challenge would be to keep on believing even if, *when*, all seemed lost. But she'd best keep doubts hidden or risk tanking morale. "We've got this. For Luna."

"For Luna." He clutched her hand tighter, shaking her hand once in confirmation of their shared commitment.

They were comrades in arms now, the reach of their bond extending beyond the bounds of husband and wife. Whether that would be enough, well, impossible to say. But the moment of truth was afoot, and there was nothing to do but hope and try.

His phone buzzed. She swallowed hard and let go of him.

Julian glanced at his phone, stashed the cell in the pocket of his cargo pants, and said, "He's downstairs."

She took a bite of the dry bagel she'd gotten earlier from the lobby café. The chewy, boiled bread tasted like cardboard, and her stomach closed around the dense hunk, but she forced herself to eat more. Maintaining baseline nutrition was crucial. When she finished as much of it as she could get down, she said, "Let's pray."

Julian raised his eyebrows, likely startled by her sudden reversal from agnosticism.

Instead of challenging or questioning her, he simply took her hands and bowed his head. Yet another reason she loved the man—he knew exactly when to press and when to take her at face value.

"Whoever is listening," he murmured in a deep, rich voice, "Great Spirit, God, Jesus, ancestors, whoever hears this, please watch over us as we embark on our quest today, grant us your blessings, and keep us safe. Please watch over our baby girl, and our baby boy and his caretakers, during this difficult time. May good triumph over evil. Amen."

A jolt of electricity jetted through his body and into hers. Her heart leapt as a series of swelling tides moved from her core to her nerve endings. She gasped and locked his eyes, watching his pupils dilate in recognition. He'd felt it too, she was sure, but no need to unpack.

Some phenomena were better left as good omens.

She brought his hand to her cheek and kissed the palm. "Amen."

On that quiet yet profound note, they marched out of the room and boarded the elevator.

Their faces were stern, reflected in silver doors that opened to an older white couple, the unbothered visages of the boomers cheerful. Each of the sockless retirees in golf shorts wore a visor and an air of blissful ignorance. Taylor envied their vacation breeziness with a bitter potency she'd hadn't guessed she had in her.

"Going hiking?" the man asked, his goofy grandpa voice as high-pitched as expected.

"To the park, actually." Julian spoke politely, but in a way that provided no avenues for more conversation.

Taylor watched the floors ding down, red numbers counting backwards, ignoring the pleasant oldies. They didn't understand. Their shared metal box was, for Taylor and Julian, a purgatory delivering them to the starting line of an unthinkable tribulation.

"Wonder World is nice this time of year," the lady said with a wide grin that showed off the gleaming spoils of cosmetic dentistry. "And I think that the two of you have a good little thing going, making the trip before you have kids. I see all these young couples such as yourselves out at the parks with their babies and toddlers, and nobody is enjoying themselves."

Julian clutched Taylor's hand, and she held his, two lifelines stitched together. It wouldn't be right to lose her cool and pop one off at these clueless, well-meaning innocents. But that didn't make their comments hurt any less, didn't stop their chatter from opening the wounds in her heart and womb.

"That's the plan," Taylor said with deliberate crispness. If one of them spoke any more, she'd get out her phone and pretend to take a call.

The elevator reached the first floor, and the gray heads exited. "You kids have a good time, ya hear?" the old man said. "Maybe you'll make some Wonder World babies." A cheesy wink, and off he went, his wife in tow, and they began to prattle about golf.

The mini ordeal already fading into a fuzzy memory, Taylor and Julian breezed across the lobby, sounds of *Muzak* and the babbling output from an artistic water fountain offering illusory normalcy.

The last bits of ordinariness she'd see or hear for awhile took on a mournful, pre-nostalgic preciousness. She soaked up the scene. Small groups congregated on sofas sipping coffee. Packs of tourists were suited up for their expeditions, Wonder World's signature bunny ears on their heads and phones stuffed in clear waterproof cases hanging from strings around their necks.

All that faded when they pushed their way through revolving doors and into a blanket of hair-curling humidity. Mad Dog looked over the tinted edge of a partially rolled down window, a stocking cap hiding his deformed head as he peered at them from the front seat of a gray sedan.

She bit her tongue and didn't flinch. Their contact's demeanor bothered her, his vats of endless rage festering just below the hangdog surface of a beaten man.

Or maybe Monty was getting inside her head. Sucking down a damp breath ripe with the miasma of a summertime city, she got in the backseat and committed herself to the mission. A cocoon of generous air conditioning chilled her out, literally and figuratively.

Julian assumed his post beside her, and the vehicle took off with a squeal of tires once his door slammed shut. Automatic doors locked. No retreating now, they were on the move in an ambulatory cell redolent of bleach used to scrub who knew what.

Her skin fit too tight. Thoughts spiraled downward in loops of menace. What if this was all a setup? If this driver took them to a warehouse where executioners awaited, at least they had weapons. Their captors had probably accounted for that. Maybe she'd get stuck with a needle and shot full of knockout drugs like the last time she'd tried to infiltrate Scarab.

She did her best to remain calm while the mystery man behind the wheel guided them onto an interstate, rolling over a bumpy ramp pockmarked by potholes. Her bottom jostled while the tang of her own fear and sweat reached her nose. If she could smell her own distress, the others in the front sure could.

She clenched her jaw, mad at her physiological betrayal, and scanned the road's shoulder for one of those universal green mileage signs.

A question from Julian broke tense silence. "Let's see your maps."

Mad Dog unzipped a polyester backpack resting on his lap and handed Julian a stack of white paper. The one on top was marked with handwritten writing and pink highlighter. A teeny sticky note crowded with words occupied an upper corner.

"The first five maps are the most likely to be accurate," Mad Dog said. "Those first few have been verified by multiple, credible sources. See for yourself. The top ones on the stack show almost total consistency in the charted area."

Julian flipped through pages, soft rustling sounds loud in the otherwise silent vehicle, while Taylor looked on. She anticipated Mad Dog saying more. He'd inflected his final syllable in a tapering manner, suggesting that his thought wasn't finished.

Sure enough, he added, "That's the good news."

Taylor spotted a mile marker alerting them that the exit for Wonder

World was one mile away. Semi-reassured that death wasn't imminent, she engaged their accomplice. "What's the bad news?"

Their driver veered on to the exit lane, further allaying a worry that the bad news involved her and Julian wearing concrete shoes and ending up at the bottom of a swamp.

"The bad news." Mad Dog cleared his throat. "The intel Julian is looking at is fairly surface. We have an alternative way in that allows us to circumvent metal detectors and most security personnel and the entrances to the underground lair. Sure, that's helpful, but I have it on good authority that most of those initial spaces are abandoned, tram parking lots, or storage. Nothing that we want is hanging out near the surface. We'll have to go deeper."

She leaned against the resistance of her locked seatbelt to get a better look at Julian's papers.

He laid those first five on the middle seat between them and spread the sheets out like a parachute. Some were official-looking blueprints, others hand-drawn, all appearing to show a near-identical layout of large and small rooms.

She picked up one of the easier to read pages and traced lines until she could identify staircases, doors, and elevators. Otherwise known as passages down. "I take it the second group of maps isn't consistent."

"Bingo," Mad Dog said, glaring at his papers like he wanted to burn them.

"He's right," Julian said before handing Taylor the second batch. "Prepare to feel more terrified yet less informed."

She spread three sheets from the inconsistent group across her lap while holding two others in each of her hands.

Mad Dog was right. After perusing only the first two, she felt as if she'd tumbled into a psycho circus run by an evil clown. The page in her right hand, etched in sloppy penmanship, depicted a vertical layout with a central pipeline dropping down, shooting off into three horizontal lines spaced at equal intervals as the main line commenced its descent.

The result was like a graph with three X-axes, the rectangular spaces created by the intersection with the Y-line all marked with its own distinct, disturbing, label.

The left and right ones closest to the surface: Reprogramming and Rehabilitation.

Next level down: Training, Experimental projects, Labs.

Below that: Kill Room (the box on the left). Kitchen (right).

Taylor swallowed a jolt of bile, bad coffee mixed with adrenaline and dread. She didn't care to think too much about why the kitchen lay to the right of the kill room. Nothing good. She read on.

Level four was designated for "rituals," "extractions," and "catacombs," all contenders for where they eventually needed to end up. The first two were possible places where Luna was being held, the third where what was left of her would go when her captors were through.

"Jesus." Her whisper was a ragged benediction, a halfhearted plea that the savior in question would lift them from their nightmare.

"He ain't coming," Mad Dog muttered, cynicism as thick as motor oil.

"Look what it says on the very bottom." Julian spoke as matter-of-factly as a person could in the present situation. "It's the only consistent piece on the unverified maps."

At the bottom of the vertical line was a small, lowercase word rendered gargantuan by the largesse it communicated: Titans.

The promise of a good clue shimmered on the surface of her frontal lobe. "Of what, industry? Science? Magic? All of humanity?" Paper stuck to the sweat and oil of her palms as she pushed sheets aside and compared.

That exact same word was typed or written at the bottom of every single page. Problem was, that was literally the only consistency among the unverified pages. Every other element, from the map or blueprint to the handwriting/typing to whether rooms were demarcated and/or labeled or not—was different.

Radically, completely different in shape, size, and layout. Except for the titans thing.

A sinking sensation pulled her low as realizations surfaced. She made a neat pile of the unverified sheets and set the stack on her lap, trading examination for staring blankly out the window. Beyond the car, a concrete expanse larger than a football field sprawled, packed with a rainbow array of vehicles.

A pearly gate and cheerful pink sign that said "parking" assured visitors that they'd arrived. As did the frosted, bubble gum castle looming beyond the lot, all spire-capped towers flying glittering flags, crystalline windows to catch the sun, and a doorway shaped like a heart.

Some genius had downloaded the aesthetic right from the wildest dreams of a six-year-old girl. Had the situation been different, Taylor might have been able to enjoy such a spectacle ironically.

While the driver pulled up to a staffed gate, she reviewed her papers again. "What you're saying is that we can't use any of these maps, only the superficial ones."

Before Mad Dog had a chance to respond, Julian did. "Not necessarily. Look closely in the upper-left hand corner of the consistent map, along what would be the east wall of that room. You'll see a square. Might be a hatch or doorway. But whatever it is, it corresponds with an identical spot on the unverified maps. The reprogramming area on the first one you looked at has the notation."

She returned to the first map. A tiny box, perhaps a crawl space or storage cubby, outlined the area in question. It was present on the same area of every single unverified map. None of the blueprints had a single feature in common besides the itty-bitty square, a black box leading to the unknown. "You're right." She went back through the pages, chasing that initial, miniscule hit of victory amidst setback and letdown. "You're absolutely right."

The car moved up a spot in line, only one place away from the attendant who'd process their party. She pored over the papers a third time, devouring as much as she possibly could in case another a-ha clicked before they entered park property.

Mad Dog added a thought. "At first I thought it was an oubliette or bottle dungeon, being small, but the fact that it tracks from surface level to deeper ones in every case kinda nukes that theory. Somebody was careful to identify and mark a passageway leading to the surface. Discreetly, I might add."

His words haunted. "What the fuck is an oubliette or bottle dungeon?"

"A dungeon within a dungeon, basically. For when you *really* don't want someone to escape or get rescued. There would only be one way in

and one way out if that's what our mystery box was, and a slope too steep
to climb. They throw captives down a chute, basically."

Her guts turned over for the hundredth time that day. Was this even
real life? "Seems like you're quite familiar. Do they have those where
we're going?"

The driver pulled up to the ticket window in a slow crawl, slicing
Mad Dog a look that made him shake his head at Taylor. For the best.
She didn't want to know the answer to her bottle dungeon question.

A blond, white guy with the clean-cut aesthetic of a nineteen-fifties
milkman hung out of the cashier booth's window, his uniform gumdrop
yellow and his smile plastic fantastic. "Welcome to Wonder World." His
voice was predictable. "Will you be purchasing a full-day, half-day, or
overnight parking pass?"

"None of the above," the driver spoke for the first time in a
businesslike tone with a commanding accent. One of the harsher
European ones, German or Dutch. "I'll be dropping this group off and
returning to pick them up at an undisclosed time."

Yikes. This driver could at least try to sound normal. Now that her
lowkey fear of getting murdered had mostly subsided, Taylor wondered
who this guy was, how Mad Dog had found him. Though chances were it
didn't matter. Likely a hired gig worker from the dark web who came
with flexible morality, didn't ask questions, and collected his cut.

The Ken doll behind Plexiglass bent forward in a conspiratorial lean.
"Are you sure that you don't want to join your friends on an unforgettable
Wonder World adventure?"

"Positive. I trust that you'll lift the gate if I exit in under fifteen
minutes?" The driver pointed at a sign listing the parking rates.

"Of course," Ken Doll said, looking bewildered but doggedly
cheerful. "Have a stupendous, magic-filled time."

If only he knew. Or maybe he knew who Scarab had trapped in the
bottle dungeon.

The driver proceeded through the lot, zigzagging and looping around
throngs of people until he stopped in front of a soaring purple-and-pink
gate made entirely out of shiny materials.

The sparkly entry point into Wonder World opened to a faux-
cobblestone pathway that wound into a promenade lined by storefronts.

They wouldn't be going in through the main gate, not with their weapons, but it helped to have a fix on a possible escape.

She voiced a lingering concern. "We don't have a sense of where we'll end up once we go through our trapdoor entrance."

"Unfortunately, that's correct," Mad Dog said.

"We'll have to wing it, true." Julian became the voice of optimism, piercing the gray cloud of doubt. "But who knows, once we're down there, maybe we'll notice patterns that weren't apparent before. Consistencies. Or maybe there's clues coded in that second set of maps that will unveil themselves once we're on the ground."

She loved him fiercely. A bulwark of good sense, problem solving, and the best blend of optimism and pragmatism. Crucial on a harrowing expedition like this. "Thank you," she said.

Taylor tucked the questionable maps into her backpack and reviewed the location of the secret entrance again. She looked at Julian and locked his eyes, acknowledged Mad Dog's role by meeting his weary ones, and glanced to her husband one more time for anchoring. Time to follow the proverbial yellow brick road.

FIFTEEN

JULIAN KEPT HIS STARE PINNED ON A LONE SECURITY GUARD UNTIL THE buff brute meandered closer to the main entrance, turned his back, and pried a cell phone from his pants pocket.

A glint of sunlight shone off a bald spot near the top of the guy's head while he texted, snorting at whatever was on the screen. Nice and distracted. Julian could have taken the rent-a-cop if the situation led to a showdown, but violent confrontation was never his first choice.

The guard safely categorized as a non-issue, Julian swept a quick assessment across the scene behind the theme park entrance, his eyes sharp for trouble.

The delivery driveway they'd followed led to a small parking lot and alcove for truck deliveries. Taylor and Mad Dog stood watch at the entry point.

Julian cased the area. Evenly spaced palm trees, their leaves swaying in a slight breeze, lined the service road until its terminus at two grungy dumpsters. Greenery sprouted through cracks in concrete, evidence of neglect. With any luck, the lack of care extended to patrolling and surveillance.

Mad Dog stood post at one of two access bays meant to accept supplies from big rigs. "I'll take up the front." He swooped a hand, ushering.

"Are you sure this is the right way in?" Suspicion etched in her frown, Taylor stayed put, reviewing one of the allegedly verified maps. "It seems a little run-down and forgotten."

"Valid." Julian looked over the grounds with fresh eyes, the trash receptacles abutting a patch of swampy green space strewn with litter, the blacktop of a street visible through trees. "Though if they don't care enough to send security personnel back here, that works in our favor."

Mad Dog scoffed, riding out a quick seizure. "Pretty sure. The secret entrance is supposed to be nondescript, and part of their M.O. is hiding in plain sight. Let's hurry, before someone comes back here to smoke pot or whatever."

Julian didn't blame his wife for her skepticism. This whole operation couldn't be any shadier if it tried. He pushed back on Mad Dog. "Pretty sure but not positive. Meaning you haven't investigated."

"No." An engine hummed somewhere in the distance. Mad Dog craned his neck in the vicinity of the sound. "Not personally. But I know people who have, and I trust them."

Taylor opened her mouth theatrically wide. "You're kidding."

Great, another curve ball. When would they stop getting walloped with unwanted surprises? Julian fought to keep his tone level, but a trace of his frustration hissed through. "You told us you had firsthand knowledge of the layout."

Mad Dog's lips thinned into a line. Sweat beaded at his temples, giving him a guilty sheen.

"You lied to us at the hotel." Taylor fanned herself with the maps. "Why?"

"To get you moving forward," their accomplice said with annoyance. "But do as you will. No skin off my nose if the two of you wanna turn back and regroup without me. Just hand over the maps and we'll go our separate ways." Shock flared in Mad Dog's eyes, and he turned to face the wall, his hands fumbling quickly near his groin. "Ah, shit." Splashing sounds of pee hitting concrete, accompanied by a grunt of relief, followed.

While the man saw to his emergency business, Julian took a step closer to Taylor, closing the space between them until they stood at kissing distance. Instead of kissing her, he did his best to communicate with her via his eyes and mind. He felt certain that merging magic had augmented the soul-connection that they shared as their wolves.

This is the best shot we have to save Luna. Unless you have an alternative.

A twinkle in her eyes paired with the slight parting of her lips showed him that she'd gotten the message. Nice. They had a new asset now, a secret way of talking.

A vein popped into relief near her forehead. *What if he goes rogue and double crosses us? Turns us over?*

He pulled on the straps of his pack, hiking the cumbersome thing higher to relieve some strain. *First sign of any deception and we'll deal with him.*

She pointed a finger gun in the air. *Deal with him?*

If we must. The mere thought of committing gun violence against anyone, especially such a broken man as Mad Dog, made Julian sick. But he needed to soothe Taylor's fears and convince her that surrender was not an option. He'd better assure her that their safety came first and would prevail. *Tell me you're with me, babe.*

Her countenance was fierce and solemn. *Okay.*

The piddle tapered and gave way to a zipper's zing. "Y'all hear that car coming? Let's go. Now."

The monotonous engine song grew louder with each second. A gray truck with a covered bed bumped down the pavement at the far end of the service road, at a safe distance but not for long.

Julian snagged Taylor's hand and jogged them to where Mad Dog stood. That vehicle would pull up in around ten seconds, and then the mission would be blown.

His pulse thumped as he interlaced his fingers to form a step and bent his head at Mad Dog. The guy stepped on Julian's hands, his rubber boot heel pushing down hard, and vaulted into the delivery port.

Her blue eyes narrow with determination and step just as deliberate, Taylor went next, disappearing between strips of heavy plastic sheeting split into even pieces like giant black linguine noodles. He winced while watching her exert herself, but she didn't show the slightest sign of pain. Hard to determine what instigated her flares, but he wasn't about to bring up the matter and risk creating an issue where there wasn't one before.

Julian planted his palms on the hard surface, pushed up using upper body strength, and swung his legs and lower body through the rubber slats.

As a corner of one of sheets smacked against his cheek, it occurred to him that the setup was unusual. Every loading dock that he'd seen, admittedly not many, was equipped with a lockable door. Either this rubber strips arrangement was different by intentional design, or the doors hadn't been pulled down for a reason. Quite possibly a reason involving the encroaching truck.

Speaking of, time to hustle. Julian crouched, then rose, his quads and hamstrings burning against the extra weight of his pack. A gray, nondescript warehouse floor stretched in front of the trio. It struck him as strange the loading zone contained no pallets or forklifts, no trash bins or vending machines, no nothing. Just a smooth plane of slate, polished to an eerie sheen, the air tinged with an unpleasant farm smell like bacteria and hay plus a hint of copper. Not right.

Outside, the clunk and rattle of aging car machinery tapered to silence. He looked at Taylor and Mad Dog with urgency. They caught it and started walking in unison, Taylor reading the map.

"There's a door at the end of this room, on the left-hand side, that takes us out of here. If we can get through a few more of these rooms undetected, we'll make our way toward reprogramming." The low, smooth timbre of her voice matched the goal of remaining undetected.

Julian's chest tightened. Speaking of undetected, they had yet another loose end with the truck. Mad Dog, magic, surveillance, and now Gray Truck populated a rogue's gallery of suspicious, unknown elements.

He glanced back, halfway anticipating meeting eyes with a potential combatant, but saw only that waxed expanse of slate and slices of daylight piercing the gaps in the slats. He returned his attention to his companions. "I don't think that truck driver's coming in this way."

Taylor picked up her pace as if the mere suggestion of interference lit a fire. "Well, he's outnumbered three to one. Even if he is, let him try."

"He's outmanned unless he's transporting others," Mad Dog put in, his voice neutral enough to be unreadable. The guy really did come off like the quintessential disinformation asset at times, sowing confusion as he cycled through counterpoints.

Julian sized up their third wheel, halfheartedly trying to poke around in his mind, open drawers to omissions. The guy obviously knew more than he cared to let on, although he seemed comfortable dropping breadcrumbs. "Like who?"

"I don't know, man. Nobody in particular. But it's not outside the realm of possibility."

Once she reached the door, Taylor halted her motions and jangled a knob. "Locked, of course. And Julian has a point. Why did you say transporting others? Is this space used for trafficking purposes, that you know of?"

"This is Scarab we're talking about," Mad Dog said dryly with a condescending touch implying that the question was stupid. "Everything they do, or are, is used for trafficking purposes."

Taylor sighed, running her hand along the seam separating door from wall. "We haven't heard a car door slam. Maybe they turned around. Can anyone pick locks?"

Eager to focus on a task besides obsessing over Mad Dog and his mind games, Julian stepped in close and took an old credit card out of his wallet. He stole a moment of solace, of vacation, in Taylor's fragrance, her body heat.

For a fraction of a second, he felt home. To preserve that speck of escape, a grain of sand ensconced in a glass bubble, he lobbed her a playful look while maneuvering the card through the crack and under the mechanism until the lock popped.

A rogue's smirk stole its way onto her lips, another tiny theft reminding them that their bond was unbroken. "Checkered criminal past?"

More like an embarrassing incident involving forgotten keys and too many beers that ended up with him locked out of his own house, but why dull the endangered glint of their sparkle with the unsexy truth? "I'll tell you later."

She poked the point of her tongue out of the corner of her mouth, slyly erotic, only her eyes smiling now. "Uh huh. You locked them in your house, didn't you?"

Heat masked his face, though his heart was full. Nobody but Taylor saw through him with such loving, effortless ease. He bumped his hip into hers and pushed the barrier separating them from the next room, odors of dust and mothballs killing his buzz as the slab opened with a creak. "I plead the fifth."

She bent her thumb in the direction of the opposite corner of the warehouse, mission mode overtaking play time when she said, "Did you see those?"

He tracked her vector until his line of sight landed on six black cubes, each about three feet tall and shiny as obsidian, evenly spaced in placement against the back wall of the main warehouse floor. "No, I missed those when I first looked around. They blended into the background I guess."

He sprinted over for a closer look. Orange crosshairs within circles painted on top of each of the surfaces didn't blend in, and as he examined the chunky stations, an idea popped into his head.

They were docking bays for drones that launched from the loading alcoves. A scenario which explained the rubber strips. The drones could come and go smoothly without human involvement. A chill zapped him as he examined the empty launch pads—where were the machine scouts right now, and what were they doing?

"What do you suppose they are?" Taylor asked from the doorway, dim light from beyond the threshold painting her face with shadow.

He rejoined his party. "Charging hubs for electronics, like an enhanced version of a power strip." For safe measure, it didn't hurt to keep a few things off Mad Dog's radar. The guy didn't need to know everything all the time.

Julian cut Mad Dog a discreet glance with the intent of gauging his response, but their tenuous ally was busy sucking on the tube of his canteen and didn't react.

Taylor led the way, stepping over loose wires and assorted industrial debris. A single, naked light bulb of minimal wattage hung from a cord in the ceiling, their only light source.

She tapped her finger on a filthy sink, then kicked a nearby hole in the ground where it looked like a toilet had been ripped out of the floor. "Remodeling stalled out."

After shutting the door and relocking it, Julian followed his wife through the smashed remains of a decimated wall, the wound weeping with ripped slabs of insulation and frayed wires.

He pried loose a board with some ugly, rusted nails poking out of the wood. Holding the makeshift weapon at his hip, he glanced to the ground, where the trio's footprints stamped a floor coated in white plaster dust. He smeared his tracks away, and Taylor and Mad Dog did too.

Everyone deployed their flashlights, beams jumping over ruins and rubble.

They kept going despite haunted house vibes, passing through the hollowed wall into another, larger room trashed with the flotsam and jetsam of abandoned renovation.

Taylor kicked a medical mask and a used caulk gun out of their path. "If the map is correct, we just have two more rooms to clear before we're in one of the unverified rooms. Any idea who or what we might meet in there, Mad Dog?"

"According to my sources, all the work done on the first secret level is mechanical. Reprogramming and updating drones, clones, and robots, also real mundane stuff like wiping compromised computer hard drives and shit. Anyone you'd run into there is likely to be a desk jockey or computer geek if it's occupied at all. They don't staff the place regularly. All work is performed on an as-needed basis."

Mad Dog knew about the drones. Noted. Julian popped another locked door and moved his light over walls marred with gashes and holes, seeing only junk and waste as they crossed the first of two more rooms.

"Good to know that we won't be stumbling upon any mind control or torture," she said, dirty flooring yielding with soft creaks beneath her steps as they hung a left and proceeded into the final room separating them from the unknown.

"Oh yeah, they keep the human capital stock and other live materials tucked way far away." Mad Dog paused for a tremor and resumed his march, stepping over a rotten cardboard box peppered with white slips no larger than playing cards.

"Some lovely terminology there. Rolled right off your tongue." Julian kept his sarcasm pointed without crossing over into caustic, crouching by the pile of paper. He didn't want to antagonize Mad Dog, but he wasn't above goading him now and again in hopes of pulling out fresh insights. Upon finding a bunch of junk, he stood and forgot about the old paper.

"Yeah, well, I've seen it all, buddy. Calling me jaded would be like referring to Satan as mildly unpleasant." Mad Dog lifted his stocking cap an inch. "Care for a reminder of why I'm disillusioned?"

"No. Point taken. You develop any more theories on what happened to Gray Truck Person, since they didn't appear to be trafficking anyone using the same route that we came in?"

Mad Dog nursed the straw of his hydration pack, his bushy brows drawing together. "Who knows. Probably just some low-level grunt. Chances are, they were on the premises to do yard work or empty those Dumpsters."

His fluorescent beam landing on a rusted metal filing cabinet, Julian peered in the drawers only to find them empty. "Meaning there's a chance they were up to something else."

"I mean, they could have been transporting product out in that truck bed, but I couldn't tell you what, why, or for what purpose. All bets are on."

Julian coughed into his elbow when a deep breath brought in a payload of throat-tickling dust. *All bets are on.* Now there was a motto for their team. They commenced a silent march down a rusted metal staircase, clomps of their feet playing a sober, staccato melody.

Taylor, a few feet up front at the foot of the steps, opened the door. She must've found a more finished area and flipped a light switch, because a bright glow spread from the opening to smear the room with light. Dust sprites dancing in the air, she asked, "You find anything good back there, babe?"

He advanced to her side, his grip on the wooden board tightening as adrenaline circumscribed his concentration and focus to protecting Taylor. "Nah, just crap destined for the landfill. What's in here?"

Taylor staggered backward, both hands pressed to her nose and mouth. "Fuck."

Leg muscles pumping and board raised, he got out in front of Taylor fast and charged the room, only to freeze upon seeing what had shocked his wife.

A cramp seized his stomach, his mouth flooding with saliva as the entirety of his perceptual field collapsed to the obscene intrusion of a visceral, grotesque assault so abject and incomprehensible that he was convinced, for several beats, that he was dreaming.

A nude man lay on a wheeled metal cot, immobile as a corpse. White, with a muscular build and red hair, he stared at the ceiling, the colorless parts of his wide eyes reflecting the light.

But his lifeless body, though a shocking sight, wasn't what upset Taylor.

The man was split from throat to groin. Metal clamps held his ripped, pale flesh apart to make a bloodless wound. Instead of guts and organs, a green motherboard as long as his torso filled his abdominal cavity. Silvery microchips and assorted specks of color decorated the slab of machinery like ornaments on a Christmas tree.

Hypnotized by the twin forces of horror and curiosity, Julian leaned forward for a closer look, the sight of freckles dusting the guy's young face striking a blow of empathy. His insides had been cleaned out, drained, and replaced by all this gadgetry. Had he suffered, physically or emotionally, when some psycho had done this to him?

The man blinked twice. This horrid sight alone made Julian jump, like the time when a punk kid named Will Yazzie killed a rattlesnake to show Julian how it moved for a little bit after.

While Julian was still reeling, the dead man turned his head in both directions, his face expressionless, and said in soporific monotone, "Trouble communicating with the printer."

Vertigo effect sucked Julian's perception in and out. The edges of his world blurred. He must have retreated from the scene because he bumped into Taylor and felt her grip on his wrist, damp and hard.

"Please load paper in the auto sheet feeder." The dead guy's shoulder jerked to his ear in gruesome puppetry of how the living moved their bodies. "Trouble communicating with the printer. The paper is jammed. Please load paper in the auto-sheet feeder."

Laughing darkly, Mad Dog pushed past Julian and Taylor and made his way to a stainless-steel basin mounted to the wall. The corpse's bare feet an inch from his waist, Mad Dog turned a handle, and the flow of running water joined the babble about computer paper. He refilled his wearable canteen, put it back on, and drank a few gulps from cupped hands. "You two babies act like you've never seen a robot before. Congratulations. We have officially found reprogramming."

Clutching Julian's forearm, Taylor croaked out, "They made him into a robot?"

Mad Dog walked to a cheap plastic desk, moved it away from the wall, and went to the opposite corner. He bent over, looking under a tabletop crowded with desktop computers and other office junk in various states of age and disrepair. "Cut the 'him' and 'into' out of your sentence, and you've got it. He's always been like that, a robot. Don't worry about him. They can't feel pain. Someone probably uploaded that printer program into his mainframe as a practical joke."

Stunned disgust dissipated, grim understanding filling the gap. Julian glanced at the abomination on the table. At least the man hadn't known any differently. Well, he wasn't a man at all. He'd never known much of anything except what his masters programmed into him. "I hate this place."

"Hard same," Taylor muttered.

"Please load paper in the auto-sheet feeder."

Mad Dog, on his belly now, grunted as he yanked on an object embedded in the wall. "You hate this place? Good. We're all in agreement. Now get over here and bring your maps, because it looks like I've found our portal to the craziness down below."

The portal to craziness was a silver door with a handle on it, no bigger than a trash chute, yet gargantuan in the potential it teased. As Mad Dog opened the door, Julian crouched for a better look and stared into the bowels of a dark tunnel.

SIXTEEN

ABANDON ALL HOPE, YE WHO ENTER HERE. ON THINE BELLY, THY WILL crawl.

Weren't there sayings like those, foreboding in their anachronistic language, hung above the gates of hell? Or maybe one was a warning in the Bible. Either way, both expressions fit.

Taylor hadn't given up all hope, no way, but as she wormed along using her elbows for traction, stuffed into the tunnel like sausage meat packed in a casing, she'd be remiss to ignore the hell allegory. It sure fit the team's belly-crawling descent into the underworld.

Lightheaded, she drew a shallow breath and tried to ignore reality. Dark, dense walls closed in. The beam from her headlamp shot from her forehead and over Julian's shoulder, where it merged with his light, melding into one ice-blue blur before fading into the black void.

The play of light and shadow was almost hypnotic, a strange prism of reflection absorbed. The presence moved in, out, and in again, ejecting her before pulling her back. She waved her hand in front of her face, watching the companion look at her wiggling fingers, trying to figure out the process and agenda. It seemed to like to watch, take in information through her viewpoint, as if learning through study.

She bumped her head, cursed the sting, and whacked her funny bone as she realigned for better leverage. With a jolt, the presence fled, leaving her more centered. Discomfort, physical and mental, defined every bend and jerk, but at least the pain knocked out her passenger for the time being.

She forced herself to imagine an opening at the end of the line, a nice big clearing full of oxygen, instead of fixating on how she couldn't take real breaths anymore. Some time had passed, twenty minutes perhaps, maybe more. Too much claustrophobic time spent without adequate light or decent airflow, but a panic attack wasn't allowed to derail their efforts.

Instead of drawing inward, she turned her attention to the environment. The smell of the chute was odorless, the impact of its smooth surface punishing as the trio wiggled single file down the length of the tube compressing their bodies from all sides.

"This has got to be manmade. Like sanded rock or concrete," she said to Julian's butt and thighs, his sculpted muscles flexing beneath jeans as he led the way. "Literally the only good thing about this is the view, I might add."

Superficial given the circumstances? Sure. But a girl had to take her wins where she could.

Julian matched her banter, "Glad it suits you because you're stuck with it for a while. As someone once said, life is like a dog sled team. Unless you're the lead dog, the scenery never changes."

Despite herself, in defiance of her goal of self-rationing air, Taylor let out a mirthful laugh. Felt good, that emotional break.

The sharp, acrid smell of body odor and more embarrassing excretions betrayed Mad Dog's presence at the rear as he pushed out through labored breaths. "Apt. They used to repeat that saying, during our sessions. Remind us of our place in the pack."

Seemed too perfect of a coincidence to be anything other than a lie or a manufactured memory. She'd be remiss, however, to squander an opportunity to coax a bit more out of the guy. He came off as little more than a pathetic victim, but she could tell that Julian's trust in their companion was waning, and a divided or fractured party didn't do them any good. "You had to be reminded? I thought that all the Mad Dogs were at the bottom. Omegas, as it were."

Mad Dog huffed, and when he spoke his scratchy voice told of dehydration. "We were. But they knew that we had abilities, talents that were enhanced if we worked together. They had to keep us scared. Divided."

Literally and figuratively, she inched forward. "Do you have any idea who any of them were? Anyone significant?"

Significant people circled Scarab's orbit, like her politician father and his finance cronies. Who, in retrospect, all seemed like mid-level minions. Surely there were proverbial top dogs closer to the center. What was their endgame?

Their companion let loose an extended whistle of fake astonishment. "Lots of the types I encountered, the goons who ran experiments, were blackmailed criminals and rogue intelligence assets who made deals. Nobody goes to college to make mutants and run mind control."

Julian, who Taylor now noticed was slinking along at a faster clip, added, "Is that why they wanted to give you Mad Dogs those Medusa powers, for intelligence purposes? Make you into a walking weapon and point you at their kill list?"

"Bingo, buddy. More efficient even than a high-tech heart attack ray gun or sonic waves that fuck up your internal systems. Untraceable, undetectable. No hardware to disappear or chemicals in the bloodstream."

Though he couldn't see her, Taylor smiled at Julian. They were getting some good bits from Mad Dog, even when solving one puzzle unlocked a new chamber full of more conundrums.

While crafting her next question, she knocked on the arched walls of their confinement. Had the space enlarged or was she getting used to it? "What's with the Medusa symbolism?"

Mad Dog succumbed to a violent coughing fit, and when he spoke again after a long pause, he sounded clearer. Must have stopped for a water break. Poor bastard. "At first, I thought it was showmanship. A calling card, or just screwing around out of boredom. Like the same motivation behind making that 'bot talk like a printer."

"At first," Julian pressed. "Meaning that new input prompted you to reevaluate your stance."

"I don't know, man. Sure. Like I said, I saw and heard a lot of crazy shit. Most of it was bad, some of it was nonsense, and some was truly fucked." After offering up one of his trademark deflections, an insubstantial non-answer delivered with sufficient punch to give the appearance of weight, he asked an unnerving question. "Did you two feel that?"

Taylor rolled her eyes. They'd gotten too close to a subject he didn't care to broach, and, true to form, he'd thrown up a smokescreen. "The overwhelming desire to stand upright? I totally did, yes. Are we not allowed to talk about the Medusa thing anymore?"

"Shut up and listen," Mad Dog hissed, a naked urgency to his plea incongruous with her theory of disingenuous misdirection.

"He's right, babe." Julian stopped moving, going still with an abruptness that left Taylor no choice but to mimic. "It's subtle, but you can hear it if you concentrate hard. Like a rumble."

A spike of fear shot through her, fizzling in her extremities. A *rumble*, down here? No, hell no. That might mean a precursor to an earthquake, boulders sealing them in until they died clutching their throats and gasping for breath. Maybe if they hustled, they could turn around and get back to reprogramming before the tunnel got buried. In any case, freaking out wouldn't help.

Her stomach lodged in her chest. She quelled the thumping in her ears until she'd won enough inner silence to pick up on the sound.

Well, she didn't label it as a sound. A subtle feeling, a vibration, reverberated up from below and trembled through her flesh and bones. The worst of her fear morphed into fascination. The sensation passed, and Julian whispered, "Count to six."

Her stare focused on a random spot, her mind empty save for the count, Taylor moved through the numbers. And sure enough, right as she finished five-Mississippi, the pixie version of a seismic aftershock quaked again. "It can't be detonations. Or an earthquake. They don't get those in coastal Florida." Her mind latched onto one conspicuous feature of the event. "The number six matters. Are you two noticing it repeat?"

Could be the Baader-Meinhof effect, where noticing a phenomenon creates the illusion of its ubiquity, but simple solutions weren't necessarily more plausible in their clown world.

Six witches, she told Julian with her mind. *Six books*. Best to keep Mad

Dog somewhat clueless to avoid priming him. See what he came up with independently.

"Yeah," Julian said, his word solemn. One syllable didn't do it justice. "Now that I think of it, it's a significant number all the way around."

"Absolutely." She craned her neck to look back at Mad Dog, averting her eyes upon discerning that he was peeing in his inconvenient position, one knee raised like he had a fire hydrant to whiz on. "Does the number six have any more weight around here that you know of?"

He fixed his pants, his smirk ugly in the low light. "Six? You bet. Six is huge. Six-six-six, the number of the beast in the Book of Revelations. The smallest perfect number. The letter 'f.' A hexagon. A guitar has six strings, which can be used to play six whole tones in an octave or six semitones in a tritone. On the sixth day of Christmas, your true love gives you six fat, fecund geese. God made the world in six days. An insect has six legs. According to Aristotle, Mythos is the first of six elements of a tragedy. Did you know, Taylor, that the first known six was found in the number two-fifty-six, etched in Sasaram on the walls of a cave, circa two-fifty BCE, in Ashoka?"

She shook her head at his tiresome bullshit. Did the guy get off on reaching into his grab bag of deflection, doublespeak, and vacuous blather cheaply disguised as substance? Was he playing dumb games at random intervals to frustrate earnest efforts at truth seeking? She swore sometimes it was all a mind fuck with him, a power play. "Let's keep moving."

"No, this is fun," Mad Dog said with flat, cynically sarcastic inflection. "Shall I go on?"

Julian intervened, "Man, leave her alone. I don't know what your deal is sometimes, but you aren't helping."

Thanks for standing up for me, babe. She could do without Mad Dog trying to annoy her on purpose for whatever twisted impetus motivated him.

Julian acknowledged her telepathic gratitude with a nod.

"Can we stop navel-gazing and keep moving, then?" the mutated man asked.

Julian resumed, and the procession continued its undignified, slithering march. Some of those tidbits Mad Dog dropped stuck with her, burrowing in.

Hexagon. The letter f. Guitar and music facts. Number of the beast, Mythos as the first element of tragedy.

Perfect number, insects...wait, had she deemed nearly all of them significant? Did the number six implicate her possession issue, a problem that she'd all but forgotten about since it hadn't bothered her in awhile? Was it bad she'd sent her thoughts and energy to the subject, just now?

Taylor ground her teeth and swallowed frustration, ripping herself out of her internal monologue when she spotted the faint glimmer of an outside light source over Julian's shoulder.

Whatever lay ahead, she welcomed the change of pace. Her hands and knees hurt, and the ammonia-tinged evidence of Mad Dog's unfortunate problem had spoiled already stale, muggy tunnel air with an offensive urinal quality.

"Can you make out specifics?" she whispered to her husband in case people—or whatever—lurked on the other side.

He lowered his voice to say, "A grate. It ends at a grate or vent."

Her body was thrumming now, pumped with an urge to move faster, to discover, to finally be productive. To even begin to think about the prospect of holding Luna to her breast. Such an outcome was within the realm of possibility. They were closing in. Hands slippery against the rock as she began to sweat, Taylor scurried up on Julian's heels, fumbling for purchase, uncoordinated but fueled by urgency.

"If the room is empty," Mad Dog whispered, "we can pause there for a moment to compare maps and scour for any more consistencies."

Emotion overcame her, seeping up from the well where she'd buried it, and all she could picture was Luna's tiny body, her little fingernails, the birthmark on her right cheek. Tears blurred her vision, and her voice trembled as she said, "Yeah. Okay. Sounds like a plan."

Mad Dog grabbed her ankle and shook it a few times. "Hey. You. You hang in there. We've got a shot here if we're smart and keep our heads screwed on."

She nodded, wiping her face. His words resonated, a low-key pep talk realistic enough to earn her respect, the jerk on her ankle a bit of touch she could appreciate as endearing in its own awkward way. "Roger that."

Taylor laughed softly at her weird, random comment. Along the way, she must've absorbed Mad Dog's penchant for old-school, macho expressions. "Babe, can you see anything up there?"

Julian, abutted now against a tan vent with horizontal slats, held up his switched-off flashlight. Taylor followed his cue, and Mad Dog must've obeyed from the rear, because instantly darkness draped them, punctured only by the slivers of halogen glow seeping through slits.

He spoke in a low tone. "I'm about eight feet up, looking down into a room about the size of a high school basketball court, but there aren't any hoops or markings, no bleachers or anything. The floor looks like heavy-duty vinyl siding. There are dummies, like crash test dummies and rubber torsos from a martial arts studio, up against the walls."

She lacked the space to wrestle a map free, but fortunately Taylor had her mathematician's memory to rely on. "Training equipment. One of the levels below reprogramming was marked as training."

Mad Dog injected, "Training, experimental projects, labs."

A current lifted her, prompting her to square her shoulders even in the confined space. "If the rooms line up, that means we have a workable map for the unverified levels."

"Don't get too excited," Mad Dog said. "These people love disinformation, sowing seeds to excite the truth-seeking community that ultimately push us off the trail. These levels might be promising, but don't rule out the possibility that the real layout is distributed among these maps. We have to spend energy and time mixing and matching, assembling a puzzle from dispersed pieces."

She wanted to be angry at him for being a downer, but the argument was sound enough to consider. "Makes sense."

"Nah, but that's cute that you think it does. Nothing here makes sense." Mad Dog snickered.

This time, her chest crunched, and she scowled, irritation pinching her like ill-fitting clothes. Too much more of this guy's aggravating little one-up, gotcha routine, and she'd tell him how she really felt and where to shove his attitude problem. For now, she focused on Julian. "Can you undo the grate?"

"Working on it." He spoke in a mild tone, his arm moving. "Four screws, not that tight. Anyone have a dime?"

Their tool kits weren't immediately accessible, but a small coin or comparable object might loosen the screw enough for Julian to defeat it. Wincing as the points of her elbows whacked hardness, Taylor pulled her charm necklace out from under the collar of her shirt.

Steadying her fingers as much as possible, she worked free the charm of the smiling half-moon, a trinket she'd picked up at the Iquitos market when the doula told her that one of her twins was going to be a girl. Luna, her lunar goddess girl. A brief intrusion by the passenger passed as suddenly as it arrived.

Swallowing a lump in her throat, Taylor tapped Julian on the leg, and he took the charm with a look of empathy, recognition of their shared struggle. She liked to think that her action held meaning, mystical import, that the symbolism inherent would setoff some good luck ripple effect of synchronicities and auspicious occurrences.

Magical thinking, sure, but why not? Magic was afoot.

A few more seconds of fidgeting and waiting, her knees achy and her resolve unflagging, and the barrier yielded with a tinny squeak. Julian passed the charm back to Taylor, and she clasped it back on before taking the grate from him. "We need to at least try to cover our tracks and replace it."

Anxiety wound her nerves tight. How would they escape from this hell hole *if* they saved Luna? What if they were all stupidly leading themselves to a slaughter no matter what? But all there was to do was act in the moment and hope for a miracle.

"Correct. You'll sit on my shoulders and put the screws back in. They'll be loose, but the naked eye won't catch that," Julian said.

Reassured for the time being, she clutched the plane of metal, running a finger over each of the gaps. Were there holes in their plan, blind spots, weaknesses that their enemy would exploit? She worked to regulate her distressed breathing. They'd come this far. That had to count.

"Ready?" Julian asked.

"Ready," she said like she meant it.

"Let's fuck up some bad guys and save a baby," Mad Dog said.

Now *this* version of the guy, scrappy and full of salt but ultimately a solid team player, she liked. Not that he had any obligation to conform to her preferences. She validated him with a smile and a thumbs up, and he stuck out his fist. They bumped, her moment of solidarity with him shaky but welcome. She didn't love him, but he was the ally they had.

"Alright. You two back up. I need to turn around," Julian said.

They did, and he did, but as he switched to the feet-first position, an unwanted sound slashed their mundane repertoire. The noise was high-pitched and tinkling. It made contact one, two, three awful times before going dead.

"What the hell was that?" Taylor's whisper was harsh, her head buzzing with the residual impact of the jarring sound. "What made that sound?"

Julian crunched his face into a grimace and cursed under his breath. "The screw. Fuck. I thought that I grabbed all three but missed one. It fell on to that court down there."

"Calm down, guys," Mad Dog said. "You two are shifters with hearing hypersensitive to high decibels, right?"

"Right." The gist coalesced, sending a cool wave of relief through Taylor, loosening her muscles. "Nobody else heard that."

"Right," Julian said, though he didn't sound so sure.

She tensed once more, her belly hardening. "I feel like there's a but in there."

"There isn't." Julian looked over his shoulder, so fast his ponytail whipped his cheek.

The surface of her chest sizzled. "Why did you check your back?"

"Just to be sure."

"Of what?"

Mad Dog groaned. "Can we get a move on, please? If anyone who was paid enough to care heard it, they'd be over here already, given how much time you two already wasted bickering."

Unconvinced, Taylor forced a nervous fake laugh from her throat. "The voice of reason. You're totally right."

"He's totally right." Now Julian sounded like he was working to convince himself, but Taylor wasn't allowed to overthink this loose screw nonsense anymore. She was simply, at this point, driving herself insane. Maybe she was the one with the screw loose.

Mad Dog said, "I'll accept my certificate and engraved

commemorative paperweight after we get out. Can ya scoot now, Julian?"

Julian' lower half disappeared out the opening, foot by foot, until his head dropped from sight and she saw only his fingertips, tendons straining against skin.

Once his nails slipped below the ledge, feet hitting the ground with a muted thud, she flipped to her back and slid toward the gap. Taylor shoved her legs out and dangled, kicking air beneath her, until Julian grabbed her hips and eased her to the floor.

She looked around, acclimating her stiff body to an upright stance while Julian helped Mad Dog out of the hole. The scene was exactly as Julian described, a gym stocked with naked plastic torsos on poles; creepy, soft mannequins; and assorted supplies like boxing gloves and helmets.

The room didn't smell like gym socks or disinfectant. She caught a whiff of unsettling, beastly fumes, like wet dog and iron. Sweaty fear. Like a slaughterhouse. Her "lambs to the slaughter" fear roared back in a dark wave.

To quash her disturbing thoughts, Taylor removed her pack, groaning when the weight left her body. She got out the maps and had begun to attempt to identify a downward route to the kill room and/or kitchen when a haunting yet familiar sensation made words and drawings run together into black squiggles.

The tremor wave returned, shaking her from heel to scalp. The force was greater this time, mighty and booming, and bringing with it a screeching sound that scrambled her brain.

Her teeth chattered. Nausea clamped down on her midsection. She rocked back and forth in an involuntary attempt to clear the disturbance violating her body.

Taylor covered her ears and looked to Mad Dog and Julian, who were doing the same, each doubled over.

Once it finally passed, leaving behind a trace of an electronic whine, Taylor cradled her head until a muzzy, dumbfounded haze left her, and she could think. But before she could, an image caused her to gasp.

Near the middle of the room, a huge mass was taking shape from a fuzzy blur, at least seven feet of something bulky with brown fur, blinking in and out like a scrambled television signal.

SEVENTEEN

THE WEREWOLF HAD A WHOLE HEAD ON JULIAN AND TWICE HIS muscle mass.

Chills dashed over his skin when he looked into the hairy behemoth's yellow eyes and saw recognition, awareness. Hatred. The monster-man knew that it was being watched and didn't like who was watching it. The urge to kill burned all around the creature.

Despite the feelings he got while staring into those ugly eyes, the open mouth full of sharp teeth split by a red carpet of despicable tongue, Julian made a play for diplomacy.

Maybe he shared some common ancestry with this fiend he could use to get through to it.

Holstered gun pressing hard into his hip, he put up both hands, palms out, in a show of peace. "Are you trapped down here? If you stick with us, we can get you out."

One corner of the beast's upper lip curled, revealing black gums and a better look at its carnivorous canines of murder. Claw-capped paws hung at its sides as it slashed a deathly glower among the trio. Sizing them up. A growl bubbled from its predatory depths, rising above the monotonous hum of a cooling system with twisted resonance.

The stillness of time and space was unbearable, worse even than the monstrosity hulking in the training room. But the visitor hadn't torn them to ribbons yet, and Julian had no reason to give up on level-headed techniques. He tried a simpler question, "Do you know where you are?"

The werewolf snarled again, drawing its lips back in a naked posture of aggression. Its mammoth, barrel chest rose and fell as it continued to gather them in that contemptuous, evil look. A bushy tail flicked once, twice, quick jerks signaling agitation.

Taylor whispered, "It's escalating. I say we draw our weapons on the count of three."

"Hold up," Mad Dog said. "If it's a hologram, it can't hurt us. These things work like a security system, responding to noises. One glimpse of motherfuckers like this hairball will send any petty thief running to the nearest door, but they pretty much embody a bark that's worse than the bite. If we fire our weapons, we play ourselves."

"Oh yeah?" Julian kept staring into the creature's eyes, not yet buying the scare tactic theory. Too much texture and depth to those yellow eyes. He experimented with telepathy, "Can you hear me?"

He got a jumble of noises back, the auditory equivalent of scribbles. But the being could communicate with him. He presented Mad Dog with a follow-up. "Do holograms have independent thoughts?"

"They can." Mad Dog started moving in large, sideways steps, toward a set of double doors, the only way in or out of the gym. "It's just adaptation to their programming, though, man. Don't read too much into it."

Still unnerved by the look in the abomination's eye, rage that seemed to temper into something more tragic as the seconds passed, Julian made another mental attempt. "Do you know *who* you are?"

"Murder." One heinous, bloodied ruin of a word sliced through the disturbing chaos of garble. "Death." Another mess of static noises. "Kill."

"I'm telling you," Mad Dog said, pinched and testy, "these guard dogs are cheap and basic, older prototypes. Sophisticated artificial intelligence by the standards of what's theoretically possible, but not one of Scarab's most cutting-edge holdings."

Julian stepped away, not once turning his back on the menace as it stared him down. He walked backwards to Mad Dog. "It's becoming self-aware."

Taylor joined the others in moving to the room's lone point of exit. "Is it becoming corporeal, too, as in able to rip our guts out?"

"No," Mad Dog said. "Holograms and virtual reality programs can't transform into carbon-based life forms or even robots or androids. Not yet. Scarab doesn't have the tech or magic to pull off an alchemical feat like that."

"Never say never." Taylor pressed her palm against the metal bar across one of the doors.

"Believe me, I didn't," Mad Dog said.

"Unlocked," she added in a tone that said time to move.

Julian pinned the werewolf guard in one more strong stare before turning his attention to Taylor. "Mad Dog, will someone that we need to worry about get word that the security system's been tripped?" He scanned the ceiling for cameras and didn't see any black domes or red dots in white boxes. But surveillance tech might be hidden.

"In my experience, they rarely have to send reinforcements. Unauthorized personnel are usually scared off or dispatched with minimal effort."

"Lucky us." Taylor pushed open the door, slowly, the hinges barely making a sound.

"Clever us," Mad Dog amended. "Since we didn't shit our pants and run away shrieking at the sight of that werewolf projection, that puts us, easily, in the ninetieth percentile of bunker infiltrators. Hell, even the most dedicated researchers don't know that this place exists."

A threadbare shawl of cold comfort, but Julian would take it. He peered through the opening that Taylor had made, which led to a three-way intersection of wide, darkened hallways with linoleum flooring and funky atmosphere that smelled like cafeteria food.

One possibility was following that food smell downward through the kitchen. Beat the level-three alternative.

Rhythmic clicks, like a dog's nails on pavement, echoed in a steady succession of encroaching taps to break his analysis. Julian made fierce eye contact with Taylor, and she shut the door as fast as she could without having to make noise.

Julian looked through a vertical slice of dirty window glass about as wide as the board he'd grabbed and ditched a while back. A black metal mass, dimensions like those of a beagle, trotted by in jerking steps supported by four skinny bug legs with gears at the knee joints. His skin crawled at the pitiful yet creepy presentation of a robot mimicking dog behavior without mastery.

Before he had the chance to ponder the uncanny sight more, a tablet where its face was supposed to be rolled in a semi-circle, flashing webbed grids of green light that flickered off the walls.

"Get down," Julian said.

Everyone ducked in succession, crouching below the window before it reflected the light in glittery specks, that damn werewolf still heaving about ten feet away.

"What the hell was that?" Taylor, on her haunches, grimaced.

"Multi-purpose drone," Mad Dog filled in on cue. "Land and air applications. They deploy facial recognition technology and fire various styles of bullets, gasses, and nanotechnology tracking material. That's our real concern down here, not that Halloween decoration." He pointed at the werewolf.

"You think that my scramble spell will protect us from them?" Taylor tugged her book free from the bag.

Mad Dog shrugged. "Worth a shot."

Taylor recited the words quickly, and while putting her book away added, "I've been pain-free since I teleported back to the hotel room. I wasn't going to jinx it, but it helps me puzzle things out to think aloud."

He hoped that her work had also stymied the progress of the possession effort. Watching her attempt to scramble the drones made a sudden hypothesis burst to the surface of his thoughts. He spoke to her telepathically, keeping Mad Dog at a proverbial arm's length just in case. "I wonder if your magic has antidotal properties to cancel their programming, and that's why they want it."

"Interesting," she said with her mind. "Like immunotherapy."

"Which might be why they infected you. To test in a controlled environment the effect your magic has on whatever they compromised you with and monitor the results."

She stood, peeked, and pushed open the door once again. "Which begs an important question. Now that I'm off the grid, the flow of data has been interrupted. Someone could easily figure that out and come looking for me. I might be all over their radar in a new sense and not know it."

"Maybe. We just have to keep moving." He reached for his wife's hand, squeezed, and added, "I'm proud of you."

Mad Dog cut out in front to take the lead, and Julian let him, hanging back with Taylor to continue their conversation in the hallway. Everyone's shoes squeaked against the flooring, and within seconds another round of robot click-click steps came calling. He blinked away spots, eyes adjusting, stale food smells ripe in his nose as his senses sharpened to face a threat.

They'd find out soon enough if her scramble spell worked.

"Give me the unverified maps," Mad Dog said, pausing his strides with hand outstretched. "We need to find a staircase, and I'd rather not take my chances with robo-puppy."

Taylor passed the tube of rolled papers to their companion. "I take it they prefer using those to employing human security?"

"For sure." Mad Dog, walking again, compared maps, the tune of machine footsteps a relentless backdrop. "They make the most money off the tech stuff, which has the most saleable applications. Those freak shows don't get sick or ask for raises. Scarab's getting away from human capital stock all together, from what I hear." He tossed a sly look over his shoulder. "Too many whistleblowers and others traumatized by what they've seen. We meat bags are mostly just used as experiments now, fodder for rituals."

Like hell his daughter or wife would end up in one of those categories. The idea brought Julian back to a dormant but still troubling loose end. While he walked side by side with Taylor, he mentally asked her as casually as the subject would allow, "Have you had any more possession activity?"

She shook her head. "After those initial flare-ups, no. Every now and then I get a feeling, a sensation I hadn't experienced before I started in with my book, but the voice in my head seems to have left."

He'd be remiss to let himself forget about the possession issue or pretend it hadn't happened. Assuming that a problem had been solved because it had slipped down on the priority list was dangerous. "What kind of feeling or sensation?"

Taylor bit her lip. He watched her, the cut of her chin and steep nose in profile, searching for clues to maleficence in the face of the person he loved.

An awful thing, but he couldn't afford to lull himself into false security because he cared for Taylor. For Luna's sake, he couldn't afford sloppiness or oversights.

Cinderblock hallway surrounded them, barren of lockers, posters, anything. What did they use this space for, moving bodies back and forth? Speaking of bodies moving, the metal dog feet kept tapping, the unnatural creature making its rounds.

"I feel like I have a passenger in my head," Taylor finally spoke through telepathy, matter of fact. "A tagalong, someone who isn't me hitchhiking a ride in my brain and observing. It's a very sentient energy, like this presence is taking in information and learning. It has curiosity, but beyond that I can't discern a motive. Except to say that it for sure has one."

The creeps crawled over him. Her confession hardly counted as good news. Unknowns never belonged in the good news box. "Did Eve mention anything to that effect? Or Helen?"

She shook her head. "I should have brought it up, but I didn't want to overload them or scare them off, you know? There's really no way to say 'hey, I'm possessed' when you first meet someone."

"Has the passenger's behavior changed, ever?"

"Yeah," she spoke the word with a hint of resignation, as if facing an inconvenient truth. "When my pain stopped. That's when it lost its voice. At first, I thought, great, maybe it learned to avoid pain, but my intuition says it's more complicated."

"Always good to go with your gut."

"If we get through this, when we get through this, I'm going to call both Helen and Eve again and debrief—"

Her voice in his head cut off abruptly. Taylor halted her steps fast enough to produce a squeal of rubber on cheap siding, the abrupt screech triggering Mad Dog to turn around. She laid her hand on her holstered gun and said, out loud, "Shit."

Julian didn't have to ask what because he saw it right away. The canine drone, blinking lights giving way to dark mass, was tip-tapping its way right toward them, marching down the hall in a series of awkward, eerie steps. He blinked when additional flashes of movement joined the fray, squinting for a better look down the dim hall, and his stomach dropped.

Six of the drone dogs, marching in a line of three symmetrical pairs, were headed their way.

Mad Dog snorted. "Of course they deploy this shit in a brigade of six. Symbolism this, symbolism that."

Julian curled his fingers around the barrel of his gun, watching the pack of devils with their blinking green, iPad faces. "Stay cool but be ready."

"Yeah, symbolism city." Taylor's shoulders cranked high, her hand dropping to her holster. "I'm convinced that they're either trolling us or that we're unwitting participants in some prelude to a mega-ritual."

"Equally likely scenarios," Mad Dog said. "Or both, which would be peak psychotic genius for these people."

The battery-operated battalion trooped on, six squat bodies trotting in authoritarian lockstep. The rows of them stopped in unison, a foot's distance separating Julian from the two dogs in front. His heart rate elevated, he looked over his adversaries, scanning for weak spots, and settled on the screen-faces. He ran his fingertip over the smooth half-moon of his trigger. A few fast, well-placed shots would, hopefully, take out their primary detection system in shattering sprays of glass.

Taylor and Mad Dog, who must've independently reached the same conclusion, stood poised as he was, characters in an old Western prepared to draw and duel.

Gleaming, obsidian rectangles lit up in a synchronized light show, projecting messes of lines over the trio's bodies until they all looked like they'd been caught in bioluminescent fishing nets.

Julian tuned out the sound of his inner workings and listened for clicks, clunks, snaps, or other auditory signs the robots were engaging their weapons or otherwise applying combative measures.

But the lights blinked off in unison, swallowed into those square-headed slabs of darkness, and the sextuplets commenced their prowl of the perimeter. Julian moved to stand against the wall, affording them clearance to pass, and Taylor and Mad Dog did the same.

He waited for the creatures taking up the rear to drop out of sight as they rounded a corner. "Good deal," he said to Taylor, releasing a huge weight of air. "Your spell worked."

But she had a troubled look on her face and was chewing a nail, a nervous habit she rarely indulged.

"What's wrong?" he asked with his mind.

"I can't be sure," she replied via telepathy. "I synched with their programming for a few seconds there. They said a lot of things. I can't tell what's relevant."

With Mad Dog distracted, dithering with the maps, Julian rested a hand on his wife's shoulder and looked deeply into her worried eyes as he spoke telepathically. "What did you hear, babe? No secrets. We can't afford to hold anything back right now."

She shook her head, more vehemently than he'd ever seen her do in the past. "You know what? The more I think about it, the more I'm certain I didn't hear anything meaningful. Just senseless chatter."

He examined her, wishing that he could read her mind. But that space was fundamentally private, Taylor's domain, and he wouldn't pressure her to give up access. If she had valuable information she'd picked up from the robots, it would come out eventually. "You sure?"

Her smile was thin, tight, and unconvincing. A new smile. She didn't look quite like herself, and he didn't like the change. "I'm sure. Yeah. It's fine." Her voice was different, too, more monotone, and lower in pitch.

It wasn't fine but pressing her when she didn't want to give would accomplish nothing but wasting valuable time. Julian knew his wife. She'd share when she was ready, and if he fought her or showed irritation, she'd get even more stubborn. "Okay." He slid a hand up and down her silken forearm, offering gentle assurance as an effort to disarm resistance. "As long as you remember that you can tell me anything."

"I do." In a swift, conspicuous change of subject, she walked over to Mad Dog. "Find a route?"

"Bad news." Their mutated scout scratched at his stocking cap. "Don't shoot the messenger."

"What?" Julian looked over the other guy's shoulder, dreadful anticipation supplanting his frustration with Taylor. Sheets crowded with crude renderings of rooms and doors stared up at him like a mystery. Confusion was their currency in this place, a fourth companion.

Mad Dog said, "There's a service elevator and a stairwell on this floor, I'm pretty sure, but both are too risky if we don't want to be spotted. Staffing is light, like I said earlier, but we're damn near guaranteed to run into some in or around both the kitchen and the kill room, if those spaces are in fact what's below."

Taylor added, "I feel like it's significant that we haven't seen hardly anyone except for that truck driver. Where is everybody? Down here?" She pointed to a spot on the map near the "Titans" marking.

"Likely. There's a big project underway, Song of Virgo, and they're all on deck for that. Nobody's doing inconsequential reprogramming or running training sessions. The action's beneath us, and we're moving toward it."

Julian touched a sketch of what looked like a ladder, scribbled in messy haste outside of a window. "Looks like a fire escape."

"Yeah," Mad Dog said. "That was the second part of my bad news. We'll have to approach the lower levels via the outside and scan for a return entry point that way. Cross the park and pass as tourists. Best bet is to stash our guns and try to come back for them. We don't want to risk an incident with park security. Not ideal, but we'll do our best to blend in. I wish that there were alternative paths that were halfway safe, but no dice."

"That's not such terrible news," Taylor interjected. "At least a fire escape exists. I assumed we were below ground."

"We are, at least partially. There's stairs up ahead that I'm crossing my stumpy fingers lead to this fire escape."

Another one of those rumbles, like the aftershock he'd felt after experiencing a mild earthquake while visiting a buddy in California, bent the air with formidable seismic prowess. The strength of the shake trumped the one preceding the werewolf. "Another hologram, incoming, or is it wishful thinking to assume that it's not something worse?"

"Maybe." Mad Dog compared two maps, his tone noncommittal. "Or some other subterranean event or space-time manipulation."

Taylor squinted. "Elaborate?"

"Alright, I found the fire escape. Let's hustle." Mad Dog took off in a slow jog, gaining a few feet of distance on Taylor and Julian until he dropped from the vision field.

He shared a dour expression of frustration with his wife. A bleak imposter of camaraderie, but that was what they had. "He's always pulling shit like that, isn't he?" he spoke aloud, yet soft enough to escape earshot. "Selective circumspection in accordance with his whims."

Taylor scoffed. "Drives me nuts. I can't get a fix on him, you know? It's like he honestly wants to clue us in on things but makes sure that we have to figure it out ourselves. It feels like a game, but he doesn't strike me as manipulative in any other way. Weird. We're all in this together."

"Unless we aren't."

They shared a heavy glance while hiding their guns in a dark corner with a bit of debris for cover.

"Come on," Mad Dog hailed, his call bouncing off the walls.

Julian shrugged, his eyes on Taylor, and walked. For now, Mad Dog was an asset.

They found him at the foot of a staircase, planted at the nadir of ugly metal rungs stained with patches of rust, little more structurally substantive than a cheap ladder. At the apex sat a lone window, as small as one you'd find in a typical bedroom. Mad Dog bounded up the groaning steps and went to work at a crank sealing the pane shut.

"Doesn't look like any fire escape I've ever seen," Julian said.

"That's because it's one in name only. This is an escape hatch, man, a secret crawl space offering easy access to the front operation. I told you those maps were prone to be wrong." Mad Dog pulled out the lever and pried free the panel until a slice of light slipped through the crack.

More than light. Voices, far away but audible, streamed through the gap. In addition to the voices, he could make out laughter, music, and a bunch of indeterminate sounds sprinkling the medley. Julian tried to see but failed to catch a glimpse of what lay beyond. He had a feeling that a lot more surprises, not all of them good, awaited them on the next phase of their journey.

EIGHTEEN

TAYLOR HAD BEEN TO WONDER WORLD AS A PRETEEN, WHERE SHE'D admittedly reveled in a magical experience, basking in a cascade of childish delights. Childish delights that were, in retrospect, far superior to marching across the grounds, years later, hot and dusty and clenching hope against horror.

Hindsight of age gave her new perspective on her surroundings, too. Or maybe that was pessimism. Either way, her surroundings were *weird*. She felt like a character in *Fear and Loathing in Las Vegas*, swarmed by claptrap storefronts painted livid shades of purple and sunburn-pink. Dens designed to separate guests from money oozed frigid, processed air, lures baiting traps sprung with bug-eyed unicorn and bunny rabbit kitsch.

Kiosks peddled cotton candy and other junk food dyed unnatural hues to match the park's pastel palate, but she felt more nauseous than hungry, overwhelmed. An animation strip of color and noise spun all around her in a frenzied monument to plastic consumerism.

"You alright, babe?" Julian asked, his voice suggesting he knew the answer.

Taylor stepped to the left to avoid bumping into someone costumed as one of Wonder World's signature cartoon characters, a pink duck with plump, red lips. "Sure. The trip down memory lane is making me feel things. Discombobulated and nostalgic at the same time."

Once upon a time, she'd lacked putrid knowledge of what lay beneath the sparkle.

Between giggles, she and Chloe had screamed as rollercoasters inverted, then had their photos taken with gown-draped princesses, trying to ignore how the employees sweated under frilly costumes, miserable despite their smiles.

She tramped across the pedestrian mall lined with shops and eateries, breathing odors of roasted nuts and bypassing packs of people with painted faces and bunny ears atop their heads, forcing everyday thoughts to overtake despicable ones. She thought about how South Florida in mid-September was still crazy hot, slicking everyone in her vicinity with a sheen of perspiration, half-moon patches darkening underarms.

Heat waves glimmered above sunbaked pavement, a dreamy character to their watery translucence evoking a mirage, well-suited to the park's public mask. Sweat glued her backpack to her body, a trickle running down the back of one thigh.

Julian kept looking over at her, every now and then his knuckles brushing hers, but she pretended not to notice his attempts to reach out. Reaching out might lead to confession, and she wasn't there yet. She wasn't ready to confess to *herself*, let alone Julian, that the possession was getting worse with no solution in sight.

As they passed a clump of tourists waiting to be seated on a patio, a middle-ager in sensible sandals, highlights freshly frosty and spiked to razor ends, gave Taylor the up-and-down. No doubt she had a coating of grime on her by now in addition to looking out of place.

Not that it mattered. The real stain was on her soul, a blemish that she lacked a clue how to scrub into invisibility. Out, damn spot.

Julian raised his voice over the din of chatter and recorded pop vocals streaming from somewhere. "Based on the maps, how sure are you that we can use a ride as an access point?"

"On a scale of one to ten? A seven," Mad Dog said.

"I don't see is how we narrow down our options and pick a ride," Julian said.

"Neither do I." Mad Dog used a hankie to sop sweat from his brow, the stocking cap no doubt causing massive discomfort. The trio had to make for quite a sight, messy and encumbered by backpacks, a bit too old to fit with the family-focused crowd. "We'll just have to use our noodles and hope for signs."

The severity of Taylor's problem grated on her with each step they took, a horrific situation incongruous with the relentless crush of Wonder World conviviality. Happy people laughed, and whimsical pastels frosted others' moods with fantasyland tones. Such pretty, pure joy knew not of the demons festering below. "Level four is rituals, extractions, catacombs, right?"

Mad Dog looked like he wanted to peel back the candy coating of her blasé tone. "Yeah. Why?"

"What all do they extract, as far as you know? One substance or magic only, or is it a catch-all?"

"I imagine it's nomenclature that covers a lot of practices." Mad Dog's shrewd expression softened to one almost sympathetic in nature, rare for a guy who was as jaded as they came. Maybe he sensed her plight. "Trust me, going over hypotheticals in your own head just makes it worse while giving only the thinnest illusion of control."

"We'll get to Luna in time." Every aspect of Julian's delivery was a promise wrapped in warmth and strength. "Nobody's going to be extracting anything from her."

For the first time since their tribulation launched, Taylor wasn't thinking about Luna. No, she couldn't let go of the sinking realization she'd made a misstep, an error, an oversight that threatened to recast her as a detriment to the entire mission.

The instant she'd faced the leader of that pack of robot dogs, she'd felt the passenger churn with a new turbulence, robust and emboldened.

Then the words, *let the reaping commence*, issuing from the dog yet seemingly vocalized in her own head, showed up as a sexless voice not her own. A draining sensation followed, like a plug had been pulled near the base of her spine. But the passenger hadn't left, her hitchhiker had not gone willingly into the dog when it tried to play its role as siphon and container. Whatever was brewing in there was undercooked, not ready yet. Getting stronger, smarter.

She was still drawing lines between points, shoring up connections, but she damn near had the answer in her hand. Scarab had infected her with their virus, encouraging possession when they'd tried to extract Luna. Initial infiltration. Contagion.

Her study of magic enabled the formless, inchoate presence to take form, to change and grow and strengthen. When she'd started reading up on spells, that's when she'd consented.

That's when she'd played her part and unwittingly agreed to let in the essence from beyond. She was no better than a dupe, a patsy.

Looking in the final section of the book and failing to safeguard herself against its machinations had been a fatal error. She knew damn well where the occupying force was coming from, whose domain, whose realm. Ms. Sixth Letter of the Alphabet was running the show.

Her immunotherapy antidote theory was wrong. They were growing something inside of her, incubating an entity in her body and soul. The incubation phase was almost complete, and now they wanted to remove the possessing force for a nefarious reason. Extraction. And after they'd gotten what they wanted, she'd surely be of no use, little more than a piece of trash to discard.

Julian tugged on the strap of her pack, playful enough to disarm her and break through her morose state. "Please talk to me."

Secrecy wasn't helping. She hadn't wanted to demoralize Julian or fill him with fears that might undermine his will to keep fighting for Luna, but her lack of honesty was distracting and confusing him.

They passed by a stall selling water, and Taylor fanned herself for emphasis. "Would you mind picking up a big bottle?" she asked Mad Dog. "I need to sit down for a minute."

He nodded and walked to the vendor, empathy in his eyes. He likely assumed she was having a pain issue. She ushered Julian to a bench and perched on the edge, opening her mouth once Mad Dog was out of earshot and engaged with the employee. "I don't know what it's doing or what the agenda is, but they are incubating some formless being inside of me."

Julian blanched. He buried both sets of fingers in his hair, freeing enough strands from the ponytail to emphasize his distress. "Thank you for telling me. I've suspected for awhile now. I didn't know what to do."

She looked at the ground between her feet, an itch nagging in some corner of her mind, frustration pulling her in and shame dragging her down. "I'm sorry. I didn't know what to say."

"You're saying it now." He rested a hand above her knee. "Is there anything relevant you can think to share, facts that might help us?"

Seconds of opportunity ticked in her mind while Mad Dog collected his change from a tanned woman with a sleek blond bob as molded as a construction helmet. "I worry that it's a trap. That they're luring us down there to involve me in the process somehow. We've always known that was part of their operating procedure, on the island and now." She wrung her hands. "But I don't know how to subvert that. We need to go in. We have no choice."

"Let's try to find you some more time to study your book. Figure out how to ward off possession, put stopgaps in place." His eyes glazed over as he trailed off, a frown wrinkling his forehead.

Mad Dog, jumbo water in hand, ambled across the ten-foot gulf separating the kiosk from the bench. She bobbed her stare between him and Julian's puzzlement-contorted visage. "What?"

"I'm sure it's nothing."

Mad Dog stopped to fumble in his pocket, buying a few more seconds. Not that she had any reason beyond customary precautions to fret, but still. "You don't sound sure. Tell me, before he comes back over here."

He rested his elbows above his knees, face going stony. "A memory surfaced. It's probably trivial."

Her heart vaulted. Trivial, her ass. Julian was trying to placate her. While not always good, new information at least enriched the existing perspective. "A memory of what?"

He groaned.

"Come on."

"Hardly a smoking gun of any kind, but when we were on the plane ride over, I had a weird dream. It started with the flight attendant acting like a robot, repeating this phrase—*let the reaping commence*. Then I'm on a boat deck, there's wind and a storm, and this Cthulhu-type monster comes out of the water, and the phrase repeats. I wrote it off as random dream imagery, but some of the symbols seem to have resonance. The stewardess being a robot. That reaping phrase."

Bile coagulated in Taylor's gut, and she zipped her lip just in time when Mad Dog stopped at the bench, sweaty bottle of clear liquid in his outstretched hand. She accepted with a word of thanks, Julian's comment bumping through her brain like a pinball. The stewardess could have easily been a Scarab bot, tasked with servicing the flight from South America.

Which would explain the phrase, sort of, but only if the machine was able to synch up with Taylor and *by extension* Julian's thoughts. They hadn't even done that collaborative spell to get her to teleport yet. Much of Scarab's scheming was beyond her grasp.

And what gave with the sea monster? A repressed memory of the missing, long-lost Salazar? Anymore, it seemed damn stupid to believe in coincidence. She didn't realize that she was clenching the unopened water with one hand while picking the label with the other, until Mad Dog asked pointedly, "Lost in thought? I thought you were parched."

Wow. Had the passenger stolen several seconds from her, just then? Where had she gone? Zapped from her stupor, she twisted off the cap and chugged, wetness cooling her throat and cleansing her mind. She finished and wiped her mouth. "I'm fine, thanks. A little spacey from the heat is all."

With two flicks of his wrist, Julian motioned for Mad Dog. "I have an idea. Can I see the unverified maps?"

Mad Dog set his pack between his knees and claimed a spot on the bench beside Julian. Taylor scooted to the end to accommodate the third body.

"Yeah. Sure. What are you thinking?" Their companion handed over the documents, pages now smudged and crumpled from repeated use, like a trusty tourist's map worn down during an extended vacation.

Julian handed a page to Taylor and another back to Mad Dog, wielding two pages himself to make a lineup of sheets. "My first thought was to target rides that explicitly go underground, into cave structures and tunnels and whatnot. This type of setup could easily be used to transport people and supplies in a more seamless fashion than a secret passageway or elevator system. Discreet, yet ordinary on the surface."

"Hiding in plain sight." Taylor scoured the markings on her own paper. The one she had was sketched in broad strokes, with "workspaces" scribbled over the level three rooms, including the training studio where they'd had a run-in with the werewolf. The number and shape of boxes was different too, with a handful of unmarked areas and some staircases she didn't remember seeing. "Yeah, that sounds like their M.O."

But one feature of her vaguer map distinguished the document from the more precise blueprints. Someone had marked symbols near the very bottom, triangles and a single circle arranged along the points of a pentagram, a layout of elements reminiscent of her book.

What looked like a crude etching of a handprint with curlicues instead of regular fingers was stamped in the middle, the placement of the whole thing drawing the eye to the "Titans" note.

"See this?" She nudged Julian with her elbow and pointed at the sigil. "This makes me think that they do have a place for us, all six of us witches, in whatever scheme they're concocting."

Her husband looked on, studying on a long current of silence. "Yeah." His word was thick, worrisome in its modulated stillness. "I get such a creepy feeling when we notice a synchronicity or coincidence of that magnitude. Like this whole thing is preordained."

An idea galloped through her, the presence in her head piloting its chariot. "A prophecy." Despite all the water she'd chugged, her words came out cottony. "Destiny. Fate."

Suddenly she felt sick, woozy. There were people everywhere, all around, herds of ripe bodies shuffling.

Julian tapped his foot. "But that can't be the case because our free will was required to keep the process moving. We didn't have to come here after Luna was taken through that portal. We could have made any number of different, alternate choices."

She shook her head. "But we didn't. That's the entire point. We never would have chosen differently, never would have abandoned Luna. They knew this, knew how we'd react. And that's just speaking to us being loving parents. Which doesn't even get into how we were monitored, spied on, possessed. All moves are mapped. Like you said, preordained."

"Hold up." Julian faced his palm outward. "I didn't mean that it was hopeless, just that there is obviously a much bigger narrative that we've been sucked into. We've noticed this before. I'm not saying that we give up, but that we ought to be on high alert from here on out to how we're being manipulated. Because that's what it is, manipulation. These people aren't gods, they're people. Evil, crafty, cunning people who have the upper hand on us, but people all the same. Mortals."

She crunched the paper in her fist, enough to let out a bit of aggression but not destroy the document. How badly she longed to shred it and spit on the remains. Maybe a bald gesture of defiance would demolish this sick machinery of *fate*. "We don't know that they're mortal people. They're into magic, spells. Maybe they're gods or demigods or demon-human hybrids or sorcerers or fucking *Titans* or who the hell knows anymore. They can read our thoughts, predict and drive our actions. They have everything on us." Her voice shook, a wound on her heart festering. "They took everything. They have everything."

Julian swept both of her hands into his, leveling her with the conviction in his eyes. "We don't know that. For all we know, our negative energy propels and emboldens them. Try to stay focused on progress, as hard as it is. We've made it this far."

Pain threatened to tear through her chest, a solid entity forged in helpless heartbreak and oil-black sorrow. Her throat thick with swallowed tears and a rising threat of defeat, she asked, "Why did you make that comment about our situation being preordained? Because when I heard that, it almost sounded like you were giving up on saving Luna. Giving up on us having any significant degree of agency in this whatsoever."

"Never." He swallowed and held her with that strong, anchored stare. "I shouldn't have made the preordained comment. I was thinking aloud without considering the ramifications, trying to get a handle on what I saw happening, but the remark was insensitive. I see now how that was unhelpful, and I'm sorry."

"It's okay." She squeezed his hands in return, thanking him while sitting with the shame of her own reaction. "It's not your fault."

Mad Dog's bitter, sarcastic chuckle neutralized her anger and remorse in a single stroke, redirecting intense, pointed emotions into messy ones blunted by confusion. She was more than a little embarrassed, having forgotten he was there. The guy had a knack for slipping away only to reassert himself and command the stage.

She glowered at him, her pain a lens distorting the world until she saw only his mockery and narcissism. "I'm sorry, what exactly is funny right now?"

He had that smirk of perverse pleasure on his stubbly face, a look at once gross and interesting, dark secrets cradled in the quirk of a sneer. "You guys are looking at this in the wrong way."

Julian handled the follow-up with authority and enough reproach to make his point. "Then enlighten us, please. But don't be a dick, okay? Our daughter's been kidnapped."

Mad Dog closed his eyes, opened them to his pages, and leaned against the bench. "You're right, I shouldn't have laughed. If it's any consolation, I'm not laughing at you. I'm laughing at this whole crazy-pants universe."

"Alright. That's fair, I suppose. The joke's on us. What's the punchline?" Taylor asked.

"Of course, it's prophecy. Or, like you both intimated, a manmade version of fate, a cheap facsimile. We're dealing with complete megalomaniacs here, sociopaths on a massive power trip. They *want* to be gods or whatever, no doubt, but whatever they've engineered through puppeting their love child of magic and mad science is fallible. A shitty hack job of a prophecy." He snorted again, curling his upper lip in contempt. "They were always pulling crap like this, you know? Trying to weigh down the scales of fate."

Julian said, "Our free will does matter. Even if we're stumbling through some approximation of a prophecy, we have the power to change it."

Mad Dog's eyes went dreamy, like Julian's words pried open a locked attic. "Power's not quite the right word, think of it more as a perfectly timed choice made possible by an auspicious collision of timing, events, speech, and individual drive."

"Kairos." The word leapt from Taylor's mouth.

"Definition?" Julian leaned closer.

"It's a concept I learned in the rhetoric class I took a few semesters ago. It's an ancient Greek word that basically means saying the right thing at the right time. Speech as action. The act of identifying and seizing upon impeccable timing."

Julian piggybacked, contributing to the impromptu brainstorming session. "That's how we subvert the prophecy. We look for our shot at a key moment, an instant where a subtle tweak could make a huge change, and we take it. No second-guessing or overthinking."

"More or less," Mad Dog injected. "Except that you guys shouldn't be fixated on units of size. Big, small, tiny, large. That's not what matters. It's all about identifying the precise beat where one turn can restart a process. Turn the computer off, then back on again. Tweak a dial." He held his fingers an inch apart and jerked them ninety degrees. "Reset."

A tweak, a restart, a butterfly effect of cascading dominoes to change the route and instigate a novel course of events. Okay. Duly noted and saved for later. Taylor went back to studying her map, cross-referencing notes with rooms and comparing the blueprint with the outdoor layout until the three agreed on a ride.

She stood, ready to fly into the pit atop the wings of a capricious, fickle butterfly in charge of her fate.

NINETEEN

HE HATED TO ADMIT HE'D NOTICED TAYLOR CHANGING.

In small ways, at first. Changes that a casual acquaintance would not have noticed. The kind that were easy to write off. How she sat with such formal posture on that bench when Mad Dog got the water. Military straight, ramrod.

How, when they crossed the floor of the training gym, her steps were different. Heel to toe in a stiff, self-conscious way. Terse.

She'd been carrying herself like a different person since the plane ride to Florida, the first moment where he'd shoved his observations into a crevice and trooped on. Easier that way, and preferable to cultivating bitter feelings toward his wife and her possibly catastrophic dalliance into magic.

Julian pushed the bar of the turnstile, crossing a boundary to enter some ride called The Enchanted Waterfall. A fog of mold and chlorine leaching up from wet pavement engulfed him, olfactory reminders to focus. With that shove into the new space, he banished dour thoughts back into their hidey-hole where they belonged.

As the three stood at the end of a line of texting teens interspersed with parents attempting to entertain bored children, he tugged on Taylor's waist to urge her closer.

He'd try to save her when the time came. Work hard to heal her with his magic. For now, he said in a low voice close to her ear, "The elevator we want is on the other side of the waterfall. When everyone's distracted by the spray effects, we jump off as one and make a run for it." At least that was his best educated guess based on the sparse hints offered by the maps and Mad Dog's input.

Waiting for her reply, he tried to ignore the severe cut of her shoulders, this newly aggressive body language now emanating from her like an unwholesome aura.

At least her voice sounded normal: "Then straight down to level four. Unless the elevator is protected by key card or fob or something. Then what?"

He puffed out his cheeks. Before he could hazard a workaround, the flat voice of a disaffected teen girl raised her voice over cheers and splashes. "Backpacks, please."

Julian turned to see a redhead in a pressed Wonder World uniform, pacing the length of the line on her hunt for contraband. Checked backpacks and large purses sat in a heap against a fake stone wall, tagged.

Taking out an old smile he once used to flirt, Julian ran his hands up his straps in a way that accentuated his forearms. "Sorry. We need them."

The young woman studied the trio and pulled a face of consternation. "You need three backpacks to ride a water ride." The skeptical remark was not phrased as a question.

"Yes," Taylor put in. "For medical purposes."

The girl's eyes hardened, glassy, and self-satisfied as she leveled her follow-up. "That's fine. I just need to check your park passes for the medical permission stamp." The gotcha was strong, and the notion of a medical stamp on a theme park pass borderline absurd. She was screwing with them for fun.

Of course they didn't have passes, either, though in retrospect it would have been a smart bit of base-covering to buy some.

Mad Dog leaned in, urging the trio into a huddle, his funk mixing with the musty, pool-water smell. "She's a bot or android meta human. Scramble her signal."

The curveball whammied Julian's brain. He whispered, "You know this how?"

"I can spot these chip-heads from ten feet away, and even if I couldn't, I know this park's practices. Cheaper to maintain a fleet of tech than hire minimum wage kids and undocumented folks. Don't look now, but look at her when you can do discreetly. Take note of what doesn't feel right for a person, and then never unsee those features."

Guilt bit down as he looked at Taylor instead, the regretful feeling giving way to grief.

She used to have such expressive ways of communicating through her body—hands tacked on the hips, elbow propped on the top of a couch in an expansive stretch that somehow incorporated the furniture into a demonstration of her confident identity. Now she stood like a toy soldier, awaiting her drill sergeant's orders.

He swiped his stare to the employee before he let himself feel any worse. Mad Dog was right. There was a dreadful dullness to the staff member's green eyes and a coldness oozing from her skin. The longer he stared, the more he felt repulsed and fascinated and just plain *wrong*.

"I said, don't look now," Mad Dog hissed, but it was too late.

"Sir, I'm going to have to ask your party to vacate the premises." The redhead stalked up close and reached for a handheld radio clipped to her belt. He caught other oddities now, too, like how she blinked frequently and at odd intervals.

"We haven't done anything," Taylor protested, her pitch muted enough to avoid drawing attention. Fortunately, the members of the slowly shuffling line were too distracted or apathetic anyway, lost in their own worlds as they inched to the ride's entrance.

A wave lurched over the wall, making a few teens squeak as droplets rained down, some of the runoff connecting with Julian's neck in a tepid splat. "We'll leave after we ride this ride. We've been waiting all day for this one."

"I told you not to stare, they can register it as a threat," Mad Dog grumbled. "But you blew it. Scramble her. Hurry."

Taylor sucked up a loud breath and spoke the hushed words of one of her magic spells.

"No, you." Mad Dog jabbed a finger into Julian's chest. "I wanna test a theory here."

"You can't be serious," Taylor said. "He doesn't know my spells. And now's not the time for testing anything."

"Sirs. Ma'am," the worker snapped, loud enough to swivel the heads of a couple of parties farther up in line, where a bald guy herded riders into a seat car shaped like a log. "Please come with me. We can get this sorted out with my manager."

"Concentrate and go for it, Julian." Mad Dog's eyes glittered now, his excitement freezing time into a capsule of opportunity. "I've seen enough mind meld work in Scarabland to know that you've got the chops. None of their subjects were half as skilled as you clearly are with Taylor. You'll need to know this stuff when we're down in the pit. It's a weapon. Tap into Taylor's subconscious and go, go, go."

Pushed into the deep end, Julian flailed until he achieved telepathy with Taylor, beginning with a relatively straightforward feat. Rather than accessing her surface thoughts for their usual private conversations, he sunk, feet first, deeper into the swamp of her hidden mind.

"Sir." The worker's admonition was distant now, and of as little import as dialog spoken by a character in a show stumbled upon while channel surfing.

The lower levels of Taylor's mind were far more interesting than some robot yelling at him, deep-sea depths of blue velvet bathed in the violet, alien phosphorescence of blacklight.

The walls around him flexed, alive, giving off puffs of cerulean mist as they undulated with serpentine sensuality.

As he watched in awe, this play of light and motion, a fact dawned on him. This sumptuous place was where her spells lived. Her magic's abode. He wasn't alone there. One or more sentient presences accompanied him.

Amazed to the point that his mind blanked, he walked, picking up input from different sources along the way. As best he could gather, stumbling through luminous corridors with no signposts to guide him, he traversed a collective arena owned and populated by all sorts of magic users, past, present, and future. Taylor shared a collective unconscious.

He ran a hand along the wall, and to his surprise, the juicy material sucked up his appendage like a hungry mouth. Instinctively, he pulled back against the wet heat, the sensation both perversely sexual and akin to being devoured by a predator.

"Don't resist," a strange, androgynous voice said. "Come in."

His whole head fuzzy, buzzing, he crossed the threshold to enter the soft wall, stickiness enveloping him like a spiderweb until he popped free of the gum. He staggered over a ledge, and coasted in free fall through formless, unlit humidity.

Julian didn't gather his bearings until he drew his first good breath in awhile, crisp and salty, his stare fixed on blurry blobs of light that coalesced into night sky stars the more he blinked.

Next, he was gasping, his body afloat, the fluid all around him changing temperature from bathwater tepid, to icy, to various gradations in between and back again. He kicked into the void beneath for a couple of seconds before returning to float belly-up, volleying his eyes in either direction in confirmation of a hunch.

Choppy black waves swelled and fell in all directions, lolling forever. He floated in an endless expanse of open water. Panic threated, pounding his gates, a hostile takeover of pure survival instinct.

Julian staved it off with mindful breathing. He had to wing a scramble spell now. "Sink or swim" never felt so accurate, and the wild ride through Taylor's magical subconscious was ten times more harrowing than any Wonder World rollercoaster could hope for. He didn't know water magic, but he improvised with his understanding from basic chemistry of how water behaved.

He had to use water to scramble the signal of a robot, mess up her mind, cloud her thoughts, and make her dumb.

The closest function he could approximate to this was the effect some gasses had on the human body, like the stuff used by dentists to make patients spaced out and giggly. With any luck, the effect was transferable.

He concentrated the flow of water until it transformed into gas, interference, invisible particles with the power to stupefy and sedate.

All that is liquid. The thought came to him in a beautiful, easy flow of spontaneity. *Melts into air. Stop you here. Start you there.*

From a turbulent pocket near the golden tips of his protruding cowboy boots, a cloud of white steam emerged. The vapory substance gathered into a column and shot upward into the cosmos.

Right as the cloud became imperceptible, some star burned as bright as Venus, then extinguished.

"You're all going to die down here." The androgynous voice, malice sharp in its unbothered neutrality, echoed through Julian with contempt fit for a vengeful poltergeist.

He refused to be cowed. Eventually, he'd have to fight this presence. Might as well start now. "Oh, yeah? Says who?"

The resulting laugh sickened him with its ring of pure evil. "We were here before time began, in advance of the world as you know it. Formless, boundless, endless."

"What are you then? A demon? An alien?"

More chortling at his expense, the trill of a ghoul who'd eat your skin while giggling like a toddler. "Original filth, unspeakable and devoid of name. The mistakes that haunt your kind."

He swallowed, aware of his vulnerable body prone to the depths below. To sharks, snakes, creeps of the deep. "What kind? Shifters? Humans? Both, and?"

"All that is wrong, diseased, disordered, issues from us. We are legion. Sin. Error. Enumerable. A multitude of Other Ones."

"Are you what's possessing Taylor?"

Maniac laughter intensified, the primordial cackle of multiplicities, a hydra bleating through a surplus of heinous heads. "We go wherever magic does."

Every instinct he possessed to survive, to thrive, to be clean, thrummed with an urge to be done with this interaction. To be free of this being. But he needed to take as much value from the chance encounter as he could and bring maximum data back with him, because the more he had, the better of a position he'd be in to help Taylor. "Are you inherent in magic, or the creator of it?"

"A part, and thus the whole. The shadow against which light can bloom. Inescapable, inextricable. These links have been forged since it all began, and they are unbreakable."

He went in hard, hoping that a sudden change in direction would skew his companion's equilibrium. "Scarab is manipulating you. Tapping your energy like you're little more than a resource to deplete. Once they're done, they'll discard what's left and laugh at you. Don't play the fool."

The entity bellowed loud enough to bend the sky, "You will not. You will never, ever, besmear or besmirch us. We submit to no peon. We rule. Peons serve. We are the greatest of all time. Now. Then. Always." The final yell echoed through the waves, rolling over crests like sonorous thunder from hell.

Julian smiled to himself. Good to know that their foe had a weakness. It seemed a little odd that a being this powerful was commanded by pride, however he supposed that an overblown yet tender ego fit this particular adversary especially well, with their blathering about being the greatest of all time. "Yeah, okay. Got it."

"I'm through with you," the disembodied voice screamed. "Get out."

Before Julian could tell the alleged G.O.A.T. that he was happy to oblige, he found himself standing on solid ground, albeit on a surface that threatened to give way beneath his feet.

He stumbled, chunks of color and shape swimming in his vision, bracing his hand on some flimsy support that clattered to the ground before strong grips clamped both of his arms.

"I got you." Taylor's voice, thank God. "Breathe, open your eyes slowly, and count backwards from ten. We're at Wonder World, about to ride The Magical Waterfall." A long, dense pause. "Do you remember what we discussed?"

Ten, nine, eight...

Nausea tightened his stomach, pushing a scarfed fast-food meal upward. He struggled to order the mess in front of his eyes.

Gradually, blurs took form. People. The fake stone wall. Silver poles to mark the line, faux-velvet ropes stringing them together, one laying on the concrete.

Taylor's queenly eyes, finally, big, and bold and the color of wild Texas bluebonnets.

Breathing in smells of sweat and chemically treated water, he nodded, recalibrated to the theme park after his journey. "Yeah. Did it work?"

Mad Dog crouched, picked up the fallen post, and replaced it to stand among its comrades in crowd control. "See for yourself."

Right, their run-in with the employee had almost ended in getting bounced from the park.

He spotted the woman near the turnstile. She ushered people in while giggling hysterically.

"I can see Russia from my house," she blurted out in a baby voice before doubling over in a fit of hysterics. "Ground control to Major Tom."

A pair of men in glasses and Birkenstocks, each leading an elementary-aged child by the hand, looked at the girl in horror as they brought the kids into the ride.

"All aboard," she let out on a gasp until another unbridled laughing spell took over.

Julian, Taylor, and Mad Dog shuffled up in line, past the gray wall and into the replica of a cave where patrons stood prior to boarding. Taylor looked over her shoulder with a snort of bemusement. "How did you do that with water magic?"

While the employee lapsed deeper into her spell, two other workers arrived and hauled her away with their elbows linked around hers. She dragged her feet while shouting cackles fit for a deranged lunatic.

Julian would have felt guilty if she'd been a person, but he figured that the only thing she had in store was a trip to reprogramming.

"Since liquid transforms into gas, I tried to channel something equivalent to a high dose of laughing gas. To debilitate her, basically, but not be too conspicuous about the whole thing. Didn't want the operation to grind to a halt."

Mad Dog said, "Good thinking, man. We'll need that kind of brainpower underground. From all three of us. In case, especially if, we get separated." His lips twitched. "That's why I wanted you to start practicing spells, J-dog. Can't have anyone running around underpowered."

The "underpowered" comment probably should have offended him, but Mad Dog had a point. Julian wasn't going to be taking down their enemies with healing magic, or probably even wolf-shifting. He took a few forward steps, closing in on the loading area. A Wonder World staffer filled the log from the back.

"What's your superpower?" Julian asked.

Mad Dog tapped his temple. "An abundance of gray matter in my ugly-ass head."

"Can't argue," Julian said.

"I like our team," Taylor added with a sort of cheer. "We've got a pretty cool Three Musketeers thing going on." She stuck out a fist.

As Julian bumped Taylor's fist, Mad Dog added his into the mix, tipping his chin down in a manner so earnest, profound almost, that Julian couldn't help but conclude Taylor got through somehow.

"You bet," Mad Dog said, sincere in an easy way Julian had never seen on him.

Maybe the man just wanted to be accepted, foibles and all.

Circumstance intervened, halting Julian's considerations, when the big guy at the mouth of the ride asked, "Are you three together?"

Taylor squeezed Julian's hand and offered Mad Dog a friendly smile. "Yeah."

The employee frowned, scanning their group. Behind him, the log car sloshed lazily in a murky stream. Lumpy walls making up the imitation cavern were pockmarked with mounted red lamps, adding a moody atmosphere. "They didn't make you check your backpacks?"

Julian liked those pleasant red orbs, the dimness of the ride. Better to make their moves under cover of semi-darkness. He was pleased about the understated lighting and didn't even have it in him to get annoyed about this stubbornly recurring bags issue. "No, man, we have an exemption."

The employee folded buff arms over a barrel chest. "What kind of exemption?"

"Hey, buddy," some guy way down in the queue called in an exasperated tone. "We ever gonna get on, or what? My kids are getting tired."

"Put that *stuff* in your laps, I guess." Mr. Wonder World led them to a spot in the very front. From the tone of his voice, he clearly wanted to drop an s-word unacceptable to the family-friendly establishment that was Wonder World.

Taylor didn't follow the cranky man. "Can we ride in the middle, actually?"

He sighed passive-aggressively, moving to the middle seats and yanking up a safety bar. "Any more special requests?"

A sweet smirk played on her lips. "That'll do it. Bless your heart." She kicked up her drawl, no doubt just for fun.

He loved his wife. And once they got out of this mess and back to Peru, they could get back to living and loving as a family. Julian climbed aboard, the flooring shaky beneath his steps, and settled in. The safety bar smashed his pack against his torso as the employer pulled it down a little harder than was required.

Taylor was next to him, stoic, dignified, and just off kilter enough to remind him they had a lot of feats to accomplish before life could return to normal.

TWENTY

TAYLOR'S LATEST METHOD FOR STAVING OFF THE ENTITIES IN HER HEAD was to ignore them. The more that she obsessed, the more frequently she felt herself recede to the background as *they* crawled to the front.

She clenched the ride's safety bar, their buggy bobbing on grungy water as the car commenced a slow part of its journey. This intermission of action served as an opportunity to weigh options. She had to figure out how to gain control of and harness the phenomenon.

The log ride whipped a hard left, adults and kids ponying up obedient screaming fit for an advertisement. The force smashed Taylor's side into Mad Dog's, and she couldn't help but notice, with the awkwardness of unwanted intimacy, how soft and squishy his body was. A plume of water surged up at the front of the ride before raining down on everyone in a lukewarm spray that spurred on a fresh round of delighted shrieks.

She craned her neck, exempt from the thrill aspect of the experience, concerned only with getting a visual on the waterfall in enough time to prepare.

The log bumped and slid down a tributary a few feet wider than the ride itself, surrounded by molded walls that glowed cherry red thanks to a smattering of lanterns. In front, gray wetness and shadows lurked.

She tilted her head up to Julian, the pain behind his eyes palpable despite the dimness. It tore her up how he noticed that the possession had gotten worse, less manageable. He was worried about her, rightfully. She'd give anything to put an end to the ordeal, and with any luck they were one step closer. "Any sense of where the waterfall is?"

"No. If I had to guess, I'd say it was a grand finale type of experience, but I can't be sure."

Let the reaping commence. Louder than ever before, insistent, like the speaker was issuing a command. Getting bossy. There had to be a reason why it had started addressing her again.

Taylor ground her molars. If only she knew what was happening when the possession piped up, what bad stuff the speech-act was putting into the universe.

The ride lurched, shooting her forward hard enough that her nose connected with her pack, the impact violent enough to sting.

From the locomotive area of the aquatic tram, the guide bellowed theatrically through a magnifying device that made his voice surreal, scratchy. "And if you look to your right, you might just catch a glimpse at some of our most magical, enchanted inhabitants."

Underwater lights popped to life, bathing the walls in fantastical shades of emerald, ruby, and sapphire, transforming the space into a prism where jewel tones and black film layered into a parfait.

"Mermaids," a little girl said with reverence, her declaration setting off a landslide of squeals and claps from her fellow kiddos.

The flickering gemstone show whisked over ecstatic young faces, glimmering sprites to humor the children.

"They're beautiful."

"Wow."

Taylor, though not in the spirit, peered between two blond heads for a better look. This exhibit would be the first big viewing, and perhaps a sign the ride neared its climax.

She turned to see a part of the wall structure replaced with a clear front, filled with water to transform cavern replica material into a giant aquarium. The tank was stocked with fluorescent fake seaweed that floated all around in gauzy, slothful motions. Some swaying plants at the bottom, anchored by a bed of translucent pink pebbles, sparkled in the soft blessing of gentle overhead lights.

Two women and two men, pale green fishtails beginning at mid-waist and fanning into fins, swam in circles, waving at visitors. Their hair was long, hot pink for the women and violet for the men, tendrils melting with the water and seaweed to create a truly magical effect.

For a second, Taylor was hypnotized, as taken by the fairytale spectacle as the swooning young girls. Her head swimming in that massive tank along with the miraculous debris and bewitching people, she waved back, squinting at how the scales of one mermaid's fin spread seamlessly up her midsection until they covered her nipples. Stellar costuming, unless—

"Babe." Julian shook her arm, his word falling safely below the register of the children's oohs and ahs. "Change of plans. We gotta go."

She shook off the fuzz of her spellbound daydream and stared at him. "Go? Where?"

"The elevator. I spotted it a few feet back. There's a clearing next to that tank, probably where they service it."

Devoid of a plan, her mind went blank. They'd have to what, hastily jump overboard? Stage a distraction? "How do you know that's the one?"

His jaw was tight. "I don't. But we can't afford to second guess."

The car jerked, began to move at a slow pace, but then stopped again when the announcer resumed his guided tour. "If you keep close watch, you might see more of these special creatures. Or even..."

"What? What?" The children went berserk.

"Shhh. Be quiet. They are very, very shy, and sensitive to noise."

"What are shy?"

"I want to see!"

"Sssh. There are only a few of these rare creatures left in existence."

Julian spoke in a low, urgent tone close to her ear, "Something big is in the works right now. We can't let it slip by."

"I know, but shit." Taylor pulled at the bar squashing down on her stuff, palms slippery, failing to budge her personal shackle. "We weren't ready."

Julian leaned down as much as possible given their minimal leverage in the sardine tin, his hand roving to something out of sight. "I think I saw him spring a latch near the floor."

He fumbled for a minute, and sure enough, the bar loosened and gave.

The light show changed, beams of amethyst and gold drenching surfaces at a frenzied pace.

Taylor looked back into manufactured twilight and churning, sloppy water of indeterminate depth. "We have to jump and swim for it?"

The kids were still fired up, calling to the mermaids as they waved goodbye. A decent enough cover when combined with the flickering colors, but surely someone would take issue with three people disembarking in haste and going overboard. She gulped. This was not good.

"We'll move in one line," Mad Dog said. "The water's deep enough to swim in. We'll duck as low as we can, slip into the water, swim to the alcove Julian mentioned, and pull up."

There were people right behind them, directly in front. She counted heads, ticking off at least thirty witnesses. "We'll get caught."

"Wait one more minute," Mad Dog said. "Yeah, we still might, but a decent smokescreen is coming up."

She sucked in a breath and held it, practice for holding her breath underwater.

Up front, a mechanical groan shot up the anticipation level, followed by the lowering of what looked like a drawbridge. Then, lights bounced across the walls, an array of sherbet colors intense enough to create a dizzying strobe effect.

"What's happening?" Yet, an invisible muscle in Taylor loosened, the makings of an opportunity unfurling.

And sure enough, opportunity trotted out right before her eyes.

Bedlam erupted among the children.

A girl let out an eardrum-shredding screech of amazement. "A unicorn!"

The pearlescent horse, cut glass hooves reflecting a rainbow of dancing rays like diamonds in the sun, marched across the bridge with a graceful, trained gait obviously learned in dressage. Or over in reprogramming. Who the hell knew anymore?

A full fall of thick, silvery mane accented with baby braids trailing behind its sculpted neck, the animal preened and pranced while children lost their ever-loving minds.

Flicking a tail that sparkled like Christmas tree tinsel, the mythical beast tilted its long head to face the crowd, giving spectators a good view of the coiled icicle emerging from its forehead as a starburst sparkle flared at the tip.

"Now," Julian said. "Now, now."

Fuck. It wouldn't work to go for it, even with a stellar equine distraction in play.

A bubble shot from the pit of her stomach to her head and burst into an epiphany. "I have a better idea. Hold up."

Of course, there were no spare seconds to fumble in her backpack and wrench out the book, let alone start reading. Taylor closed her eyes and focused on the energy inside her.

She'd used her water magic intuitively the first two times she'd tried it, the first time they'd infiltrated a Scarab facility, and initially attributed the positive results of her novice efforts to beginner's luck. But what if accessing her magic sans book was just another method of wielding it, and equally valid? No time to weigh pros and cons. Her gut had to be her guide.

She closed her eyes and instigated a mini meditation, dropping in and down, low, past the place where her white wolf slept dormant, tucked into a ball, tail grazing snout.

Below the wolf's den, the most surface level of her subconscious, lay a swampy realm, teeming with all sorts of life, an endless horizon of dampness laved by the hot tongues of blue flames.

Let the reaping commence. The voice echoed all around her, riding the wind, omnipresent, closing in to pound against the bone boundary of her skull.

Taylor ignored the demand and concentrated, pulling with her thoughts, trying and failing to tug heavy-duty water magic out of the dark place. It was as if a barrier separated her from the energy, keeping her at bay, relegating her to pawing at a smooth gate with no knob or knocker.

She was close. She could sense the goodness, its moving tide of electric pulses, but she couldn't seize it in her hands.

A swell of indigo tentacles burst from a blue-black pit, tingling as they grazed her fingertips, shrinking in retreat when she reached out to grab them. *Let the reaping commence.*

Anger ignited her blood in incendiary bursts. The force down deep was teasing her. "No."

No more. The tentacles coiled up her body, alive and humming with power; power she craved more than anything in the world. She tried to catch one, but the serpentine tube exploded into particles of soot and dissolved into the air. *No more for you.*

Her ribcage tight, muscles knotty, she tried to suck one of the remaining curls into herself by sheer force of concentration. The snaky thing inched towards her, tentative, while she slurped at it like her brain had a straw poking out from her third eye. "There, there, it's okay. Come on. Come here."

A few more nudges forward, and the coil of magic nearly kissed her forehead before exploding into ashy shards. Her heart plummeted. Close. "Damn it!"

The voice laughed, amused at her expense.

Taylor dug her nails into her palms until her hands flared up in pain. If this stupid voice had a corporeal form, she'd punch it out. But unfortunately, the being had something she wanted and total control over the resource in question. "What do I have to do to take some of this back with me and keep it?"

Let the reaping commence.

Dread weighed down on her as her intuition flashed a warning. But what choice did she have? If she went back up empty handed, she risked ruining the entire operation. Losing her shot at saving Luna was not a choice. She'd do anything for her precious baby girl. Fucking anything.

"Hurry," Julian spoke from afar. "We're losing ground."

Their shot was sliding away, down a lazy track of water. All she needed, more than anything else in the world, was a reliable ruse to buy them the seconds to get to that elevator. Nothing else mattered.

"Fine. It can fucking *commence* all day long. Just give me enough magic to move water with my mind again."

You consent to the reaping.

"Sure. Whatever."

Say it.

She ground her teeth. "I consent to the reaping."

Not quite.

Tears of frustration in her eyes, at what she was about to do, Taylor squeezed her lids shut and pushed out the filthy phrase before she changed her mind. "Let the reaping commence."

The entire energy field changed, giving in like a cracked egg. Magic poured into her, timeless and otherworldly and charged with the supernatural chants and hexes of many, many witches before her. Visuals came fast and unspeakable, beings with sheets of eyes and scaly skin ending at cloven toes.

Serpents crawled up a caduceus, their fangs dripping venom that mixed with Taylor's saliva until acid fried in her mouth. The taste of evil. She let her tears free, streams of lava and regret against her cheeks. She was corrupted now, utterly, but she didn't stop taking.

She shook, gasped, took it all until the boiling, liquid pressure slammed in her temples and overloaded her blood, threatening to stomp her heart like an overripe peach.

Very well. You consort with us now. Folly into skull, possession complete. Shape the water as you wish from here on. Poison gasses and fluids of all kinds are yours to manipulate now, to wield as you choose. Leach all moisture from the land. Boil the sea. Blow a pestilence across the globe. Do as thou will.

Taylor bungeed upward, rejoining her body with a bang. Magic still ran wild inside of her, fecund and eager, wearing her skin as a suit. Instantly, a headache crunched into her brain, accompanied by unbearable nausea, but too bad. She didn't have the luxury of falling prey to any symptoms.

Instead of going into her body, she turned outward. The unicorn presentation went on.

Apparently, time moved differently in the dimension of magic. She held on to Julian's arm as a buffer against the urge to be sick. She stared at the water, throwing her concentration into it, an anchor and a sponge, sinking to the proverbial bottom to soak up its essence in molecules.

She locked into a direct vibe with the flow, engaged in a push and pull of buzzy hums that slowly, gently, coaxed the liquid upward until a shimmering, translucent bubble enveloped the log car in a cocoon.

The worker, standing up in his driver's seat, frowned, though he kept talking about the unicorn's supposed ability to grant wishes. He was probably new and assumed that the water trick was part of the show. Good enough.

Once Wonder World dude looked at the unicorn, drawing attention to a little dance that it was doing, Taylor signaled Julian with a nod.

His stare burned with love and a trace of fear, but he didn't take his gaze away from her as he slung one leg over the side of the car and passed through the bubble in a smooth motion.

Her pulse was a drumbeat, but none of their companions said anything. She followed, a warm wave drenching her before she popped out the other side beside her husband, as saturated as a drowned rat.

A spray of pennies, two cell phones, one pair of sunglasses, and what looked like the remains of a broken beer bottle littered the tracks in a hodgepodge of superstition and bad luck.

Mad Dog emerged a second later, droplets hanging from his nose.

Instructions weren't necessary as they moved to the elevator access point as one row of determined bodies, slurpy sucking noises marking their steps.

She stole a minute to chance a glance. Her handiwork shimmered like a snow globe, trapping the others in a sphere. Even if they noticed three riders had disembarked, they wouldn't attempt to bust through the water wall, at least not right away.

Not right away, meaning that seconds counted. The three reached the ledge at the same time. Taylor clung to the hard, sharp surface and pulled up, throwing her legs over. Her biceps fiery from the exertion, she ran to the elevator, letting go of ten pounds on the exhale when she spotted old-fashioned buttons. No black box. No fob system to stymie them.

Julian pressed his nose against the side of her head. "Thank God." Relief made his voice tremble. He smelled like the time they'd made love in the rain, his lips on her neck, her back against a tree.

The sweet memory made her long for escape. Better yet, returning to the past moment gave her an idea on how to avoid conspicuously sloshing around the bunker, leaving sodden trails in their wake of noisy steps.

Without explanation, she laid a hand on Julian's shoulder and another on Mad Dog's, concentrating on a surface-level sense of dryness until the soaked fabric beneath her palms changed to dry cotton. She opened her eyes and smiled at her companions upon affirming that the wetness had evaporated. Magic for the win.

Positivity was scant nourishment rationed among them. But she'd accept what little there was.

She pushed the down button.

Down, again, all aboard the expressway into the pit. The doors opened to padded walls streaked with rusty brown slashes.

TWENTY-ONE

THE INTERIOR ELEVATOR BUTTONS WEREN'T MARKED WITH NUMBERS, or even symbols remotely resembling numbers in any way. Another coded, impenetrable system to remind Julian exactly who they were dealing with. What they were dealing with, the malevolence decimating his poor Taylor from within. The force was getting stronger, bolder, overpowering her as she wilted to a husk of her former self before his eyes.

He switched his focus to their immediate predicament, a problem somewhat within his control. The markings on the buttons resembled crosses between Chinese characters and the runes he remembered reading about in history books about Celtic druids. Scary tangles of indecipherable obscurity and mixed systems.

The sixth, lowest button was just a black pinpoint dot resting against the disc. As an artist, he couldn't stop staring at the display of ominous minimalism, like some modern art statement piece rendered in miniature. Too bad the whole scene was too sick to derive any inspiration whatsoever from.

The door closed to trap them in a cell that smelled like a half-cleaned bathroom, the dried blood on the walls both gross and evocative of severe unease. To foreground logic, problem solve, he asked Taylor, "Do any of these markings look familiar to you?"

Taylor was breathing heavily, the latest thing he noticed since she went away and came back with enhanced water magic and worsening psychosis. He ought to start cataloging her symptoms, tracking patterns among the changes. Repelled him to think of her as a patient, a problem, but here they were.

She scoffed, pulling at a strand of her hair in a fidgety way. "No. Totally foreign. But they do indicate to me that whoever works on the surface knows what's going on downstairs. To a certain extent."

"Push 'em all," Mad Dog said. "No guarantee that they're aligned in an intuitive up to down order."

"Fitting," Julian said in regard to the observation about the layout being a discombobulating, topsy-turvy funhouse of nightmares. "But what if—"

Mad Dog's swift pressing of every button cut Julian off before he finished making some sensible, forgotten counterpoint. Stunned mute, he gawked at the pleasing, butter-yellow glow of those sinister buttons activated by Mad Dog's impulsive finger.

Julian and Taylor looked at him at the same time, her pale face mirroring his inner shock.

She snapped, "What did you just do?"

Cool as can be while the metal box groaned and dropped a floor, Mad Dog said, "No time for dilly-dallying here. Think on your feet, guys."

Doors opened to the next phase of their fate, Julian clicking into the fight reflex with a half step in front. He shielded Taylor's body with his larger, stronger one. His heart small and leaden, vision sharp, he faced a corridor.

The floor and ceiling were brushed in dull red tones. Bare concrete. Industrial. A musty smell underscored with something chemical-sweet hung in the air. Two separate machine sounds issued from the distance, a metallic whine like a dentist's drill and the lower, clunky grunts of an engine or boiler.

He failed to get a clear read on the setting, whether to be comforted, alarmed, or disturbed by the rush of unusual input. Fucking Mad Dog.

Then, a man joined them in the claustrophobic space. A man that he didn't want to be looking at.

At least Julian assumed the brute was a man, judging by his refrigerator build and shoulders broad enough to support four heads. Work boots designed to stomp and kick were big enough to fit the tallest basketball player.

Yellow rubber gloves stretched up to the elbow, a plastic smock the color of shit overlaying a milky-white hazmat suit with a built-in bonnet that clung to his head like a shower cap. A clear face shield and medical-grade mask guarded his head holes against airborne contagions and splatter.

Splatter. The entire ensemble evoked it, splatter and torture. Murder.

Personal protective gear hid every bit of skin, save for the piercing hit of his ice-blue eyes. Handles of tools in various sizes poked out of generous pockets on the front of the heavy-duty apron.

Nauseated, Julian managed a curt nod, the blood on the walls haunting and visible out of the corner of his eye, desperate traces of someone fighting for their life.

"You're headed to the Song of Virgo, aren't you?" the stranger spoke with an accent, Appalachian, perhaps, sounding impressed even as his eyes darkened with a negative emotion.

If the glare was rooted in envy, they'd enjoy a sliver of leverage, having something he wanted.

Julian's pulse spiked as the doors closed to trap them with this freak. But the new development wasn't all bad. Here was a chance to snag a clue or two, if he finessed this right. "Yes. We're very fortunate."

The monster snorted, a touch of resentment bitter on his vowels. "The word you're looking for is lucky."

"No doubt." Taylor spoke with a perfectly curated air of humility. "I feel like we won the lottery."

Julian's fists twitched in preparation as this asshole dressed up like a torture porn villain turned to glower down at his wife.

"Yeah, no shit, Barbie." Julian wanted to kill him in that moment, for his hostile and semi-misogynistic condescension alone. But as he kept bitching, his words got juicy. "I hate this shithole. I've been paying my dues in the kill room since the drone guy was president, ya feel me?"

"Sure do, man." Mad Dog did a nice job playing the role of fellow disgruntled worker. He looked the part, unshaven and dressed in a jean jacket and stocking cap fit for a dock worker. "I cleaned up blood and guts for Scarab for three fuckin' years."

"Yeah." The big man sounded validated. "It ain't fair. I've never been late. Never missed a day of work since I started, showing up fifteen minutes before shift start to hack and slash in their slaughterhouse."

"I hear you," Mad Dog prodded, gently enough to escape detection. The elevator continued its descent. There had to be a lot of distance covered between floors. Didn't quite check out with their earlier crawl through the tunnel and walk across the training room, but apparently the consensus was that the building's layout was bonkers.

The big man scratched his head, the elastic of his cap stretched tight enough that the corners of his eyes pulled upward, brows giving way to a red line curving from ear to ear. "If you ask me, that new lottery system sucks. It's like the draft. Arbitrary. No merit-based rewards. But congratulations on getting your number pulled, brother. Gotta feel good, getting that break from ripping out organs and pulling off skins. I swear, bro, these greedy-ass, black-market buyers can never get enough."

"Thank you," Mad Dog said. "It's a relief."

The doors opened to another hallway, this one drably decorated with nubby blue carpet and walls the color of dishwater. "Well, this is my stop. Those beasties aren't gonna process themselves. Wouldn't it be sweet if Scarab invented the tech for that? Programmed their drones and bots or some shit to do it?"

"Sure would," Julian said affably as the urge to murder intensified.

This deranged psycho killed shifters because his bosses told him to. Then he went home, crashed on the couch to watch football and drink beer, and scratched his balls while awaiting payday. A truly lowly, contemptible sort of evil.

Big Bubba stepped out. "Maybe my number will get pulled in the fall. Anywho, enjoy the Song of Virgo. My buddy says it's even cooler than Ballad of Capricorn, but he's biased. At least for this ritual y'all get to wear those cool druid robes." He laughed at some memory, lumbering off as the elevator sealed itself and resumed its downward trajectory.

Collectively, tension shattered in imperceptible explosions felt on the pre-conscious level.

"Fuck," Taylor drew out the obscenity, eyes wide as she braced a hand on the wall. "Did you guys notice that his uniform was clean? He's just starting his shift and went to that lower floor to get something first. That means we went down *one* level from the surface to get to the kill room. Either the layout is nonlinear or the maps are wrong."

Mad Dog grunted in agreement. "There was a lot in there, what he said, but yeah."

Julian tried for morale enhancement. "He mentioned druid robes. Let's keep our eyes open for something like that. We might ultimately need a disguise. We can't count on a reliable path out, but we have magic. Teleportation."

Taylor looked at Julian, hard and pained. "I need to be honest with you. Both of you now. If I change, turn into something really vile, as in I'm clearly not myself, as in I'm possessed beyond recognition..." Her chin wobbled, throat working as she swallowed what came after the trail-off.

His heart ached as he hugged her, the fit and compact body he knew, the body that had born their children and fought hard for them. He didn't lie to her or spew platitudes. He just held her, touched her, cherishing the tactile impressions of her flesh. His wife. Lover. Comrade in arms. Friend. Partner. "Don't say the rest, okay, babe?"

"Okay." Her whisper prayed for better days. She fisted his shirt at the sides, nodding against his chest. "Promise me you won't give up on Luna."

He'd die first. He'd die before sacrificing Taylor, but she didn't need declarations of heroism right now. She needed support. "I promise."

The inhale she drew in was sharp and serious, the kind of breath used to quash a tide of emotion. She backed away, still clutching him, her eyes pure tragedy. Silence, her gaze, accomplished more than words.

He couldn't lose her. Would not lose her.

Mad Dog spoke at last, his voice kinder, gentler, than anything Julian had heard roll off his lips. "Hey, guys, sorry to interrupt, but I felt the elevator slow. It's gonna be go time in a second. We don't want to get caught off guard."

Whenever Julian began to wonder if their third wheel was an asshole, or worse, duplicitous, and untrustworthy, Mad Dog restored a viable amount of faith.

Julian held Taylor's hand as the doors parted, the seam in the middle widening to deliver them to—wait, what?

"No way," Taylor whispered.

They were back in the training room. Same props and dummies. No werewolf.

Wind vanished from his lungs, an avalanche of blood and chemicals making his body feel not like his own. Same smell. He ventured out onto the gym floor. "This is good. We can recover the dumped guns."

Mad Dog exited and took a few steps. "I don't know if I'd go as far as good. I swear that this elevator shaft wasn't here before."

Taylor went out next, reclaiming Julian's hand as she did. "There's a possibility that we didn't notice it before, since we had that werewolf to deal with."

A creepy feeling slid through Julian. He would have noticed metal doors on the wall. They'd combed the perimeter for potential exits. "Option B is what, that Scarab is changing the terrain on us intentionally? To keep us going in circles?"

Breaking the hand clasp to chew a nail, Taylor looked toward the tunnel they'd crawled through, the vent still intact from when they'd replaced it. "That means they can see us. The fact that we pushed our way into this gym in the first place doesn't square with the environmental manipulation theory. If they can alter things, why didn't they trap us in the tunnel? Seal the exits, fill the crawl space with rocks, block and kill us that way?"

Julian's mouth soured as he spoke. "Psychological manipulation, maybe. A long game where they screw with our heads, break us down psychically. Demoralization."

Mad Dog took off for the original exit, which fortunately still existed. Small miracles and all. "Unless it's semi-random. We know that they can alter matter, since sending a hologram to a specific location requires molecule adjustment. Maybe that kind of stuff messes with the space time fabric."

Taylor frowned. "Making elevators appear where they weren't before seems like a stretch."

Another one of those aftershocks, faint enough that Julian might have missed it if not already aware of the sensation, wove an energetic curve through his bloodstream. "You two feel that?"

"Yeah," Taylor said. "This room is a hot zone, or it sits right above an activity epicenter, I'm guessing."

"That's what I'm saying." Mad Dog peeked through the window of the double doors. "If we're dealing with timeline manipulation here, the changes occurring could be internal or external, or some combination."

Confused, Julian looked through the rectangular slice of glass opposite Mad Dog, seeing no drones upon first sweep. "Come again?"

"Mandela Effect," Mad Dog said casually, as if everyone ought to be able to define this phenomenon easily.

"I think I've heard of that," Taylor interjected. "Doesn't it refer to a kind of collective misremembering, like how lots of people thought that Nelson Mandela died in jail, but he actually got out and went on to live a long life?"

"Precisely," Mad Dog said. "Curious George never had a tail, and Pikachu never had a stipe on *his* tail. The monopoly man never wore a monocle, and there was no cornucopia, ever, on the Fruit of the Loom underwear packaging. But people swear on their mom's lives that those features once existed. Common side effect of timeline manipulation. Maybe that elevator was always there, or maybe they went back and added it for whatever reason."

Julian looked over his shoulder, the sight of the silver doors, the trio's reflections watery apparitions against metal, suddenly spooky. He halfway expected the slabs to part and blood crests to pour forth, *The Shining*-style. He used humor as a calming agent, "Curious George had a tail, and that's a hill I'll die on. And in your example, the elevator is still an exception. Everything else is a subtraction, whereas our case study is an addition."

Mad Dog shrugged. "I don't make the rules, man."

Someone did, however, and working around those rules before Luna died was more important than philosophical brain teasers. "Coast is clear," Julian said.

They retraced old ground, no patrolling robot dogs in sight, and reclaimed their guns.

Taylor slung the soft case of her rifle over her shoulder and asked, "Do you think that they have a patrol route and moved on to some other wing of the building?"

"Yeah, that's a solid theory. They also transform into flying drones. Remember the charging bays in that loading dock? Maybe they're out scanning the park for theft or filling the air with chemicals to drug people into spending more money." Mad Dog suited up, wearing his shotgun diagonally.

"That's a thing?" Julian asked. "Drugging customers into opening their wallets?"

"Oh, yeah." Mad Dog led them down a hallway, smiling like he enjoyed having insider knowledge. "One of their primary functions is as delivery vectors of consumer narcosis substances. It's a special, lab-created formula they make here, sort of like a synthetic amalgam of heroin and amphetamines with an added dopamine payload. The park visitors breathe it in and literally get hooked on spending money."

Just when he thought his urge to nuke Scarab's theme park couldn't possibly intensify. "That's the grossest, most craven example of shameless capitalism that I've ever heard."

The three ended up at a door, a red exit sign flickering above it. Mad Dog changed the subject. "We need to go straight in now. No bypassing by way of the park."

The stairwell that they'd nixed before was still there, untouched by the Mandela Effect. Julian applied a mind over matter technique to calm his nerves. "Now that Taylor's magic is more enhanced, I'm feeling more confident about blazing right in."

"Always the eternal optimist." She gave him a small, intimate smile before her face adjusted into severity. "Magic first. If it fails, or if I go out of commission in any way, we shoot to kill."

"Right." Julian conferred a nod.

"Roger that," Mad Dog said.

"Alright." Julian stepped out in front, his heart a war drum, hoping that the others saw him as a cool, composed, and steely leader.

Taylor grabbed his elbow. "When I played Dungeons and Dragons, one of the cardinal rules was to protect the healers first." She moved in for the lead.

He didn't want to be a sexist caveman about the whole thing, but fuck if he was about to let his wife occupy the front lines in battle. With a bump of his hip, he urged her back behind him. "If the breast milk and formula stores run out or go bad, you're the only one who can feed Luna. Besides, we just discussed how your magic is our soundest bet. We can't risk you."

She shook her head. "Well, actually—"

Mad Dog butted in between the two of them, shoving each to the side as he pushed his way to the front. "For Christ sakes, quit with your little charade conflict for my benefit. We all know who's the most expendable here."

Julian heard the pain behind the guy's snarky speech and reached for his arm, intent on clearing up some misunderstanding that had arisen. "I wasn't thinking that, and neither was Taylor. It's not cynicism and abuse with us. We're better than that. Better than what you've gotten used to. We're friends."

The expression the man wore was soaked in both acid and residual traces of trauma. "Kumba-fuckin-ya. We can all trade friendship bracelets and braid each other's hair after this is over. Well, maybe Taylor and I will just braid Julian's hair. Anyway. Now. I'm the human shield here, you got that? We'll try to stay undetected at first, but I have a strong feeling that plan will dissolve pretty quickly. You two ready for action, or what?"

"Yes," Taylor and Julian said in unison as he filed the vestiges of his anxiety into spears.

"Alright." Mad Dog pushed open the door. Instantly, the earthquake aftershock feeling, those reverberations coming in swelling waves at timed intervals, bubbled up from below. "Get ready to see some truly wild shit that is sure to boggle the outer reaches of your imagination."

As Julian descended the dingy stairwell, a depressing medley of stained concrete and ancient, painted metal, he knew those words to be true. Hated them to be true, as he took his wife's hand for his comfort and support as much as hers.

TWENTY-TWO

TAYLOR FINISHED CASING A GENERIC, EMPTY BALLROOM AND JOGGED out into the hallway. They'd gone down two floors and ended up in some level used for gatherings. Mad Dog stood watch by the door, glancing over his shoulder every few seconds like something was going on. Julian wasn't at the lookout post he'd assumed while she surveyed the big room.

"What's up?" Taylor asked Mad Dog.

"Julian's checking the room across the hall. He said that he heard some guys leave and got a hunch that there might be a lead."

Unfortunately, since she and Julian had to make eye contact to communicate telepathically, she'd have to see for herself. She bypassed the door they'd emerged from that led right back to the stairwell, poked her head into the new space, and scowled, not seeing much of anything.

Slightly larger than a master bedroom and laid with distressed hardwood flooring scuffed by much foot traffic, the area was bereft of furnishings. Its most interesting feature was a three-sided mirror, the type found in dressing rooms, built into one corner.

And where was Julian? What of possible value could he have found in here?

"Hello?" she said tentatively, her soft question echoing in the emptiness.

"I'm in the back." Excitement crackled across his statement, enough to widen her eyes. "Come check this out."

Following the origin of his voice led her to a doorway shielded with a curtain, this discreet entrance tucked away next to the mirror. She pushed the fabric aside, smelling mothball musk, and instantly found herself in solidarity with his interest.

Racks of clothing were arranged in rows with the aesthetically bland efficiency of a thrift store. The fabrics that hung on the hangers were thick, lush, lacy, velvety.

Julian stood between two clothing-filled towers, their heights dwarfing his six-foot frame, and pawed through items with gusto. Each arrangement was separated into two sections, the lower batch of hangers easily reachable without ladder assistance.

Several card tables pushed against the wall supported a lineup of severed Styrofoam heads. Some were capped with wigs, while others wore masks molded to look like animal faces or smooth slabs as reflective as the polished cutlery on the table.

A costume shop. She permitted herself a modest laugh, joining him at a rack. Hangers grazed bars with metallic zings as she leafed past poofy Victorian dresses, gowns spun from decadent, slippery silk, and a few different styles of tuxedos.

There was no order, with men's and women's outfits mixed together, unsorted by era or occasion. She pulled out a cow costume complete with a goofy rubber mask stuffed in a plastic bag. "Find any druid robes?"

He flipped through frocks. "Not yet."

She chewed her bottom lip, taking a second look at some ensemble involving lots of sequins and a fluffy boa, crimson feathers slipping silkily between her fingers. A black block caught her eye from a few rows away, a gaggle of skirt hems grazing the support bar of the collection below it. She went to the curious development and ran a hand across the cluster of around ten dresses, robes, or whatever they were, finding the material smooth yet thick, blended to balance sturdiness with a sumptuous look and feel. Her heart surged when she touched a very druid-y hood. "I think we've found our contender."

Julian spoke from the opposite side. "Yeah. They're robes alright. And they have an entire batch in red."

She ducked around the corner, where, sure enough, he held the lower half of a costume out far enough to reveal its features. A robe indeed, like one a druid would wear, with a hood and bell sleeves. The spot that housed these robes was less densely packed than the section with the black ones, suggesting that the red group had been picked over.

He said, "I say we each put on one of these and start moving around like we're supposed to be here. No more ducking and hiding. If we're out in the open, we increase our chances of overhearing something that could lead us to Luna."

Anxiety came on like a plague of grasshoppers. She and Julian were little more than puny playthings enslaved to the whims of fate. Choose the wrong costume? Dead. "What if we pick the wrong color? Then our cover is blown the moment someone sees us."

His nostrils flared, eyes shadowing with clouds. "I mean, they are planning a blood sacrifice. Stands to reason that the color of the day would be red."

Her gaze drifted to the robe, its hue as sanguine and saturated as the outpouring of a heavy flow day. While Julian's plan was sound, aspects of it didn't sit well. Hiding in plain sight was hugely risky in the best of circumstances, and they didn't have a strong grasp of the territory, let alone its inhabitants. "What if someone thinks we're one of them, starts talking to us, and we say the wrong thing and arouse suspicion?"

"Mad Dog's good at bullshitting. Remember how he worked that guy in the elevator? We'll put him in charge of communications and figure out how to improvise."

An aftershock roared through, that disturbing calling card of something big happening or about to happen. She worried her lip. There wasn't going to be a fail-safe, perfect solution. "Let's find the ladder."

Following a brief search, she ended up twisting the loose knob of a wooden door.

Inside was a basic storage closet with a broom and dustpan, some paper towels and a spray bottle of fabric freshener, and the step stool they sought.

About a dozen pixelated photos on computer paper, run off in color from a printer, were stuck with push pins into a hanging corkboard. The subject in most of them was the gray truck from the loading zone, snapped from various angles and distances, captured at locations ranging from a home driveway to a gas station to a stoplight intersection. A close-up showed that it had no license plate.

Several snaps of an attractive, red-haired woman, leaving a house or entering a different one, rounded out a plethora of truck pics.

"Bizarre." Taylor worked her phone free and snapped a few shots. Someone at Scarab was interested in this gray truck and redhead, meaning Taylor was too. Was the woman an investigative reporter, or a jilted former employee like Mad Dog? FBI?

"Speaking of bizarre." Julian pointed to the adjacent wall.

She shuddered when she saw what was displayed there, a blatantly macabre decoration.

A plastic human skeleton, a couple of feet tall and to scale, hung upside down and crucified. A note hung from its toe, words in blocky penmanship reading, "This little dummy tried to push a number through. Don't let this happen to you."

She took a picture. "Have we gone over yet how much we hate this place?"

He made a noise of acknowledgment, steering her away with a pull on her side. "Let's get those costumes."

They'd gotten three robes off the rack and even managed to return the stool and close the supply room when the front door opened. Calm male voices travelled, muffled slightly, the frocks absorbing a syllable here, an inflection there.

"Shit," she mouthed it wordlessly, slipped the robe on, and slid between two random costumes. She could only pray they didn't look down and see her feet, didn't notice the robe out of place amidst the colorful hodgepodge of fabrics.

Julian did the same, landing right in front of her, the hood of the robe intended for Mad Dog slung limply over his shoulder like an unconscious body.

A fog of adrenaline undercut by the unpleasant smells of other people's underarms, persistent against aggressively perfumed detergent, made for a stifling miasma.

Her pulse jacked. She slid a stare past Julian's arm, craning to see over a frilly dress, and listened.

The first guy sounded young, confident, and douche-y, like a frat boy. "Dude, for real. I'm just asking a question. What's so great about immortality that we gotta do all of this? I'm, like, not that afraid of death."

Metal scraped against metal, a second one speaking as he perused options. "Who cares. The whole thing about becoming godlike is bullshit, bruh, and everyone but the true believer crazies know it. This is about networking and meeting important people, donors and mentors, shit like that. If we get through Song of Virgo without fainting or freaking out, we're *set*. I mean set for life, hooked up. Cushy Wall Street jobs, big cash injections for Silicon Valley startups, public office. That's fire-ass pussy guaranteed for *life*, son."

Bro Number One laughed heartily, the thought of objectifying women apparently renewing his zeal for black magic. "Better be. Like, I thoroughly expect to pick a new piece of ass out of an underwear catalog every night for the rest of my life. Have it delivered and shit, naked, to my doorstep. Enthusiastic about servicing my sexual demands without being too slutty about the whole thing."

Now it was Bro Number Two's turn to laugh, though his was hollow enough to haunt. "For what we've gotta tolerate? Hell yeah. I thoroughly expect to shoot a hot load in a supermodel's face this evening. Or butt fuck that chick that just won three Oscars."

The gross comment tapered into a pause, no sound coming except those metallic scratches.

"Do you think that the Harvard senior from rush week was telling the truth?" he sounded skittish, as if begging for a no.

"Nah." His "a" sound went on too long, exaggerated enough to discredit him.

"Liar." A clattering noise. "Whatever. I'll lie naked in a coffin or pour goat's blood over my dick, but I'm not digging out a baby's brain with an ice cream scoop or whatever. That's, like, a hard no."

"Tell that to Satan, when they summon him." He stretched out his s's, mimicking how snakes in cartoons hissed, and they both chuckled like ritualistically murdering Taylor's daughter was the funniest thing in the entire world.

Her heart crushed further back into her chest. Julian's shoulders jumped as he tensed. She tried to swallow the root of her tongue in some instinctual effort to beat back vomit. The room spun, hot and smelly, colorful clothing barfed up everywhere.

Ice cream scoop. Baby. Brain. Luna.

"It's a rumor, dickweed. Pure fiction to haze the recruits." Yet the doubting Thomas now spoke with anemic upswing, his periods question marks, consonants and vowels huddled together in a blurry, mealy-mouthed quiver.

Conversation halted, and the scratching of hanger over bar soon stilled. All she heard was her breath and pulse, the cries of her child rising from some distant place.

"Boo!" Bro Number One shouted, closer than before, booming enough to make Taylor slap a hand over her mouth and leap backwards.

Bro Number Two shrieked, the sound shriller than she'd imagined a man was capable of uttering. "Fuck you."

"No way. I'm holding out for something better. Go grab us masks." Bro Number One enjoyed a belly laugh at his pal's expense. Following rustling noises and a muted thump, audible traces of a scuffle, perhaps, the door to the main entrance shut with a click.

Taylor held on to Julian for support. He turned around in a swift motion and hugged her until she felt grounded enough not to scream or cry.

Brain. Baby. Ice cream scoop. Hazy, unspeakable images whipped her beleaguered mind into a heinous compilation reel of bloody nightmare shots.

"Stop thinking about it," Julian said with a loving husband's strength and authority. "We're close now, getting closer. That stuff we heard was coming from the vicinity of the inner circle. We must keep going. Have to stay strong."

"I'm trying." The words eked out, weak and shaking, but in his arms, she found the ability to stand tall again and reassemble herself. A big inhale and exhale steadied her breathing, her resolve, what remained intact of her composure. She had black magic to use if need be. She wiped unshed tears. "Let's see if these robes are baggy enough to conceal our guns and backpacks."

Julian stepped into the open and turned around. The bulge of his pack gave him a mild hunchback appearance, but nothing too conspicuous. She offered thumbs up and turned her pack to the front for balance. It'd look weird if all three of them had those sloped, round backs.

His eyes misted, lips pushing out into a soft pout. "You look...passable."

Pregnant. She looked pregnant, and the emotions that state evoked were too painful to talk about. Her mouth twisted into a pathetic fragment of a smile, and she patted her fake belly. "I do, don't I?"

He touched the outer corner of one eye, sniffling. "If those two needed face coverings, then I'm guessing we do also."

Trouble was this decision presented another mind-boggling dilemma. The model heads sported every manner of animal mask, elaborate masquerade ball number, and plastic political spoof costume imaginable. The setup was nothing like the costumes, where at least robes were grouped.

"Let's ask Mad Dog if he knows anything," she told a bulbous, ruddy caricature of Richard Nixon.

"Good call." Julian hiked the third robe into the crook of his elbow, and they passed through the empty room with the mirror.

Mad Dog stood at his post, face slack with boredom, and dropped the canteen straw out of his mouth when Taylor and Julian approached. "Looks like it's time to suit up, eh?"

"Yeah," Taylor said. "Except we weren't sure which masks to pick."

Mad Dog scowled. "They didn't have any ski masks?"

"Not that we saw," Julian said. "That's what we're after?"

Mad Dog put on his smug smile. "Follow me, kids." He led them back into the costume warehouse. "FYI, I've got a catheter situation set up, in case opportunities for bathroom breaks become rare."

A few seconds later, he pulled a box out from under the table and whipped out three black ski masks. Instead of holes for the mouth and eyes, each was stitched with a grid of delicate mesh netting.

Taylor spied red masks in the box. "You sure we don't want red on red?"

Mad Dog bent one shoulder in a shrug. "I'm not positive, but based on my research, I think it's a safe bet that we want to go with red robes and black masks for the Song of Virgo. Red because the sacrifice is the main event, black because supposedly, Virgo is where new initiates spy the black goo for the first time. Hence, a black shield over the face to signal fealty to our lord and master, the black goo." He shimmied into his robe, opting to slide his pack to the front for the full-bellied look.

Julian pulled the black mask over his face, transforming into someone disquietingly unknowable in an instant, and finished off the setup with a pop of his hood. "What the hell is the black goo?"

"The essence of pure evil, allegedly." Mad Dog reached into his robe and pulled his drinking straw to peek up from the collar. "Dredged from the pits of hell, they say. They worship it, make sacrifices to it, in hopes of drawing from its formidable power. My contacts say that their scientists figured out how to make it reproduce. They extract bits of it, grow them in petri dishes, and put the offspring in their various chemical and bio products."

Taylor tugged the thin, stretchy cloth over her face. Her breath came out muggy against used fabric incubating trapped traces of sweat and halitosis, and the eyepiece shrouded her vision in a network of miniature tic-tac-toes, but at least they'd be able to see while remaining obscure. "This black goo is basically like a sentient, evil Kombucha starter?"

"Scarab's pride and joy." Mad Dog sipped water. "Shall we?"

Out they went, but not before Taylor checked the three-way mirror for keys, notes, or anything else helpful that could have been slipped between panes of glass and the wall. She found nothing but figured that canvasing any object that stuck out as unusual was a good habit.

Julian touched her lower back before they settled into their incognito roles.

The hallway they chose to traverse, undecorated but laid with bland carpet, bottomed out in a T-intersection around twenty feet up.

They opened doors to investigate rooms along the way, excuse about a lost phone at the ready, finding nothing of import. Anti-climatic emptiness included conference rooms without butts in their many rows of chairs, a unisex bathroom that Mad Dog briefly used, and a closet stuffed with cardboard boxes of bulk coffee pods and nutrition bars. Everyone was elsewhere, in the epicenter of the action.

A red robe legion, ten people at least, crossed the intersection in a sea of purposeful movement.

Taylor killed the urge to freeze and walked in their direction, thankful that none of the disguised were speaking. Easier to blend in without having to introduce or explain oneself.

The trio caught up to the new people, joining them at the back of the pack, and all marched silently down a hallway. Taylor lost a bit of her footing, her steps quickening as her feet escaped from her total control, and it didn't take her long to grasp why.

The hallway sloped into a downward incline. Awkwardly shuffling in overly self-conscious motions—she did *not* want to fall and make a spectacle of herself—she stopped when the others did.

Weaving and bobbing for a better look at what lay ahead was useless. There were too many bodies, and of course the vision-impeding properties of the ski mask didn't help.

The red-clad others began sliding out of sight feet first, and she soon caught a glimpse of slotted metal steps in motion. An escalator. Okay. She boarded, checking her sides for Julian and Mad Dog. Confirmed. Beads of sweat stung her eyes, salted her lips.

When the escalator opened into a clearing of sorts, white marble walls and matching floor tile suggested a ritualistic element. Good. Meant they were in the right place.

There was no escalator going back up. They'd damn well better be in the right place.

The other robed bodies divided evenly to stand against each wall in single file, twin lines straddling an arched doorway she couldn't really see into. She assumed her place, Julian beside her, and Mad Dog across the hall.

Like a ghost floating up from an abandoned well, a white-robed person in matching gloves walked out of the doorway in big steps of leadership. They carried a wand, shiny obsidian sphere capping a staff of porcelain. Their face covering was a fat drop of blood on ivory sheets.

Suddenly, and with great urgency, she wanted to kill this sick freak. Rip out his throat so he could choke on real blood as it flooded his lungs. But not before Luna was safe. After, well, some of the tormentors might have to pay.

With rounded, bold command, the man in white said, "Welcome, initiates and hopefuls. The Song of Virgo will commence shortly. Before undertaking this most special of rites, we shall swear fealty to Chaos and recite the Prayer to Folly in efforts to pledge our eternal souls to our exalted sister and The Ones whose essence She carries within. Then, as you know, we must weed out the unlucky as a blood offering to Her. Follow, now."

He turned and re-entered the pit, an apparition swallowed by darkness. The moment bodies started moving and merged into single file, Taylor was up on the heels of the person in front of her. She wasn't scared anymore. She was ready. Beyond ready.

Eager, as she stepped over the threshold and smelled spicy incense fit for a church.

These appalling wastes of oxygen were about to be sorry they'd crossed her. A dark plume of power, arousing as any intoxicant, flared in her center. Bring. It. On.

TWENTY-THREE

THE SCENE WAS LIKE A HALLUCINOGENIC PORTRAIT OF AN ILLUMINATI conspiracy ball but crazier and on steroids.

Julian felt like a mule had kicked out his wind. Unreal, the stuff he was looking at. Things that seemed wrong to look at, desecrated, sickness to the soul. Out of context, the imagery would have appeared benign enough. Not in this twisted church.

Flanking the doorway, an equally divided number of robed bodies made a semicircle. His fingers twitched with an urge to seize Taylor, but of course he couldn't, or they'd be made on the spot. Instead, he sent her a telepathic pep talk, *We're close. We've got this.*

The person beside him kept shifting on his feet, restless, smelling of marijuana and anxiety. Julian empathized. The entire thing was madness and drenched in the terrible excretion of what was to come.

The legion of the cloaked waited in a white room forged in creamy marble with vaulted ceilings that aspired to poke spires into heaven. In the dead center of the room was a black cube the size of a dinner table, ebony polished to a sheen that absorbed and reflected the bright light emanating from overhead. A golden bingo ball cage comprised the table centerpiece.

Someone had burned large quantities of bitter herbs, resulting in a smell thick with the threat of ceremony.

The red-masked, white-robed man who'd come out to deliver the greeting stood behind the cube, holding his wand.

In the belly of their gilt prison, caged onyx spheres lay idle, miniature versions of the bulb capping the man in white's staff. Didn't take a genius to figure out that whatever had been planned to involve this bingo game was dire.

Silence was oppressive, formidable, an invisible monster. Moments passed in torturous agony.

Without warning, the leader of the shit show slammed the butt of his staff into the ground, producing a booming echo. Julian bit his tongue as the reverberations vibrated, tasting blood.

A flurry of red as everyone knelt, Julian bringing his knees onto the punishing press of the hard ground in unity with the herd.

From this new vantage point, he saw that the floor was carved with an intricate network of grooves as deep as his wedding ring and just as wide. He swallowed, sweat pooling on his lower back as he shifted the point of his aching kneecap off a gap with as much discretion as was feasible to muster.

Rubber soles squeaked against flooring when the guy in charge approached the semi-circle and stopped before a person at one of the far ends. "Initiate, or hopeful?" his voice was mild yet proud, curious, like he genuinely believed in this.

The suggestion of fanaticism gave Julian the heebie-jeebies. Something about the smug disdain of those punks in the outfit rental room nursed his nerves with a false sense of security. If this was all a big joke, like he'd halfway convinced himself, nobody involved would fight that hard for it.

"In...initiate," a young man stammered, his voice cracking.

Julian cringed, thankful that not a soul could see the facial evidence of his embarrassment sympathy.

"Loyalty oath," the master of ceremonies demanded.

"I swear fealty to Chaos, and the elemental sister Folly, who governs this most mighty element, until I draw my last breath." He got the words past his throat amidst stutters and verbal stumbles, barely.

"Very well." The ringleader used the cap of his wand to tap the kid on the forehead and moved down the line, pausing at the next genuflector. "Initiate or hopeful?"

"Hopeful," a woman of indeterminate age spoke, her voice wooden like she was working diligently to overcompensate for oppressive fear.

"Prayer to Folly."

"I embrace myself as a fundamental mistake, forged in the disorder of filth and slime. As an initiate of yours, I call upon you and your command of chaos, to curse me with your exalted blaspheme. May I embody the essence of sin and spread misery as your caprice sees fit."

That was horrendous. Worse, how to know which declaration to pick? The loyalty oath sounded remotely less bad.

"Very well." The young lady got the same treatment as the first dude, and the boss man went to the next person.

Hopefuls and initiates named themselves in roughly equal number, and identity aspects like age, gender, and what he could determine of ethnicity didn't seem to matter in terms of who went with what.

Red on White reached Taylor. Julian could smell his feet, noting at the close range how he was short for a man, with sloped shoulders. Beatable, even armed with that staff.

"Initiate, or hopeful?"

"Initiate." Her tone was hard to read, smart how well she was able to compose herself, but the speed and ease at which she delivered her line upset him.

Suddenly, initiate sounded more formal and further along in this vile, secretive process. He didn't want that for Taylor. He didn't want her advancing in the ranks, clearing milestones.

"Loyalty oath."

He held his breath like stopping air would plug his ears.

"I swear fealty to Chaos, and the elemental sister Folly, who governs this most mighty element, until I draw my last breath." She spoke as smooth as butter, accentuating the words "Chaos" and "Folly" with a kind of satisfied, ceremonial lilt.

She had to be acting to fit in. Had to be, couldn't be enjoying the recitation for real.

The disdain in him spread, bottomless and alienating. He fixed his stare on one of the cracks that dug tributaries into the floor, ran the wound on his tongue over his top teeth, and tried not to think about anything other than which choice to pick.

The speech for hopeful was grosser and more dehumanizing, but in theory mimicking Taylor might arouse suspicion since people saw them arrive together.

A wall of white imposed against his little grated eye holes and pushed him closer to a decision. "Initiate, or hopeful?"

Fuck it. Julian didn't consider himself an egotistical man, but he had too much pride in his heritage, family, and ancestors, to recite that crap about being a filthy mistake. "Initiate."

They went through the routine, Julian bothered and distracted by Taylor's behavior even as he said his loyalty oath. Something wasn't right.

When the time came, Mad Dog picked hopeful. The way he said his piece was lowkey amusing, delivered in a self-aware fashion suited to his trademark self-deprecation.

He wasn't taking this ritual all that seriously, Julian could tell by his snide, cheeky over-affectation as he talked about being a mistake. A small ding in the tension amidst glum intensity and formal prognostications voiced in quaking doom. Sharp pain stabbed his knees, the stress position becoming increasingly less bearable.

But his comfort wasn't the priority. He'd let a mobster smash those same kneecaps with a rusty pipe if it meant that his baby girl would live.

Once finished with the hopefuls and initiates, Red on White took his wand and foot stink back to the black cube, where he turned a crank on the cage to make the balls bounce. "As you know, our Exalted One is fickle, with an appetite for pain."

"All hail!" A few participants shouted, likely a calculated risk or educated guess on the best way to reply.

"Silence, pigs," bellowed Red on White. "She revels in the senseless, the random, the power of luck, good *or* bad, to sate her whims and fancies."

Nobody said a goddamn word this time, good little pigs who'd lost their squeals.

The leader pulled a ball and held it up between pinched fingers, a marking Julian failed to make out drawn on one side. Without warning,

Red on White tossed the ball on the floor, where it clattered and rattled before finding a grove and sliding down it, pinball-machine style. The floor must've been subtly slanted or been moved by a mechanical force underneath.

One of the tremors quaked up from underground, replacing Julian's guess work with explanation. Whatever was going on down there, they used it to make these ceremonies happen.

The ball stopped at the knees of a guy two people down from Julian, one of the costume room shitheads judging by how he'd talked during the pledge.

"Retrieve your token and rise."

The man obeyed, his hand shaking. When he looked at the sphere, he started to whimper. "Please. No."

"Silence!"

He couldn't fully shut up, resorting to gurgling gasps instead. A small puddle formed below his blood red hem, pale yellow against new snow.

"Read your numbers, as gifted to you by the fateful hand of Chaos."

"Six. Four. Two." Followed by a keening wail of defeat, prelude to a death knell.

"What is your birthday?" a taunting element came with the prod, the sound of perverse delight.

"June seventh, two-thousand and two."

"A fifty-fifty probability split goes to Chaos!" Proclaiming with gusto, Red on White raised his arms. "Come forth."

The hapless victim hung his head and complied, sobbing.

Julian wanted, more than anything except saving Luna, for this hell to end. He closed his eyes, tried to dissociate, or daydream, but being able to hear but not see made it worse. He nixed the fantasy of escape and braced himself.

"Lie on the desecrated cube and prostrate yourself to Folly, in preparation to receive her gift of chaos. Remember, unluck is luck. A curse is a blessing. Entropy is harmony, for us who believe and worship."

Nodding weakly, the guy did as ordered, filling the slab with his vulnerable body.

Red on White procured a tiny bell from somewhere and rang it, the trill a razor slice through funky air.

A wraith of a figure appeared, coated from hair to toes in black fabric that ended at a flowing train oozing over tile like an ink blot on computer paper. The sword they carried rounded out their dark bride ensemble.

True to the grim reaper character they also evoked, the new factor in the equation brought the sword down on the initiate's soft underbelly.

There were screams, unmoored cries of animal agony, spliced with moans from the audience. Julian looked away, a piece of his innocence dying along with this sacrifice from the costume shop, but he didn't escape the sight of blood as it filled the marble grooves on which they all stood.

Invading, sick smells wouldn't allow him to forget either. Meaty, rotten, coppery, and sharp, it sang a dark reminder of what had happened, pounding in space like a tell-tale heart.

Julian didn't know the deceased, hell, from what he did know, the guy came off like a jackass, but he mustered a silent prayer for his soul all the same. He'd died in vain, for meaninglessness and evil. No one deserved a wasted life.

"Do you have a grievance, hunchback?" Red on White shouted, pointing his staff at Julian. The wand hovered over the dead body, the slain man's guts heaped on the outside, where they should not be.

Shit, what had he done to give himself away? A solid reminder that they were being watched at all times, never below the radar and not allowed to get lazy despite wearing the outfit of anonymity. "No."

"Very well, then." Red on White turned the handle and spun the cage once again.

The grim reaper type grabbed the corpse by the wrists, and dead flesh hit the ground with a sickening thump before being dragged off, leaving a streak. The sword stayed on the cube.

Six more rounds of the lottery happened, one more poor person meeting the blade, screaming during the selection that the ball that came to her wasn't even supposed to be there.

Julian guessed that the "push a number through" reference from the storage closet referred to the act of somehow surreptitiously removing damning birthday numbers. Mercifully, no balls of fate landed at Julian, Taylor, or Mad Dog, though it wasn't time to celebrate yet.

"Folly's thirst is *temporarily* quenched," Red on White exclaimed snidely while the reaper dragged the butchered remains of the unfortunate woman across the bloodied floor. "But do not rest easy, initiates and hopefuls, for She has been known to grow quite insatiable during the Song of Virgo. You may yet be called upon to appease."

Julian hated this fucking guy, from his breezy, sneering sadism to his stupid clown getup. The bastard got off on it, an inconsequential and runty moron who felt big and powerful, for once, underneath his baggy dress.

"Let the reaping commence," Red on White called out abruptly, an announcement to serve a celebration of the highest caliber.

Cheers erupted, boisterous and hearty, complete with clapping that Julian forced himself to join in on. He glanced at Taylor and sent a telepathic message of calming, but she wasn't facing him. He couldn't be sure if the communication got through.

Red on White let the conviviality happen until it began to die down naturally, bobbing his staff in the air to quell the final stirrings. "Your fidelity today does not go unrecognized, and in honor of your brethren who courageously gave themselves over to sustain Folly, I have authorized the conference upon you of a curse most sinful and lovely. Initiates and hopefuls, I present to you, the daughter of Titans."

An aftershock gripped the room, and as it faded to shivers, a woman blinked into existence the same way the werewolf in the gym had. She was pale enough that he could see her vessels and blue veins from ten feet away. Her eyes were an unnatural shade of violet.

Her hair was twisted up in a black turban, and she wore a red turtleneck dress, conservative in coverage, shielding both wrists and ankles.

An object was concealed by her neckline, popping into relief in a ring shape against the material.

"Disrobe and unmask." This from Red on White, with his usual flair.

Oh, no. Was a sex magic event afoot? How would he shirk that?

In his peripheral vision, he caught Taylor shake and twitch. *Stand straighter*, he urged.

Her posture stiffened. *I'm scared.*

Instead of removing her dress, the new woman undid the bind

securing her hair, and as she unraveled a long reel of fabric, Julian could tell after a couple of inches that she wasn't right under the wrap.

When it hit full force, his eyes bugged, though he'd suffered a mini-preview of such an atrocity back at the hotel. A mass of squirming, writhing, agitated snakes in a variety of girths and color patterns wiggled where her hair should have been. Several were coiled, tight and angry with readiness to strike. Rattles like the one in Mad Dog's head buzzed. A fat beast the color of muddy grass snapped at open air, hook of a fang catching a glimmer.

His lower back muscles clenched, the fear in the room permeating his senses with a jab of hot, sharp quiet. He could sense in his marrow the tension, clenched jaws, and censored yelps, no one daring to show weakness.

"Bequeath, daughter of Titan." Red on White banged his staff into the floor again.

The snake-haired woman approached a quivering person, cupped their masked face in her hands, and brought them into kissing distance. She whispered words in a lost language, incantations that sent her serpentine locks into a twisting frenzy.

One struck, and his guts bolted up his throat, locking down as the man yelped in pain and rubbed his shoulder.

A similar version of the original incident happened to everyone until she got to Taylor. The Medusa stared into the red curtain of Taylor's veil, her features softening as snakes went relaxed then fully flaccid. They faced off for a while, transfixed.

Time condensed to a droplet while he stared at an exchange so uncannily prophetic that he was sure he wasn't supposed to see it. The effect was like witnessing seductive propaganda, dreamy and stupefying with a dirty aftertaste.

Movement resumed as it had stalled, the Medusa speaking a phrase that riled her snakes into aggression. He reviewed a couple of crackpot, implausible strategies for preventing Taylor from getting bitten, though intuitively he knew to let the scene play out.

A lithe, indigo ribbon of a serpent hit Taylor near her ear. She didn't react save for an iridescent, aquamarine sparkle that engulfed the surface of her for less than a second before fading into errant flecks of glitter that died off individually.

The snake woman played it off cool, dealing her blows to recipients who moaned or hollered in protest.

When she reached Julian, he looked past the snakes into her unnatural, purple eyes far enough to see the buried trauma. She didn't want to be here. She was trapped. Suffering. He studied the object under her turtleneck. A collar.

He scanned her for other anomalies, pilfering a glimpse of a chunky black box attached below her ankle by a strap. Looked like a tracking bracelet like the equipment used on house arrest prisoners, a device that ensured her submission.

She held his face and whispered her line in disconnected monotone.

He whispered, "Why are you here? What's in this for you?"

She said things he couldn't understand, showing no recognition, though mist formed over her eyes, someone trapped in there begging to be free. A small cobra reared back, flaring its hood.

"We can help you." Julian reached for his healing magic, reached in deep to pull forth the person locked in her, imprisoned under brainwashing. "Me and the woman who sparkled when you bit her. Don't tell me you didn't see her reaction. We're like you. Magic. Abilities."

Her chin quivered, and for a second he thought he'd flipped her, but her face hardened into an aloof mask before a breakthrough occurred.

An electric stab of pain punctured his neck, a poison setting in fast to space him out, drain his thoughts in preparedness for input to go into the emptied vessel. But his healing magic kicked in, swift, shoving the toxin out of the hole made by the fangs. A warm trickle seeped over his collarbone.

She moved on. Julian lobbed a question Taylor's way in case connection through the masks was possible.

What impact did the bite have on you, babe? How do you feel?

Taylor turned her head a few degrees in his direction, a deliberate, slow flow to the swivel of her neck, and he caught a flare of the blue sparkle igniting under the fabric.

TWENTY-FOUR

THEY WERE JOINED NOW, TAYLOR AND THE CHAOS WITCH. SHE'D drunk the forbidden elixir. Venom murmured secrets into her bloodstream, mysteries of a forbidden bite.

Enhanced by her coven sister's power, her own magic shifted, merged, mining to depths previously unimagined. Soon, she'd be unstoppable. And she wouldn't stop. Not after saving Luna.

She'd keep going until the hunger no longer demanded feeding. An abyss within her gaped wider, a cosmic serpent to swallow the world.

The snake witch finished her task and joined the man in white at the altar. They stood side by side like a pair of sentinels. Streams of blood branched across the floor.

She focused on the glint in Julian's brown iris, just enough shining out beneath the mask to establish contact. *I'm augmented. I made contact with her. Collaboration. Partner work. This is good.*

Are you sure that it's good?

She was sure. Set right. Calm with resolve. Purpose. Dormant energy. A sleeping shark drifting through a mellow ocean current. Soon, she'd strike. But not now. Now, she'd bask in the depths of herself, bathed in blue lightning, bathed in potential. Fierce. Hot.

Light behaves as a particle and a wave based on the nature of the observer.

The thought didn't originate from Taylor the person. Did it go to Julian anyway?

What does that mean, babe? For us? For what we're doing?

A realization shot up from a recess. *I need the spirit witch. The enlightened one. We need her, to harness the light. Move at the speed of light and win this war.*

Helen from Minnesota? We need her to win a war?

All of us. A teardrop struck the center of a placid lake to create concentric circles that stretched to infinity, touching the remotest corners of the universe with magic consequence. Six witches, connected, far-flung yet tethered by thin wisps of spider webbing. *The prophecy comes by all of us.*

You're scaring me, Taylor.

The next thought was both hers and not hers, a product of many, *don't fear.*

A speech from the ringleader quashed the telepathic interlude before Julian had a chance to reply, shoving the possessed part of Taylor into a crevice. "You have drunk of the filth, now, sipped of the blasphemous cup. Ye shall feast, taste of the sweet meat, and ascend to your posts from which ye shall serve."

Initiates and hopefuls spoke at once. "Let the reaping commence."

Taylor wasn't compelled. Her magic had saved her from the mind control. Also, the king's English bullshit that Casper insisted on spewing was tiresome and pretentious.

"Feast, and ascend," the head honcho cried.

"Feast," the crowd threw back, pliant, and the call and response chant continued.

Taylor stared at the chaos witch, her squirming hair and serene countenance, the glow of her youthful skin. She needed to get her alone. Isolated and on their side. First, she sent a question to Julian. *Were you impacted by the bite in any way that you can tell?*

I don't think so. My healing magic pushed the poison out. A pause in which she could hear him think, formulate. *Are you feeling like yourself again?*

Unless she paid active attention to the possession, the influence ebbed. She had to figure out how to harness and control the passenger, establish total control. *Yes. For now. Can you tell if Mad Dog was affected?*

Not sure.

Call and response chanting ended with Casper whacking his staff on the ground. A bone-rattling earthquake followed. The disturbance got the chaos witch's snakes worked up, coiling, and hissing as a few lashed out. She stood unbothered, hands clasped below her navel.

The ground started to move. In a circle, then sliding downward while the roundabout motion continued. The floor tilted, not much, but enough to nauseate by vertigo.

The marble room lowered, exposing granite behind it, dark gray walls covered in grooves like the ones that lined the floor. The pathways were carved into shapes, sigils, and charts, and the longer she looked, the more she could tell that these etchings resembled ones in her book.

Her axis of perception tilted, equilibrium disoriented by the onslaught of different motions at once.

Vision spinning with dizziness, she watched more and more graphs slide into view. Lines connected symbols into a diamond shape. She saw her water symbol in several of the drawings.

She'd do anything to take pictures.

Movement ceased, the room still whirling for her. She looked up in search of more meaningful scars on the rock face and swallowed a scream. The spatial configuration of their confines had changed into a cone shape, with the white room rendered into the narrowest point of a funnel that opened to reveal a hall of horrors.

Evenly spaced and built into the rock were six prisms of light, hexagons, emitting bright white glows shimmering intermittently with all the colors of the rainbow.

Squinting against the glare, she forced herself to stare into light nearly as blinding as the sun for long enough to make out that each one contained a shape. A creature the size of a dinosaur.

There were dragon's tails and leather bat wings, their span larger than a bungalow. Open mouths full of teeth, scales, red eyes. Blood from the recent sacrifices filled the carved symbols in-between cages, delivering red lines into each of the prisms.

These had to be the Titans. Bloodthirsty ones.

The man in white said, "Divide evenly now, initiates and hopefuls."

Following a logic known only to their brainwashed legion and master, the robed participants split up to make small groups. Each assembled beneath a Titan.

There was just one problem, a big enough one to crater Taylor's spirits. By adding three people to the group, her party had created an odd number. Her best bet was to hide behind a tall person and pray that the leader didn't notice the odd group of four. Julian was the logical choice for cover.

As a bonus, they'd be sticking together.

She'd set her sights on her husband and moved one foot in front of the other when the man in white pointed his staff at her. "The water witch, by contrast, shall join her sister at the altar as we begin the Song of Virgo."

Her world went black. Shit. How long had he known? Shock careened through her. This whole thing could have been a setup from the get-go. An elaborate ruse to lure her into this very pit. Was Mad Dog in on it? Monty? Tim, even? Who knew? But she had to play it cool.

On her way up to the cube, she messaged Julian, *I'm busted. Going to try and use magic to incapacitate him if things go bad.*

Be careful. He's the only potential lead on Luna.

True. Taking him out too soon didn't serve the recovery effort. She walked to the black box, no entrance or exit in sight.

The man in white flicked his wrist to urge her to move forward faster. "Disrobe and unmask, Taylor McClure. Guns won't help you here. Lay your book upon the altar, and your coven sister shall follow suit."

Fuck. Fuckfuckfuck. If nothing else, she was buying time. At least he hadn't mentioned Julian or Mad Dog, possibly assuming that they were brainwashed and complacent.

She stepped out of her robe, peeling off the mask with a traitorous rush of pleasure as she finally got a good breath after over an hour of stewing in others' bacteria.

Propping her gun and backpack against the cube, she removed her book and laid it down closed, her palms sweaty against the leather cover.

"Daughter of Titan," the ringleader said.

The chaos witch opened a drawer in the cube. A book sat in there. A key did, too. Snakes curling and angry an inch beside Taylor's face, the other woman laid her tome beside Taylor's.

A blob of energy the color of concrete bloomed in the space between the volumes and stretched to a wire, connecting them.

Black smoke issued from the books, undulating in the air like ectoplasm.

The man in white waved his wand through the sooty clouds, collecting a good amount around the bulb of his wand until it looked like cotton candy spun from dust.

He walked to the wall etchings, singing in a creepy, lost tongue, and touched them one by one with the black orb surrounded by dark steam.

The patterns lit up on contact, black and blue with flashing lights.

Taylor whispered to her companion, "What the hell is happening?"

She replied, hushed and breathy, "They are dead, but dreaming. With the help of the coven daughters, the Song of Virgo shall supply the opening note of their reawakening."

Bad.

Hopefuls and initiates began to dance in weird, interpretive choreography well-suited to evil ritual. The man in white sang louder, stoking the dancers into ecstatic, whooping frenzy.

"What happens when they reawaken, and why would we want that?"

She turned to Taylor, violet eyes piercing with an ominous sheen, the beady glares of two dozen serpents fixed on Taylor right along with the head of their hydra.

A bitter taste spread over her tongue. She felt as if she was staring into the darkest corner of all existence.

The chaos witch moved her lips with methodical deliberation. "The black goo rewards us."

"Where is this black goo?"

"Not yet. Soon." Her whisper came quick, a hypnotic hiss on the exhale.

The singing and dancing reached a level of utter bedlam, pagan and crazed.

"Is my daughter alive?"

Serpents wove the atmosphere into their hideous curves, scaly underbellies pressed out in wretched displays of deathly pallor.

"Not long now." The chaos witch's lips went slack to present small white teeth with a gap between the two front ones, something pathetic in the dental normalcy, a hearkening to being human once. "Ascension, claiming, and sacrifice, then the crescendo of Song of Virgo."

"Answer me. Is. My. Daughter. Alive?"

"The sacrifice has not yet occurred." The chaos witch looked at Taylor like she was the dumbest person in the world.

"She's alive. Where is she?"

"Exalted, in the place to which we shall ascend. Not long now, and along with the Other Ones, we may claim her."

Over by the light cages, the ceremony boss stopped singing. He waved his wand. Dancers promptly stilled, chests heaving with exertion.

"Open." The boss man shook smoke in front of a masked person's face and did the same to the next. "Open and receive, then give. Your essence unto Titans. Servitude is freedom."

"What's going on?" Taylor asked the chaos witch, who was staring with her jaw slack.

"Not long now. Ascend. Claim. Sacrifice. Crescendo. Then the age of Titans shall reign once more."

Worry wound her system in knots. How were they going to save Luna now? Where was the way out of this place? The chaos witch was under a spell as strong as the one gripping the dancers. If only Taylor had the means to disrupt it. She eyed the hard ring that jutted into relief against the other woman's turtleneck. Could she break the chain, snap her out of her stupor? Would it work to rip the collar off with brute force?

Bodies cloaked in red swayed, the effect ghastly, control of their faculties gone. A short person dropped to their knees first, head lolling to one side, and hit the floor with a dead smack.

Others followed. A few went down without incident, others suffered brief seizures before they expired.

Please, please, please. Her plea wasn't as much a message to Julian as it was a general cry into the universe, for help and a blessing. For this miserable moment not to be the end.

The man in white faced the Titans and spread his arms in a wide V. "Drink, now, Titans and Other Ones. Drink of the soul essences of those who serve you and grow strong."

A feathered beast twitched in one prism. In another gleaming prison, a spear of a tail whipped at its confinement. Lips curled back to show several rows of layered fangs. The threat of tears stung her nose when she realized none of the bodies on the floor were moving.

Shit. *Can you hear me, babe? Are you there?* A quiet void stared back. She clenched her fists, unable to make telepathic connection with him, since he was face down. Was he…no. Impossible. Maybe one of her spells would help. Push air into his lungs.

The man in white turned his back on the fallen and approached the cube. "Water witch, summon your fire and spirit sisters to complete the dark trinity and awaken three Titans."

The chaos witch snatched Taylor's hand in a cool, silky hold and opened her book to a section near the back. "We read together now," she said with girlish excitement. "To craft the chorus of Song of Virgo. You lead the way. Light summons dark."

A lifeless body pushed up to hands and knees before rising to stand. A burst of hope injected her, intensifying as he rushed the altar.

"No," the chaos witch cried out. "You must not meddle in the Song of Virgo."

But the interloper ignored her protest and meddled away by catching the man in white off guard. He wrestled the staff out of his hands, raising it high in the air amidst startled yelps, and slammed the bar into the side of his head with a sickening crunch of flesh and bone yielding to much harder material.

With a groan, the man in white fell forward, his upper half slamming against the cube before he crumpled to the ground. A red stain seeped out from a spot near his ear and grew to merge with the slab of cloth over his face.

Taylor already knew, but when the person who'd clubbed the ringleader reached up to drop his hood and tug off his mask, she saw the flash of gold banding his ring finger.

She ran to Julian right as his face came into view and threw her arms around him. "Is Mad Dog dead?"

"Playing possum." Their third party staggered to his feet. "Scarab shit doesn't get to me anymore. I've got immunity."

An ear-piercing shriek rang out from behind. "How could you?" yelled the chaos witch.

Titans jerked and shifted, and their adjustments set off an earthquake that made Taylor's teeth chatter. "How could I what? Stop us from being killed? Stop you from slaughtering my baby? Stop you from unleashing a legion of monsters?" she called over the ruckus, clenching Julian's arm for steadiness and support.

The chaos witch's angelic face twisted into a scowl of hateful fury. "The Song of Virgo might be compromised beyond repair."

"Good." The tendons in Julian's hand strained as he clenched the staff. "Now take us to our daughter before you end up like your friend on the ground."

Instead, she clucked her tongue in a snide, upsetting way before stretching out both arms, palms facing Taylor and Julian.

Taylor stepped forward, flexing her biceps in case she had to throw a punch. Magic was afoot, but she wasn't about to cower in its wake when she had serious water power of her own. "What do you want?"

"To guide the Titans as I am destined to." A slick sheen, gray with an olive finish, coated the snake mistress's hands from fingertips to wrists. "Upon my throne, lord and master of chaos, I am the rightful, ruling queen of the coven daughters."

"You aren't gonna be ruling anything," Taylor shot back. "You're literally wearing a shock collar and an ankle bracelet. You're a useful idiot, and when they've exhausted your usefulness, they will kill you. You know that, right?"

Julian added, "She's right. You're a prisoner with Stockholm Syndrome. Stick with us, and we'll get you out. What's your name?"

A shriek so curdling that Taylor had to cover her ears ripped from the chaos witch's throat. The earthquake worsened, chunks of rock breaking off and rolling down the walls.

A Titan butted its feathered, feline head into the chamber trapping it. Walls of light bent, trembled.

Mad Dog looked around in fast motions, shoulders bunched. "Hey, guys? The prism walls seem to be thinning or dissipating."

A cloven foot the size of a motorcycle poked out through shiny light that wobbled like water.

This situation was deteriorating, fast. They had to hustle, but to where?

"Please," Taylor yelled over the ruckus. "I'm like you. Julian and Mad

Dog are too. Let's help each other escape. Is there a door, or portal we can get to?"

Twin blasts of magic shot from the chaos witch's hands and hurled right at Julian and Taylor.

They ducked just in time. He shoved down hard on her shoulder to get her out of harm's pathway, and the beams hit the walls with an acidic fizzing sound. She turned in horror to see the impact site dissolving, rock eaten away by gunk.

Additional shots sailed over their heads. The chaos witch kept firing. Near-misses grazed their waists while they shuffled, ducking and weaving to become moving targets.

Glop covered the floor and walls, sizzling every point it touched, releasing plumes of unwholesome steam. Toxic waste flew in all directions, spreading ruin and decay.

She'd about given up, resigned to rot in a noxious vat of poison, when Julian said, "We can cleanse her. Purify her magic. Together."

Deadly blockages reformed into solvable problems, obstacles to clear. "Pair work. Collaboration. Your healing and my water."

"Exactly." He took her hand, assurance in the flesh. His healing energy reached her as an elevating, subtle, essence of harmony delivered in packets.

True and right, meant to be. Just like them.

Working quickly, she dove into where her magic lived, buttressed by his influence against further compromise by malicious or ill-intentioned agents. She bypassed the efforts of those who would interfere, drew up a plume of water power, and purified it through the infinity loop yoking her and Julian.

"Water into chaos washes away evil." She held out her palm, mimicking the chaos witch's stance as best she could from her crouched position. "Sister Water, I, a water born, humbly call upon your assistance. Cure my sister of all that is unclean and foul, banishing your darkest aspect who governs chaos and halting the efforts of Other Ones from other places."

Pockets of pale blue enveloped the goop hills on the ground. Ugly crap changed to plain water. The chaos witch staggered to the side, a dazed stare locked on her palms as they dripped with benign liquid. She whimpered helplessly and sunk to slump against the cube.

"The damage to the structural integrity has been done." Julian pulled Taylor to her feet. "We gotta go—now."

"Damage, among other issues," Mad Dog put in as he ran over, arms covering his head.

Yikes. She saw what he meant. The Titan who'd stuck its foot out had worked a leg free, the hairy appendage hanging out up to the haunch. Massive muscles engaged as it kicked into nothing, a swift motion that would no doubt wreak more damage than a head-on collision.

"Too bad there isn't a way out." Yet as Taylor spoke, she mentally amended her position. She sprinted to the cube, shoving an unconscious but breathing chaos witch out of the way to get to the drawer, and grabbed the key. "Correction, there might be. We just have to figure out what this opens. I'll look. You two take pictures of the drawings on the walls. I think they're significant. Keep an eye out for keyholes, doors, escape hatches, anything."

"You got it, boss," Mad Dog said, his phone camera clicking.

Julian's device joined with an identical sound. "I think you might be on to something about these markings."

Stabilizing herself against a fresh, fierce quake, she ran to a wall opposite the two men and combed with vision and touch. Nothing but more drawings and a steady trickle of falling rocks, the moans of earth yielding. They didn't have much time. "Yeah. If I could only find a way out of here."

"I'm looking where the doorway in used to be, the one at the foot of the escalator," Julian said. "But it's been sealed off. Nothing but wall."

A mighty roar entered the scene, guttural and fearsome.

Think, think. Taylor raced back to the altar and looked in the drawer again. Empty. But a hunch nagged as she stood there, pebbles falling all around her like hail. The ceiling of the sacrifice room had been vaulted before, built to draw the eye up.

Up meant something. Mattered. Ascension and exaltation. She looked up.

Eureka. They weren't at the bottom of a funnel, they were in the center of an hourglass that tapered again after the flared, wide part cleared the Titans.

A pale-yellow circle of light glowed at the highest point of her visual field. An opening. A way out. Not like they could fly. Taylor muttered a curse, a rock the size of a bowling ball sliding across the bloodstained floor. She shifted her focus back to the cube.

The altar was placed right underneath the spherical opening, but the port was far off and appeared as small as a basketball.

Cool, hard smoothness slid past her flesh as she pawed at the cube, finding only planes of ebony. "The drawer." The earthquake intensified, and the bleat of a second titan entered the fray. "They kept her book in there. It has to matter."

She tugged the drawer free and nearly jumped for joy. Behind it were six slots. Keyholes.

"I got it!" But she slid the key into the first one, and it didn't engage. Didn't fit. "Fuck."

Julian and Mad Dog rushed over, arms above their heads as cover from rocks falling at a faster and faster pace. Julian picked up Taylor's book and used it to shield her skull.

She tried hole number two. Nope. "Shit."

Pebbles bounced off her book, tapping her shoulder in little stinging jabs before striking the ground and cracking into pieces. She grabbed the chaos witch's arm and dragged the dead weight of her snake-haired sibling underneath the minimal protection offered by the book.

Fortunately, the serpents slumbered along with their mistress.

Hole three. Access denied.

"Let's go back to the walls." Julian had to yell over the Titans' increasingly agitated vocalizations.

The fourth hole yielded with a meaty, satisfying snick of engagement. Every muscle and organ in her body unclenched. Thankful beyond speech, all she could do was exhale the air she hadn't realized she'd been holding in.

With scrapes and a groan, the lid of the cube slid open several feet. The whole thing lifted to levitate a few inches off the ground. Inside, empty. Enough room for all, if they squeezed.

Taylor entered first. Julian hauled the chaos witch, dragging her by the underarms as he stepped over the ledge, and plopped her limp body in a corner.

Mad Dog boarded, and she crossed her fingers while reengaging the key.

The lid grumbled shut, and the cube zipped off into an upward trajectory.

"Almost there, baby." She prayed to every God she could think of to make her declaration true. "Almost there."

TWENTY-FIVE

RIGHT AROUND THE TIME THAT THE FLOATING CUBE'S UPWARD HURDLE slowed to a gentle, bobbing float, the chaos witch began to stir and moan. Her soft noises of distress pierced the darkness the same as signal flares.

Clutching the key as a lifeline, Taylor fumbled and groped, bumping Mad Dog's knee and Julian's boot until she located the keyhole. Metal butted against metal in stubborn refusal as she cursed, fingers slippery. Everyone was breathing hard, trapped in wait.

A couple of failed efforts later, she managed to unlock the lid of the cube.

Taylor blinked until spots cleared from her vision. She feared the unknown but was grateful at the same time. Wherever they were, it helped to be able to see.

The chaos witch reacted to the sudden change by wincing and rubbing her temple, nudging aside a listless viper that lazed beside her ear.

Her serpents were as slack as dreadlocks, loose waves of scaly muscle framing her grimacing face in a slithery array of earth-toned camouflage patterns. Taylor took in the grotesque spectacle of mutation with weary and clinical detachment. Made sense, how those critters easily hid under sticks and leaves.

She was actually getting used to the sight of someone with a nest of snakes sprouting from her head. Outlandish, but here they were.

"Ow." The other witch's voice sounded different, animated by a rising tide of panic. At least she'd lost that creepy cult follower's monotone. "Where am I? Who are you people?" Her lips parted like she was about to scream.

One of her live extensions perked up and reared back, flicking a gray tongue into the air.

At least they didn't seem to strike without orders, but that didn't make the sight of them any less worrisome. "Stay calm. We're friends, here to help." Taylor frowned at the snake as it grew more curious and poked its head this way and that.

The chaos witch seemed unaware of them.

Julian leaned forward and took the Medusa's hands. "What's your name?"

"Rachel," she said in a quiet stammer, eyeing Mad Dog and Julian before fixing a long, open look on Taylor. "Was I unconscious? How did you find me?"

Empathy brought an ache to her chest. Not only had the poor woman been brainwashed and freak-ified, she'd been memory wiped and suffered amnesia. "Rachel, what's the last thing you remember?"

Rachel shook her head and squeezed her eyes shut, the grooves of unease deep on her forehead. "I was in this lab, on a hospital cot. Hooked up to tubes. These people in lab coats came in. They had clipboards and told me that I was about to be on the vanguard of a new project and ought to be excited. I was nervous because what they talked about wasn't what I was there for. I felt like they'd done a bait and switch."

"How did you get there in the first place?" Julian asked.

"I answered an ad to take part in a research study. The compensation was unbelievable, enough to wipe out my student loans. But when I got there, it seemed shady. I guess they drugged me?"

Mad Dog hummed a sound of confirmation. "Yeah. You were lied to. Like me."

One of the snakes twitched. Rachel scowled and said, "What's wrong with my hair?" before reaching toward a lively squirmer with scales trailing down its body in a Hershey's Kisses pattern.

Uh oh.

A high-voltage waterfall of adrenaline spurred Taylor into action. She got to Rachel in time, swatting her wandering hand away and covering her mouth just as the wily copperhead swung around to stare directly into Rachel's face.

Rachel's pupils dilated until black eclipsed color. Her lids stretched to capacity. The wail of absolute, animal terror that cut from her throat slammed into Taylor's palm, vibrating through flesh, bone, blood, soul.

Rachel thrashed and kicked her legs, flapped her hands. Chilling cries didn't stop for a long time.

She'd never forget that sound.

"You were an experiment," Mad Dog yelled to be heard. "So was I." He took off his hat, which didn't help ease Rachel's episode in the slightest. "We were ruined and made into monsters, but we can't let them win. We have to fight now. For Taylor and Julian's baby, to save her. To avenge what was done to us in the name of this greedy mad scientist experiment. For justice. We gotta stop these psychos, Rachel, and we can't do it without you."

Tears sluiced down Rachel's cheeks in fast falls, wetting Taylor's skin and breaking her heart as the expression on the chaos witch's face crumpled from terror to mourning and grief.

"Listen to me," Taylor told the other witch. "First and foremost, the snakes won't hurt you, or anyone else, without your permission. They recognize you as their master. I'm going to take my hand off your mouth and explain some things, but I need you to stay calm. I know that this is traumatic. But I swear to you that there's an upside. Do you want to hear it?"

Rachel nodded weakly, shaking as sobs wracked her body.

Taylor removed her hand and pulled away an inch at a time, watching Rachel closely in case she went haywire and lashed out. With the four of them packed in the floating cube, a physical outburst could do real damage.

All she did, though, was hunch over and dry heave, howling ugly cries as she hacked up nothing.

Once she calmed down, Taylor stroked her arm. "Before this happened to you, were you aware of your magical powers?"

Rachel sighed and wiped away tears. "Sort of. I've had prophetic dreams since I was a kid, and I see and feel things before they happen. I had a little set up in the back of my grandma's bookstore for awhile, reading Tarot." She looked at her knees and pulled a thread on her sleeve. "Grandma died when I was in high school, and that's when things started to get really strange. Dark and scary, to be precise. I think she passed a curse to me."

Julian looked to the partially open lid. "Did you all hear that?"

Taylor had been engrossed in Rachel's story and not heard anything. "No. What?"

Rachel shook her head, causing a couple of snakes to weave and bob in the air. A few more forked tongues slid out like ribbons. Maybe they, too, sensed a disturbance.

Mad Dog rose to a crouch and pushed on the lid. The stone slab groaned as it let in more light. "Harp music, or other stringed instruments. Things are happening. We gotta get out of this cube before we're ambushed."

Taylor jammed both her book and Rachel's deep down in her backpack. "Tell me the rest of the story when we're out of here, okay?"

Rachel didn't look convinced that the condition would be met. "Yeah. Okay. Thank you, guys. For...bringing me back to myself."

"Things will get better from here," Julian said in that assuring way of his.

Mad Dog drew his gun and left first, followed by Julian, who was equally armed. They'd gotten into the cube with their weapons and packs.

Taylor rested one hand on her holster and used the other to guide Rachel out of the box. "Do you know how to shoot?"

"No, sorry." Rachel stumbled upon stepping over the edge of the altar. "I'm starting to regret my commitment to pacifism."

The crew was back in a white room like the one where the sacrifices happened.

No point at the apex of the ceiling this time, just a dome of unvarnished ceramic.

The top of the hourglass. Emptiness. The harp music sounded sinister.

Abruptly, the cube slid into the floor, white tiles closing over the gap, seamless. They were trapped in this bubble, encased in the inside of a ping pong ball.

"Oh, shit," Rachel said.

Taylor squatted and knocked on the ground where the cube used to be, her rap absorbed by the dense material as white filled her visual field. "Yeah, for real. But we can figure this out. Rachel, you talked about claiming a bit ago. Any memory of who is doing the claiming, or what's being claimed?"

The voice that followed was mellow, androgynous, and uncannily familiar. "You."

The hairs on her neck and arms stood at attention as her danger systems turned on.

She sprung to her feet and looked around, her pulse hammering even as her insides turned to icicles.

Julian, Rachel, and Mad Dog were gone. They'd been transported—or Taylor had.

She was alone with this voice, the one she'd met at Wonder World when she'd agreed to take a big blast of water magic despite the price. "Me what?"

Smooth laughter made a mockery of her inquiry. "We take you now, as our conduit, water witch. A powerful proxy on this earth, you shall serve us. We've come to collect on your debt. Let the reaping commence."

Taylor's ears rang. She pushed her hands against the sides of her head, the metal of the pistol cool against her cheek. Her eyeballs heated and throbbed. Pain clamped her skull like a vise. "No."

More laughter at her expense. "Too late. She is ready to imbibe the goo now, peon, and carry out our total impregnation of earth, the cosmos, and beyond."

"No." But Taylor was rapidly losing her fight against pain, disorientation, and loss of lucidity. Her vision swam, skull full of glass and nails. She sunk to her knees, the change in center of gravity nauseating her beyond tolerability. Saliva pooled in her mouth, and she might have thrown up, but she wasn't sure. It hurt, pure agony inside and out. With a feeble, weak arm, she aimed her gun in a pathetic last-ditch effort at self-preservation. "No."

"Oh, yes, Taylor McClure. Oh yes. Water witches such as yourself are uniquely capable of claiming. You'll be a good little stooge in our efforts to release the Titans."

An aura of phosphorescent light shimmered in her peripheral vision, contracting, and expanding in time with tides of pain. She squinted to block it out, the weapon falling from her hand as she lurched forward and planted her palms on smooth ground. She cried, on the verge of surrender.

The black cube slipped up yet again, a menacing trespass against the blanched walls. The man in white emerged from the top of the box like the transporter was made of jelly.

He moved via levitation and drifted to stand behind the box. The side of his head was still marked with the red blotch where Julian had clubbed him, and he wielded his staff.

He held a separate item—a test tube half-full of dark liquid—which he placed in the center of the altar.

"That's the famous black goo," Taylor slurred, slouching to the side as she reached for her gun. The room whipped in a drunken circle as she pawed blindly for her firearm, sick and and hurting and nearly blind.

The man in white sauntered over, crouched to retrieve her gun, and cupped her chin in his gloved hand. "You should consider your invitation to participate in the Song of Virgo a true honor and privilege. We'll have to skip a few steps now, alas." He grabbed her roughly by the arm and dragged her to the altar, her feet clumsy and uncoordinated as she staggered behind, unable to keep up without crumpling.

"Where is everyone? Julian and my friends? Where is Luna?"

The man in white shoved her at the black cube until she had to grab the sharp ledge of the top to prevent face-planting on it.

The disembodied voice laughed. "Your little friends? They reside in the Other Places, now, slaves and playthings for the Other Ones for all eternity."

That explanation felt plain wrong to the point of nonsensical. "Bullshit. I know that Rachel is of use to you in your scheme, probably Julian too. You wouldn't be stupid enough to discard them."

The voice from beyond barked, testier than she'd ever heard it, "Process her, peon. Hurry."

Hurry, huh? Taylor had an advantage here, but what? The demands of an unseen and more powerful party? A ticking clock? "Or else what?"

"Silence, witch. Peon, let the reaping commence. Begin with the claiming in two phases."

The vial of inky fluid sat in a little plastic holder, the kind used to transport tubes at a medical clinic. She stared at it, grounded by her breathing. While she felt awful, she maintained control. "I'm supposed to drink that, and my takeover is complete?"

"Yes," the disembodied voice said, calm and patient again. "You will drink, and the reaping shall commence."

"What if I refuse?" Would the man in white hold her nose and force the foul contagion down her throat, put the gun to her head? Why hadn't he done so already? Why the pomp and circumstance?

The voice said, "You won't refuse."

A whirlpool swirled upward in her, bringing epiphany to the surface. Here was her leverage. She had to consent to drink the shit, and she held the means to make a deal. She'd pretend to honor the deal until she figured out how to beat these two. "I'll drink it if you bring me my daughter this instant."

Silence, save for the sickly-sweet tinkle of that harp music, crashed down over the walls of the porcelain globe.

"Very well," the voice without a body said, but their concession was mild to the point of smug, and Taylor wasn't able to feel like she'd scored a victory. She was missing vital pieces to this puzzle.

The voice said, "Peon, bring out the child."

Taylor gasped, convulsed, her body filled with stress chemicals and confusion. "Luna? Luna, baby? Where is she? Is she here? Let me see her." In her emotional frenzy, she hadn't noticed the man in white going anywhere. But when she jerked her head to and fro, he was nowhere.

The next time she looked at the altar, however, there he was.

Holding Luna.

Her brown eyes big, she was clean and alert, unharmed, wearing a frilly, virginal white dress fit for a Christening.

"Luna," Taylor eked out, beside herself, caught up in the unspeakable maelstrom of feelings clawing at her. She reached out her arms. She itched and ached to touch her child. "Please, let me hold her."

Luna fussed in the robed man's arms, wiggling her shoulders to get free. She bounced a chubby foot.

Taylor covered her mouth with both hands. Her heart hurt. Empty pain clenched her womb as her breasts swelled. Tears streamed down her cheeks. "Please, please give her to me. I'm begging you. I'll die without her."

The disembodied voice laughed. "Humans, shifters. Sniveling and pitiful, all of you. Place the cursed sacrament on the altar, peon, and let the reaping commence."

Taylor's insides crashed to the floor. Acid sizzled in her chest cavity. Her legs threatened to quit. She fumbled out through cottonmouth, "What? What is this?"

The peon did as ordered, setting Luna in the middle of the slab by the black goo. With Taylor's confiscated gun in hand, he dissolved to translucence, then faded completely into the air.

Luna whined, scowled, balling tiny fists.

Taylor locked eyes with her baby, doing her best to impart reassurance, calm, protection.

There was no way out, but she could pull off a teleportation spell. Grab Luna and start reciting, visualize Julian and the rest of the group zapping back to Peru.

But then, the voice from beyond kicked in. "Other Ones, come forth from Other Places. On this most impure day, the onset of the sacrificial season, we sing the Song of Virgo to guide us on our travels."

The harp music notched up, soporific and dream-spun nightmares, a narcotic rainbow of tinkling, sprinkling angel kisses of death.

Taylor swayed, her eyelids lead weights, Luna's cries drifting to the background of her conscious mind. Painless hooks stabbed into her spine, putting a negative essence in her.

She was flooded, losing herself, presences from that dark place with the water magic storming her all at once before she could stop them. There were too many to fend off.

The voice kept going, "A witch's womb, of offspring torn. Feast on the fruit of water born. Use this wolf bitch, her teeth and cries. Eat the skin, devour the eyes. Rend the flesh from tender babe, wake the dead from sleepy grave. Other Ones, our time is now. Use our vessel, take our cow."

"I'm not a cow. I'm a wolf," Taylor garbled out, her tongue too large in mouth full of molasses, hunching forward. Her sweat dripped on to the black cube. She was weak now, depleted as she desperately scratched to hang on.

"Take and eat. Consume the child to sate the Other Ones and carve space for our essential medium of transport. Drink, now, drink of the black goo."

Her hands slipped against the ledge, scraping a layer of skin from her palms as she fought to remain upright. She'd at least make them work for it. "Fuck you. And fuck your black goo."

But the magic was too strong, whooshing, crowding out Taylor's personhood as hordes of Other Ones stormed her gates, shoving her to the margins as they made space for themselves with their dirty claws, taste for torture, and ghoulish smiles. They just kept coming, lots of them, endless.

"Do you see, now, water witch?" the voice crooned. "Do you see as we see?"

Taylor's ego and all that went with it burned to ash.

"Make a rope from those ashes, water witch," an Other One goaded in their favorite, teasing tone, pushing to the front of the line. "And your child shall live. Last chance."

The ashes dissolved into dust while what was left of the water witch grasped and flailed.

Very good then. No rope for her. It was fun to taunt idiot shifters and humans with impossible riddles that none could solve. Haha.

The Other Ones stared at the baby, that little tasty bundle.

Eating shifter and human children was always a delightful perk of these conjuring rituals.

They picked up what remained of Taylor's soul, a ghostly wisp of broken, vestigial limbs, and threw her in the oubliette.

The Other Ones giggled, warm and toasty at the memory of throwing pieces of scum into the pit, left to rot in the bottle dungeon once they'd outstayed their use.

The water witch's body felt good to experience, snug and young, a skin suit made hospitable thanks to the obedient preparations of a peon who'd put just a nip of the black goo inside of her in anticipation for this very moment. Tremendous.

Once they filled her body with the special juice of her own baby's brain, the meat sack would be fully ready to receive the rest of the goo without threat of rejecting the filthiest medium.

Then, all Other Ones could finally come over, using the witch's body as a conduit while enjoying her magic to spread their influence across the universe and claim all souls.

The Other Ones reached forward, curled their hands around the infant's butter-soft neck, and pressed their thumbs against the hard resistance of its windpipe.

This one was an ideal age, plump and healthy.

Good for feasting.

They had just begun to push and start the process of extinguishing the infant's life when a pair of sapphire eyes glowed in the depths of the bottle dungeon.

A white wolf came charging out of the pit, and before they could grab the beast and throw it back in, the animal sprang up and scattered the Other Ones like a swarm of flies.

TWENTY-SIX

As his wolf, Julian was able to escape the spell that bound him in mute, paralyzed invisibility along with Rachel and Mad Dog.

Whoever had done that to him to get him out of the way couldn't touch his wolf aspect or disrupt the telepathic connection he shared with Taylor.

Now, all he had to do was chase away the horde of demons clamoring to complete the possession of Taylor. He had to guide her back to herself. He told himself that he'd done more difficult things over the course of his life.

In the battlefield of her mind, he stood in the middle of a replica of the Peruvian jungle. With any luck, the beloved trappings of home would help to stabilize her.

Fiends advanced upon him from every point of the perimeter, packs of slimy things with lolling tongues and bug eyes, reeking with the stench of corruption.

Sinkholes pockmarked the scruffy underbrush, and while he snarled at a creep that looked like a cross between a goat and a horsefly, a flash of white propelled up from one of the pits.

He locked eyes with Taylor's unmistakable blue ones and howled in triumph. She'd sensed his presence and used it to crawl out of her prison.

His effort worked; the hunch he followed proving true. A possessed person could be guided out of their lost state if the connection forged with them was strong enough.

"We don't have to fight them," he called to her with his mind. "We need to move through this place with confidence and get you to overcome them."

She bounded over in a smooth, canine gait, all lean muscle and pristine fur. "Yeah, but we also need to get them gone. That'll require purging the black goo that was put in me."

He started to run, her at his side, the demons looming and lurking but barred from taking over. "My healing magic isn't there yet; I don't have the skill to pull foreign elements out of your system. Once we're back home, I'll get to work on that. I think the best we can hope for now is to subdue these demons or whatever they are. Repress them. Make them dormant."

"How?"

They sprinted in tandem, clearing fields and dense packs of trees with hefty trunks. He could feel Luna's life force in the physical world beyond this psychic dimension and raced to get to her. "I think if we work together, we'll be able to throw up a wall or force field in your psyche. A barrier to keep negative forces away from you."

Her eyes lit up with intelligence. "By joining our magic."

Terrain morphed from forest to rocky slopes, cliffs overlooking an ocean. They had to be creating and changing the landscape with their minds, molding their surroundings from unconscious power of suggestion. "It's worth a shot. We did it to stop Rachel from shooting toxic waste. I'm hoping we'll be able to pull it off internally. Seal you off against evil."

They stopped at the edge of a bluff, sea breezes ruffling her thick fur. She panted, a pink tongue slipped over sharp teeth and black lips. "It checks out to me. A water-based seal with a healing intention behind it."

Her vote of confidence scared him a little. The pressure was on.

At the farthest point from the water, where the cliffs abutted shoulder-length weeds and crabgrass, commotion stirred blades.

Debris crunched underfoot.

Propelled by a cacophony of grunts, clicks, and howls, a phalanx of malformed flesh stormed the cliffs. Cloven hooves clacked on rock, creatures with bull-like snouts snorted.

Piercing screams rose above it all, the cries of things that craved malevolence.

Now. The word didn't even need to be uttered, for they both felt the urgent slam of its impact, one body tethered into a united front.

Working as fast as he could without sacrificing care or precision, he drew from his healing magic, pouring the entirety of himself into the intention of keeping these filthy formations away from Taylor.

They were close now, close enough to smell and feel on every level. Hot breath. Craven greed. Sin.

Julian purified her, baptized her in the crystal pools of health and innocence, absolute detox realized as a frosty flood. Like joyful tears from heaven, rain fell, gathering in intensity until the floodwaters took form in a shimmering sheet of solid transparence that stretched to the horizon in both directions and thrust up until it merged with blue sky.

A nasty, hirsute frog-thing as big as a linebacker butted its head against the wall, snarling in frustration.

Taylor yapped victoriously. "We iced them out. Literally."

No clue if their collaborative spell would hold forever, but for now it bought enough time to get Taylor back into herself. He nuzzled the side of her face. "Close call." He looked out over the slab of aquamarine ocean. "You think that's where we want to go?"

She cocked her head at the ice wall, which barricaded off the woods for miles or more. A scaly mistake with a dog's head scraped sharp teeth against the ice, grating off shards. It was obviously going to keep working, chipping bit by bit until it made a hole.

Taylor said, "I think that's all we've got."

He walked to the edge. "Ready, babe?"

She rubbed her nose against his neck, the affectionate contact tickling him with pleasure even beneath a thick coating of fur. They'd both been starved for the touch of the other. The smallest taste of contact registered as poignantly intimate. "There's no one that I'd rather jump off a cliff with. Now let's get our baby and get home."

"Count of three?"

She arched her back, straightening it out. "One."

"Two." He pressed his side into hers.

"Three."

In tandem, they hurled their bodies over the precipice of the abyss, the sensation of free fall exhilarating and all-encompassing until his perception snapped to black.

＊

WITH A BANG, SHE HURLED FORWARD INTO THE EDGE OF THE CUBE, sucking like a fish to take in oxygen. Taylor returned painfully to herself with a whimper.

Her head throbbed, and all she was able to hear was the ringing in her ears. She slurped against knocked out air, her vision still blacked, scrabbling to remember where she was and why.

The baby's cry came as a sharp plea and went right to Taylor's center.

Her instincts took over. Her baby was distressed, and she needed to get to her.

She groaned and clutched the sharp stoniness in front of her, fumbling for clarity though every part of her screamed in agony. Luna was alive. She herself was alive. Not possessed.

"Mama's here," she stammered, forcing the heel of one of her hands to her eyes. She rubbed each one until darkness transitioned to jumpy smudges, blurs of color. Lots of white. Black.

A strong arm looped around her waist, the stabilizing hold marked by Julian's scent. "You're okay. You're back. We've got Luna, and we've got you."

Taylor collapsed into his strength, clutching the sides of his shirt, her stomach sour as her breath came in shallow huffs. She was lightheaded but must've had a pulse. She didn't manage to say much. "Okay. Okay."

"She's right here," Julian said soothingly. "We did it. *You* did it. You saved her."

She dropped her lids then pried them open. Though white flecks danced in front of her eyes, she could see what was most important to her. Luna. Tucked into the crook of Julian's arm, chewing on her foot.

A scream tore up from Taylor's depths, the raw and primal urge to release. But she smashed her tongue between her teeth before she did it. Because screaming would make Luna cry, and they weren't safe yet.

She trembled as her body rebelled with an urge to let go, tears bleeding down her cheeks. She clamped a hand over her mouth, composure unraveling thread by thread, and stared at her child.

After what seemed like an eternity, she whispered, "I thought I'd never see you again."

Luna showed off her gums.

"Let's go home, okay?" Julian whispered into her hair.

She nodded, emotions rushing out, soaking her shirt as she slowly recovered. They hadn't come here alone. "Where are Mad Dog and Rachel?"

"Here," a female voice said, and a hand rested on Taylor's shoulder. The snake-haired witch stood behind her, a combination of tragedy and gratitude behind her eyes, vipers cascading past her shoulders in arching curves. "You saved us."

"Both of us," Mad Dog said from beside Rachel. "I'd tip my hat to you guys, but, well, you know."

Taylor managed to acknowledge his quip with a kind chuckle as her faculties returned to relative normal. "You guys are coming back to Peru with us, right?"

"No place I'd rather go," Rachel said. "We can be witchy together, coven style. It'll be fun."

Taylor smiled, her well filling a little, and wiggled Luna's big toe. That did sound fun, collaborating with her long-lost sister witch to join forces and hone the craft of magic. But talk of Peru evoked two inconvenient issues.

First, the Other Ones weren't eradicated. They were trapped behind a wall, a solid and tangible barrier erected in a vulnerable recess within her, sure.

The portal to her consciousness was plugged with a stopgap for now, but she could feel them working at it. They were far away, but ceaseless in their efforts. Working tirelessly. Doggedly obsessed, desperate to take her over.

And they wouldn't quit, ever, until they busted down the ice sheet and claimed their second chance to possess her. "I haven't been cured. As long as the goo is still in me, the Other Ones have what they need to grab on to. Who knows how long it will take them to smash that wall. Weeks? Days? What if it happens in my sleep, while the babies are in the next room?"

As long as the Other Ones had a hold on her, she was a danger to Luna, Mal, and maybe others.

"We'll get to work when we're home," Julian assured, squeezing her upper arm. "I promise you I will focus day and night on nothing else until you're cured, sealed, and safe."

Her second concern, she vocalized right away, for the benefit of her new friends as much as herself. "We haven't served justice. Where did the man in white go? Did he fade into nothing or just change locations? Are we just going to let them get away without any consequences?"

"I'm at peace." Rachel looked deeply into Taylor's eyes. "Justice will come. I truly believe in the law of karma. They'll get what's coming." Her lids narrowed. "Like we talked about a minute ago, we'll be practicing witchcraft together. Sure would be a shame if we came across a hex to take these bastards down."

Taylor washed out her guilt and remorse with a big exhale. She'd gotten lucky, sinking that original Scarab outpost into the ocean. There was a certain hubris in thinking such good fortune would strike twice. Rachel was right. With patient effort and a pact to remember who deserved punishment, vindication would arrive when the time was right. There was an auspicious quality to Rachel's perspective, an honoring of synchronicity and the machinations of the universe, that Taylor found alluring. "Yeah. That's valid."

Mad Dog's features softened. "Hell, I'm just happy to have a home to go to where I'm not alone anymore." He leaned forward slightly, twiddling his thumbs. "If your South American crew doesn't mind taking in a grizzled old piece of meat with a messed-up head."

"Watch it," Rachel said in a jesting tone, a snake coiling.

"Note to self, do not get on the Medusa witch's bad side." Mad Dog ducked as a rattlesnake got pretty close, but the reptile seemed more interested than aggressive.

Taylor patted Mad Dog on the upper back. "Of course you're welcome. It's the least we can do, after all you did for us in here.

Seriously, you were indispensable. I just feel like we're running away. Leaving with unfinished business. Without resolution or closure. What about the red-haired woman with the gray truck?"

Julian said, "We won't forget. I know I never will. But I agree with Rachel, that's a battle for another day." He kissed Luna's forehead, making her coo. "And we have the most important closure right here."

"No doubt." Taylor rested her temple against the firm support of his bicep. She'd have to put her drive for revenge on hold for a bit and forget, for the time being, about suturing loose ends. Unsatisfying, but perhaps for the best. Not like she had a solution on deck. Maybe once she and Rachel got to work, they'd arrive at one. "Let's get home."

They stood in a circle and joined hands, with Mad Dog clutching Julian's forearm since he was partially occupied holding Luna.

"Here's the deal," Julian said. "Taylor and I will key in with each other, and the two of you concentrate on holding tight to us and following us wherever we go. I think that I'll be able to bypass the seal that Taylor used to stop the Scarab magicians from coming back to the camp after they kidnapped Luna. But I'm no expert, and this isn't foolproof or tested. We'll all need to focus as hard as we can and just plain hope for the best. It's going to be disorienting. Stay calm and use every ounce of concentration in you to target getting to exactly where we're going. Got it?"

Rachel pressed her fingertips to her lips. "Lead the way, guys."

Mad Dog rolled his shoulders back and tilted his chin to rest on his chest. "Beam me up, Scotty."

Julian stared into Taylor's eyes, and she stared back, the bleached walls surrounding them melting into a pool. They slipped into the deep end.

A vortex of white light and rainbow color pulled them in, out, down and around, upside down and inside out until reality vanished into the total power of a hurtling energy field.

Her face battered by an incoming headwind—she supposed she still had a face—Taylor gave herself over to the bliss of surrender, abnegation.

The moment when her butt smacked against hard ground came impossibly soon.

She crawled onto her knees, her ass numb. Portal travel never got easier.

The good news was that she recognized the patch of land where they'd landed. The clearing by the wide, slow part of creek where folks washed clothes. Less than a quarter-mile from the cabins and communal buildings.

The hour was dusk, meaning that they wouldn't have to get out their flashlights and deal with a walk in the dark. Not a huge deal, but small bonuses counted. Once oriented, she asked, "You guys all here?"

"Here with Luna," Julian said. "We're both fine."

Beside her, he stood, Luna in his arms. She yawned.

"Yep," Mad Dog grunted in a distressed voice. "That was a hard fall."

She glanced over to see him face-planted in the dirt, a sad sight in the prone position, and crouched to offer a helping hand. "Yeah. It's a rough ride every time. I hope we don't have to go through it again."

He got on his feet and brushed grass off his legs. "You and me both. This is home, eh?" He looked around, nostrils flaring as he smelled the air and closed his eyes in what looked like a moment of serene enjoyment. "I always dug camping. Roughing it."

Julian said, "You've come to the right place. We do have running water and three home cooked meals every day."

"Good deal. I was eating burritos and McDonalds every day before I met you guys."

While the men chatted, Taylor scanned the area for the fifth head and came up short. She didn't see Rachel. Had she not made it? "Guys, I don't see Rachel."

Julian stepped closer. "There are a few sub-openings scattered through the jungle, a network of nodes. We'll take Luna to Sasha and Crystal and get a team out in the jungle."

The plan didn't come to that because Rachel called out a moment later, "I'm over here." She sounded about twenty feet away, judging by the slight echo of her words and the way they faded after she spoke. "Be right there."

Rachel stepped out from behind a Kapok tree, a jungle behemoth with a twisted trunk wider than three people, many stories tall with leaves to eclipse the sun.

She'd been easily camouflaged behind the giant with its tangle of dangling vines pouring down to the earth.

Empathy wound around Taylor's heart when she saw why Rachel had chosen to go off by herself for a minute.

The chaos witch had re-wrapped her snake hair in the turban, which she patted sheepishly with a sad blip of a smile tugging her lips. "Wouldn't want to scare off my prospective hosts."

Taylor jogged over and surprised her coven sister with a big hug. Rachel flinched at first, but her body relaxed to return Taylor's sisterly embrace. "You're okay. You made it."

"I'm worried this won't work out," Rachel confessed, her voice small and shaky with the trepidation of an insecure girl at a new school.

"They won't reject you," Taylor said to Rachel. "We'll prepare them and get them used to the circumstances, but you're home now. I won't let anyone hurt you again. *We* won't. We'll protect you. We're family now."

"Thank you," Rachel whispered, breaking out of the hug, tears pooled high to wet her eyes. She touched the hunk of hardware under her collar. "Not that it's urgent or anything, but this is really uncomfortable."

Bouncing his arms lightly to offer Luna distraction, Julian said, "Taylor's right. We'll take care of you from here on out and get that thing off your neck. You're safe. Let's check in with Tim first. He's the alpha— the leader. We'll get him up to speed, then go relieve Sasha and Crystal. The two of you can stay with us until we get you set up and situated."

As Julian started walking, Taylor kept pace at his side. Mad Dog and Rachel, hesitant newcomers, hung back in tow. A few blocks' worth of paces, and the welcome sight of log cabins peeked out from gaps in the trees.

The first person that Taylor spotted was Kathleen, the ancient woman with her cobwebs of hair and a loose grip on her mental acuity, walking barefoot in the opposite direction of the dining hall. Her wrinkled hands were full of sticks, and she wore an iridescent evening gown dyed to an amethyst hue fit for a prom queen.

Kathleen followed the whims of her hidden, unknowable mind, fashion-wise and in various other ways. She had a predilection for playing kitchen with nature's detritus, hence the twigs.

"Hi Kathleen," Taylor said with friendly affection. The clan watched out for its elders and stayed vigilant where their safety was concerned, but Kathleen never wandered far and hadn't yet posed a risk to herself. "We have two new friends joining us today. Are you making your special tea again?"

Kathleen stopped abruptly and stared. A childlike grin split her wrinkled cheeks. "Two witches, two witches, two witches," she proclaimed gleefully before skipping off.

Taylor looked at Rachel, who had a highly amused but clearly interested look on her face and shrugged. "I'm going to go ahead and call that a good auspice."

As they approached Tim's cabin, Taylor took Julian's hand. A new era was afoot, with plenty of unknowns and variables, but Kathleen's words spiraled up and around her like a magic spell of their own.

Two witches, indeed. Let the crafting commence.

TWENTY-SEVEN

TENDRILS OF FIRE TOUCHED SULTRY AIR WITH CURLING STROKES. Flames soared from a bed of smoldering wood that cracked and popped as fragrant smoke blew its campfire perfume.

Laughter, conversation, and the melodious plucks of somebody's acoustic guitar rose from the benches circling the fire to create a soundtrack of harmony and love. While only hours had passed, the ordeal now felt like a lifetime ago.

Taylor snuggled into Julian's side, the log bench supporting their bodies, the lively presence of the shifters and other clan folk soothing her soul. "I never thought I'd be this happy to be sitting around a campfire." She leaned down and adjusted Luna's blanket while her daughter slept in her portable carrier, Malcom dozing in his carrier right beside his sister.

Side by side, two little sleepy beans, one with a mop of hair and the other bald. Right. Reunited. Whole.

Her husband put his arm around her back, stroking her side. "While I was picking up Mal, I talked with Crystal a little bit about strategies for your healing. She works with aromatherapy and meditation and has a theory that if we combine those modalities with my magic—"

She placed the pad of her finger against his lips. "Can we put the action plan on hold until the morning? I just want to enjoy this night before we get serious tomorrow."

He took her finger away and kissed it, looking a little thrown. "Yeah, sure, it's just that you seemed pretty concerned before we left Scarab."

"I did." She stretched out her legs, kicking up puffs of dust in the dirt, reflecting for a moment. Awareness of the Other Ones behind the wall had been fading reliably since they arrived, and now she felt nothing more pressing than a faint itch. Still there, without a doubt, but fainter each time she remembered to notice. "Now I think that being here might be healing me. Buying time, at least."

He held her tight, his touch free of doubt or apprehension, in trust of her word. "Good news."

"Check that out." She pointed across the circle, where Tim sat beside Rachel, working on her collar with a tiny screwdriver. The ankle monitor was beside her foot, disassembled.

The lock popped, hinging at the back to spring free from Rachel's neck. He used both hands to pull off the wide metal circle with slow, meticulous hands.

She leaned her head back far enough to bare the pale column of her throat, lips parted in ecstatic rapture, and stroked her fingertips over the skin right above the dip of her collarbone.

Rachel said words heard only by Tim, perhaps an acknowledgement of how long it had been since she'd felt air against the skin there.

Tim was staring, hard, as he leaned forward. He reached out to caress her face before pulling back, stopping himself once she opened her eyes.

"Oh, boy," Julian said. "Interesting indeed."

Taylor quit spying on the new development and watched their babies sleep for a bit before scanning the fireside circle. Bottles of wine and beer in various stages of consumption sat at the feet of community members, the skunky smell of weed layered in with wilderness odors to create a social atmosphere. A young surfer named Earl, shirtless and sporting a California tan, played "Wish You Were Here" on the guitar.

"Destiny is such a strange thing," Taylor said.

"You're philosophical tonight."

"Well, yeah." She bumped him playfully. "We've been through a lot."

"Hey, Sasha," Julian called and waved, hailing one of the women who'd taken over Mal's care. "Can you pass the zinfandel and a couple of cups this way?"

"I can pump and dump." Taylor's reasoning allayed her brief prick of guilt. If she disposed of her breast milk after she finished the wine, she wouldn't run the risk of passing along any alcohol to the twins.

"Absolutely. You deserve this."

Instead of merely passing the bottle, Sasha breezed over, all hippie princess with her long skirt and sandaled feet dripping with rings and anklets. She handed Julian the wine along with two kiln-fired clay cups that she'd made, then squatted by the baby carriers. "He was perfect. A dream." She tapped Mal's chin and hugged Taylor, fragrant with her favorite patchouli. "I'm glad everything worked out."

Taylor squeezed her friend tight. "We appreciate you."

"Thanks again, Sash," Julian said.

"My pleasure." Sasha went back to sit with her wife and some other folks, who had commandeered the joint.

Julian poured two measures of wine, the burgundy liquid flowing with an inviting gurgle, and handed Taylor her cup. He clinked his glazed mug into her beaten metal one and said, "You were saying?"

She treated herself to a long drink, flavors of pepper, oak, and cherry exploding on her tongue before going down with a silky finish. "Wine is the answer." She closed her eyes as the fruity, spicy goodness warmed her belly. "I don't remember the question."

He gave her foot a gentle kick. "You brought up destiny. I was interested to hear what you had to say."

Taylor opened her eyes to a web of stars, radiant diamond nodes connected by shimmering threads all stitched into the ebony blanket.

A long breath of sweet air unmarred by pollution and laced with that woodsy campfire essence complemented the splendor of the heavens. "I wonder where magic came from. Why I was supposed to meet you, fall in love with you, have the twins with you. Find Rachel. And Eve, and Helen. I wonder when I'll find them again, and how that will happen. Even those Other Ones, you know? Why am I connected to them? I just wonder what it all means."

She took another drink, tasting subtle whispers of chocolate and blackberry. The flavor of cinnamon lingered on the base of her tongue after the drink went down, the palate changing along with her thoughts. If there was a prophecy, and she was one of the chosen ones, did she have free will? Who was doing the choosing, and why?

Julian stargazed along with her and sighed, his own contemplation registering in the peaceful aura he exuded. "I've wondered that. Why I was born being able to shift my shape. If the stories my grandma told me were true, that our kind came here through a portal from somewhere up there." He pointed at the stars. "I wonder if everything happens for a reason, and if our kind inhabiting the earth is part of a grand master plan or occurred by random accident."

A buzz set in with the slow fall of a weighted blanked draped over covers. "It's existential for sure. You know what else I've wondered about?"

"Hmm?"

"Where magic goes, and what it does when it's not being used. Is someone always using it, is it working on its own accord when a magic user isn't manipulating it, or dormant? Then there's the whole issue of those places it lives, when we're not using it. I wonder what they are. What to call them."

"The places where we went to take it?"

A slight shiver raced over her arms, raising bumps, though it wasn't all that cold. "Yeah." She hugged herself, huddling into the crook of his arm. "Was that another dimension, or an astral plane, or even deep in our own minds, like our subconscious?"

"I have a theory. It's not a personal theory that I invented, but I think it fits."

Anchored by his warmth, touch, smell, while the heavenly bodies worked their mesmeric sway, she knew everything would be okay. Perhaps the sensation of knowing made it true. "Elaborate."

"It's a kind of collective unconscious. A place of memories and dreams shared by all and stored in a place accessible to all. In different ways, at different moments. I think it's been in existence ever since there were minds. Like a kind of psychic supercomputer, storing all our output in a massive hard drive."

"What a concept." Before she could ponder Julian's notion too deeply, a glittery streak as faraway as the distant constellations overhead flew across the sky, winding in curves, miles long with sparks flaring at its tail.

"A shooting star," a little boy squealed. Others followed suit, oohing and clapping.

A different kid cried out, "Make a wish, make a wish."

But as Taylor watched the thread of light stitch through darkness, maintaining its brightness as it traversed a distant galaxy, she got a different idea from the depths of her heart. In the collective unconscious, the murky place Julian had mentioned, a truth took shape.

The light in the sky was Salazar, wherever he was, her familiar gone of this earth but out there blazing his own path. Watching over them.

He'd guided them through the water dimension, shown them the spells, taken them to those mystery places where his kind thrived. Her familiar, always, and forever, doing what he could even if only in spirit.

He'd been there the entire time, during their journey.

Never gone. Never forgotten.

She kissed the tips of two fingers and lifted them skyward. The inside of her nose stung, but she had no space for grief or sorrow, for there was nothing to mourn.

Salazar might be gone in his physical form, and she missed the physicality of him, seeing him fly above the treetops. But he was there, wherever there was, travelling the collective unconscious of magic. Perhaps he brought her to Rachel, the witch crowned by his lesser brethren.

Taylor took herself out of the sky and turned to Julian, her fated one here on this earth.

There were a finite number of questions they could answer. She looked into his brown eyes, into his soul. "I love you."

His gaze was love to match her water, two elements, joined in synchronicity from now until the end. They were boundless, magic bound, for eternity. "I love you," he said.

And on that night on the cusp of autumn, with her wine and the stars, her husband and family, she reunited.

With her babies, the lineage of magic that she'd inherited, her everything. She moved into the new era, a part of herself still poised to tarry with the other realm. If she accepted the full breadth of her gifts in their complexities and contradictions, she would prevail.

The next phase stretched before her like that endless horizon of celestial gems. Destiny was afoot, prophecy abound. In time, the universe would unveil those pieces to reveal her role.

But for now, all she had to do was flow along with the river of stars.

***

Thank you for reading! Did you enjoy? Please add your review because nothing helps an author more and encourages readers to take a chance on a book than a review.

And don't miss book 4 of the *Coven Daughters* series, FALLEN ANGEL, available now. Turn the page for a sneak peek!

Also be sure to sign up for the City Owl Press newsletter to receive notice of all book releases!

SNEAK PEEK OF FALLEN ANGEL

Where does magic come from? Where does it go?

The errant thought tapered into a fuzzy memory as quickly as it arrived, but not before rocking Cynthia Fields. She rode a wave of ripples that shook her like déjà vu.

Standing at the side of some California highway as the relentless beat of a midday sun baked her skin, she stared into the blue dome of a sky, certain that a thread of magic stitched her into the fabric of the mystical unseen.

A trio of vultures circulated above, scouting for carrion in their endless black loop of death, yet her realization filled her with a renewed zest for life.

The thought of magic had not originated in her own mind. She'd made contact with a witch who shared her bloodline. The spell that she'd cast to mind-meld with one of her long-lost coven sisters had worked. Now, all she had to do was gather and assemble all six witches in the same place, and the prophecy would commence.

But first, she had to get to Hollywood. And figure out what exactly the fabled prophecy was all about.

She held her hand up to her forehead, craning her neck to see around the side of the mountain where the two-lane highway curved behind a hill. Cars tended to come around the bend fast, meaning she had to be ready to signal quickly.

A bead of sweat slipped down her temple, the acrid taste of dust chalky on her tongue. She'd only been hitching for an hour, but dehydration was a consistent threat in the Northern California climate. As she reached for the hook securing her water bottle to her hiking pack, a coil of brown and tan patches camouflaged to blend with the rocky landscape caught her attention.

She came face-to-face with a small rattlesnake who regarded her with beady eyes. The nub capping its tail shook in a blur, cutting the still air with a tell-tale buzz.

Cynthia grinned at her new pal. Sister Folly was visiting her in serpent form, a good auspice and sign that her journey was unfolding according to the prophetic plan. The chaos and fire witches resided in southern California. They had to be there. She crouched on her haunches and met the snake's predatory stare with a question, "Where does magic come from? Where does it go?"

The low bleat of a truck horn aborted her communion with the visiting familiar, and she leapt to her feet. The silver plate of a big rig's grill barreled right toward her, the sixteen-wheeler lengthened by a typical cargo load. It honked again, and she stuck out her thumb.

The truck ground to a halt, kicking up dirt and rocks under its wheels. Cynthia squinted to get a look at the driver, letting out a breath when she spied feminine features and tousled gray hair.

Cross-country hitchhiking was a harrowing crapshoot, and she'd rather not have to use her air magic to leach the oxygen from the lungs of another sleazy guy who assumed she was some hooker or runaway that he could rape and discard without consequence. Dead bodies were logistical nightmares, and the the two she'd dealt with were plenty.

The trucker's passenger window slid down before the driver hollered in a gravely, smoker's voice, "Where ya headed, blondie?"

Cynthia tipped her chin in goodbye to the snake before sidling up to the side of the truck. "Beverly Hills."

The woman laughed, brushing some items off the passenger seat. "No offense, but you might need to grab a shower before your audition."

Once she gathered those two keys to the Coven Daughters Prophecy and set her part of the phased plan in motion, nobody would care what she looked or smelled like. They'd be too busy hailing her for saving the world. "Yeah, well, I'm not exactly going there to see my name in lights." Not in the conventional way that the trucker assumed, at least.

The trucker leaned forward, brows raised, and opened the door. "Okay, I'm interested. Get in."

Cynthia stepped up without hesitation, sticking her hiking pack on the floorboard beneath the dash as she settled into her seat and buckled. The truck's cabin was tidy and smelled like the pine tree air fresheners that hung from the rearview window, promising a pleasant ride in one sense. But as she glanced to her sandaled feet, she spotted a cluster of religious pamphlets in all different shapes, sizes, and levels of printing quality.

Uh-oh. She gritted her teeth, bracing herself for a long trip involving proselytizing and gushing declarations to a lord and savior. Not the best topic of conversation for an advanced witch with two killings on her conscience and a predilection for the darker aspects of the craft.

The driver revved the engine and got them moving, the truck taking several seconds to return to full speed. "You think you're in for a lecture about the salvation of your eternal soul, don't you?"

Cynthia looked to her driver, a woman so petite and whisky-thin that the belly of the big rig swallowed her whole. The lady practically needed a booster seat to reach the steering wheel. As they whizzed by a green mileage sign posting over ninety miles to Los Angeles, she resolved to humor the little old lady in the big truck. She'd endured far worse in her travels, from high-pressure sales pitches that verged on threats to unnerving screeds about ex-wives ranted by psychos with thinly veiled misogyny issues.

"We can talk about whatever, or not talk at all. Thanks for picking me up." Politeness never hurt, and occasionally religious conversations lent fresh insights to Cynthia's understanding of the magical tome stuffed into her backpack.

"I collect those. Those papers at your feet. Which isn't to say I believe what's printed in them."

Cynthia used the toe of her hiking sandal to sift through a few pamphlets. There were some from a few different sects of Christianity, a couple of Buddhist ones, and some of unrecognizable origin. Her interest piqued, she asked as casually as possible, "Why?"

The lady pulled a fast-food cup from the middle console and slurped the dregs through a straw. "Now that my grandkids are older, I think that I'd like to go back to college and study world religions. People are always shoving these into my hands at truck stops. Figure I can make the most of it by getting a head start, and accepting them is less awkward than saying no."

A fondness for the truck driver emerged as an unspooling warmth in Cynthia's chest. She might be a staunch follower of the Left-Hand Path, but her sinister predilections of the diabolical sort didn't stop her from harboring an affection for industrious types.

Spending the past five years roaming around the country in a tireless, dogged search for clues to the prophecy, including an off-grid stint living among animal shifters in the Peruvian jungle, had instilled in her a healthy appreciation for improvisation and thinking outside the box. Talking to people, she'd come to learn, fed her mind more than any book or article. "Nice. Which concepts interest you the most?"

Intellectual analysis of the subject matter might spark clues. The likelihood of a revelation was certainly higher than if she'd met some jolly, boring convert droning on about salvation.

The truck hugged a hairpin curve, the driver slipping Cynthia an odd, sly look. "What's your name, dear?"

Cynthia beat back a frown, forcing herself to exert dominance over her stubbornly expressive face. Thirty-three years alive and she still hadn't mastered her poker mask. She'd inadvertently given something to this woman to make her think that she had the upper hand. Not that it mattered. They weren't there to lock horns, and all that Cynthia needed at the moment was a lift to Beverly Hills. Appeasing the trucker didn't come with a cost. "Cynthia. You?"

"My given name is Denise, but I work under the nom de plume Nerissa. I have five other aliases that I rotate, depending." The words hung like runes in the space between them, codes to unlock destiny.

Where does magic come from? Where does it go? This time, Cynthia wasn't able to discern whether the questions came as memories of her own thoughts or the implantation of someone else's. As the engine moaned out its rumbling song of monotony, she stared at her chauffer's sharp-cut profile.

Cynthia had never been particularly good at circumspection or indirection and lacked the finesse required to play situations cool. Rarely was there time to meander, in her estimation.

Bluntness worked the same as air itself, blowing away clutter and dust, clearing out stagnation to make room for new energy. "You're part of the network, aren't you?"

That's what the esoteric tome sandwiched between a t-shirt and some dirty socks called the alliance of magic users supposedly scattered around the globe. The coven daughters were the most central to the prophetic unfolding, but their mentors, guides, accomplices, conduits, and foils all played roles.

Now all Cynthia had to do was figure out how Denise-Nerissa fit in.

The woman tipped her chin at Cynthia's bag. "You didn't even need to ask, now did you? What all have you learned from that book in there?"

Chemical reactions set off sparks in her bloodstream. She'd amass as much as possible over the next hour or two and do her best not to push too hard and drive Denise-Nerissa into a shutdown. "Am I the first person whose book you've seen? Either normally or through an extra-sensory ability?"

A long, agonizing pause emphasized the whizzing noise of tires spinning over pavement in endless loops. "No, I've seen them all, at one point or another. I've played crucial roles in ensuring that all six tomes make their ways where they need to be." Her tone dropped an octave lower and went flat, as if to suggest that this reunion of book and rightful owner was not an altogether positive development. "Whether by my own design of free will or through auspice and synchronicity, I can't be certain."

Frustration, dread, and irritation fought for control of Cynthia's emotions. Her research into the Coven Daughters Prophecy led her to conclude that the six witches finding their respective books was good. Otherwise, humanity had a holographic prison universe, a future of high-tech mind control technology, and some scary-ass energy harvesting programs waiting in the wings. "You seem troubled about this."

The trucker clarified, "I'm worried. Wary. My dreams are telling me that there's a twist coming. This conclusion we're marching towards isn't all neat and tidy." She sighed like the exhale weighed a ton. "My problem right now if that I can't figure out what the book represents on a deeper level. At first, I concluded that they were instruction manuals, but they also contain elements of warning. And language written in code, which suggests a need to hide or pass off the knowledge in covert form."

How much to hold back versus what to reveal? This woman seemed on the level, for real, but one never knew. A few varieties of scammer, fake, and lying nutcase had crossed Cynthia's path since she'd started opening up about her relationship with witchcraft and journey into the far corners of occult belief. She went with vague yet honest. "Directions written in code strikes a chord. Have you had any hunches?"

The vehicle approached an intersection, then a ramp that led them on to a sparsely populated highway. "I used to think they were lost texts of the Book of Revelations. I spent a lot of time with one of them before releasing it to the whims of the universe. It wasn't suited for me, apparently."

"You used to think they were lost books of the Bible. But now?"

An icy, knowing, blue-eyed gaze came Cynthia's way. Denise-Nerissa merged onto a new highway clogged with traffic. "I think that their origin is not of this world, and they have the power to control us if we aren't careful. These books have an agenda that seems separate from our own. At times in conflict, at times in accordance. All but the chaos sister is supposed to avoid working with the sixth section of the book, but I have a feeling that's a moot point in your case."

A chill slipped up Cynthia's spine. She couldn't quite land a read on Denise-Nerissa, whether she was being completely earnest or playing some game of misdirection and subterfuge, and to what end. But they'd come together by the machinations of fate or destiny, landed side-by-side in this truck on route to Beverly Hills, so Cynthia's best bet was to treat the older woman as an ally until proven wrong. "I believe that. I also believe that the Coven Daughters have agency. More than we may even know. And yeah. I've worked with the sixth circle. I've never been one to follow the rules"

"Rules exist for reasons."

"To be broken with intent. I believe in that adage."

"What do you seek?" They passed rows of palm trees, the ocean offering glittery peeks of its waters from over a cliff.

"Chaos and fire. Chaos is easy. The chaos witch is one of my opposition elements in the hexagon sisterhood. I think that she manifests as a serpent of some kind and is connected to snakes. I saw a rattlesnake back where you picked me up and have reason to believe it was a familiar visiting me with a message." In any other context, she would have felt like a crazy person spewing tinfoil hat drivel, but this driver knew the score.

Yet, the sober look on the older woman's face plunged Cynthia into dread-laced doubt. "Be careful. Nothing in this system is easy or obvious, ever, and thinking so infects the practitioner with virulent hubris." The driver pushed a button on the radio and scanned through static and pop songs.

"Why do you say that?" She wiped her palms on her lightweight cargo pants.

"Experience." Denise-Nerissa settled on a news program and turned up the volume. "Everything that's important in this world is something that we don't see. Take that for what it's worth."

Denise-Nerissa would have to do better than dropping a passive-aggressive hint by turning up her radio. "I'm not sure what it's worth, actually. Does it have to do with why you have five aliases? Six names total, one for each Coven Daughter, right?"

The older woman turned the volume dial higher, filling the cabin with dry talk of geopolitics. "Excuse me. I'd like to catch my show."

"This talking head garbage is all surface-level theater. You realize that, right? Besides, you're the one who just told me that the important stuff is unseen."

Denise-Nerissa slowed to let a motorcycle pass. The helmeted pilot, drenched in leather, flashed a quick wave of thanks. For some odd reason, the signal pleased Cynthia. Must've been the unexpected element of it, violating expectations. She watched the biker shrink to a black dot on the horizon.

"I'm tired of turning over rocks. Every time I did, I wasn't actually helping. I ultimately did something concerning that I can't seem to reverse," the old woman said.

"Oh, come on. You can't dangle that and not follow through."

"Sure I can. Don't test me."

"What'll it take to get you to talk?" Everyone had a price, financially or otherwise. Everyone wanted something and responded to incentive to get it.

"You're slick, aren't you?" Begrudging respect infused the rhetorical question.

"Lady, I've been living the nomad life for five years. I've gotta be savvy and pragmatic."

"Fine. I'll give you one piece of my story in exchange for a promise."

"What is it?"

Denise-Nerissa held a ferocious stare until traffic forced her focus back to the road. "Promise me."

"How can I make a promise without having the terms?"

"You're a practitioner of the Left-Hand path of air magic, correct?"

"Yes. How did you know that much detail?"

"Advanced members of the network, myself included, we see. You'll be more than capable of fulfilling your obligation to me in exchange for what I'm about to give you."

Cynthia balled fists so as not to fidget with her messy ponytail. She might be digging herself a hole here, but what choice did she have? She hadn't picked up any new leads in weeks, and the Beverly Hills excursion was itself a faith-based launch into a blind alley. If she wasted a chance to glean insights from this stranger in the truck, she'd kick herself. "Okay. I promise."

"If you find one or both of the Coven Daughters out here, I need you to facilitate an introduction to me. Don't lose touch. We need to be in regular contact and make a plan to meet once we have all six of you assembled. I'd stick by your side, but for various reasons, I can't."

The plan didn't sound terribly daunting, but it didn't make much sense, either. "You picked me up because you knew who I was. What I was."

"Of course. I've been tracking you through remote viewing and astral travel. Managed to pin down a rough read on your coordinates and come get you. But my spells to locate the others are failing. Fire and chaos are elusive, and I can't figure out why."

"Are you connected to earth, spirit, and water in addition to me?"

"Yep."

If true, this fact alone warranted keeping Denise-Nerissa close and opening lines of communication.

Cynthia's insides jumped. "What's in it for you if you collect the entire set of us?'

The trucker's jaw tightened. "I'm invested in this prophecy the same as you are. Plus, it's starting to look like a combo spell of the daughters is required to undo a mistake I made. There's discussion in the books of a practice called partner work. I'd ask to see your book, but I don't trust myself with those texts anymore."

"This has to do with what you initially didn't want to tell me." Though air conditioning blew from the vents in a generous stream, Cynthia's face heated. She sensed herself already drifting into the deep end, and Denise-Nerissa with her cryptic talk wasn't the flotation device she would've chosen. But the trucker was a lead and the only tenable one at the moment. "The concerning action that you can't reverse."

Denise-Nerissa nodded with intent. "After I identified my first coven daughter, I got too eager and enthusiastic about tracking down the other five. I used spirit magic spells to scatter myself. Long story short, I broke my consciousness apart and implanted it in six bodies. It didn't entirely work out according to plan, so now a little bit of me shares a physical form with parts of the original host." She patted her jean-clad leg. "The original trucker lady is in here with me. Name's Denise. We've learned to share. She's a real good sport."

An icky feeling made Cynthia's skin crawl even as excitement chased through her. This was no doubt the work of possession magic, the entire dark underbelly of the system. "You want to gather back into your original form. Leave Denise and whoever else and go back to being strictly Nerissa."

"Yeah. And dispatch the hitchhiker."

Cynthia reached for the mace on her key ring. She'd try a non-lethal solution before resorting to magic.

Denise-Nerissa snorted. "Not you, silly. It's not in my best interests to harm you. When I split my psyche, I let in something else. A traveler from another dimension. I assumed I was advanced enough to prevent this side effect of psyche splitting spells, but as they say, assumption is the mother of all fuck ups."

"I see. And I'll do my best to help."

Without warning, Denise-Nerissa veered onto an exit ramp and drove toward a gas station. "I appreciate it. We'll exchange contact info here."

Cynthia's stomach hardened. "We've got to be an hour away still."

"Yeah. Sorry, hon, my contracted route extends to the east. This is as far as I can get you without getting poor Denise fired." She pulled up in the refueling area and turned off the ignition, stilling behind another truck with pinup girl silhouettes on its mud flaps. "Gimmie your number, please." She reached under the seat and pulled out a cell phone. "This way's more polite than stalking you through the astral plane."

Cynthia rattled off her digits, and Denise-Nerissa texted her with a ding, cementing their connection. Though bummed to be stranded again, she supposed that she should count the day's development as a win, having wrangled a lead on a possible node in the Coven Daughters network. Unless the old lady was full of shit. "I'll be in touch if it's worth reaching out. Thanks for the lift."

"Be safe and all of that nonsense." The trucker winked.

"Never. Safety's overrated." After returning the tease, Cynthia hopped down the big step onto the pavement and shut the truck's door.

Once she got her pack secure on her shoulders, she blazed a path across the parking lot, figuring that she'd pause for a decent meal at the truck stop diner before gathering her bearings and plotting her next move.

She passed a row of motorcycles, pausing by the line of chrome beasts when one machine struck her as uncanny, like something she'd ridden in a dream or when spellbound in astral travel. How did she know of this mysterious motorcycle?

✳

Don't stop now. Keep reading with your copy of FALLEN ANGEL available now.

Don't miss more of the *Coven Daughters* series with book four, FALLEN ANGEL, available now, and find more from Kat Turner at katturnerauthor.com

✳

Cynthia Fields, a powerful witch with a troubled past, is so close to cracking the code of the Coven Daughters prophecy. She just needs to unlock the secrets of Fire and Chaos and connect with her five coven sisters, and she'll be set to save the world and maybe even herself.

Cynthia's search takes her on a cross-country hitchhiking trip where she meets a strange truck driver who claims to have the ability to jump into different bodies before the journey lands her in the arms of a sexy, mysterious drifter who goes by Raven.

Following what was supposed to be a one-time, steamy encounter, Raven reveals to Cynthia that he's a shifter with his own agenda—revenge—for unraveling the prophetic mysteries. His knowledge of the prophecy runs deep, and they form an alliance that's as intense as their burgeoning desire.

Bound by sizzling romance and magical obsession, Cynthia and Raven hop on a motorcycle and chase the secrets of witchcraft until Cynthia's quest to enhance her power tangles her in the snares of a malevolent entity, Folly, who claims to rule over the prophecy. Reluctantly, Cynthia agrees to Folly's demands, a bargain that must be paid with the blood of those she loves. Will Cynthia and Raven beat this witchy game of cat-and-mouse before it's too late?

✳

All reviews are **welcome** and **appreciated**. Please consider leaving one on your favorite social media and book buying sites.

For books in the world of romance and speculative fiction that embody Innovation, Creativity, and Affordability, check out City Owl Press at www.cityowlpress.com.

ACKNOWLEDGMENTS

Writing is a solitary endeavor, as they say, but shepherding a book from inception to publication requires the steadfast support of many.

First, thank you to everyone at the City Owl Team for your continued championing of my books and author career. Knowing that all of you believe in me keeps me going during the darker moments. A special shout-out to my awesome editor, Tee Tate.

This acknowledgement includes the wonderful group of City Owl authors. I cherish you all and how we support each other continually.

Thank you to my critique partners and beta readers, especially Jaqueline Snowe for reading this book chapter-by-chapter and giving detailed suggestions to help me make it the best that it could be.

Of course my readers, who keep picking up my stories and buoying me with reviews and kind words, deserve all of the kudos. Thank you, thank you, thank you to anyone who has ever read, recommended, reviewed, or shared one of my books! Readers are an author's lifeblood, and every one of you is precious.

Finally, a massive debt of gratitude is owed to my husband, Mark. Your ongoing support of my writing and author career is priceless. I couldn't do any of this without you, and I love you dearly.

ABOUT THE AUTHOR

KAT TURNER is an award-winning author of paranormal romance and urban fantasy as well as the occasional thriller. Her favorite stories to write are those that combine action and adventure with magic, dry humor, and steamy romance if the situation allows. She lives is Kentucky with her family, where she can mostly be found practicing yoga, taking nature walks, or getting lost in the corridors of her own imagination. Kat loves to connect with readers, so don't be shy about getting in touch!

linktr.ee/katturnerauthor

ABOUT THE PUBLISHER

City Owl Press is a cutting edge indie publishing company, bringing the world of romance and speculative fiction to discerning readers.

Escape Your World. Get Lost in Ours!

www.cityowlpress.com

facebook.com/YourCityOwlPress

twitter.com/cityowlpress

instagram.com/cityowlbooks

pinterest.com/cityowlpress

www.ingramcontent.com/pod-product-compliance
Lightning Source LLC
Chambersburg PA
CBHW020647030726
47498CB00002B/411